<u>Advance praise for *Boys, Lost & Found: Stories*</u>

"These fascinating, often funny, stories that engage the heart, lead us on quite a safari through the perils and joys of gay life. Casillo's characters sexy Italian-Americans with operatic, roller coaster emotional lives—search unstoppably for love, from feverish New York to exotic Los Angeles. Congratulations for a fine-tuned, courageous performance!"

—Edward Field

"Casillo's surprising and accomplished collection reveals a heartfelt observer of life's emotional emergencies and indignities told with immediacy and feeling."

—Felice Picano

About the Author

Charles Casillo was born in New York City. He has spent many years exploring and documenting his interests and obsessions—such as Marilyn Monroe, strange encounters in various Manhattan bars, unusually talented individuals, eccentrics, sex, tragic figures, and antidotes to insomnia, insecurity, and loneliness. His novel *The Marilyn Diaries* combines these themes. It is a fictitious recreation of the infamous lost diaries of Monroe and is written in her voice as he imagines it.

He is also the author the biography *Outlaw: The Lives and Careers of John Rechy* which tells the story of the legendary literary lion, provocateur, and sexual renegade. Casillo's profiles, short stories, articles, reviews, and poems have appeared in *The New York Times, The Los Angeles Times, Christopher Street, The Lambda Book Report, New York Magazine, Frontiers, Men's Style, The Harvard Review* and many others. He divides his time between New York and Los Angeles.

Boys,
Lost & Found:
Stories

Charles Casillo

Gival Press

Arlington, Virginia

Published by Gival Press, an imprint of Gival Press, LLC.

For information please write:

Gival Press, LLC, P. O. Box 3812, Arlington, VA 22203.

Website: *www.givalpress.com*

Acknowledgment is made to the publications in which some of these pieces appeared in a somewhat different form.

"Buying And Selling" in *Christopher Street/Stonewall News*

" Woods" in *Off the Rocks*

"The Finer Things In Life" in *Alex Magazine*

"The Legend Of Denham Fouts" in *Alex Magazine*

"John Rechy At Home" in *The Gay & Lesbian Review*

First edition ISBN 1-928589-33-2 (ISBN 13: 978-1-928589-33-4)

Library of Congress Control Number: 2006924425

Photo of Charles Casillo by Nathan Yungerberg.

Format and design by Ken Schellenberg.

For love, support, and inspiration through complicated emotions, in assorted ways, at various times, I would also like to thank Stephen Barbara, Bill Brownell, Francine Civello, Tricia Civello, Steve Curtis, Hugh Daly, Terri Fabrice, Harry Fini, Skip. E. Lowe, Robert Giron, Mona Miles, Elena Nelson-Howe, Arlene Sparaco, J. Randy Taraborrelli, Damian Wild, my brother and his beautiful family, and most of all my parents.

Contents

A boy who is loved can never grow old or die.

Hafiz

Buying and Selling

For Jeff Dymowski

I am not a hustler and I have never been one in the real sense of the word, but I can probably trace back to where those rumors started. Occasionally I hang out at an infamous bar on the Upper East Side that caters mostly to Upper East Side gentleman, older out-of-towners, and very beautiful young callboys. But it's not the money that lures me there. Usually it's my last stop on a bad night. A lonely night. A night of not getting the attention I crave.

Though I don't see it in myself because I'm not my type, I have a look that certain men desire. A Mediterranean look: dark hair, dark eyes, hirsute. So I stop at this bar to test my powers of attraction. To make sure I'm up to snuff. To learn, once again, how valuable I am. There is, of course, a danger in this. What about the night I may go there and find out I am worth nothing? But for now, I find a certain comfort in the place. My skin absorbs the attention, the men's stares, their hard-ons, their offers of money. This is all taken in, processed, and churned out in a sexual force-field that many mistake as absolute arrogance, but in reality is a shield to cover up inner emotions too tender to expose, unprotected, to strangers.

It was at this bar that I met Boyd. During the course of every day life, I often see guys whom I find drop-dead gorgeous: in a club, on the subway, walking down the street. But every once in a great while, maybe two or three times a year, I see someone I want so badly it actually hurts to look at them. That's how it was the first time I saw him. He was talking to someone else when our eyes met and it occurred to me that if I didn't end up with him it would actually be painful.

Boyd was talking to a hustler. I knew he was a hustler because I was close enough to hear him talking and there was something in his voice that was so consistent with all the other boy-whores I have ever heard speak: optimistic, phony, confident as hell. Mediocre charm pumped up to the tenth power. Boyd was nodding at the hustler, but he kept looking at me. Sometimes he locked eyes with me and nodded in unison with the hustler's story. Thank you God, I said to myself. Sometimes I don't get the ones that are painful for me to look at.

Boyd was not handsome in the traditional sense. An older man, mid-forties, a slightly fleshy face, brown wavy hair graying at the temples with a solid and robust build. Yet he carried himself with total assurance, as if he thought he was the most desirable man in the room, and that made others, me included, believe that he was. He would not be mistaken as one of the male prostitutes, of course. More likely he was someone that they would target, an affluent man out on the town, looking for rare delicacies. But for me he had a magnetic chemistry that had nothing to do with money. I recognized in him the qualities I so lack in myself, qualities that come from a lifetime of succeeding: cocky arrogance, supreme confidence, a casual comfort with any situation set before him. A man who was able to surround himself with luxuries, a man who had made it, a man who wasn't afraid. I was terrified. My heartbeat doubled as he made his way towards me.

"So, why did you follow me here?" he asked, charming me and setting the tone of mild kidding that would continue through the night.

I was game. "I always follow attractive things," I said.

Through my drunkenness I knew he thought I was beautiful and so I presented my face to him full attention, without hesitation. And I also presented the best package I could muster. I tried to give my opinions with wit and charm. We talked about recent movies we had both seen, the club scene in New York City, and how it wasn't what it used to be. We talked about his real estate development company; he bought old buildings, renovated them and sold them at great profit. I told him I was an actor.

Usually I didn't tell people about my real life. There are too, too many people running around Manhattan saying that they are an actor/model/dancer/singer/producer/writer/blah, and I didn't want to put myself in that category, so I usually just said I worked in construction. That worked like an aphrodisiac to most—they liked the stupid silent type, making a meager living from hard labor. This time there was no lying on my part. I didn't want to start off on the wrong foot with Boyd, so I told him about my struggles as an actor, trying to get in some of my earnest passion about the profession, being vulnerable but in (I thought) a self-confident way.

After about an hour of sitting on a couch in the back, he leaned over and started kissing me, lightly at first, then building steam, growing more and more passionate. The kiss lasted for a good long time, thrills a mile-a-minute. When we pulled apart, he looked at me with the kind of excitement that only comes with newness. He cocked an eyebrow and lifted one corner of his mouth into a sexy leer.

"So why do you find me attractive?" he asked.

"I can't help myself," I whispered, and his smile grew wide.

Then, as if to protect himself, he said, "You're not a hustler are you?"

"No."

"Good," he said. "Because I'm not into that."

It could have been so. Maybe he had his own reasons for being in a well-known hustler bar. After all, I was there, and I had mine.

He asked me if I would like to go back to his place for a drink.

I found myself in a dilemma. He seemed to be everything I was looking for in a man. Smart, witty, engaging, successful, and terrifically sexy. His conversation kept me on my toes, and his charisma kept me longing for him. I wanted to mean something to Boyd. What I didn't realize then was that I was at my most powerful with him that night because I had mystery. I could have been his fantasy, his perfect love. I wish I had known what that was and I would have constructed myself into it. I didn't know. I tread lightly. So did he.

I could go with him tonight and risk being thought of as a one-night adventure (and there was a chance his life was filled with them), or I could give him my number and risk being a forgotten, drunken memory whom he would never call. Sometimes people forget the magic that was shared. I thought of old movies I had seen on late insomnia nights where Doris Day meets Rock Hudson, has a lovely evening, goes home to her own apartment, and receives flowers the next day. But my life wasn't any movie and I certainly wasn't any Doris Day.

"It's not too late for a drink," I decided.

All night, desire had been rising up in us like mercury near heat. Alone in his apartment, sex began immediately, with urgency and need. Our mouths met and bonded. The taste and feel of him left me weak with excitement and surrender, as if all my previous sexual encounters had been practice sessions for this one. Sessions that had mixed passion and disgust, pleasure and emptiness, curiosity and pain, boredom and longing, all leading up to this moment—a moment of magnificent culmination. I had nothing else to offer so I gave him myself completely, every part of me, every pore, every cell, every atom in my make up. We rolled over and over on his giant bed, this way and that, limbs crossing and uncrossing. His strong hands roamed forcefully all over my body, arms, back, ass, thighs, and I silently thanked God for all those aerobics classes of late.

"So why are you in love with me?" he asked afterward, as we lay exhausted in each other's arms.

This time I didn't answer. I closed my eyes and gasped for breath, and wondered if I was.

Early the next morning, I was hustled out of the apartment. He had a business meeting, he explained. But I had his business card tucked into my jeans and when I arrived home later that morning, the phone was ringing. It was Boyd.

"Rick," he said, "I just wanted to tell you what a pleasure it was meeting you, and what a good time I had last night. I like you more than I like anyone I've met in a long time."

That phone call would become one of the threads that kept me hanging on to him. Taunting me with the possibility.

We had dinner plans for the following week. "I must be worth something to some people," I said to myself as the cab pulled up to his Central Park West address.

At this time in my life a feeling had taken over me, a weariness that left me unable to fight back. I had spent my childhood hiding my true self, my real identity and that had left me confused, unsure and very exhausted suddenly. I had been fighting for too long, trying to get other people to accept me and like me. Now I was struggling to let my true self emerge and I wasn't sure what people thought of *him*. Little by little I was breaking down walls, taking off masks, discarding old skins. I had dropped out of high school to pursue acting and since then there had been too many auditions, too many subway rides, too many one-night stands, too many disappointments. And I was only twenty-two. Yet I have a tendency to compare myself to the people around me and most of my friends were in college and their lives seemed so much more promising.

I knew it was time to start making some serious strides in my life. If I was going to survive I needed something to happen. A jackpot. A score. By now, fame and fortune seemed too much to hope for. I'd settle for a great job with a touch of glamour and good pay. Or I needed to meet someone who was crazy about me. Someone I could love and who would love me so we could find shelter in each other. Or something, anything that was good. I needed something...something...something....

The first time I had been to Boyd's apartment it was dark and we had feverishly headed straight for the master bedroom. But this time he gave me a full tour, room after room, my boots clacking noisily on hardwood floors, or sinking into lush carpeting. There was a grand foyer larger than most New York apartments, a sort of game room with leather bar stools, a gigantic white tiled kitchen, and a huge guest room I would have gladly called home. And then that vast and opulent master bedroom.

Many months later, it occurred to me that this was part of the thrill for him. Walking the new guy through his spectacular show-palace, staggering him with his success. The boy, in my imagination, would always be working-class and young, and ecstatic at the thought of what a catch he had made in Boyd.

After the tour, we settled into the living room on a white linen couch, looking out through the floor-to-ceiling windows to the park. Boyd had set up canapés on a silver tray in front of us; these were hunks of cheese on dainty water crackers. I was terrified to pick one up. I come from Brooklyn, and what do I know about hors d'oeuvres and the way to eat them properly? Do I grab one or wait to be offered? Do I stuff them whole into my mouth? Take tiny, delicate bites? He picked one up and handed it to me. I carefully bit into it and the cracker broke into a million pieces, leaving me holding the cheese. I demurely picked up the crumbs from my lap with two fingers and placed them in my mouth. What a clumsy mess I am, I thought.

I felt so awkward and out of place here, but I wanted to belong so desperately. He wasn't all that brilliant or good-looking. Why was it so hard to talk to him tonight? If I wasn't aware that all this belonged to him, we'd be settled into a nice cozy conversation by now. Rarely am I at a loss for words but everything I thought of to say seemed boring or idiotic. Topics presented themselves to me and I examined them in my mind, turning them this way and that way, so that when the words finally left my lips they came out sounding (to me) neat and polished and very dull. He watched me with a quizzical smile. Obviously he was studying me and I wasn't sure if I was coming across as an interesting mystery or a lobotomized moron.

The night we met I had suspected that he wore a hairpiece, so I stole quick glances of the back of his head, looking for tell-tale signs, bumps or something. If he did wear one, it was a good one and it was impossible to be sure. Eventually, he caught me sneaking a look. He was totally unfazed.

"I wear a hairpiece," he said without a bit of hesitation, "and I have for many years." It was as if he wouldn't even consider having a full head of natural hair like some men—this was the right way for him.

I blushed from top to bottom. Actually the fact that he wore one so confidently only endeared him more to me, that he had the nerve to make an admission that was so clearly a sore spot to so many men. "It looks very good," I said stupidly, "I would never have known."

Obviously this whole night was going to be a disaster and I resigned myself to just get through the evening and then go home and nurse a freshly broken heart. But Boyd came to my rescue.

"I've thought about you a lot this past week," he said. He sounded sincere. After all, there was no reason to say something like that to a nobody like me.

"I thought about you, too," I said. If only he knew how much—how many tissues were used to absorb the aftermath of my masturbation sessions in which he had been starring.

At the restaurant, I stroked his knee under the table and he smiled and winked. The wine was helping me feel at ease with him. There was a three-piece jazz band playing and he sang the words to old standards while looking directly at me, and a lifetime of struggles melted away. He was so strong, so sure, I felt totally safe in his presence. It was the only time in recent memory that I was completely, unadulteratedly happy.

My dates with Boyd went on like that for many weeks. It was always the same thing. He'd call me in the middle of the week and ask me out for Saturday night (sometimes skipping a week). We'd go out to dinner, have sex, and I was out of there in the morning. He always made it clear to me that he had an appointment early the next day, a building up for sale that he had to look at, a family commitment, something. It *did* seem strange to me that he would never have a Sunday free, but I reasoned that he was a busy, important businessman.

I wasn't familiar with the strategies and intricacies of love and in my mind I was slowly building up a relationship. Trying to get him to trust me. I really did like him and I wanted him to know I wasn't out to use him for his money. If he asked me what restaurant I wanted to go to, I always picked an inexpensive place. On some nights, we went to a movie before going back to his apartment and I always made sure I paid for it. He was always very attentive to me during these dates and seemed genuinely happy to be with me and the sex got better and better. He said so himself. However, he never called me during the week just to see how I was doing, or to see how the audition went that I told him about on the previous date. If I called him, he was polite but curt—it always seemed that I was catching him in the middle of something—so I stopped doing it.

"Rick, he's just using you," my best friend Joey said when I told him about all of this. But Joey always said this when I started to get serious about someone, and now I harbored a secret resentment. Part of me wanted to believe that Joey cared, the other part felt that he was jealous because Boyd was such a great catch.

"Oh Joey, face reality," I snapped. "I'm using him too. I'm not in love with the man. It makes me feel good to be with him. I'm just in it for the fun. I can handle it." I knew this wasn't exactly true, but it made me feel safer saying it.

To everyone else in the world Boyd would seem to be a brick. A lumbering, cast-iron presence impervious to daily trials and tribulations the common New Yorker has to deal with. The obstacle course of city life. His status was his fortress. In a way, I saw him like that as well. Looking back now, I realize I was in love with the idea of total protection. When I touched his body I touched pure success. But I saw other qualities, too, which made me feel tender towards him. Feelings that he would not allow to emerge in his life of high-powered lunches, wheelings and dealings, buying and selling.

The thing about him was that he had spent so many years building his success, climbing up the ladder, putting up protective walls, so that his simplest emotions—warmth, love, caring—lay hidden, underdeveloped, under tons of cement and steel. These small green seedlings of emotion are what I related to. Sometimes I'd glimpse a look of unguarded vulnerability in his steely eyes. He, too, was afraid that no one would ever love him for the true person he was so he learned to discard before being discarded. But this sensitivity was quickly cloaked if he caught me looking. He refused to let me in. I longed to cut through layer after layer after layer of his shields, his masks. I wanted to contact him down deep where it mattered, where few people have been allowed to visit. Maybe I could touch this place and find a safe place for myself there. Perhaps we could teach things to each other.

Of course, there were crumbs thrown from time to time and, starving, I accepted them. Sometimes as we lay in the darkness, Boyd's hand would search out mine and hold it softly. Other times, he would reach across a table in a restaurant and stroke my cheek with tenderness, not caring what the other patrons thought. But then, if I responded, he would back off and become impenetrable once more.

I started to want Boyd with the kind of longing that only comes with the unattainable. I'd charge clothes on my credit card to wear on dates with Boyd, things I really couldn't afford but it became necessary for me to feel good about myself and new clothes often injected me with a booster shot of confidence. I'd plan dinner conversations for days in advance. I borrowed witty anecdotes that friends had told me, changing them around so that I was the center of the story. Sometimes I'd make notes on things to talk about with Boyd and I'd carry them in my wallet and study them on the subway as if preparing for a test.

Lying in his bed, it was an impossible thing to sleep after having sex with Boyd. First of all there was my mind, a scaffolding of emotions and questions (was I good enough for him, did he enjoy my dinner conversation, will I look horrible in the morning, can I keep his interest, etc.) Then there was the fear of waking him. I was acutely aware he had to get up early in the morning. He always made sure I knew this before we went to bed (or was that just an excuse to get rid of me as soon as the day began?) As a result I was afraid to move. He liked to sleep with an arm around me, a position I enjoyed for about one minute. Soon his arm became a lead weight pinning me to the bed. My body became rigid, my nose itched, and a cramp formed in my legs. Unable to move I lay there, my bladder rapidly filling up, but there was no way I could get out of this trapped position without waking him. Nervously, I'd become aware of the loudness of my body. Each breath, each swallow, each movement, was amplified. I tried to close my eyes and find sleep but my bladder would keep reminding me it needed to be emptied.

Clocks ticking. Boyd snoring. The huge bedroom mocking me with its richness. The traffic of the city murmuring below, and eventually a breathtaking sunrise painting the bedroom with a fiery orange glow. The rays of the sun scorching parts of my heart as well.

In the morning there would be the usual rush to shower and get going—and to get me out and on my way. He dressed hurriedly, occasionally smiling at me. Insulted that he couldn't wait to be out of there, I took my time, languidly pulling myself together, hair in my face, eyes downcast. Resisting him. Resenting myself for wanting him so much. His kiss good-bye was quick and dry, when I would have liked it to be wet and lingering.

Every once in awhile I'd ask Boyd if it was possible that we spend an entire day together. He'd pause and reply, "We could do that, someday." But he never made solid plans. I set my sights on someday.

There were other definite telltale signs that Boyd's attitude towards me would always be the same, would never grow deeper. For example, he was constantly commenting upon and flirting with other guys in my presence. Men on the street, actors in films, and waiters in restaurants were all appraised and coveted right in front of me. Hurt, I would follow his gaze as it traveled down the back of some guy, like the blonde surfer type who waited on line in front of us for a movie. One thing I could never be was blonde.

I overlooked these things. I glossed things over when telling Joey about my dates with him. That Boyd didn't want to meet my friends was an unspoken rule and I wondered if he thought them beneath him, and if so, if he thought I was beneath him as well. I never met any of his friends—that was another unsaid rule. The reason I put up with it was because he made me feel valuable (even while, in other ways, making me feel worthless). It was hard to believe that someone so educated, so rich, so powerful, would actually want me. I didn't understand the reasons.

He was a fat cat. He bought and discarded boys all the time. When he found me—innocent and stupid—with no ulterior motives, he was delighted. Maybe even infatuated for a few weeks. But once he found out I actually loved him he couldn't believe his good fortune. To have one of "them" truly love! He could take everything out on me. He could rip me open and feel around the inner mechanisms of emotion, examining pieces of feeling this way and that, and then stuff everything clumsily back inside and go along his way, whistling merrily.

Late one night near the Christmas holidays at a small cafe in the Village, he flirted with two overly confident, gum-snapping queens. It embarrassed me terribly because the mod-haired things gave me looks that silently conveyed they thought they had something that I lacked. Boyd smiled and flirted with them. I sat there like a lump. Then he told me a story that was the beginning of the end for us.

He said he had gone shopping for a new TV as a present for his mother. He talked about the salesman who helped him. The "kid," he said, liked him. He discovered that the guy was Irish and German. And that he was a student at NYU. And that he was nineteen years old. So what? That wasn't so much younger than me! Why were so many men attracted to teenagers? What was up with that fetish? Man, I was glad I didn't have it even when I was a teenager. Youth is beauty in its own right! But I silently prayed that I wouldn't become a slave to craving men half my age when I was middle-aged. That's how many a fool had been created and will be created.

I was shocked Boyd felt it necessary to tell me all this info about the "kid", as it was not the usual conversation you extract from a sales boy, and certainly not something you would tell a boyfriend about while on a date. Was he doing it on purpose? Was it to make me jealous? If so it was a huge mistake. I felt my face flush. I, however, smiled in the face of his bravado, and silently hoped he couldn't see how small he made me feel. But a brooding resentment rose up out of me, a smoldering smoke screen of resentment, creating a thick barrier between us, which only I knew the reason for.

"...and I told him I'd like it delivered," he was saying, "and the kid says, 'Sorry, sir, we don't deliver.' So I said to him, 'Why don't *you* deliver it, just for me?'"

He was smiling, as though I might actually find his flirtation with the teenager amusing. Instead, I silently looked down and sipped my beer as if it contained the magic potion that would transform me into something he could love.

"What are you thinking about?" he asked.

"About you actually."

"What are you thinking about me?"

"I'd rather not say," I replied. "But it's very insightful and sad."

That was enough to communicate, even to Boyd, that something was wrong and he quickly changed the subject. "I've been debating in my mind all week whether or not I should invite you to spend the holidays with me in Florida."

I looked up sharply. "If it's something you have to debate about I don't want to go," I answered.

"You're very good with your movie-script answers," he said, annoyed.

What would life be like with someone like Boyd, I wondered. If we spent years together building a life? Me: constantly worrying, feeling jealous, having to always compete, on a strictly physical level, with the more beautiful boys he was seeing for the first time. Always knowing deep down inside that I would never be enough. Him: always looking at other men, always wanting them, craving their newness. It would be impossible to put up with the constant strain, of that much I was certain. Still, I had hopes of changing him. Of making him fall so deeply in love with me that he wouldn't want to have sex with anyone else, out of loyalty for me. That was my dream, my goal with all the men I've loved since.

10

The next morning was cold. He couldn't get a cab so he took the subway with me to his office. All around us the early rush hour mob scurried to their positions, dodging through the homeless, the deviants, the garbage. It seemed weird, seeing Boyd with the backdrop of my world. As we stood there waiting for the train, suddenly the whole previous evening hit me in the face and I knew the time had come to do something.

"I can't go on this way with you," I said abruptly. "Either you give me some kind of commitment or we should stop seeing each other." I thought that this would take him by surprise but he was not taken aback at all.

"Can't you just relax with it? Can't you just be satisfied with what we have," he asked.

"No, I really can't," I said. "Because we're not going anywhere."

"Which means you want me to call you every day and see you three or four times a week?" he said. "Well I can't give you that."

"It doesn't have to be anything so drastic," I said. "Can't we slowly ease into something more? I have to know there's some sort of future with you. I can't make love to you the way we did last night, and then not hear from you for two weeks."

A homeless woman with hair askew approached us babbling insanely, and Boyd grabbed my arm and walked me to the other end of the platform. I leaned against a column. The train roared into the station. The doors opened. We didn't get on.

"I want to be more important in your life. I want to matter to you. I can't go on just being one of your things."

His expression softened. He looked at me carefully. I was wearing a baseball cap pulled down low and sweatpants rolled up and a leather jacket. Usually I didn't dress this way with Boyd because I knew this type of look turned him on and I wanted to be more to him than a look. I wanted him to look inside. On this particular morning, however, I figured I needed all the support I could get.

"I have to think about it," he said.

Boyd said he would call me the following Saturday night between eight and nine. At seven, I checked to see if the phone was working, placed it at my side, and climbed into bed, and waited. And waited. At nine, still no call. My favorite Saturday night situation comedy began. Figures, the bastard wouldn't call when he said he would. He'll probably call during the show, I thought. Numbly, I watched the comedy, but I had to force myself to laugh when a line was particularly witty or clever.

At nine-thirty. Ring, ring. My heart jumped. I thought: Just to show me whose boss, he had to make me wait an extra half-hour. The caller ID said, "private."

"Hello," I said, trying to sound light, and airy, and busy.

"Hi, Rick, did you watch your show?" It was my friend Joey.

"Yes! Yes! It was so funny. It was hysterical!" I gushed, still forcing myself to sound fine. Perfectly fine.

"Did Boyd call?"

"No. Do you believe it?" I asked, now attempting to sound only mildly-pissed-off, but inside my heart was broken.

"What are you going to do?"

"Nothing. It's over as far as I'm concerned."

"I think that's best."

"A boy can only put up with so much humiliation," I said, trying to imitate Audrey Hepburn in *Breakfast at Tiffany's*. Joey liked that movie. We both laughed, but suddenly I was weak with sadness.

Joey felt these vibes through the phone and said, "Why don't you come over tonight? I rented two movies."

"I'm so tired, Joey," I said, "I think I'll just stay in."

"Don't feel bad about him."

"I don't. Actually, I think I may go out," I decided suddenly.

"Why not come over and spend the night?"

"No...I uh...am going out."

"Okay," Joey said. "Cheer up."

"Why? Do I sound depressed?" I asked. I had been putting a lot of effort into sounding cheerful and it was exhausting me. Joey was a good friend and knew better.

"You sound a little gray. Like the weather."

"Goodnight, Joey."

"Have fun."

I went to take a shower. Boyd would probably call when I wasn't standing at attention beside the phone. A watched pot never boils, the old wives say. But when I returned to my bedroom fifteen minutes later, the answering machine stared at me, the message light defiantly not blinking.

From the night I had met him, I had been faithful to Boyd. Not that he had given me the slightest indication that it mattered but I had never even stepped foot into a bar or a club in all the time we had been together. Even when I masturbated, I only thought of him. Going out on this night was my foolish sort of revenge.

I wasn't in the mood for the carnival atmosphere of Chelsea so I decided to go to a more sedate piano bar in the East Fifties, a large, two-level bar that attracted a mostly business type crowd. As it was a Saturday night, the place was packed. I ordered Dewers on the rocks and wandered around with the panicky feeling that I no longer belonged to this scene. With Boyd, I had been looking for an escape hatch from all this; if he decided against me I would be adrift again.

The bar was so crowded on the first floor that there was no place to lean or stand without getting in somebody's way. On top of that, it was as if there had been a casting call for all the men in the world who I wouldn't be attracted to. A loathsome, slovenly man strolling leisurely around used his considerable girth as an excuse to press up lewdly against people, me included, as he passed.

I decided to try the downstairs section. As I made my way towards the back, through shifting bodies, I saw Boyd talking to a blonde man so beautiful that all my defenses for competition faded away. I never expected to run into him on this particular night, but it did add another dimension to the type of thing that might happen. I was stripped, standing there experiencing the awful, raw feeling of giving me very best—being used and judged—and coming up short. Feeling terrifyingly naked. And this feeling hurt me very much. Very much. I wondered where I would get the strength to walk out the door, take the subway home. Not finding it yet, I ordered another drink.

"Please, God," I said to God. "We're friends, aren't we? Please take away this pain. This feeling of rejection is too much to bear at the moment." But God is God and he had His reasons for making me feel what He thought I should feel.

Boyd had told me that he was too busy to see me this weekend. That he would be thinking about me, thinking about us. And that he would call me. Okay, I said to myself trying to wrestle my emotions back under control, maybe he *is* busy this weekend, maybe he just needed to get out for a drink, maybe this guy he's with is an old friend. I'll watch and see what happens. I stepped back into the crowd, hidden by small groups of chattering men and their shadows.

And Boyd kept talking to the blonde, becoming more and more physically intimate, squeezing his shoulder and so forth. The guy seemed disinterested, and that hurt me, too—what did he have that I didn't that protected him against Boyd's spell? I remember writing on a napkin, "There's a horrible knife in my heart, my darling. But that's okay, maybe I'll live." I stuffed it in my pocket and kept watching, foolish and exposed.

To my surprise, the blonde turned away from Boyd, so he moved on to another guy, a completely different type. This time it was a fey looking young man with a long wispy hair. But Boyd's technique was the same. The same shoulder squeezing, the same intimate whispering. Soon this guy rejected him too.

Undaunted, Boyd continued his hunt. He moved upstairs and I quickly downed my drink and discreetly followed. On the upper floor, he approached one man after another and struck out again and again and still he moved on to another, and another, and they were all completely different types, and as the evening wore on, he went for lesser and lesser in quality.

Having made his way downstairs again, he finally met someone receptive to his advances. A handsome model type with dark sculpted eyebrows—known to regulars at the bar as a hustler with a superficial magnetism and a sinewy, defined body that he presented to interested men in the same style that a used car salesman would show off his latest model. I kept watching, by this time completely numb with humiliation and scotch, as Boyd steered him to a corner couch where they both sat down. And then they kissed, the same way Boyd had kissed me on the night we had met, and I was suddenly struck with a realization. All the time I had been with Boyd, I could have been anybody. In the months that we had been together, I had presented him with the finest pieces of myself—inside and out. Yet I didn't have to. I didn't have to be particularly beautiful. Or charming. Or witty. Or intelligent. Or elusive. Or loving.

I could have been any body.

He had mattered to me and I had done my best to make him want me. From the beginning I tried to make him value me but it didn't matter. He wasn't buying. I could never again be new. The lesson that Boyd was teaching me was that some people want the real thing—warmth, honesty, commitment, comfort, trust, love—but for others it's enough to be able to go through life buying the moment.

The next thing around the corner was a present waiting to be unwrapped—who knew what you'd get? He would leave with him, the model

14

type. Take him to his place, his apartment. And tomorrow this new man would wake up in Boyd's bed in that luxurious apartment and think, "What a score!" But the next week Boyd would be out again, hunting for something new. And maybe then he would be in the mood for a beauty, and he could flash some bills and have another.

Boyd and his new friend separated from their kiss and our eyes met. He was thrown for a moment but then he gave me a look that tried to convey the fact that we both knew the score. But I didn't. Relationships don't come with instructions.

They got up to leave, and Boyd passed by me and winked and patted me twice on the ass on his way up the stairs and out into the night. I could have been anybody. I said to myself, He's got a stranger now, and that's more exciting than knowing what you've got. And I knew that he was out of my life forever. He didn't even give me the dignity to stop and talk to me, to end it properly. He knew how I felt about him but the moment is now and now is what's important.

And I could have been anybody. I could have been anybody! I could have been anybody! It played before my eyes. A litany. A eulogy. And I knew it was true. I had given him my all. But I could have been anybody.

I am not a hustler and I have never been one but I say that with regret. As time goes by you learn that it's about survival. I always presented my true self, without guile, hoping that eventually honesty would win the jackpot. Usually I came up empty handed. I should have sold what they valued and gotten what I could while the getting was good.

I stood there in a stupor, waiting to see if God was going to grant me my wish and take away some of the pain. How many people in this room right now were desperate to know love and how many people were afraid of it? "Was it a sick joke on me, God," I asked. "To send me here as a stranger to glare and recognize the inconsistencies and mysteries of the others? Or is it that we are all born feeling the same way about each other? Alone. Strangers among strangers. That, God, is a truly sick joke."

Just as I was finishing my rant, I noticed two men looking in my direction. I could hear them talking.

"Oh, wow," one of them said, "look at that."

"Appetizing," the second man said.

I looked around to see who they were talking about. I was crushed for sure, but things like that were still important to me. And I realized, through my sorrow, that it was me they were desiring—me! But if it wasn't me they found appetizing, it would have been somebody else. The next guy.

"Are you all right," the first man asked, approaching me. "You look out of it." All the same, I smiled because I was grateful for the attention and for whatever concern he had.

He was right. I was out of it. I didn't even try to speak. I knew my voice was gone. I simply nodded. I felt around in my pocket and handed him my note on the crumpled napkin. He thought I was nuts, I think. So what? I was on my way up the stairs and out the door while he smoothed out the wrinkles in the napkin. I heard him reading aloud to his friend: "There's a horrible knife in my heart...but that's okay, maybe I'll live."

And you know what? I did.

Woods

For Andrew Harte

Earlier that day there had been a promise of sun but now the weather had grown dark and chill. I walked through the entrance of the woods and experienced the same feeling of anticipation and guilt, which always mixed together and produced an incredible excitement. There were, as usual, a number of men leaning against trees with a practiced casualness, waiting for something to love. I too was out looking for something, but there was no need to be hasty. The woods were lovely, dark and deep—and all my promises had been broken. I started down the main path.

It was an anonymous encounter I craved. The kind where I wouldn't have to think but could quietly feel. The exchanging of souls without a contract. The acquiring of knowledge without words and, maybe, an unexpected tenderness.

The first one I saw who was a welcoming possibility was standing on an offshoot of the main path that circled around a small area of trees and rocks and led back to itself. If you walked a few feet off this circular pathway you would be too covered by brush and trees to be seen by a passerby. I took a few steps on to that path to view him better.

He had a balding patch in back of his head and was slightly worn out, but was still quite handsome. He made a rubbing motion with one hand on his crotch, but I did not follow. With the motion, his wedding ring glimmered and even if it hadn't I would have been able to tell that he was married. I had this kind of discerning ability by now. I could also tell that he would not want to kiss or suck my cock. He would hold my penis with his left hand, his own with his right. He would turn his face if I tried to kiss him. He would take a step back if I tried to touch his ass. This was out of the question. I needed to kiss today.

I left him standing there and headed back down the main path. A black queen, walking with a friend, saw me and screamed in my direction: "Hey you! Frenchie! Frenchie!" He was calling me "Frenchie" because I was wearing a brown cap cocked to one side that, I suppose, did make me look French. "Hey you! Watchu doin' wit my coat?" I was also wearing a brand new black jacket with a hood. When walking through the woods I always wore black, or brown, or muted green so, if needed to, I could camouflage. This queen probably belonged to the gaggle of young men who usually huddled at the mouth of the woods (but who weren't there today)—envious, observing what came in and out and, not being able to attract most, grouped together and scorned them with their acid tongues. Sometimes, of course, you must stop in the woods and acknowledge a stranger's words, if for no other reason but to be polite and avoid hurting feelings. But on this one I wouldn't waste my dignity. What little I had left.

I continued walking deeper, tripping half the way. There were large embedded rocks and thick roots growing out of the ground, like the gnarled hands of a giant old man who died while trying to claw his way out of the earth. Above some birds chirped a steady stream of consciousness in neat little patterns. Others—the big black ones—emitted high-pitched screams that sometimes became hysteria. It was as noisy as a bird sanctuary. I became exhausted from listening.

Somewhere not too far behind me I could hear footsteps crunching through dried out leaves and twigs but when I stopped (dead in my tracks) and turned around I saw nothing. I was frightened but fear was something I constantly lived with.

This thought led me to Orlando my friend who had died years before. I thought of myself clutching a glass of red wine as he told me about his illness. I thought of his last few months. A horrible hacking cough. And I thought of the dreams, sick dreams, that had haunted me ever since. "I must put these thoughts away," I thought, "or they will spoil this for me." I was determined to get through a day without fucking tears.

Something else was following me. Now I was sure of it. I stopped and stood on a slab of broken cement that seemed to be a fallen tombstone but, on closer inspection, turned out to be the remaining skeleton of an ancient park bench. Heading towards me, around a curved path, I recognized a man I had seen leaning against a tree at the woods entrance. He was not hideous, but he was not my type. He had casual, uncombed wispy hair, sparse mustache, sloppy clothes, dirty, loud-colored jacket—white, red and navy blue. He walked in my direction, smiling broadly and he looked like he might speak to me. Anyone who liked to talk to someone here was not my kind of person.

I didn't enjoy making friends in the woods. On subsequent visits I'd run into them and they'd want to chat, ignoring my hints that I would rather be alone. I was not bored in the way that they thought I was and I might miss out on opportunities. It had happened before. This was not a place I came to be social. It was a private thing and when I saw something I wanted I followed it.

I looked beyond the man and started walking quickly past him in the opposite direction. This was the most polite way I could think of to show him that I was not interested. He chose to ignore the sign and made

18

a complete about face and started following me again. Even when I was almost running he continued following, not heeding the negative signals. I did everything in my power to prove that I was not attracted. When I felt him close behind, gaining on me, I abruptly changed course. If we passed each other on a path I looked to the ground and quickened my stride. He kept pursuing me nevertheless. I thought he might force me to be rude or hurt his feelings.

My mistake was that I had locked eyes with him momentarily when I first walked into the woods. For me he was taken in and dismissed as a "no" within a split second. But that brief connection was enough for him to interpret my glance as desire—and overrode all my efforts to negate it.

I stopped suddenly. He was only a few feet away. He had been trailing me for quite some time and if I didn't do something now it seemed he would follow me for the rest of my time here, the rest of my journey, and I would never get what I had come for.

He walked up to me, face to face. "I'm not interested," I said as neutrally as possible.

"Fuck you," he said and continued down the path.

As much as I hated to admit it, I was offended. When someone doesn't look at me when I go by I know he doesn't want me. If I am following and he quickens his step and turns abruptly, I get up, dust myself off and continue hunting. I can accept the fact that I'm not attractive to everyone in the world (although it hurts me, too). Why couldn't he accept that fact in himself?

Throughout all of this the sky had remained one color—an even gray. Now darkening it turned the horizon into a cryptic Oz. The wind swept through trees and activated black plastic bags to life. For a moment I stood perfectly still and allowed the movements of the forest to happen around me.

I never told my friend Orlando that I loved him enough during his lifetime. Although now I found myself saying it all the time. I didn't want to think of Orlando but it was too late. The thought of him earlier had already opened up a Pandora's Box of sadness. Memories rushed back to me. Memories once comforting, now torture. I remembered us during a vacation in New Orleans, staying in a cheap hotel, which we soon learned was haunted. Ghosts swirled above the room in a watery blue haze. Even though we were just good friends, Orlando and I decided to share a bed. I never believed in spirits before but lying there in the misty darkness it seemed I would never doubt their existence again. Orlando and I turned to each other at the exact same moment. We drew the sheet up to our necks and we stared into each other's face.

"I'm afraid," Orlando said.

"I love you," I replied. It is the only time I could clearly remember saying it. It isn't enough.

"Hey you," the queen from before called out. "You still didn't get no dick yet?" He was alone now and I was surprised to see that he had traveled this deep. Some queens are very quick and clever. This one was not one of them and the only adornment he had to draw attention to himself was his loudness. His voice hacked through the woods like a hunter's blade on a safari.

I had been trying to fight it but I was starting to grow gloomy and angry, partially because I kept running into these people I did not want to see. I had been here almost an hour and the woods had not even offered me in a faint flicker of hope. To escape him I followed a sudden narrow trail up a steep hill. When being patient enough the woods usually yielded something. This trail was not very used or clear but I followed it through overgrown paths and winding burrows. My feet became entwined in vines. These had snares and prickly substances I needed to be protected from. I traveled this way for a very long time without seeing anyone.

Then suddenly, when I wasn't looking, when I least expected it, the way it always happens, I saw the one I wanted. A cleft in his chin, perfectly groomed hair like a 1950s matinee idol, and a chiseled face much too handsome for normal, everyday life. A movie star. A fantasy man. A dream boy on pinup posters hanging above teenage beds. I was overcome with a longing so severe that it was no longer desire. It was a desire that approached agony. I wasn't even horny anymore. I was desperate. How dare someone have this power over me?

He saw me too, now, and gave me a cocksure look that I found hard to read: "What are you waiting for?" or "What the fuck are you looking at?" Both questions were at opposite ends of the spectrum. I hoped it was the former. I could end up in love with this elusive beauty or wake up mutilated by him. I couldn't help myself. I had to look. I had to look.

He lit a cigarette, sniffed loudly, and smiled. His smile to me was as mysterious as the distant landscapes. I awkwardly smiled back with my mouth pressed closed. My lips were trembling. I wanted him too badly. Now he turned from me and stared down the path and began walking (indifferently?) in that direction. I was still unsure but I followed him. Occasionally, when I got close enough, I could smell his aftershave, or perhaps it was some sort of hair lotion. It was a masculine fragrance that made me think of locker rooms after the showers, or scents advertised in commercials during football games. Each time I inhaled it the pain in my groin became so severe that I thought I might collapse in the grass from longing. Probably if he felt the same way about me, my wanting wouldn't be so strong.

It wasn't a farfetched notion that I could have been beaten or killed here. There were always vague rumors about men who had disappeared in the woods in the not so long ago past. And once I ran into a friend who I hadn't seen in a very long time. He explained to me that he had been beaten unmercifully. He had been in the hospital for weeks after they—three young men—had chased him through these woods and terrorized him, screaming obscenities and eventually breaking his bones. I thought of my friend, Eddie, running through the forest, terrified and helpless. He was a nice person.

Once when I was waiting outside Orlando's hospital room I heard him angrily yelling at someone in his sleep. Was it me, I wondered? He was wasting away and I was healthy yet our lives, up to the time he became ill, hadn't gone down very different paths. Why did I deserve health? I went to his side and held a hand that, by this time, was bony and cold. Often in the past we would joke about what we would be like when we were old. Now—even though we were both in our twenties—I had to look away.

If I stayed in the woods much longer it would be too dark to see. The dream I had been following, I noticed, had gotten far ahead of me. If I let him get too far in front he might not be there when I arrived. "Maybe he's trying to elude me," I whispered to myself. At that exact moment, however, he stopped, turned around to see if I was still following, spit a quick, neat glob, waited for me to catch up a little, and then continued walking. I checked for the handkerchief in my pocket.

Now he was leading me to a place I had never been before. The path was narrowing and the bushes and weeds grew more wildly here. It was difficult to see too far ahead of me and at times the only trace of the man I had been trailing was a hint of his cologne. The trees held there black arthritic arms spread wide—doing their best to seem welcoming.

When I was a child my father would take my sisters and me to a different part of these woods on Sunday afternoons. We would run ahead of my father, giggling devilishly, our yellow Labrador happily leaping behind us, his tail wagging. In those days I felt as if I were simply going through the motions of life. I never really felt I belonged to the woods—or anywhere. Never until now.

I walked a few yards further down the pathway and it suddenly ended on a great precipice that looked out over another valley of twisted trees and complicated pathways. Looking around I saw that there was indeed a way to get to the hollow. To the right was a steep sloping trail that led down there. But when I scanned the darkness there was no sign of the man I had been following. It seemed a dangerous risk to make my way down, chasing something that might lead to nothing at all. A powerful wind rushed towards me pushing me in the opposite direction, blowing off my cap, whipping fiercely against my face and through my hair.

Then I saw him standing below in the distant valley, waiting patiently beneath a tree like a beautiful phantom, sinister and lovely and, at the moment, as easy to touch as loneliness.

Prozac, Insomniac,

Half-Cracked

For Scott Lesko

When my grandmother gets depressed she rides the bus. She just gets on a bus and rides to the very last stop. Well, she lives with my parents and occasionally grandma and my mother will get into a fight. Okay, more than occasionally. The bus ride, of course, is also grandma's revenge on the entire family because she feels we don't give her enough attention. She knows my mother—the queen of spreading bad news—will instantly be on the phone, telecommunicating the story of the missing grandmother to the masses. And grandma is well aware that everyone will worry and talk about her while she's gone. She loves to be the center of attention, even if she's not there. She also knows that eventually someone will have to go and pick her up, wherever that might be, depending on what line she decided to take on that particular day.

The unlikely image of my grandmother, in the mid-stages of Alzheimer's, taking a bus to nowhere helped me devise a fantasy which, for awhile, would help me to fall asleep each night. This may sound crazy but for months I was obsessed with the idea of selling all of my belongings—books, clothes, furniture, music, toiletries, computer—and buying a one way ticket on a Greyhound bus. For a long time the planning of this adventure was the only thing that would settle down my nerves enough to put me to sleep. And believe me I have tried everything. You're talking to the king, the high priest, the god, of hot baths, warm milk, sleeping pills, special herbed tea, scotch—nothing worked. Until my bus fantasy.

Night after night as I lay in bed I'd imagine myself with no possessions, no wallet, no appointments, no memory, sitting on a Greyhound that was speeding down desolate highways, through darkened tunnels, expertly negotiating hairpin curves. Soon I'm the only passenger left. When I reach the end of the line I discover my destination to be a vast and visually pleasing wilderness. I walk and walk—don't forget I have no baggage—through wide open spaces, around lush botanical gardens, past welcoming trees and friendly animals directly out of a Disney film.

Eventually I happen upon a deep, dark cave, which, after further investigation, I recognize as home. Exhausted, I crawl into this shelter. It is incredibly warm and cozy and comfortable. There are no bugs. Everything is black and peaceful. Each night, for well over a month, I would fall asleep just as I was settling into a snug little nook in this magnificent haven. To me it felt like paradise.

When even this fantasy stopped putting me to sleep I decided it was time to see my doctor again.

Maybe you remember me? Anthony DeMicello? I played Tony Angel on the daytime soap opera *A World Away*. Well maybe you don't remember. It's been off the air for two years now and I was...I mean my character was...killed off six months before the cancellation in a canoeing expedition up the Amazon. In other words, my contract was up for renewal and my character had become tiresome.

Oh how happy I was for a time—when I was on that show. It was my first real part and the character's first name was my real first name and it made me so happy when I'd walk down the street and my "fans" would yell, "Hey Tony," because that was really who I was. Hardly anyone ever recognizes me anymore. Except for a badly paying infomercial for skin care (I shot a "before and after" segment and truly thought I looked better "before") I haven't worked since. My savings are going fast.

A year ago I left a spacious, one-bedroom apartment in Chelsea and moved back to my old neighborhood in Ozone Park Queens in the area near Aqueduct Race Track. Talk about a step down. I live above a saddle shop. I figure if I don't eat more than one dollar's worth of food a day I can pay my rent for the rest of the year. This shouldn't be too hard since I lost my appetite soon after the cave fantasy stopped putting me to sleep.

Really, I've lost thirteen pounds in the past two weeks. Me, Anthony DeMicello, who has spent the last ten years of my gluttonous life on a diet, struggling to keep my weight down to a fighting trim 175 pounds, now has no desire for food. Me with the hugest appetite this side of Mama Cass. After my soap opera went off the air I slowly climbed up to 188 pounds and I occupied myself each month with losing and then gaining back five or seven pounds. Now, without any effort at all, I'm 165.

Recently I went to my doctor—Shapiro's—office, sure of one thing. I was dying. I mean, sure, I've been through depressions before in my life. Although I prefer to describe it as bouts of melancholia—I like to think of myself as the brooding Montgomery Clift type. But this time it was different. This time I was going through a depression so overwhelming that most days I could not get out of bed. And now it was turning physical, what with not being able to sleep and having no appetite and all. Throughout my life I've wished for an easy way to lose weight without diet or exercise. Now, by God, here it is. And I am terrified. Food terrifies me.

Every morning I wake up and ask myself, "Are you hungry?"

"No" I answer.

"Don't worry," I assure myself, "you'll be hungry later on." But I don't believe me. Just the thought of food makes me sick. I find myself thinking about all the unnecessary food I've gobbled in my life and wonder how my stomach had the patience to digest it all. And food is all around—mocking me with its undesirability, just as it once taunted me with its desirability: on TV, in magazines, on ads in the subway. I could just vomit. I fit into clothes I haven't worn since my soap opera hay day. I am horrified and delighted.

I never feel hungry but there are certain moments when I feel like I could get something down without gagging. During these moments I find myself attempting to eat the things I've spent a lifetime longing for while at the same time trying to resist. Salami and mayonnaise heroes, peanut butter sandwiches, pizza. I drink heavy cream out of the container. All of it makes me sick. I eat it anyway. I'm terrified of losing more weight (or of course of gaining a single pound back.) Then again, I am terrified of everything.

Dr. Shapiro is one of those men who has been tragically trapped in the period of the time that covered the best years of his life. And I'm assuming that, unfortunately for him, this was during some groovy era in decades past. Today, except for some gray strands around the sides, he has no other hair on his head of which to speak. And these few on the side he scrapes back into a wispy ponytail. He has a pierced ear with a hoop going through it. He wears muumuu inspired psychedelic shirts and granny glasses.

Once, when I was being treated for what I thought was a urinary tract infection but turned out to be my imagination, I even smelled the traces of marijuana in his office. Worst of all, even though he is at least sixty-five and I am at least twenty-nine, he sprinkles our conversations with phrases like "let's rap about your symptoms."

Hey, I'm desperate. I rap. My biggest fear is finding out I have this aggressive new form of AIDS that can't be treated. And, because every symptom there is, is a symptom of AIDS, I can't help but torture myself over every discomfort, every toothache, every headache. I obsess over every minor infection. My life is as empty and lonely as ever but now with the added terrifying real fear that something may be wrong physically. Even though people tell me worrying about AIDS is old hat, that people don't die from it anymore, that there are drugs that prolong illness, I occasionally see news items that state emphatically that there is a fast-moving unconquerable form of the virus that people die very quickly from. It's horrible living this way. With the threat constantly hanging over you. I mean, it's bad enough being ambitious and not moving fast enough, being lonely, being broke, being frustrated...but to have to worry about getting ill too? It's devastating at times.

"Frankly, Tony," Doctor Shapiro says, "I don't think there's anything wrong with you. You're just depressed. Man, we've been through this scene before, haven't we?" Then he prescribes the antidepressant Zoloft, the tranquilizer Klonopin, and sends me downstairs to the lab for a battery of tests. Zoloft is out of date but it's cheaper than some of the more up-to-the-minute drugs currently in vogue. Still, he charges me $150 for the office visit. The lab charges me $350 for the tests. To have the prescriptions filled will come to a whopping $150. I have no medical coverage. Even if I manage to develop an appetite it seems I could never eat again.

It was a slow progression—my decent into madness. First, after I was fired from the soap opera, I found it difficult to get parts. They told me I'm a "challenge" to cast. See, the problem is I'm big and burly and hirsute and swarthy on the outside and kind of tender and sensitive and sweet and insecure on the inside. And the outside persona always fights for dominance with the inside persona, and the inside usually wins, which always makes me come across as something I'm not. A casting director once told me I look like a cross between Sal Mineo and a young Truman Capote crossed again with Marlon Brando and Ernest Borgnine, which, you gotta admit, ain't the most compatible personalities in history to cross. See? I've never been normal.

Yet, I remained optimistic. Instead of allowing my mood to plummet. I pumped up the optimism volume. I signed up for an acting class being conducted by a respected coach, now half dead but still renowned. I attended every audition, even the ones that I considered beneath me. I continued to work out every day. Then the auditions started dying down. Then my agent stopped calling altogether. It seemed unfair, that life was giving me so little in return when I was giving it so much of myself.

Soon, the phone wasn't ringing at all, except occasionally from my best friend Miles and his lover Les who were still in the first few months of their romance and, therefore, relegated my friendship to back burner status. And then I started to gain weight, stopped working out, and my biggest fear was that I'd turn into Marlon Brando circa 2001—uncrossed—instead of the way he looked circa 1950 in *A Streetcar Named Desire*.

Is it any wonder I felt bleak? Forced, everyday to stare at an answering machine light that never blinks, and a mailman who brings only bills and advertisements for Off-off Broadway shows featuring tired drag queens. Living in a two-room apartment with only my dog, Pooch, for company. And an every growing hairy little pot belly.

But then, of course, I suddenly lost my appetite altogether and I realized that I'd rather be fat and healthy than thin and sick...but by then it was too late, the weight was melting off so fast that I had begun to cast myself as an aging Tony Perkins in the 1980s, also uncrossed.

Waiting for test results is the worst. The doctor had said that the Zoloft would take about a month to kick in. A month! Meanwhile I'm left thinking about how it would be if I were really physically ill. How it would bring my parents shame. Of course there are all these new drugs to extend the life of HIV positive people but how could I afford it if I turned out to be so? I have no job. No money. No health insurance. I began to shake with fear. I walked around with a headache. Not my usual slight, thumping, behind-the-eyes headache. This was a dizzy, vertigo, migraine, pounding, whole-head kind of a headache. And the Zoloft gave me furious diarrhea. Another AIDS symptom! God! It was difficult to get out of bed. And yet, sleep still eluded me.

On the third day of Zoloft and Klonopin the phone rings. The caller ID on my bargain basement phone doesn't work, so every phone call is a grab bag. It's too soon for the test results. One ring. And one thing I know for sure—I'm in no condition for conversation. At this point I'm practically catatonic in bed. But there's a problem. Two rings. Whenever I let the machine answer the phone whoever it is always hangs up. Now, off course, I'm sure it's my agent with some fabulous audition information. Three rings. If it gets to the fourth ring the machine will get it. Yet I'm thinking, "If I don't pick it up my agent will hang up on the machine." He's too impatient to leave a message. Even though I'm too sick to work, even if I did get a part, I still don't want to miss out on the opportunity to screw it up myself. I pick up just before the machine. "Hello?"

"Grandma's on the bus."

Shit! It's my mother. Not even a hello. No, "howya doin' Anthony?" Nothing. Just "Grandma's on the bus." And, yet, even as she says it I know what was coming next.

"Mom, no," I say, "I can't get her. Not today."

"She's on the Q-10. Chickie from—Senior Citizens—saw her get on at the Kew Gardens stop. If you leave right now you can head her off at Kennedy Airport."

"No, mom. I'm not going to pick up Grandma at the airport. I'm afraid of the airport. I get lost at the airport. I don't know how to get out of the airport."

"You'll have Grandma with you. She'll help you get out."

"Are you out of your mind? The woman gets lost going through a tunnel. Mom, listen. I'm getting panic attacks again. I can't get lost in an airport at this stage of the game."

"Oh, before I forget I saw something on Regis the other day about panic attacks, um, let me think...yeah!...if you're in a grocery store and get an attack, you should just get out. Leave all your belongings, your shopping cart—everything—and just get out into the open."

"Mom? Are you sure you saw this on Regis? Who was the guest and why were they talking about panic attacks? Why didn't Chickie stop Grandma from getting on the bus?"

"Well maybe it was on Matt Lauer. I don't like his crew cut. Chickie is eighty years old—she can't stop a bus. Anthony, I'm not foolin' with you. You have to go. First of all it's gonna rain and she's got a sore throat. Second of all if she makes it to the airport, who knows what she'll do? Maybe she'll wander on to a plane and wind up in one of those foreign countries where they kill old people."

"Why don't you go get her? Matt Lauer looks good with his hair shorter, Mom."

"Me? I'm one step out of a nuthouse with her. This morning she was feeding a picture of your grandfather."

"Why can't Daddy go...?" I stop dead in my tracks. "What do you mean, 'feeding a picture?'"

"That framed picture of grandpa? She had it propped up on the kitchen table. She was feeding it sauce with a spoon. She's nuts, let me tell ya. Sauce was running all down the glass and everything."

My head started to throb again. "I'll go," I say.

28

"Come for dinner on Friday, I'm making stuffed peppers," she replies. "Don't worry, Anthony. Grandma will help you get out of the airport."

Between love and madness lies my grandmother.

It had started to drizzle. Sure enough there she was in front of the Delta building with a plastic bag tied around her head as a kerchief. Leopard coat, pocketbook wide open, sucking ferociously on a hard candy. I beeped the horn and waved her over. She was expecting me, or somebody to get her but she got in the car angry.

"Your mother is impossible," she said with a violent slam of the car door.

Luckily there was a yellow cab in front of me and I decided to just follow it out of the airport. Cabs in airports are always either coming or going, so already they know more than I do.

Grandma yammered away a mile a minute with laryngitis. She sounded like a sick Italian frog. It was a nonstop tirade against my mother ("She's impossible. You should see how she talks to me! The troubles I got all around the world. I'm going to live somewhere far far away—maybe with Chickie—where the people are friendly. Of course she hasn't got a house like ours! It's all a shambles.") I turned a deaf ear and switched on the wipers, refusing to get involved. I was in no mood for putting up with grandma's shit. When it comes to getting people in hot water the woman is scalding. I know even the slightest comment to my grandmother about her relationship with my mother would later be taken out of context and can and would be used against me.

I let the windshield wipers do the talking for me. But grandma's not that easily dismissed. Her one function in life is to lead the conversation, any conversation, and to get as many people as possible embroiled. Even after her mind flew south for the winter—a sudden lull in the conversation is death to her. And, as I was the only other person in the car, she focused on drawing me in. She loudly unwrapped another hard candy and tried another approach.

"Grandpa won't eat," she said solemnly. "He's turning into a skeleton."

"Grandpa is dead," I told her for the millionth time.

"So what?" she sniffed. "I still have to feed him."

It was just about rush hour and it had begun to rain really hard. The drive home stretched out endless before us. As I was heading for the Van Wyk Expressway I thought of just stepping on the accelerator and letting go of the wheel, bringing grandma and me to a fiery but quick end. It would probably be a mercy for both of us. Instead I gripped the steering wheel tighter.

The only thing I fear about death is dying. That is to say dying before I have a chance to fulfill what I have inside. I know I have a few great acting performances in me. I've never really had a chance, outside of a few forgotten episodes of *A World Away*, to really show what I can do. But I can feel these performances lying dormant inside of me, waiting to explode. I need to release it—the way I did in those few soap opera scenes and maybe in a couple of acting classes. If I were to die now I would hate for *A World Away* to be my legacy. I want to do things that are powerful and funny and biting. There is so much more I have to accomplish.

It was like being stuck at the starting line waiting to hear the word "GO!" with all this energy flowing through my limbs, but the race never starts. I also want to accomplish my great things—get them out of the way—so I could love someone in that all consuming earth shattering romance I've been waiting for. Was oblivion inviting? Sure thing. But at this moment I felt I was not ready. Yet.

"I'm very depressed, grandma." I said. "I'm taking anti-depressants."

For the first and only time I've ever been in her presence my grandmother was knocked speechless. There was a long pause. "If you need any money for the doctors, you come see grandma. Grandma'll take care of you." When I dropped her off home 25 minutes later she left a hundred dollars on the car seat.

Since I was already out and about I decided to stop at Barnes & Noble to read up on Zoloft. Just standing in the "Health" section of the bookstore made me feel dizzy and faint. Who ever thought that I, Anthony DeMicello, would come to this? On anti-depressants. Living alone above a saddle shop. Skinny, no less. Too broke to buy a book and forced to do my research in a public bookstore.

But was I dizzy and faint because I hadn't eaten in nearly three weeks? Or had I always been dizzy and now, with all my fears never far from my mind, was I just more in tune with my feelings, which made me feel faint? Or, possibly, was this vertigo simply a result of my nervousness over the entire situation mixed in with new medications and lack of sleep? Or, worst of all, was the room spinning because of some serious, more complex illness yet to be diagnosed?

Oh, it was all too complicated and overpowering. Before sitting on the floor with a ten-pound book on medications and their consequences in the hope of finding some answers, I scanned my surroundings to see if anyone was watching me—the poor sick boy—with sympathy.

Shockingly everyone seemed to be going on with their own lives, taking no heed of me whatsoever. Did they recognize me as a television star and were just ignoring me for the sake of privacy? Didn't they know I was ill? Maybe they were avoiding me? Perhaps they thought I had some contagious wasting-away disease? Oh what was the use? I knew I could go on with this line of thinking indefinitely, each thought linking to another more horrible web-sight of despair in my brain, but this, perhaps, was not the time to worry about being socially acceptable. Still I had to wonder.

I opened the book and began reading. Aha! Murphy's Law was upon me once again. Everything that the medical book said could happen on Zoloft—would and did happen to me. Diarrhea, blotchy skin, dry mouth, shaky behavior. When I got to the part that said one of the side effects could be hair loss—that was the last straw. I can take almost anything as long as I look fairly decent. Bald—forget it. It would only be a matter of time before I'd be turning on the gas. Well, actually not gas. I'd already concluded not to use gas. I've been thinking a lot about how I would do it. If I did it. Suicide I mean.

Sylvia Plath—the great lady-poet who managed to build up quite a reputation for being a genius while at the same time being dead—used gas. She just taped up the windows and the doors, lay her head down on a little folded towel she placed in the oven, and turned the gas on full tilt. A few deep breaths of the ghastly fumes and in no time flat she pleasantly drifted from here to eternity. No mess no fuss. It sounded good to me. During a burst of energy and optimism, I started Brillo-ing my oven but then I suddenly remembered that Mrs. Nussbaum in the apartment below me, just above the saddle shop, is a chain smoker. With my luck some gas would seep down to her place and—one flick of her bick—the whole building would be blasted out of the stratosphere. Even dead I didn't want that on my conscience.

When I arrived home I started calling Dr. Shapiro to tell him he must change my prescription. "He's out to lunch," his scatterbrained, bleached blonde secretary informed me in her two-pack-a-day voice.

"Tell him it's very important." I hadn't noticed any hair loss yet but, come to think of it, it did have an unusual texture. A bit like Brillo, actually. Never mind that my hair always had an unappealing wiry texture. By now, I was sure of it; the antidepressant was making it worse.

"Howya feeling?" Dr. Shapiro asks when I finally get him on the phone.

"I feel a bit more hazy but I still can't eat. I need to talk to you."

"Come back to the office tomorrow," he says. "Are you free around two?"

The next day, when I told him about my fear of losing my hair he laughed in my face. "Hair loss, hair loss," he snorted, running his hands over his spotted, bald head. "Never heard that one before, Tony." Hrmph! I wasn't that easily brushed off. I persisted. He took his own huge medical book down from the shelf and looked up Zoloft for himself. "Well what, do you know?" he asked. "Alopecia can be a side affect."

"Alopecia I can live with," I said. "It's losing my hair that's out of the question."

"Alopecia means losing your hair," he said in an annoyed tone usually reserved for imbeciles. "But it happens in less than one percent of the people taking it." Those odds were good enough for me. With my luck I knew I had to get off Zoloft at once, lest in a matter of week the only other parts I'd ever be up for again is Mr. Clean commercials and the lead in the *King And I.*

"Luck—without it you might as well throw yourself in the river."

This pearl of wisdom was drilled into me while I was growing up by my Great-Aunt Mamie, whom knows of what she speaks. Luckless herself, she is now a vegetable living in Flushing with only a humongous, sadistic, foreign-born nurse to sustain her.

Poor Aunt Mamie. The only memory I have of her, besides her quote, is the time that during a family reunion in upstate New York a bat landed on the top of her head and carried off the curled wiglet worn to disguise an unsightly bald patch. How unsettling the thought that, to this day, a family of bats is nesting in the hair of a wig belonging to an aunt of mine. No wonder she lost her mind.

Dear Aunt Mamie—with her crooked horn-rimmed glasses, bad false choppers, sagging bosom, and lurid floral-print housedresses. Is that all I had to look forward to? But if I gave in and followed her advice surely by now I'd be floating face down somewhere in the Hudson. Whether it be for the big gambles in life or the minor games of chance, I have no luck.

"Change it," I demanded of Dr. Shapiro. He prescribed the ever-popular Prozac—a very similar drug, he said, without the risk of hair loss.

This entire interaction took but five minutes. He charged me seventy-five bucks. Oh man. Seventy-five bucks! And being clean and sober, childless, single, and born in this country, the government isn't about to reimburse me. My doctor knows this. He's giving me a special rate he says. "How's show business," he asks as I get up to leave. How should I know? I'm living in Queens above a saddle shop. I haven't been in front of a camera in 18 months. To anyone else I exaggerate the hope of some future projects. To him I paint a realistically bleak future. "I'm not in show business," I say. "I just put an application in with the post office."

"Something will turn up," he says, much more optimistically than my agent ever sounded. "My second wife used to watch you every afternoon. She had quite a crush." Hrmph, again! Well, he'll have to bill me. I have to use the hundred bucks my grandmother gave me to fill the Prozac prescription.

From my doctor's medical office it was a short walk to religious sanction—St. Patrick's Cathedral. The cool, quiet cavern always seemed so comforting before. Yet, the moment I sat down my brain started annoying me again, "You can't believe in God as a back-up plan," my mind scorned. "You're either with Him or you're not. There is no in-between."

"Oh, shut up," I snapped back. "Mind your own business!"

In her best-selling book *A Return to Love*, Marianne Williamson, the popular and charismatic spiritual guru explains that God is all love and automatically forgives us for whatever we do. She writes: "When we choose to love, or to allow our minds to be one with God, then life is peaceful. When we turn away from love, the pain sets in." Surely, then, God forgives me for my teensy-weensy lapses of faith.

Being able to quote Marianne Williamson on a whim made me feel smug with myself. Yet I knew this time my mind was right. If it is indeed a sin to turn to God only when in distress I am destined for hell. Each time I need something, want something, or fear something, I turn to the only One who patiently listens to me full attention. Each time He listens I swear I'll remain faithful. "In the light," so to speak. I walk down the streets praying. I read the New Testament each night in bed. I switch my car radio to the religions stations. But, usually after only a few short weeks, I'm walking in darkness and listening to Marilyn Manson. Yet, Religion had helped me throughout the rough patches before and, perhaps, it would help me through this one.

When I arrived home my message machine was blinking! Oh happy day! My agent? An ex? A secret admirer promising a glorious new life, you ask? "Hrmph," I reply. Unfortunately it was my mother's voice that boomed through the airwaves when I pressed "play," reminding me that I was having dinner at her house that evening. Pooch, my dog, sniffed at my pants leg as I sat on my bed and listened to her seven-minute monologue on how she had to plunge the shower drain because of a major water back-up in the upstairs bathroom. She almost drowned in three inches of water. "I can't prove it of course but I'd swear your grandmother stuffed something down there. What? I don't even wanna know..."

I realized my Pooch hasn't been getting the attention he's used to. He's very depressed. Now that I've switched to Prozac I thought of starting him on my left over supply of Zoloft but the last thing I need—with a beige carpet in my bedroom—is a dog with the runs. But, oh, it was with envy as I watched Pooch curl up at my feet and close his eyes. It seemed all he did lately was eat and sleep, as if he absorbed those two glorious functions from me in addition to his own abilities to do so, and now, exhausted and diminished, I was left without them.

A couple of hours later I turn onto my parent's block. A police car is parked in the driveway. "This is not a good sign," my mind warns. "Make a U turn now! Drive!" I hesitate for a moment. "Save yourself from a fate worse than life," is my advice to myself. As per usual I don't listen to me, reasoning that the only other place to go was home to my un-ringing telephone and that, in my present condition, is unthinkable.

Along with my father and grandmother there are two young police officers sitting at the dinner table. My mother is in the midst of laying down a tray overloaded with stuffed peppers.

"All I did was go shoppin' for two minutes..." my mother says by way of greeting.

"Don't worry, son, it's nothin'," my father—the high priest of under-statement—explains.

My mother's tone turns vicious: "What do you know? You were at work!"

To me: "Your grandmother called the cops this afternoon and said that John Travolta was in the house and wouldn't get out."

I shall explain: my grandmother has a collection of back issues of the *Star* and *Enquirer*. Like many of us, gossip fascinates her and she refuses to throw a single issue out often shutting herself in her room reading during lulls of arguing with my mother. I guess you could say that the constant reading of ancient tabloid news, mixed in with her selective senility, alters her perception of reality.

"This is what I came home to," my mother says, indicating the police-men. One of them nods a greeting and the other one, the one I recognize from my neighborhood beat, stares at me with a look which can only be described as pure contempt.

The cop's disgust with me started several months earlier when, unbe-knownst to me at the time that he was an off duty police officer, I refused to let him cut in front of me as I waited amongst a long line of cars backed up due to an unloading truck. Everyone else had been waiting patiently and, just when it was my turn to pass in the one free lane, his car snaked in out of nowhere and tried to cut in front of me. My mind told me, "Why should you let him get in front of you? After all, your time is just as impor-tant as his, isn't it?"

And I decided to listen to my mind for a change. Which resulted in this gorilla of an off-duty policeman jumping out of his car, screaming obscenities at me, pulling out his badge, calling my a "spic" and spitting at me. Luckily, due to the intense heat, I had the window rolled up with the air conditioner on and the glob of saliva trailed down the window in-stead of my face. Even badly shaken as I was I thought his actions wrong. Couldn't he tell that I was Italian and not Hispanic? Surely, in these politi-cally correct times, he knew that "spic" wasn't the appropriate slur and that "guinea" or "grease-ball" would have been more befitting.

Besides that one little incident, what did I do to still be an object of such loathing? Was it my fault that his eyebrows were more continuous than ever and practically melded into his hairline? Waxing and electrolysis would have been good words of advice but his angry expression made me hold my tongue.

I smile wanly and sit down.

"What did you expect me to do?" my grandmother asks. "He wouldn't get out."

"Ma, John Travolta was not in this house!" my mother bellows, taking her seat amongst us.

"Of course the cops didn't see him," grandma explains. "He was hiding in the shopping bag."

"She's a little forgetful," my father tells the cops.

"A little forgetful?" my mother sneers. "She's like the aunt on *Bewitched*—Clara. She has signs taped up all over the bathroom, 'KEEP OUT!' Meanwhile, there's no one in the house all day..."

"What do you mean," my grandmother heaves in astonishment, "I have company in and out all day. Today for instance, all she did was brag about her eight thousand dollar gown."

"Who?" I ask.

My father explains: "She read in the *Star* that Angelina Jolie paid eight thousand dollars for an evening gown."

"Was she here too?" I ask.

"Listen," grandma tells the cops, "I don't want to hear John Travolta anymore! I don't want to hear Angelina Jolie anymore! I want them out!"

Unfortunately this is not one of those moments when I have even the slightest of appetites. And not eating at my mother's is a mortal sin. I put one stuffed pepper in my dish. My mother heaps in two more, commenting on my wan appearance that I look like I could "haunt houses."

"I'll push it around with my fork and chatter away," I think. "And when the coast is clear I'll get up and empty it in the garbage as if I'm helping her clean the table..." It's not to be.

"I want to tell you something, Anthony," my mother says in a confidential tone after a one second lull in conversation. "But you can't tell anyone because your Aunt Lou has sworn me to secrecy."

I look at the two cops, deeply engrossed in the food that had been set before them.

"Maybe you should tell me later," I say.

"Oh these two aren't gonna tell anybody," she says, offhandedly. My mother trying to keep a secret is like a fat woman trying to squeeze into a size two. She's bursting at the seams.

I sigh. "What is it?"

"Your cousin, Joseph and his wife..."

"Yeah?" From the look on her face I think she's going to add, "are dead." I use her grave expression as an excuse to put down my fork.

"...are having another baby." She looks at me stricken.

I wait. "And?"

"That makes three kids and they're only married four years."

"This constitutes a secret?" I ask.

36

"She doesn't want anyone to know yet."

"Well," I sigh yet again. "Good luck to them." Being well studied in my mother and her ways I know what is coming next and brace myself for it.

"I'm very happy that I'll have another grandniece or nephew," my mother quivers over a brave smile. "After all, I know *I'LL* never have grandchildren."

Every time I eat with my parents it's like being in a cut-rate, Italian-American version of *Cat on a Hot Tin Roof*. I'm cast as both Brick and Maggie, unable to produce an heir for Big Daddy and Big Momma. By now I know all the lines for this play, we'd been in rehearsals for the past seven or eight years, and yet, in my weakened state I'm in no condition for the big argument scene.

"You don't know that, Ma. I'm still relatively young. There's plenty of time..."

"Look, Anthony—your father and I—all we ever wanted was a NOR-MAL life," she says, martyr-style, emphasis on "normal." "All our friends have grandchildren. What are we supposed to say when they ask about you?"

This gets the two policemen's attention. Up to now they had been hunched over their plates like the starving wild coyotes I had, unfortunately, once seen on a PBS wildlife special. The wild beasts ripped open a fawn and devoured the poor dears innards in a matter of seconds. Now they look up at me quizzically with the same expression as the coyotes.

"Tell them I'm fine."

"HA!" laughs my mother with the abrupt and stunning impact of a truck collision. "We did everything right! Why have we been cursed this way?" (This is said looking up at the ceiling to God). "I've been cursed," she hisses. And then she mutters: "I'm thinking of worshipping the devil."

"God gives bread to those without teeth," my father says.

I'm losing the thread.

Ann Sexton, another famous woman poet with suicidal tendencies, went into her garage, closed the door, started the car, crawled into the back seat, glass of vodka in hand, and breathed in the toxic exhaust for several minutes before a chorus of angels descended onto her and pointed the way to delicious oblivion. But the only people I knew who had a garage were my parents and the thought of waking up to my grandmother giving me mouth to mouth was enough to nix that idea pronto.

"It's just that right now I'm very into my career..."

"Career?" Big Momma says, packing the word with enough sarcasm for ten sentences. "What career?"

"I'm going through a dry period."

"Your career as dry as the cunt of an eighty year old woman," Big Daddy pipes in with a mouth overstuffed with stuffed peppers. Now it was turning ugly. Discussions of eighty-year old women and their private parts, in my opinion, are not appropriate at the dinner table or at any table for that matter, as far as I'm concerned.

To put an end to it I try to invoke their sympathy. "Look, I didn't want to tell you this—I don't want to worry you—but I haven't been feeling very well lately."

All color drains from my mother's face. "What's wrong with you?"

"I've been very depressed?"

This really gets her dander up. "Depressed? DEPRESSED? What do you have to be depressed about?" she shrieks. "Do you think my life is a picnic? Living with him (a head nod towards my father) taking care of her (a nod in the other direction at grandma), and all day long I have to listen to myself! Don't you think *I'd* like to have some peace?"

Obviously these people know nothing of Marianne Williamson and her teachings. But already I know that any attempts at enlightening them to the inner peace that spiritual awareness might bring would result in my mother commenting smugly, "Anthony is having another one of his flights of fancy." So I figure, why set myself up for the humiliation?

"Insanity runs in your side of the family," my father reminds my mother. "Look at your Aunt Mamie. And your mother," he shoots a look at my grandmother. "She has Alzheimer's."

"I'm twenty-nine," I gasp. "I'm too young for Alzheimer's. Aren't I?"

"You've always been very mature for your age," my mother says, considering.

"But I'm not forgetful. I remember everything—unfortunately. It's just that, well, my career isn't moving fast enough and I'm...well, I'm... lonely..."

I know my parents care for me deeply. I know they would each give the other's life for me. But if I should have learned one thing in my life by now it is that revealing any kind of weakness would turn into a screaming match as to which one of us has the worst life.

My mother, bogged down with an endless life of vacuuming cleaning, grocery shopping and cooking and now, at the ripe old age of fifty, branded with the horrifying stigma of being grandchildless. My father, stuck with the ever-mounting pile of bills, a wife who is never satisfied, and a flighty, actor-son without medical coverage. My grandmother, elderly, insane, spending a large portion of her social security on rag publications and public transportation, whilst trying her best to spoon feed a forty year old photograph of my grandfather. Thus were the problems of the modern family unit—at least my unit. They are the world champions of screaming at the tops of their lungs. I give them a run for their money.

Luckily for me my grandmother saves the day. It goes like this: She takes a sip of soda. An ice cube goes down the wrong way. Suddenly she's a candidate for the Heimlich maneuver: choking, heaving and coughing all the while trying to get in her two cents in between quick gasps for breath. Now's my chance. I get up and empty my plate in the garbage pale. The cop with one eyebrow slaps her on the back. Grandma spits up the ice cube.

"I have to go," I say, kissing everyone, save the cops, on the cheek. "Thanks for dinner. It was great."

"Do you need any money," my mother asks me as a parting shot.

"No, no, I'm fine."

"Sal, give him money," she tells my father and he takes out his wallet.

I don't want them to give me money. I feel guilty. After all I'm an adult. I shouldn't still be dependent on them. I walk hurriedly to the door, but my mother is hot on my tail. We pause at the door. I look at her standing there and there is real concern from her and I love her because I know that no matter what I say, no matter what I do, no matter how bad things get for me, my mother will love me and be there for me. No matter what they say to me, by parents are the ones who will always love me.

"Give me a hug, Ma," I say embracing her. "I don't want to seem like a baby but I..." I can't go on without crying so I stop.

"You don't seem like a baby," my mother says still holding me. "But you worry about things too much."

She hands me the five twenties my father had taken out of his wallet. I shrug and take them, figuring that I better start a savings fund for next months medications. Life is not cheap in the valley of the dolls.

Did I tell you I started making out my will? There wasn't much really. To my parents I decided to leave a plastic sandwich bag filled with my sperm—they can freeze it, I thought, and whenever she's ready, Mom could inject the woman of her choice with my sperm using the turkey baster. Okay, Thanksgiving at her house would never be the same and she'd probably have to put a mortgage on the house to pay the woman—and then of course there would be many years of custody battles and video taping of the saga for television shows like *20/20*—but at least she'd finally get that grandchild she's been longing for.

All the while I'm thinking that maybe I should be more masculine in my suicide plot. "Forget about famous lady suicides and their ways," my mind advises me. "Do you want to be a laughingstock even in death?" (By this time I had already rejected the two Marilyn Monroe suicide scenarios that had presented themselves: either swallowing a large dose of Nembutal while falling fatally asleep—glamorously nude—with my hand fiercely clutching the telephone, or getting romantically involved with a high profile politician who would have me rubbed out by the mob when, after being dumped, I threatened to expose the affair in a free-for-all press conference). Then my mind came up with the perfect suicide: "Ernest Hemingway—there's a man's man for you—put a bullet through your head." But the idea of the mess is so damn off-putting.

I was almost finished with my will when I was overcome with despair so deep, so consuming, so utterly unbearable that, without thinking, I grabbed my car keys and jumped into my car. In desperation I drove towards my best friend Miles' apartment. I did not care that he now had a lover named Les and a life beyond me and that our friendship was now a minor subplot in his life. I realized it was payback time. A time when all those little things you do for a friend, all the little inconveniences that you never expect to be paid back for—well, now it was payback time. I needed a friend and now was the time to see if I had any.

I was halfway there, screaming at the top of my longs, driving, and crying all at the same time. After sideswiping a parked station wagon I no longer felt safe driving so in this pitiable state, I parked my car near the bus stop and decided to take the bus the rest of the way. Mercifully one came right away and I took a seat in the back, crying all the way while, at the same time, giving the passengers fashion makeovers in my mind. I wanted to do it privately but, at the very next stop, a disheveled man wearing rubber boots took the seat next to me, eating a piece of pizza, the smell of which put me on the brink of vomiting.

I tried to be patient but it seemed the pizza would never come to an end. When I looked at the guy—horn rimmed glasses, long, lank, blonde hair, plaid shirt—he seemed to be taking big healthy bites out of it but the pizza never finished. Each time this nerd took a bite, the pizza slice renewed itself to its former state. How could this be? It was, after all, only one normally sized slice. Was it the same kind of miracle Christ performed when feeding the hungry crowds and the bread and fish didn't run out?

Why couldn't I be left in peace? Who could help me, even now?

Miles! My friend Miles, I hoped, would know what to do. At one point in his life he had been an actor and had been on *A World Away* with me and, when we met, it was friendship at first sight. I had never met anyone with whom I was more in tune with. What initially made it easy for us to bond as friends is the fact that there was no competition between us. Particularly as actors. In contrast to my dark broodiness, Miles has a blond, blue-eyed, All American, apple-pie kind of appeal. Easy going and good-natured.

Through the hectic rehearsal and taping schedule of a daily soap opera we spent a lot of time together and realized that we had many things in common, including a family life which we couldn't disentangle ourselves from, and a non-existent love life. We two struggling boy starlets had spent too many years obsessing over our careers to become emotionally involved with anyone. It seemed we shared the same vision, the same humor, the same hopes and dreams, the same soul. Yet after the show was canceled, something in him died. His ambition.

Show business is a tough life and many people, after the first five years, just sort of give up. Miles took a job in a PR firm and slowly drifted out of acting. Then, recently, he met Les and became the equivalent of a suburban housewife, content to be out of the world of auditions, rejections, headshots, and resumes, and now lived happily in the world of coffee tables, floor waxes, and three weeks a year vacation. It was during this time—experiencing his absence—that I realized how close we had been. Suddenly I had no one to catch a flick with, have a drink with, or call when the 3 AM dooms set in.

Things were different when we had both been desperate and miserable. We'd commiserate for hours about the horrors of life in New York. But now whenever I brought up my favorite topic of conversation—despair— his voice would get very low and he'd sigh, "If only you could find someone to bring you happiness, Tony. Then my life would be complete." Which on one hand makes me feel fuzzy and warm to have a friend so wonderful that his complete happiness depends on my own, but on the other hand makes me feel, well, pathetic.

Perhaps, I thought, I should find someone and settle down. But I knew in my heart of hearts that that was impossible. I would never be able to love anyone until I loved myself and that wasn't gonna happen until I fulfilled at least some of my dreams. But couldn't I find someone who was not only attractive but also bright and just as ambitious as I and, perhaps, we could push and encourage and support each other during our respective climbs? But where to find such a person (let alone snare one) in the midst of a nervous breakdown?

When the pizza slice was finally finished—the 5,000 had apparently been fed—the nerd sitting next to me started whistling a happy tune. The smell of the pizza had been bad enough but the whistling in my ear—*Tie a Yellow Ribbon 'Round the Old Oak Tree*—was really, you know, a bit much, so I blew a fart and hoped it wafted in his direction. I know, I know. "Vengeance is mine says the Lord." But I was far too impatient for that.

When I arrived (unexpectedly) Miles and Les were eating dinner. "Just dropped by to say hello," I said. I never dropped by unexpectedly before and the air was filled with a sort of "what's he doing here," quality. Or so I thought. I felt so lost and insecure it was impossible to accurately read any atmosphere. They were watching reruns of *The Golden Girls* and making small talk. I hadn't eaten a single morsel in quite a few days. Miles poured me apple wine and offered me some French fries. I drank the wine and ignored the French fries. We sat in the living room, them with their plates in their laps.

Suddenly I started pouring everything out. My fear of getting ill, at this stage of my life, with no job, no coverage, no money, no prospects. I started to cry over how much I love my parents but how their unhappiness mingles with my own and compounds it. They have always been good to me and it hurts me that I cause them pain. Yet they can't help it anymore than I could. About how I need to get a job and get out but nothing seems to work. Everything falls through. How I wanted to be an actor but how I'm difficult to cast and how I couldn't even afford a new set of headshots. And here I was getting older every minute.

As I spoke I hadn't had the nerve to look at them for fear of getting embarrassed and abruptly stopping my monologue. But now, having gotten this all out of my system—and having given a pretty damn good performance at that—I stopped crying, wiped my eyes on a greasy napkin, sniffed loudly and popped a French fry into my mouth. I felt better already.

"You're just depressed," Miles said, with one eye on me and the other on the television.

I stopped chewing. I was astonished by this remarkable insight. You mean I spent several hundred dollars at Dr. Shapiro's office only to get the same advice I could have gotten from a dear friend—who was only half-listening—for free?

Surprisingly it was Les who sprung into action. "Come and spend some time with us," Les said. "You need to get away from that familiar atmosphere for awhile."

I batted my eyes and said, "Oh no I couldn't. I wouldn't want to impose." Knowing all the time that I must. My exhaustion! I leaned back languidly, twisting my body to show off my newly svelte frame to its best advantage.

"You know, Tony, there's more to life than being a sex kitten." Les said, bemused, observing me.

"If there is I don't want to hear about it," I replied.

"We're your best friends. Tony," Les went on. "We want you to stay here. That's what friends are for...not just in the good times." Miles whole heartedly agreed.

The thought of being able to sleep in peace amongst friends who understand me, was the equivalent to a snug, dimly lit cave in the middle of nowhere.

"Yes," I said.

I moved into their guest-room for three days and three nights. I must admit that I felt much better while staying there. It was a small, cozy room, with a bookcase filled with movie star biographies, family photos and various Catholic icons. During the day I would go home, visit with Pooch, walk him, feed him, and just generally love him for the better part of the day. In the late afternoons I would drop the dog of at my parents and return to my friends guest-room and read bits and pieces about the tragedy packed lives of Lana Turner, Bette Davis, Ava Gardner and Elizabeth Taylor—relating to every heartache, every tragedy, every well deserved breakdown—in between fervent bouts of praying. The fact that the framed photos that watched me as I read and prayed were not pictures of *my* family made me feel unthreatened and calm.

I would be lying in bed when Miles and Les returned from work and I'd listen to them plan vacations, bicker about something on television, or simply prepare dinner. I think they forgot I was there. It made me realize that there are lives outside of my own. The world goes on with or without me and whatever I do with myself—it isn't going to have much consequence outside of me.

In this snug little cave there were no demands on me. I would have very much loved for Miles to brick up the doorway leading to the guest-room, but I knew that I had to get back to my real life. It was refreshing to get away from the uncertainty of my existence but time moves much too quickly to waste too much of it.

Well, on the forth day—just as I was beginning to feel alive again—my wonderful doctor called and said he wanted to see me. He stressed, "there's nothing to worry about," but if that were true why did he want to see me? Surely he would have given me the news, had it been good, over the phone. Because of this phone call I bussed myself to his office in a state of utter hysteria, hiding behind a pair of Lana Turner dark sunglasses, praying frenetically and making all kinds of deals with God to spare my life, at least until I had the guts to work my way up to suicide.

What seemed like many hours later I was sitting in Shapiro's office sitting across from him at his imposing, mahogany desk. By this time I was a ticking madman waiting to explode. Dr. Shapiro was telling me about his "cute" five-year old niece, which only added to my unease. "...she's not shy. She's very adorable and articulate and she's got a very nice way with people..."

He took out an eight by ten color department store photo of her. The kid—with a big head, tiny body, huge brown eyes, and a mop of hair—was indeed cute. Was this what he wanted to see me about? To see if I can open show business doors for this personable moppet? Yes, yes! "Maybe you could show her picture to some of your people?" Flattered that he thought I had "people," I assured him I'd send her photo to my agent with a letter or recommendation, which I knew I would do. I'm good with things like that.

"By the way," he said as I was getting up to leave, "your test results came back."

He had been waiting to give me my death sentence till after I made a commitment to help the kid out, I presumed.

He shuffled some papers on his desk. "You're fine. You have the kind of blood that's least likely to get cholesterol."

Funny. Earlier I hadn't felt like driving and I took the bus to Shapiro's office. But now I felt as if I could drive for hours. Life wasn't over after all. And I really couldn't think of any valid reasons to end it. There are always options, right? At least for now. I could get a job at the post office and fall in love with an ambitious mail carrier. I could write a play for myself and try to get it produced Off-Broadway and become creatively fulfilled. More likely, I could pack up my dog and move to Los Angeles. It was somewhere far, far away—but maybe the people were friendly.

I got on the bus and found a seat way in the back near the window. The air conditioner was on high and it felt cool and wonderful. For the first time in many months, I had a plan. Perhaps my recent trials had added something interesting to my character and someone in Los Angeles would recognize it and promote me. Maybe my tribulations had finally given me the courage to face Hollywood alone. Being thin again I was already ahead of the game.

The bus sped me to my destination and I closed my eyes and to my complete joy and amazement I felt ready for sleep. At last I had something

44

to attach hope to: I was going to borrow a few thousand dollars from my parents and move to Hollywood. I would find a new agent. I would get a small, comfortable apartment in a fashionable part of town. I would go on auditions by day and work as a waiter by night. There was plenty of fear, sure, but I wouldn't let it rule me. I wouldn't let it make me sick again

"Hey! Hey you!"

There was a ruckus at the front of the bus. Some lady was haggling hoarsely with the bus driver. "Hey you! Mister! Can you please turn down that air conditioner?"

"Lady will ya sit down, please!" the bus driver roared.

"I don't wanna sit down! Lower that air conditioner! Is it me, or is it cold in here?"

Ah New York. We were going 60 miles an hour down winding streets, hermetically sealed in on an express bus, and there was a nut on board. I jockeyed my head to see the cause of the commotion up front. I was only a few minutes from home and I was going to be okay, but even my mind was at a loss for words.

Grandma was on the bus.

The Secret Of
Marilyn Monroe

For Denis

I was no fool. I knew it was weird for a kid—me—to be fascinated with a beautiful actress who died before I was born. I mean it just wasn't done. In my neighborhood the boys my age were out playing baseball, while I was inside pouring over the TV guide wondering when a Marilyn Monroe movie would be on the late, late show. Soon I would be starting high school and I knew I'd have to leave my Marilyn interest…okay… "obsession"…behind.

The first time I saw her was about a year before. I was leafing through an issue of my Cousin Connie's *Cosmopolitan Magazine.* I was about twelve years old and at that time Cosmo, like my sixteen year old cousin, was to me was the height of adult sophistication and glamour. I remember coming across an article called "The Marilyn Monroe Only Her Hairdresser Knew For Sure," or some such title. Along with the article they published a photo of Marilyn at a movie premiere. The piece was derogatory. It was written by a man who had been one of her make-up artist/hair stylists in the last few years of her life. Mostly it dealt with how she had two distinct personalities. He saw one half of her as a lazy, sloppy drugged up woman who stumbled around from room to room in a ripped terry cloth robe eating caviar and guzzling champagne. The other half was a cool, calculating sex object oozing female sexuality who, when in her "Marilyn getup" would cause men and women alike to turn into quivering masses of goose-bumped flesh.

The article said she never wore a bra, except to bed to compensate for not wearing one during the day (to keep her breasts firm). It said she stood stone still for hours while seamstresses literary sewed her into sequined gowns so that every curve—including the crack in her rear—was show to the best advantage. It said that she was so insecure that she demanded that all the blondes around her—secretaries, stylists, agents, friends—dye their hair to a darker shade so that no one would diminish her radiance. It said that in the last year of her life she had an affair with Frank Sinatra and, with much intrigue, President John F. Kennedy.

As I read the article I kept going back to the photo chosen to illustrate it. In the photo the woman's shoulders were thrust back, her great bosom pushed forward and barely contained in a tight beaded gown. She smiled brightly into the camera with a movie star's confidence. Yet she didn't seem brazen. She didn't seem hard. In total contrast to the pose, the dress, the smile, this woman seemed vulnerable, as if part of her was a little girl begging the viewer to "please like me."

The article was intended to humanize the goddess. Make the legend real; even tarnish it a bit. But what came across to me was a complex woman, filled with self-doubts and insecurities. This was a girl who somehow rose above her extraordinarily unhappy background and overcame her emotional wounds to eventually bring Hollywood, and the rest of the world, to its knees. A film actress whose image on the screen had earned millions of dollars. A celebrity who was mobbed whenever she appeared in public. A woman who was habitually late and kept the most important people on the planet waiting—and they would wait for her. What was her secret? How did she become so famous? Why does she endure?

I had never thought of Marilyn Monroe before that summer afternoon I sat in my cousin's bedroom reading and re-reading the article but from then on the world was suddenly filled with her. Everywhere I turned there was another magazine article, a new book, a different photograph. I began collecting books and memorabilia.

I found Marilyn Monroe fascinating and I wanted to know why.

I had an old copy of Elton John's *Goodbye Yellow Brick Road* album and I would listen to his song about Marilyn over and over looking to see if he knew the answer to her secret. Elton saw her as a fragile, flickering flame trying to keep itself alive in spite of violent outside forces. Candle in the wind. Yeah. Okay. I could relate.

This was also a year of incredible change for me. I had always felt a certain separateness from my peers but I never had a problem making friends, at least on the surface. I went to a Catholic grammar school and most of my classmates and I had been together since kindergarten. We were comfortable with each other if not particularly close. But I felt the rumblings of change. The girls were becoming more distant and mysterious, they no longer wanted boys as "friends" and I was no longer privy to their secrets or welcome in their groups. Boys were getting tougher, acting more macho, swaggering to impress girls. I still had no sexual interest in girls and that panicked me. I tried to fake it. I remember once I brought in a revealing photo of Marilyn Monroe and taped it on the top of my desk. It was not taken as amusing and I remember being ridiculed for it.

Actually, I was growing afraid of the boys who had been my friends for years. They were going through their mischievous age, experimenting with drugs and, with their new body hair and deepening voices, were becoming more rugged and mean. They began t to wonder about me. It wasn't that I was really effeminate. I had long ago exorcised all sissy mannerisms from my body, at least to the best of my ability. I kept my voice a low pitch deep in my throat. I did have a funny walk, but if I concentrated I could keep it under control. As I walked down the hall I learned to balance my books on my hip rather than clutching them to my chest as the girls did. When after school sports events were organized I knew to stay away. "He throws like a girl," was the assessment of my athletic ability on one of my first cracks at the neighborhood sports scene—a crack, I've since learned, that's been made to many gay guys in sports arenas before and after me.

The problem was that I knew I was gay. Even before I had a word for it I felt separate and undefined. In my little world—my family, my friends, my neighborhood—being a sissy was the absolute worst perversion imaginable. The most awful thing in the world that you could be. The definite roles of male and female behavior were so clear-cut, so stringently observed, that I grew terrified of veering away from them. And yet, because nothing of the way the boys acted came naturally to me, I knew I didn't fit in with my set. I never had a real childhood. I could never be carefree and simply play. I was always watching myself. Careful not to make a wrong move or say the wrong thing. A little old man, constantly embarrassed by my mistakes.

So, as high school neared, I entombed all of my true self within me. All of my thoughts, opinions and personality became so deeply buried (for fear they'd find out) that even I lost track of who I was. I became a blank. A zero. A nothing. All that existed was my anxiety, my terror, my fear.

But when I was in their midst, of course, these qualities were what they sniffed out in me.

With high school I knew I'd have a second chance. I would start over with a brand new crowd. But I was aware that, naturally, this new crowd would be tougher to crack. The boys would be harder, more world weary, deeper into puberty. I made a vow that when I was in high school that I wouldn't talk about Marilyn. She would be mine. My little secret. High school would put me in a new environment with a new set of kids. It was my goal to fit in. I was determined to make it.

Unfortunately I went to a Catholic Prep school that, although it recently went coed, was still famous for its football team. Oh what a mistake to chose such a high school (though it is also known for its academic excellence). Jocks. Jocks! Everywhere jocks! I was petrified.

In retrospect I see that, even there, it should have been easy to make friends. I remember the first few weeks everyone was afraid and eager to be accepted. But my initial attempts failed because I was so strangled with the self-conscious terror of being thought of as gay. I would reach out, make an

48

attempt and then retreat. Burying myself again. Days went by. Slowly clicks started to form, and the more established the clicks became the harder it was to break into one.

Soon the entire freshman year was grouped: The brutish jocks. The snobby cheerleader types constantly on the prowl (for brutish jocks). The bookworm intellectuals who joined after school clubs. And the pot smoking hard rockers—stoned and brilliant with their spacey philosophies. And in the middle of this jumble—me! A mess. Afraid and horribly sensitive. I had missed the boat. I could not find my place. There was no place.

And the teenagers zeroed in on that. And cast me as an outsider. Or at least that's how I felt. And, thus, it was so.

In the years since high school I have walked alone through the worst neighborhoods in Manhattan at three AM. I have lost my breaks while driving and plowed head on into an intersection. I have had a knife held to my throat on a late night subway. But I have never again experienced the sheer terror of walking into my high school cafeteria alone. The sneering girls with too much makeup on their adolescent faces, smelling of the cigarettes they smoked behind the school, starting malicious rumors and spreading them fast, all in an effort to become the most popular luncheon companion. The hulking football players, scornful of everyone, eating their grayish hamburgers and soggy French fries, scanning the area like vultures for each new scrap of meat that might become the butt of their merciless jokes. Pimples, disorder, fear, anger, longing, sexuality, panic, anxiety, jealousy. This was my new world.

I would walk around the cafeteria with my tray, looking for a place to sit, my whole body trembling, my face burning. It was too crowded to sit away from everybody and I didn't want to put myself under horrifying scrutiny by planting myself in the midst of an established click that didn't know me. Yet to sit alone was the ultimate humiliation. Wandering. Wandering. Finally I would choose a table with a group of three or four girls I had known in grammar school. They were, however, already popular—part of the boy-crazy cheerleader set. They endured my presence for old-times sake, I suppose. But, as I did nothing to add to their luster, I was more or less ignored. But it was at least a place to eat my greasy mustard-smeared knish and sip my coke.

But day after day, as this group of gossipy females expanded, I became more and more conspicuous. A lone boy among a chattering gaggle of giggly girls. I could sometimes feel the fierce glares from the other tables, the "guy" tables. I could practically see the seeds of rumors and legends about me, that were soon to circulate, begin to take root and sprout right before my eyes. The fear of being ridiculed in front of these girls (or anyone else) was so horrifying that I completely stopped going to the cafeteria during lunch period. Instead I would go to the library, sitting quietly between my loneliness and my loneliness—reading books about Marilyn Monroe and other movie starts that I found in the library's "Entertainment" section.

I did my best to remain hidden. I no longer dreamed of being part of a popular crowd. Now my goal was to simply go unnoticed.

For the first few months of my freshman year I noted a group of effeminate boys who were tormented unmercifully. Weak, pale boys with spindly legs and pretty, delicate features. With a giant lump in my throat and a stoic expression on my face, I silently watched these boys as they were hit with snapping towels in the locker room or teased before classes began. I was filled with a genuine pity and a wobbly relief. Pity for what they were forced to endure, relief that it wasn't me enduring it.

I was shocked when the verbal assaults started on me.

My first clear memory of being targeted myself is while I was waiting for my Spanish class to begin. As always I was sitting quietly at my desk thinking myself invisible, when a tall, blonde guy—the class clown who I had a secret crush on—passed by and nonchalantly dropped an advertisement for a gay porn theater that he had cut out of the newspaper on my desk. I was shocked. Appalled. Terrified. And then that familiar hot rush to my face. Not only because I was humiliated in the moment—disoriented, frightened—but also because I suspected that this was only the beginning. I wasn't invisible. They could see me! I quickly crumpled up the advertisement and swept it to the floor, but I could feel the entire classroom alive and twittering. Me? Me! They had noticed me. They had actually planned this humiliation in advance and waited for my reaction—these people who I had never spoken to and who never said a word to me.

From that moment it was only a matter of days before I was being verbally assaulted with "faggot," "fairy," and "gay boy," whenever I entered a class. Just to make sure I wasn't spared any cliché, I was showered regularly with rubber bands and paper clips as I sat statue-like at my desk. To not acknowledge them at all was always my only defense. I hypnotized myself into ignoring them, forcing myself to believe it wasn't happening. There was nothing I could say to those torrents anyway without being made more ridiculous. Yet because of my silence, my refusal to defend myself, I came to represent everything that was weak and awkward and undesirable. .

My whole week, my whole life, revolved around my twice-a-week gym classes. Hours were spent trying to think up new ways to avoid attending them. Having gotten the reputation of being a faggot, now the white hot spot light was on every move I made—and, under that glare, my moves were very clumsily indeed. Eventually I stopped attending gym classes altogether, only to be sought out by the young, handsome gym teacher (and football coach) who made a fool out of me—mumbling, fumbling, and furious red—in front of the entire snickering class.

The way I walked, talked, and moved also came under delighted analysis and ridicule. I became stiff with terror as I tried to concentrate on walking normally but all I could do was wonder who was behind me. The halls of my school stretched out endless before me. The long walk. The death walk.

In reality I knew that these were really, underneath it all, okay kids. Most of them anyway. One on one I probably could have gotten along with them as friends. We were all vulnerable young boys and girls who wanted to be accepted and liked. But as a group they were dangerous, evil—predatory. They had to be to cover up their own twisted mass of fears and insecurities. They ridiculed someone else to take the attention away from themselves. I wonder if I would have done the same if I had the option. Christ! I hope not.

Funny how stupid this all seems today. How important it was to me at the time. How it would keep me up night after night, tearing, praying, trying to think of a solution, something I could do or say that would show them that I wasn't the mumbling stumbling fumbling fool they saw wriggling before them. The one deed that would convey: "Hey, I'm a nice guy. You would like me, if you knew me."

As I write this now, many years later, I realize I risk coming off as unlikable here. No one likes someone who goes around feeling sorry for himself. Crybaby! Grow up. Get over it. You're an adult, stop blaming the past. But actually, dear reader, friend, I did not feel sorry for myself at all. This was just the way things were. My plans and schemes of the time had to do with survival not self-pity. But that's not to say I didn't know loneliness.

Oh, I knew it.

Marilyn Monroe died many years before all this, without even knowing of my existence—easy enough to deduce since she was dead before I existed. But during these bleak years my interest in Marilyn was the one thing I could hang on to. She was never far from my mind—a presence, a mystery, a light, a longing, a comfort. Through her movies and photos and books about her life she would always be there and I would call on her as one would call a friend.

Even in that jungle-like environment of high school she was a thread of communication.

The girls, the sex-hawks, circling the gymnasium, the cafeteria, salivating over their lipstick, hunting for hunks of men, preferably left over from the football team. Me they passed over with a condescending smile.

I was not meat they desired. But when I sat quietly by myself before class, sketching a portrait of Marilyn on the inside of my notebook cover, they would come up from behind and watch (me draw) and comment of their own fondness of Marilyn—my patron saint of glamour.

The boys, my torturers, with their raging hormones and their hard-ons like spears, would leer over my shoulder, friendly for a change, and make comments about Marilyn's cleavage which I lovingly sketched in.

Why does everyone like her? How did she overcome? Why is she immortal?

My parents were loving and protective but my pain would be their pain so, even though I was very sad, I kept them in the dark about my life at school. Their love for me pierced my heart because I was not what they were, I was not what they wanted me to be, and I always felt they deserved better. They were approximately the same age I am now, but a hundred times more mature, together and loving. They would have loved whatever was born to them, and, by some bizarre twist of fate, they were sent me. Nevertheless my family was all I knew of love and kindness.

I realized when I walked through the doors of my high school I was utterly and completely on my own. My parents must never know what I had to endure there. It embarrassed me that I had no friends, received no phone calls, rarely left the house. Except, of course to go to school.

So I would go off on Saturday afternoons. I would ride the subways from my home in Queens into Manhattan looking for a destination. Sometimes there would be a Marilyn Monroe movie playing at one of the revival movie houses and it was wonderful to see Marilyn up on the big screen. Going to the movies alone was no small feat. By now everything frightened me—any place outside of my house had become strange and dangerous territory and all the people inhabiting these places were threatening, hazardous enemies.

But seeing Marilyn was worth it.

She is the Cleopatra of her century. Hundreds of years from now people will look at her image in photographs and on film and contemplate her secrets. Besides physical beauty what was it that made the masses single her out? What made her able to attract the most powerful men of her generation? What makes her immortal?

The most terrifying aspect of high school was—even with all the tedious planning—my inability to control every situation. No matter how many gym classes I skipped, no matter how many halls I carefully slinked down, no matter how many disasters I tactfully avoided, I never knew when it would all be out of my control.

In my junior year there was this one girl who liked me, a dark Italian girl. Marie was her name. She had a friendly, pretty face, but didn't possess the ravishing beauty or caustic wit that would have automatically designated her to one of the popular sets. But Marie didn't seem to mind. She was constantly primping herself, applying pink blush, flinging her abundant, shoulder-length hair. And her confidence made her seem beautiful. Plus, Marie was warm and good-natured—always smiling—and that to me was a breath of fresh air. I had been gasping. Why she liked me, I don't know. There wasn't that much to like at the time, but she gave me a chance and would sit and talk to me in the school library brimming with curiosity and cheer.

Eventually I allowed some of my true self to seep out. At least what I knew of myself. As it turned out she was a Marilyn fan too and although I had vowed that I wouldn't talk to anyone at school about Marilyn, Marie initiated conversations about her movies and so I broke my vow.

Well, see, I felt comfortable with Marie. It was good to be talking with someone who also was interested in my Marilyn. Who flirted with me. Who, maybe, thought I was a dish. Or maybe she didn't. Perhaps she was just being sweet. But still, it was good to be talking to anyone at all. She was in one of my classes, which was canceled one day, and she suggested we go to the cafeteria for hot chocolate. I felt it would be safe. At this hour of the morning most people would be in classes and besides it looked as if Marie was my girlfriend so I felt a bit cocky.

Funny, the things you remember.

I specifically recall not looking around the cafeteria as we sat at a table with our hot chocolates. Too look around was to invite others to look back, to be noticed. I remember we were talking about *The Misfits*, a Marilyn movie that Marie had never seen. I remember describing the plot, having an easy time, forgetting myself. And then suddenly, in the middle of the conversation, I heard the voices from another table. "Hey faggot, hey fairy." It was a low, mocking murmur at first but my antenna for miserable situations immediately went up—by now it could sense humiliation from miles away. It was, I knew—for my antenna told me—the football players who were out to humiliate. And silly, unsuspecting me had landed right in the middle of their evil web. *See what happens the minute you let your guard down!* "Faggot, faggot."

I knew, of course, they were calling to me but their voices were still relatively low—they could just as well have been teasing each other as they often did—and that's what I hoped Marie would think. It was imperative that she didn't know it was me, me, me they were mocking

To acknowledge them now would mean instant death. So what was a boy to do but pick up the pace? Talk more rapidly. So rapidly in fact that it was easy to lose track of what I was saying. "..and it's one of Marilyn's few serious films and towards the end she runs into the dessert and screams at the insensitive men 'Tortures! Killers! Liars!'"

And then the football players at the distant table broke loose into frenzied name calling to me: "Faggot...fairy...hey girl..." There was no doubt now to whom it was directed—the voices sharp, cruel, loud and crystal clear. I sat pin straight in a storm of words swirling around me like bits of ice. My monologue about *The Misfits* was now incoherent rambling as Marie's eyes darted to the direction of the noisy table. Yet my intense babbling continued. If only the cafeteria floor would split open and suck me into some place safe—some dark room with a blanket and a tranquilizer. Oh what a drastic mistake I had made, brazenly trying to do something normal like chatting in the cafeteria with a friend. How did I ever think I could get away with it? Marie's eyes returned to mine.

"Who are they talking about," she asked kindly. Of course there was no question of who they were talking about. I knew. She knew. But she was saving my face. And from then on it would be very difficult to be with Marie.

I got through it all, obviously. But something in me had changed. It was as if I had to go through that final humiliation—the big one—in order to be free of them. The football players had taken their act as far as it could go and I no longer cared. Nothing they said could hurt me now. No longer a victim, I viewed myself as a survivor, and I effortlessly exuded an unwavering dignity that caused others to step back. Oh miracles. I was stronger. In my senior year I wasn't obsessed with hiding from people anymore. I silently faced them head on—words would roll off of me anyway. And because they were stripped of their power to hurt me, I was more or less ignored.

Graduation came and went. The world opened up like a flower and I discovered the planet actually expanded outside of my high school walls. I learned that there actually were all kinds of people and room for us all. I made friends, and experienced kindness, and learned love, and climbed and grew and changed.

Eventually I discovered that Marilyn Monroe was a gay icon. That she was loved for her whispery voice, her thrilling red lips, her voluptuous curves, her pillow case white hair. Yet at the time I knew nothing of gay icons. I loved her triumph. She came from nowhere—a nothing from nowhere. Ignored. No friends. No defenders. Last in line for everything. Never noticed. Never loved. Waving her arms in front of the masses screaming "See me! Love me! After all I am a life." Nevertheless, in spite of her terrible sensitivity, she was able to rise from the ashes and demand that people see her, notice her, love her! That is what made me idolize her.

And yet I'm lying. That's not the only thing I loved. I too loved her radiance on screen. Her undeniable beauty. Her unearthly beauty. The way she moved, the ways she spoke. The way men wanted her: an incandescent angel who, for a short while, was allowed to visit with mortals and touch so many of us.

Because I was so unreasonably sensitive and felt such an amazing, unlikely connection with her from an early age, I often wondered if I was Marilyn Monroe reincarnated as a man. Then I smiled and reminded myself that millions of gay men and straight women felt the same way. The vulnerable, the lonely, the tragic—a multitude of people think that they must be her in a different form. A different life. I am no different. Then I crane my neck and look at my ass—the plump round thing—in the mirror and I see that I *am* Marilyn reincarnated. And I laugh at the very idea and hope that somewhere she sees that I like her.

After high school I was a fumbling mumbling mass of wounds and scars but I strove strove strove to overcome it. To become interesting and smart and desirable. Oh yes. I wanted to be desirable. During my teenage years there wasn't a single person in the world I could call a friend. So I thought it would be nice to walk down the street and hear a wolf whistle now and again.

A few years later men would want me and they would come to me in their expensive hotel rooms and apartments on Central Park West—by then I was meat that was desirable—bare-chested men with gelled hair and Calvin Klein underwear. They'd gaze their horny gaze down at me, lulling high as the sky in their clean white sheets, and they'd say breathlessly, "You really are exquisitely beautiful." But by then the high school boys' words had turned my skin to Formica and nothing could sink in. I couldn't absorb compliments. I mostly wanted to please.

Soon, though, it wasn't enough to be desirable. I wanted them to *know* me. For the first time they'd look into my real heart and see ME. See that I was an okay guy, a cool person, and there was some love in there for them all. So I worked and worked and worked on myself. Teaching myself. Trying to improve myself. Everything I did had to be stellar, the absolute best I could give. I had to prove my worth to every person I encountered, from homeless woman in the street, to bartenders in bars to anyone who crossed my path.

I would be drawn to the men who treated me the worst. The liars. The cheaters. The fakes. The ones who could not love. I could see through the nice guy facades to the hard, cold, selfish, damaged man underneath, the kind who would spend his life searching. The kind that I would never be enough for. Nor would anyone else. They thought they were fooling me but I knew what they were. That's what I wanted. Their little humiliations were exactly what I felt I deserved.

Although I developed my own exquisitely designed masks to cover up how I felt inside (people always think I'm this confident, together creature) on the inside I was a wreck and so terribly shy. I never felt I was good enough to be loved. Good men would reach out to me, would love me, but I couldn't feel their touch.

Do you think I want sympathy because my adolescence was unhappy? God! That would be a joke. Ha! I scorn the sympathy card myself as much as I scorn it in others. Yet I usually babble about it because it has so much to do with who I am. And for me, like everyone else, I feel my unhappiness was real.

Today, though, talking about an unpopular childhood is an adornment people add to their personas like an amusing bag or striking brooch. It's so common that celebrities use it as a hook in their publicity. "I was tall and unpopular," a gorgeous, gangly model—who has never known an unpopular day in her life—reveals on late night talk show. "I was tormented as a child," a dirty comedian might gleefully divulge during a pitch meeting for a television show. It's like the millions and millions of A-Listers who talk about the time they were so broke they had to live in their car just before they made it big. Not exactly original but it makes for an amusing anecdote.

What's going on? If there is any slight feeling of suffering let me market it to the media. It's not real unless it's on television! Let me get it to the magazines and make it glossy. Let me sell it to the book manufacturers while the feeling is white-hot.

No. I'm just trying to explain why I might not feel secure in the fact that your invitation to come visit you was insincere. Why, while sitting at your table at a formal party, I might drink a little too much in an attempt to coax out a glimpse of a likeable me. Why I may look down or away in panic during a conversation when the subject becomes too personal. Why I always feel I'm ten years behind in my affairs, my personality, my career, my life. Why, after all this time, you may still not know me.

And yet...

Still there is Marilyn Monroe. An occasional tenderness in a world that has become brittle. On calendars and coffee mugs smiling from a bookstore window—smiling her beautiful, vulnerable smile that disguises real pain. What makes her last? What makes her immortal?

Today everyone, it seems, demanding their unearned minutes. We are all trying to turn ourselves into a series of cut-rate Marilyn Monroes. Selling our pain for fame. Our sexuality for money.

Marilyn was the genuine artifact. She really was suffering. She really did use her sex appeal to try and gain respectability and love, because that was all she thought she had to offer. But she climbed the ladder the hard way, step-by-step, and really struggled. Constantly trying, working, studying to better herself, to become a good actress, a smarter person, a more complete woman—to transform Norma Jeane into Marilyn Monroe. And her compassion never left her. The pain and the ugliness and the selfishness surrounded her too, but, for the most part, she strove to make things better.

Part of her secret lives in me. Hesitant. Vulnerable. A small candle flame, flickering. Snuffing out for a moment, then soaring high. Flickering. Flickering. Trying desperately to retain some level of tenderness and dignity and still survive. A delicate feeling of humanity that longs to reach out, to feel, to connect. A gentle yearning saying, "please like me." That is the secret. That is immortal.

Terrible Darkness

For John Rechy

"Don't leave me, God, I feel you slipping." I remember saying late that afternoon. All that winter I realized that my dark-side had become a horrible obsession. It had nothing to do with the fact that someone I knew had recently died, although I was always looking for some new explanation. My slide into the Manhattan sex clubs and porn theaters had begun some time that fall. This was February.

The same doorman who stood outside of the porno theater in all weather watched me—whom he no doubt recognized—stand on the street corner pretending to read the newspaper while I tried to fight off the urge to go in. He knew nothing of the war that was going on inside of me. I watched the doorman too—watched him smoke and smoke—his lungs as black as the souls of the people inside his theater. The sky, also, was the color of smoke. Soon it was going to rain. There I stood on the chilly corner. My camera bag around my shoulder, newspaper in hand. "What does he think of me?" I thought.

A sudden powerful wind rustled the newspaper that I held open in front of me and I forced myself to read the article once more. The paper talked of the murder. I scanned the columns again, horrified and excited. I hardly knew Derek, the man who had been killed, but still it is a shock to read about someone you knew, however briefly, who died so gruesomely. It said that his body was found by a building janitor. They suspected a serial killer, currently in vogue, who had been killing homosexual men in their twenties and thirties. It said that Derek was thirty-five.

Apparently the blurred photograph that accompanied the article had been taken a number of years before, perhaps at the time of his college graduation. I barely recognized him. In the picture his black hair was longer than I remembered and he was smiling. In the short time I knew him, I rarely saw Derek smile. What struck me again in the article was the blood. It spoke of the obscene amount of blood that had been found at the scene of the crime, which was the bathroom in Derek's apartment.

After I finished reading the article a third time I became aware of the fact that I was trembling. I looked up at the theater's marquee: ALL MALE. I knew I would lose the war and go into the theater. Already control was leaving me like warmth from a corpse freshly dead. I discarded the paper in the trashcan and headed for the theater, past the doorman, through the glass doors.

As I paid I diverted my eyes away from the hideous crone (dyed red hair, sunken eyes) who sat in the filthy box office, knitting and knitting, judging all who came in but taking their money nevertheless. I pushed open the swinging door leading into the theater. A shocking heat greeted me and I was blinded by the familiar darkness. Since it had not been bright outside my eyes would adjust in a matter of minutes. In the meantime hands reached out to me, stroking me. I brusquely brushed them away. These hands were all snakes, serpents that must be avoided at all costs; at least until I was able to see and could pick and choose the ones I wanted to touch me.

The movie soundtrack droned a sparse, steady beat. Beating. Beating. Like sex itself. Moans and groans were emitted from the screen to prove this. Young men, with lean, tight, hairless, tattooed bodies, preserved forever in their twenties, frolicked on videotape. "Yeah, yeah, yeah," one of them kept moaning in a fake macho voice. It wasn't acting talent that landed him this role and so, I supposed, it was wise of the video-maker to keep his dialogue to a minimum. I was not here, however, to watch a pornographic movie. As soon as my eyes adjusted to the darkness I started to explore.

This was a place of scattered categories. The first major category was older men. Very old. Some of them in their eighties. Once they must have been effeminate men; now they were sexless masses of withered flesh—shriveled and bent and hairless and spotted. Tongues hung out of slack open mouths as if some vital nerve needed to keep the mouth closed had been severed. Time had destroyed them, robbing them of their humanness. Wasted, wanting, ravaged bodies, void of anything other than their desire, roamed the aisles. Corpses kept in motion by longing. They rubbed their crotches obscenely but their eyes stared dead ahead.

It wasn't long before one of the zombie-men moved toward me, grabbed my crotch, and mumbled something to me through an idiotic grin. A cigarette was clamped between his teeth. There was something about the way he stared, the way he approached me, and his complete as-surance that I'd want him, that made me furious. I did not understand a word the man said and did not want to. Words, of course, were unneces-sary. His smirk lasted only a moment but I saw what it conveyed: this place is sleazy and ridiculous, as we both know, but you and I are here for the same thing so why don't you let me suck you off?

"No," I said out loud, contemptuously, pushing his hand away force-fully. It is, I know, ludicrous to act righteous in this kind of place but I despise being touched unexpectedly, especially when I give no indication at all that I want to be touched.

"Sorry," he said with a backing off motion. I had sounded tough. He walked away, coughing up phlegm, spitting it on the floor, and leaving a trail of foul smoke behind him as if it were the residue flames from his rank existence. He was a creature from the blackest of lagoons. Yet in the next moment I scolded myself for being contemptuous. How would you feel if they didn't approach, I asked myself? How dare I judge these men who someday I may be exactly like? And yet I did.

Derek was saved from the savagery of aging, I thought to myself. He'll never even see forty. In a photoflash moment I imagined his death scene. Derek lying in a pool of blood on his tiled bathroom floor. The sink nearly pulled from the wall, the water pipes dripping a steady trickle of water diluting the fruity, dark blood. The image blinded me. Then, just as suddenly, it was gone.

Where was Derek now? On some stainless steel mortuary table? In a cold, dark freezer awaiting further examination, or waiting for someone to claim him? Death robs everyone, even the beautiful, of their dignity. These were the kind of images that had been coming to me for weeks in dreams and which I tried to push away. They couldn't be real, I'd been telling myself.

I continued walking through the theater. There had to be a reason for me being in such a place and so as an excuse I thought of my loneliness. I thought of ex-lovers I once felt tender towards—Michael in particular. Michael, my real love, smiling, waving, waiting for me outside of his office building in the snow that first winter we met five years before. I hadn't talked to Michael in over a year, but lately I couldn't get him off my mind. Is that why I'd been coming here so often? Was this revenge? A slap in the face to Michael who, by now, wouldn't even care what I did.

"It's over between the two of you," Derek had said when I spoke of Michael. "Just erase him and go on." As if it were possible to erase all sad memories from a person's memory bank.

Through dark shadows I wandered, I watched. Trying all the while to squelch my fear—a fear that was unfamiliar and inexplicable. The darkness was hiding things. Lately I'd been seeing terrible things in my dreams and I dreaded darkness. There had always been nightmares, but this was ridiculous. In these dreams I saw men screaming, bodies bleeding, horrible wailing, and the mutilation of young boys. Was it a holocaust? Was it a war? So clear were these visions of torture and death that I thought I might be going mad from them. Michael, my ex-lover, had been part of these dreams and that made me think I should call him—but that would be proving that I feared them—and that might give them the power to come true.

I hoped that these were only nightmares with no element of truth. Since I was a child strange people came up to me on the street or in restaurants or in elevators and they would stare into my eyes and then say, "You have the gift!"

"What gift," I would always, always ask, pretending to be baffled.

"The gift of prophecy." I always shook my head, 'no' but I knew they knew. These people had it too and we could recognize it in each other. I tried to deny it. Sex was always a way to get my mind off of things. In the hunt nothing else mattered.

Soon the heat in the theater was stifling. First my leather jacket came off, then my sweater. I, carrying these garments along with my camera bag, prowled the aisles in my t-shirt. Soon the heat had exhausted me and I took a grime-stained seat in the audience.

Another category here was middle-aged businessmen and the young men who desired them. In an odd reversal, in the row in front of me, a young man, about eighteen years old with the blonde, tousled hair of a teen model, sucked the cock of a grotesquely obese man (sixty-something, bald, greasy). The pretty boy sprung up to kiss the man, sucking his tongue, pulling on his tie with an intense passion. I had, by this time, stopped being shocked by such scenes. Now there was only fascination and a weird sexual excitement. If I stared long enough at the two, they might invite me to join in. I quickly looked up at the screen.

Another excuse for being in this place, which sounds ridiculous in retrospect, was love. "Everyone thinks they need to eat love as their daily bread. Their daily diet." That is what Derek said to me when I told him of my recent obsessions. So was it love I was looking for? The human body is a wrapped package. Through sex I ripped open layers, looking for the unpolished gem that might lie within a heart. Night after night, man after man, I rummaged through the packages, only to be awarded the fakes. The booby prize. Or perhaps that is just romanticized bullshit, the answer being more complex a myriad of reasons—another being anonymous sex itself. Sex without the investment of emotions, an immediate fulfillment.

Placing my camera and things in the seat next to me, I settled back into my soiled seat and began a conversation with myself. "I should just kill myself, shouldn't I?" I whispered. Funny, I hadn't meant to speak out loud and I looked around to see if anyone heard. The men around me continued in their seats: staring at the screen, masturbating, sucking cocks. For the moment I was safe.

"You're wonderful," the fat man in front of me said to his young companion. But the boy was already making his way down the aisle, zipping up his fly. He had cum, obviously, and now, no longer a captive of desire, he was embarrassed and he wanted to escape. Now the businessman turned to me. "You look like you got a nice big dick," he said, smiling lewdly at the area below my belt.

And this is what Derek had said to me the day we met. The day before he died.

"You look like you got a nice big dick."

I had been walking down Christopher Street, thinking about Michael, when Derek seemed to appear out of nowhere, stepping directly in front of me. I had never seen him before. Oddly the first thing I noticed about him was his hair—incredibly lush and black and combed straight back, slicked with a sweet smelling oil that made me dizzy. But after looking into his face I saw that his eyes were truly the amazing thing about him. They were big and black, like mine, but they held extraordinary power.

He was standing directly in my path and I could not go any further without stepping around him, nor he without going around me. I felt scared and trapped yet incredibly sexual. My heart, reacting to this, revved up, skipping beats, urging me to play out the scene to its inevitable conclusion. Oh have sex with him, my mind urged me. It is what you came out for. Perhaps it will help you to feel.

In the past few weeks I had felt myself overcome with a blackness that, while not completely debilitating, seemed to make my body secrete a numbing substance like Novocain to protect me from harmful emotions. I myself felt like a zombie.

There was no one reason why I felt as I did. Millions of bits and pieces came together to feed the monster inside of me. There were my nightmares, but more than that I laid some blame for my bleakness on my career, or lack thereof, which was as good a reason as any. I had been trying to become a successful photographer for a long time but I could not get my break.

My photography seemed very promising for a moment and then it went nowhere—I'd have something published in *Newsweek* or the *Times* and then not have another job for many months. Meanwhile, mediocre talents all around me—more aggressive and pushy than I—were being recognized. It ate away at me. People said I had real talent, but I was not manipulative enough. I couldn't play the game of using people. I wanted someone to recognize me for my creativity, to rescue me—and that, I guessed, meant I was lazy.

And it was the loneliness too. My friends and I had grown apart, or they were paired off with lovers or husbands or wives. My intense ambition and feelings of low self-esteem had destroyed all my own relationships. Even with Michael. I needed to be successful to feel worthy, to feel whole. I felt, at thirty-two, too old to begin again, yet too young to give up. People told me I was beautiful—but I never felt beautiful. They said I was talented but I never got the breaks. They told me they loved me, yet I always ended up alone.

Maybe I should go for a walk, I suggested to myself earlier in the day with all of these thoughts pressing against the interior walls of my head. Also, I had been longing for Michael, worried about him, and I wanted to meet someone for distraction. The day I walk down Christopher Street and don't meet at least two people by the time I reach the piers is the day I give up, I thought. It didn't have to be about sex, really. If only I had someone to talk to. Someone who interested me. Someone whom I interested.

I grabbed my camera bag and headed for Christopher Street.

It was a freezing twilight, just before dark, and the Village streets were crowded, as I knew they would be, though not festive and good natured as I remembered them. Angry groups swarmed by me, talking a slangy shit, intentionally banging into me, aggressively trying to incite incidents with others and me.

"Lady! I have to use the phone now!" screamed a stout, bald-headed, Hispanic woman to a frail, elderly lady on a pay phone. Where was her cell phone? Everyone I came in contact with seemed hostile and savage. This was part of the reason I thought I was going insane. I was worried. I was very worried. And always the nagging, nagging, nagging images of murder. And the calling of suicide. Part of my fear and hesitation of going on was that everywhere I looked I saw evil.

Was the world so evil, with its slickly edited television news of murder for money and sport, every hour on the hour? Or was my mind corrupted—seeing humanity through my own-skewered vision? Or maybe it had always been like this and I hadn't noticed. Of course some eyes on the street roamed hungrily up and down my body as I passed and that was a comfort. Now Derek's did too and he finally repeated his opening line in case I hadn't heard.

"You look like you got a nice big dick."

"No," I replied.

"No?"

"It's average," I said.

"It looks pretty nice to me."

I let it go. I couldn't understand this obsession with dick size. I refused to get involved with it. This gay talk. Trick talk. Nice-big-dick-talk. Of course we both wanted the same thing—sex—and sometimes it's necessary to go right for it and forget about pleasantries. That's what porn theaters were for. Alleyways. Woods. But did it always have to be that way? There had to be more. I needed to believe in affection. Yes! That's what I was looking for.

Suddenly I realized that I didn't want this man just once. A frantic toss in bed and then turning away from each other as if nothing happened. I wanted to feel something for him. I wanted him to feel something for me. Otherwise, no go.

I waited but he said nothing more. Yes, it was important for me to be physically attractive to him but isn't it ever about anything more? I decided to avoid a painful encounter. I stepped around him and walked quickly away without saying another word.

Once I had been in love. With Michael sex was more. With Michael I was more. With Michael sex was love. Michael, Michael, Michael. Now the moment of hope and ultimate disappointment from my brief encounter with the stranger on the street mixed in with the hammering memory of Michael and produced a hurt that was unsettling after so many weeks of emptiness. A hurt that made me long for something lost. Michael slipping a ring on my finger under a restaurant table on my birthday—the single happiest moment of my life. Michael kissing me under the sheets in a hotel room in Italy. I compared him to all the men in my past.

He was the only one who loved me, I deduced. The only one I ever really loved. Now I had been seeing him dead in my dreams. I tried not to think about it. There was the smell of the city, the feel of the cold, the sight of the traffic. Nothing more. Physical stimulus in the immediate presence. Why flog myself with memory?

As I walked I was compelled to look back and I saw that the dark-eyed man was making his way towards me through the crowd, trying to catch up. In seconds he was walking beside me. He gave me a friendly nudge with his shoulder but when he saw I was crying he grew serious.

"You're thinking about Michael, aren't you?" he asked

I was struck dumb. I had never, I swear, seen this man before. I had not so much spoken Michael's name in months to anyone. How did he know? Had he been a friend of Michael? Had he, perhaps, seen us together years before?

"No, I never met your Michael," he said. "And I never met you before either."

Now I was frightened. He had the gift.

"Don't be afraid," he said. "I'm one of you. I have the gift too." I noticed he had a slight accent but I couldn't place it. It was something...vague but unusual. "My name is Derek," he said. "And yours?"

I told him my name.

"Listen," he continued, "I didn't mean to offend you by talking about dick size back there. It's just that I could feel that you were in pain and what I was picking up from you was extremely sexual. It was the chemistry generating between us. I thought sex was all you were looking for, but it's more isn't it?"

I said nothing.

"Let me buy you a drink," he said.

The obese businessman was waiting for my reply. The movie had ended suddenly and the theater had grown darker still. I smiled but shook my head. Without the boy he had lost any erotic appeal. There was still a lingering guilt, however, for snapping at the old man earlier and I didn't want to hurt any more feelings. I got up from my seat leaving the businessman to draw his own conclusions. I had been looking at him without an ounce of desire but people will read into your thoughts what they may.

I quickly walked down the center aisle amongst slurping noises and a smell that comes out of the body when it's tampered with. Amidst all of this a white-haired black man ate his lunch—a rancid smelling meat sandwich—out of a crumbled aluminum foil wrapper. This was not uncommon. I often saw men in this theater eating greasy, smelly things. For some reason this enraged me. What kind of monsters would eat lunch amongst such filth, my horrified mind asked—hating myself all the more for being surrounded by them. By choice.

"But I could understand what you're saying about being sensitive and tough at the same time," Derek said to me in the dimly lit bar on Grove Street. That is how I had described myself as we searched for the quietest looking place to have our drink. "I think New Yorkers deserve their reputations for attitude," he said. "You've got to be very self-protective here. It sucks to be vulnerable in New York."

The bar we chose, which I had never noticed although I must have passed it dozens of times, was dark and nearly empty. I placed my camera bag on the vacant stool beside me. The muscular, long-haired bartender, pouring our scotch, smirked in my direction, as if he knew secrets about me that he found funny. But Derek's face made me feel strangely comfortable.

Yet there was something dark in him. There was no doubt about that. I, too, had certain powers. I had the horrible ability to look into people's souls. Most of the time I didn't like what I saw. I didn't view this as being judgmental. I saw it as a curse. I would much rather go blindly through life happily being fooled by people's masks. But people recognized I had this power to see through them, and they resented me and took two steps back because with me they couldn't pretend. They hid from me. Not Derek. It seemed to draw him closer. He leaned in.

My own soul felt caged in and desperate. I hadn't yet met the right people—or person—to free it. And with Derek there was the feeling of inevitability. As if he were someone I had been waiting for. Although he actually spoke very little about himself.

"And what about you?" Derek asked. "Tell me about your family."

I told him. I had been adopted. My family—dysfunctional (surprise, surprise). But mine really was. Cold. Distant. It seemed strange for an older couple to adopt children, only to ignore them. Why bother? My sister, also adopted, compensated for a lack of emotion by becoming the town pump. Now she was living a different life in Brooklyn, escaping the unpleasant memories of her childhood. Married with her own child—a little girl named Carolyn. That my sister had made a conventional life for herself pleased me, it made me believe that there was hope for me. Yet, although she never said it, I sensed she disapproved of me being gay and she rarely invited me into her life. We had nothing between us, not even blood. Of course dredging up all these things from the past was only my way of making excuses for why my life hadn't turned out the way I planned.

Derek reached for my hand. We looked at each other and at once I was again overloaded with his presence. I had never felt anything more exquisite. There was the sight of his eyes, the smell of his hair, the feel of his skin. Nothing else. I asked him if he lived alone which, I guess, is the equivalent of asking if he had a nice big dick.

"Yes," he said. And we both stood up.

YYYYYYYYYYYYYY
YYYYYYYYYYYYYY
YYYYYYYYYYYYYY
YYYYYYYYYYYYYY

I climbed a spiral staircase leading to an upstairs section of the porno theater—something they called the "lounge," but was actually a large, dank room with a few haphazardly placed folding chairs. Another porn video was being shown there on a smaller screen. The room might more appropriately have been called the "orgy room," for that is what usually took place there. Now there was the usual scattering of men in cheap suits, carrying their overcoats and briefcases.

There were also many of the usual older men who seemed to dress in the first thing they pulled from the bottom of their laundry hampers— dirty, plaid, flannel shirts and wrinkled, baggy pants, hanging below their waist without a belt. Most of these men didn't bother to comb their wispy hair, brush their teeth, or spray under their arms. They did chain smoke and the smell of stale cigarette smoke mixed in with their natural odors. Men with endless supplies of phlegm, standing around, hacking it up.

A painfully thin man of about seventy sat completely naked and complaisant on a small bench in a corner. His hands were primly folded in his lap, his shoulders stooped. There was a dog collar around his neck. Where are his clothes, I wondered, uselessly. It was shocking that these scenes no longer shocked me.

I stood quietly amongst the ruins. Mostly I felt contempt for them all, and shame for myself. So what was the hold, the incredible hold, this place had on me? Then, as if an answer, I suddenly saw someone who was unusual (but not impossible) in this kind of place. A handsome young man with sand colored hair and pale blue eyes. He was the kind of jackpot that kept me coming back to the tables. I watched him lean against a wall, his chiseled features staring dreamily into nothingness. Possibly...a lawyer? He was clean, and well groomed, and neatly dressed in a fashionable suit and tie. Married, no doubt, with a home and children in Connecticut. I thought of approaching this one for he seemed both handsome and sensitive.

It might be nice to kiss and nothing more, I thought.

Before I had a chance to move towards him, however, a disheveled-looking man with wild gray hair, like Einstein, and a walrus mustache got to him first. To test the waters the wild-haired man gingerly stroked the lawyer's crotch. The younger man did not move. Assured, the older one dropped to his knees, unzipping the other's pants as he did so. Immediately I was swept away with a longing and jealousy and despair for putting myself constantly, constantly, constantly in these situations.

Oh my God, my mind screamed. What can I do to be free of this? What mountain should I climb? What potion can I drink? I closed my eyes tightly for quite a long time but it was no use. When I opened them it was all still the same. I headed towards the men's room to take a piss.

Derek had a small, one bedroom walk-up apartment on the fourth floor of a building on West 47th Street. The floors of his place were wood, the walls were gray. As I waited for him to come out of the bathroom I looked around for clues to Derek, but here there was very little. No books on the shelves, no family photographs. A chest of drawers, some sweaters piled on shelves in a closet that had no door. The light on his answering machine was not blinking.

I took off my clothes and sat naked on the bed waiting. Suddenly, for the first time since he gave it to me, I took off the ring Michael had given me on my birthday and laid it on the night table beside the bed. I don't know why. I just couldn't stand the thought of making love to Derek with the ring on.

I lay down on the bed, arms spread out like a horizontal crucifixion. After what seemed like a long time Derek stepped into the room, also nude, and joined me on the bed. To my surprise, he took my foot into his hand and started kissing there, working his way up, licking and kissing my ankles, my calves, my thighs, grazing past the pubic area. My stomach, my chest, my nipple in his mouth. I arched my back and tore at the sheet beneath me.

For months the world had been circling around me and I, a stone in its center, had been polished smooth by the surrounding movements—but unfeeling. Unfeeling. Now Derek's arms held me and I was on fire. One of my basic problems was that with all the years of searching, and running and changing I still hadn't gotten away from my self. But with Derek I felt as if I had become who I was supposed to be.

At last, at last, his lips reached my lips. And his mouth breathed life into me. His hands flushed warm the skin on my body, a body that had turned to marble in a slow death, a starvation of the heart. His tongue rushed into me and it was the sea, fertilizing a ravaged desert. As we kissed our eyes opened and locked and Derek's eyes said: Abracadabra one-two-three, Up Lazarus—your history is wiped away. "Oh. Oh thank you, Father," I silently prayed, for this, his body his blood—his eyes, his hair. Yet even in my frenzy I realized that it was wrong to get carried away in all of this. This was only sex I tried to reason. Only another man and his body. But I couldn't help myself. I had been dead. Now I was alive.

All the stalls in the men's room were occupied at the moment, the cracks in the doors were covered with strips of toilet paper to keep the roving eyes of voyeurs, like me, from peeking in. The warm air was swollen with the vapors from rancid urine. While peeing I stared into the dusty mirror above the urinal. It scared me that sometimes I looked in the mirror and saw a face, still somewhat youthful, but without that really young, lost quality that sometimes made people want to protect me. The trouble was I still felt just as young and lost, and like I needed to be protected. But my face said otherwise.

I could not sleep. Before the sex, when I was numb, I didn't care what he thought. Now it all mattered and I became aware of the imperfections of my face and body. The failures of my life. I imagined myself taking an overdose in a tomb so far away that even bugs couldn't get me. It didn't matter if people would remember me or not because God would embrace me. Then I fell asleep.

When I woke up the following morning I was on the far corner of the bed. It was so cold. Derek was in the other corner facing the opposite direction. I hesitated then snuggled up to his back.

"That's better," he said sleepily, turning to face me. Every time he stared into my eyes for a long time I was afraid to make a move for fear of losing him. "Let's take a ride to Atlantic City today," he said out of the blue.

It seemed so whimsical. It had been such a long time since I'd done something just for the fun of it. And I had nothing else to do.

"I need to go home and get some fresh clothes first," I said.

"No, don't bother. You can wear something of mine."

"Well, I'll need to stop at the bank."

"How much do you have on you?"

"About forty dollars."

"That's enough," he said.

"Can I at least take a shower?"

He laughed. "That you can do."

"About your photography," Derek said when I stepped out of the bathroom wrapped in an oversized towel. "You need to take a different approach."

I looked at him carefully and sat down on the bed next to him. "You haven't even seen any of my work."

"Believe me, I know. I can see it now. Dying prostitutes on the West Side. An aging transvestite in his dressing room—the one who was later found dead, wasn't he? Homeless crack addicts on the subway."

He was right. The subjects he mentioned were among my best photos. They, however, had never been published or displayed. Perhaps to distract him from my fear I looked away and stared into the mirror on the opposite wall. I looked rough. I hate the mornings. "A documentation of my life and times," I said.

"It's not enough. Not extreme enough. Your emotions are extreme. Your life is extreme. Much more extreme than you're ready to admit to

70

yourself at the moment. You have to change subjects—and really document the extremities of what you feel." And then he added, "In your dreams."

As if he had planned this moment all along he walked to his dresser drawer and removed a manila envelope and handed it to me. He stood looking at me waiting for me to look in. I wiped my hands on the towel I was wearing and opened the envelope and shook out the contents. You must believe me when I tell you what I saw.

In the envelope were color photographs of corpses, each shot with eerie detachment. Men in their twenties and thirties—colored with the paint of death. The exposed faces were serene in spite of the awful violence that seemed to have been done to the bodies. Most, spattered with blood, could have only died from horrific crimes. A few of them had severed limbs. There was something strange and familiar about the photos. Of course! This is what I had been seeing in my nightmares. I wanted to study them but I felt I had no right. Of course the subjects were dead and wouldn't care now. Yet the people in the photographs, I told myself, once had life. They had histories, educations, memories. They read books, saw movies, laughed, cried, loved. What were they now?

I left the photographs in my lap but stared blankly ahead, past Derek. The pictures had affected me in a way that made me feel as if I might cry. What horrified me most was that I understood the photographs completely—the body as an object. No warmth or humanity. The way we'd come to see each other.

"Look at me," Derek said kneeling in front of me. "Tell me if this isn't true: Your photographs are very good, excellent really, deep and mysterious—but they're not getting the attention they deserve. They're not being noticed by the right people."

I found my voice. "Yes," I replied slowly. "I think that is true." I knew I should give it up but I couldn't walk down the street without seeing everything as if it were a photograph.

"But once you have notoriety people will look at your work in a different way. They'll really see it for the first time. Fame makes people look at things differently. But you have to do something to get them to notice you first."

I looked down at the photograph face up in my lap of the mutilated man who died with open eyes, as if staring into a dark tunnel, his expression sad and quizzical, though not horrified.

"No, no, no," I said. And then I added one more "no" for good measure. "I can't do this kind of work."

"Why not?" Derek asked with a short little laugh which to me sounded mocking. "If your loneliness is so overwhelming why don't you face your realities?"

"Because. Because it's not in me. First of all, where would I get the..." I paused because I didn't want to say "bodies."

"Subjects?" Derek asked. "You know where. You'd find them."

"No," I said again. "I don't want to make a career this way. It is not art."

"Who is to say what art is? Listen to me," he said taking both of my hands into his own. "There are explanations for this type of art. The public will believe it. Rally behind you. It's the only way. Do you want to spend the rest of your life on the fringe? A mediocre career? Shooting headshots for second rate actors?" (That is how I made my living although I hadn't told him that) He continued: "Look at almost everyone who is really successful today. Their success depends on scandal. Controversy. Shock. Just say yes and I can help you."

The clock suddenly seemed to be ticking so loudly. Too loudly. It was giving me a headache. How could anyone think with time passing so loudly?

"No," I said finally.

"Fool," he said.

And yet...and yet I was still happy to be with him. I still considered him a find, a prize, a golden thread with something thrilling at the end of it.

Now that I was alive again my body was nothing but vulnerable. The photographs had unsettled me in a way that made me want to be close to someone. I didn't want to spend my life alone. I didn't ask him where the pictures came from. I thought, perhaps he had bought them from the Internet where such atrocities were readily available

For now I tried to put the photographs out of my head. Yes, I was frightened of him, no doubt about it. But when your phone hardly ever rings—when the mail brings no new greetings. When, each time you check, your answering machine light is not blinking, well, you start to look for a savior.

"Are we still going to Atlantic City," I asked after I was dressed in a pair of his jeans and sweatshirt.

"Of course."

In the car there was between us the uncomfortableness of two strangers who had given too much of themselves sexually the night before and now had to deal with the presence of the whole person sitting next to them again. I wondered why Derek didn't stroke my leg as he drove, the way he did the night before. I figured that since he now also knew the mysteries of my body, as well as my mind, he had had enough. Naturally he read my mind and his hand found mine.

He looked so beautiful sitting beside me, even with the bright morning sunlight streaming through the windshield, that I was sorry that I had left my camera at his place. But even his beauty was not enough of a distraction. My mind kept returning to the photos.

"Surely those kinds of photographs have been shown commercially before. I wouldn't be the first," I said. I could think of more than one photographer who worked with similar subjects and exploited the same themes as the pictures Derek had shown me.

"I assure you, you would become the most famous. The time is right, isn't it? But I'll tell you this, if you don't do it, someone else will. And he'll get all the rewards."

We reached Atlantic City by the early afternoon. We entered a well-known casino and I was immediately uncomfortable amongst the high-spirited disorder. There was an immediate bristling among the staff—the guards, the dealers, and the mysterious men who worked for the casino who roamed around in suits, gravely observing the gamblers. They seemed to recognize Derek. They stared at him menacingly and then exchanged warning looks with each other. I felt like an accomplice. To what, I did not know. But the feeling was there.

Derek asked me for twenty dollars, which I gave him. He led me directly to a blackjack table—the rest is a rush of memory—he just kept on winning and winning. And winning. He could not lose. He could not lose! The stack of chips in front of him kept on growing. A crowd formed around us. The men in suits also surrounded us and they seemed foreboding. But there was absolutely nothing they could do. There was no explanation for the unlikely winning streak. No wrong doing that was at all obvious. Derek kept turning to me with a triumphant arch of his eyebrow. Finally after about three hours of non-stop winning he was ready to cash in.

"Wait here," he instructed.

When he returned he tried to hand me a stack of hundred dollar bills. By this time I was very frightened and would not take it.

Derek said: "No, no, I insist you take it. Half of it is yours."

"I don't want it," I persisted.

"Stop being ridiculous, it's a great deal of money."

Our strange meeting on the street the night before, the surreal sex we had, the grotesque photographs he had shown me this morning, and his uncanny winning streak now all rushed toward me at once, pushing me away. And I knew that there was something unnatural about the two of us together. Each of us was strange, separately for sure, but together it became something ominous. I felt it. I knew it. There is a line between good and evil. For a very long time I had been walking in between. It was wrong for us to be together, the power that we generated between us was dark and I didn't know where it would lead.

"We belong together," he said urgently.

I started running. Derek called my name several times but did not run after me. He did not follow me out of the casino. Yet there was a sinister under-thought. The feeling that there was no way to lose him. Not really. It seemed ludicrous. I had had sex with the man only once and, yes, it was immensely enjoyable, but now would I be stuck paying for it with his presence for the rest of my life? At the time this fear seemed very real.

In my confusion I somehow found a bus that would take me back to the city and I took a seat towards the back. I traveled home amongst chattering old ladies wearing brightly colored jackets, and they were so normal and wonderful I fell in love with them all. I leaned my head against the window and wearily listened to their non-stop gossip and it restored me to wonderful normalcy.

Before long I fell into a deep uncomplicated sleep. But when I woke with a start a few hours later we were in Manhattan and it was already dark. And I knew, even before I really knew, that Derek would be waiting for me when I stepped off the bus. And he was. Too drained to protest, I followed him to his car and went with him to his apartment. I had to get my camera anyway.

"Michael is dead," he said as soon as we entered his apartment and I knew it was true. A sacred love of mine had died. I silently mourned for that. In the moments that followed I felt as if I were in a trance. Derek was saying, "You killed him. Don't you realize? Those photographs I showed you are pictures I took of your victims. I've been following you for weeks. You haven't been having visions. You're having flashbacks of the murders you've committed. We're alike. Now, my darling, we can do it together."

He went to his dresser drawer and took out another photo. This one showed Michael in his apartment—spread on his blood-soaked mattress—dead. The way I had been seeing him in my dreams for weeks.

Suddenly I knew that Derek was the killer. Of course he was trying to make me think that my visions weren't real. But that couldn't be. It couldn't be. It couldn't be!

"You'll never be able to leave me you know." Derek said. "I know all your secrets. Who we are and what we will become is much more entwined than you think."

I walked into the bathroom to splash water on my face Derek followed me. I saw his reflection in the medicine cabinet.

"Go ahead and do what you have to do," he said. Therefore I do not blame myself for what happened next. I was so exhausted. I don't even remember how the switchblade got in my hand, or where it came from—I simply flowed in the moment as if I was spreading towards an ineluctable destiny. What can I tell you about what occurred? That it happened quickly? That it seemed to be over before I could grasp what was unfolding? There were a few moments of scuffle, some force, horrible gurgling sounds, and then a sudden relenting. Yet the struggle had been so fierce that the sink had been knocked from the wall. Was this all there was to crossing to the other side? Now I knew too. But please believe me, I needed to be free.

What time was it? How long had I been here? I stood in the reeking porn theatre men's room utterly confused, staring at myself in the mirror above the urinal without any concept of who I was or where I had been. Or where I was going for that matter. I was trying to think of what to do next. Should I wait for someone attractive? Was it almost after business hours when the horny, handsome men in suits would arrive? Or was it wiser to go home to my unblinking answering machine, my meaningless stack of mail? There was nowhere else for me to go.

In the Chelsea bars the men would be sitting casually around their beers, staring at a video screen projecting camp classics. Faye Dunaway would be screaming, "Don't fuck with me fellas...!" And they would all laugh, the way I had laughed years ago.

A disheveled man appeared at the urinal next to me. He shot me a silly come-hither look. His fine hair stood on end. His horn-rimmed glasses and crooked tie made him seem goofy.

"Are you trade?" he asked.

I shook my head and zipped up. What he had thought about me did not make me angry. What was he supposed to think, poor guy? Me vacantly standing there for God knows how long, not peeing, my penis hanging out. I always seemed to be giving off the wrong signals.

Derek was the one person who was able to read me. But of course I wasn't the murderer. He was! That's why I killed him. To stop it. Don't you believe me?

The reason I think about his death so much is that although such things are all around me, in the news, in movies, on television, in dreams, it still seems astonishing to me that I had been involved in something like it in my real life. What it made me realize more than anything is that no matter how bad my life had become I still wanted. I wanted life because of the hope of something new, of finding myself, of feeling again, of somehow becoming whole.

There was blood everywhere. All over Derek's body. All over the bathroom. Drying rivers soaking into the ancient linoleum floors. Splattered on the walls. I can see it now. My own blood soaked hands. And the numbness creeping in again, obliterating what had just recently been brought back to life—and pain—and I knew that there was no one to talk this over with or to ask for advice. I was alone. I picked up my camera and shot a photo of Derek lying face up on the bathroom floor. Then I turned around and left.

I believe in evil. Most people today, I have found, will deny that it even exists. They will give excuses for the atrocities of the world—excuses like abuse, rage, poverty. I can use any one of them. But there is, I believe, an embryo of potential evil lying dormant in every human being, lying next to the fetus of compassion. The two fight for dominance. What is it that causes evil to win then? Some leave it lying dormant in its sack. Others nourish it. Once this thing is tapped into there's no telling the things we might do. I'm talking about you. I'm talking about me.

Things we once thought of as unspeakable can become the common place. Every day I think of people being tortured, animals being tortured—living things being tortured. Sometimes I close my eyes and I can see it. When I think of all of this going on, everyday, every minute, somewhere in the world. Starvation. Wars. Mutilation. I feel so helpless, so small. I cannot bear it. I must do what I can to stop it. At least in this life.

Now that Derek was dead I feared I would never feel anything again. After I left his place I sat in my own apartment staring out of the window at the windy street below, watching an alley cat rummage through garbage. He was concerned with nothing, nothing but filling his hunger. Is nothingness better, I wondered. The cat disappeared into the shadows.

This night I didn't mind the darkness. It was the morning I dreaded. It was okay to be alone in the evening. The daylight would uncover loneliness. When it arrived I went on with the normal arrangements of my day—showered, scrambled eggs, ate, grabbed my camera bag and left my apartment with no particular destination in mind. But that gray February afternoon found me in front of the porno theatre again battling with my demons.

"Don't go in there," my inner voice warned me. But, as I already told you, I did go in.

"Hello," a masculine voice said to me as he entered the men's room.

It was the man I had seen in the upstairs lounge—the lawyer, the brooding angel with pale blue eyes and hair the color of sand. Apparently he had ditched the Einstein look-a-like I had left him with and followed me to the men's room. Now, though, his sensitive, lost demeanor was completely gone. People are never what they seem. He appeared snide and cocksure—his suit looked too flashy. He stared at me brazenly. He was one of these men who could eat you with his eyes.

He confidently placed his hands on my waist and guided me to a vacated stall in the corner of the men's room, past the gaping row of cocksuckers sitting on toilets with the stall doors open hoping that a floating dick might happen along and land happily in their mouths. I let him lead me without resisting. I was wearing my sweater and jacket again and in my jacket pocket I could feel the switchblade I had used to kill Derek. Once instilled in our humid haven I leaned against the tiled wall as the stranger worked on my belt buckle.

"You look like you got a nice big dick," he said and kicked the stall door closed. Immediately I saw an eye press to the crack of the door. Moaning sounds, low and steady, reverberated all around us. In the Chelsea bars a drag queen, giggling, would be bending over to light her cigarette. There was nothing else for me to do.

"Help me," I whispered.

He fell to his knees. The eye at the door watched us unblinking. The lawyer, finally undoing my belt buckle, unzipped my fly and pulled my pants and underwear down to my ankles with one swift movement. I felt the cold tile against my bare ass. I fingered the knife in my pocket. "I would like to suck you all day," he moaned breathlessly. It seemed like so very little to ask of life. Is this wrong, I wondered? I had been asking God to show me the way out of this kind of life. He seemed not to be hearing me lately so I felt justified. But then why am I always looking for excuses for all my faults? Why not just be? God waits for you, can't you wait for Him, asked the voice in my head. This seemed reasonable. I had no answers. I had no answers.

Unexpectedly I thought of my niece Caroline, my sister's child: Four years old. Gape-tooth grins. Tangled dirty-blonde hair hanging to her shoulders. Skinny little body that makes her head seem big. Little rag-a-muffin. She was not pretty yet and that made me feel more tender towards her. Where did this come from? I was not close with my sister and felt shy when I visited, which was seldom. But Caroline seemed to like me. She'd say, "Come color with me," or, "I love Disney films." In my minds eye I saw her hopping around on one foot.

Oh Caroline, Caroline! Darling. You've shown me that—even if only for a brief time—there is such a thing as purity. And suddenly, out of nowhere, I loved this child. This little girl. It was only one feeling. One single emotion, sneaking up on me so unexpectedly, for one tiny creature in this gigantic universe. But I didn't care. It was enough. Caroline was hope. "Oh thank you Father," I said, sobbing quietly to myself, "that I can still feel."

Eyes closed in ecstasy the man on his knees in front of me gripped my thighs tightly and encircled his lips around the head of my penis—a Communion wafer—sucking greedily, forcefully, making rapturous sounds deep within his throat as if what I had to offer him was the salvation of his soul, the forgiveness of sins, the life of the world to come. Amen.

John Rechy At Home

For Vincent Curcio

When I was just starting as a journalist people would ask me—if I had a choice of anyone in the world—whom I would most like to interview. I think they were expecting I'd answer Madonna or Princess Diana. But I always replied, "John Rechy."

Rechy's autobiographical novel, *City of Night*, about a lonely hustler drifting across the country, first appeared in 1963, shocking the literary world and becoming a controversial bestseller. It was published before I was born, but when I came across it in a bookstore as a teenager it almost jumped of the shelf into my hands, screaming for me to read it. It was one of those unexplainable omens that has happened a number of times in my life. I hear a name or see a photograph and—BAM!—I know it's going to be important. *City of Night*. I started reading it right there and then. It knocked me out on so many levels. First of all it introduced me to a world involving characters dealing with confusion of gender and sexuality—hustlers and johns and drag queens—all creating outer personas, carefully polished veneers, to camouflage their true selves which they haven't grown comfortable with. Young men who felt soft and feminine on the inside painted their faces with garish makeup. Sensitive boys who yearned for male love, acted tough and heartless and sold their bodies to other men rather than be labeled homosexual. Mature men who yearned to touch young flesh acted worldly and blasé to hide their lust. I never knew anyone could write about this kind of perverse subject matter with such poetic intensity.

Because I myself was young and hypersensitive, John Rechy took a place in my heart that had, until then, been roped-off for tragic, dead movie stars. Anyone who was isolated or lonely. Anyone in great pain. These were people I recognized and who stayed in the forefront of my mind. Rechy had the faraway, unreachable tenderness of Marilyn Monroe and Montgomery Clift.

Loneliness, sensitivity, and a gentle spirit are universal emotions. Rechy and I come from different backgrounds yet the beauty and power of *City of Night* is that you don't have to experience his kind of aloneness in order to be touched by the novel.

Rechy's loneliness, channeled in that novel, stemmed from the fact that he grew up homosexual in a Latino family in El Paso, Texas during the

1930s and 1940s. His father was a domineering, brutal man who saw (and despised) homosexuality everywhere—and sensed it in his sullen, artistic son. The seeds of Rechy's talent were always in him, but his father's contemptuous treatment isolated young John and imbedded in him a hunger to be great, to excel. So John nurtured his talent and it flourished. Yet by the 1950s—even though he had graduated from college and had been in the army—Rechy felt so alienated, the only way he could express his sexuality was through hustling. He turned his loneliness into a triumph, however, by writing a masterful book about his experiences and feelings.

I grew up in a very loving and supportive Italian-American family in New York City. But it was a tough neighborhood and male and female behavior was always very clear-cut. I was trying to construct my own mask, to play it tough, be cool—in other words, be something I wasn't. I never felt I belonged and so I felt like I didn't have any value. Feeling unworthy made me timid and meek, which I would later learn to camouflage by appearing utterly detached.

In the game of disguises I had my role models. At the age of eleven, I discovered Marilyn Monroe in a photograph while flipping through a magazine. I recognized the pain in her eyes that she tried to mask with a movie star's smile. A few years later I stood in a bookstore and began reading *City of Night*. I knew I had found someone else who belonged to me.

By the time I was in my late teens I had read other books by Rechy: *Numbers, Rushes, The Sexual Outlaw*. To me, his protagonists lost some of the innocence of the narrator of *City of Night*. They became more narcissistic, less sensitive. As I got older I came to understand Rechy's narcissism. Because he was such an outcast while growing up, his physical appearance became a shield for him. Desirability was power. Rechy's looks became the most important thing—that's why he made men pay.

In my childhood and through my adolescence there wasn't a single person I could talk to or relate to about my confusion. Later, when I started going out to clubs and bars I always found it astonishing if guys wanted to talk to me, know me, be with me. No one before, except my parents, had ever valued me. I became aware of the importance of the physical, especially in the gay community.

In 1988 Rechy wrote a fictitious book about Monroe called *Marilyn's Daughter*. I thought then that we were truly spiritual brothers.

Years later, I moved to Los Angeles. I was working for a magazine and the editor asked me for ideas. I said, "Well, what about John Rechy?" I always hoped that one day I'd take one of his creative writing classes. I sent him a letter requesting an interview. He called me up (and I remember the excitement of getting a voicemail from Rechy!) and requested some of my clips. I sent him one of my best clips along with excerpts from a novel I was working on, *The Marilyn Diaries* (also about Marilyn Monroe). Rechy agreed to an interview. But first he wanted me to visit one of the creative writing classes he conducted from his apartment.

The idea of meeting John Rechy in the flesh was so overwhelming to me, I wasn't sure how I'd deal with it. My choices were either to get drunk enough to go to the class or not go at all. That night I stopped at a bar near his place to have a few drinks. I kept thinking: *I have Rechy's address in my pocket! Soon I will meet him.*

After I left the bar I walked up and down Rechy's street in an inebriated state of nervousness. I thought, maybe I wouldn't go through with it. How do you say hello to Marilyn Monroe? How do you shake hands with Monty Clift? And then, fortified by scotch, I walked up to the door and stood there. Knock on the door, nut job, I urged myself, this is a moment you've been preparing for for years. I knocked.

I was surprised! Rechy was not the moody, broody man I imagined him to be—the aloof hustler in *City of Night*, the cocky Johnny Rio from *Numbers*.

Surrounded by his adoring students, Rechy was affable, attractive, charming, funny. We all sat around his dining room table under huge portraits of Greta Garbo and Joan Crawford. I was drunk, which is usually when I take the most astute notes, but instead I simply watched and listened. He called his female students, "darling." "She was gorgeous darling," he told one young lady, describing a stripper he met in the 1960s. They laughed. Then he turned to the work. Obviously he had read his students manuscripts carefully. He criticized them gently, praised them lavishly, sprinkling his monologues with shrewd tips. They adored him.

A few days later I had Rechy all to myself. We had breakfast—little bite-sized—muffins, at the same dining room table the class had been held. It was wonderful beyond words for me to be able to sit across from someone whose book had such an impact on me and be able to ask questions about his life and work. He was truly kind and thoughtful with me at that meeting. I adored him too.

Rechy liked the resulting article I wrote about his life and career. Soon after I had dinner with him and his longtime partner Michael and I approached them with the idea of a biography. They agreed. But we weren't sure what kind of a book it would be—if it would just be a brief introduction to *Rechy* or a full authorized biography. Rechy had been burned by journalists in the past and he didn't trust me completely. We'd see what developed as we went along.

Rechy and I often met during the week, late in the afternoon. I took two buses to get there, carrying a bottle of white wine and a loaf of bread. (When I first asked Rechy if he drank he replied, "Of course I do? What am I? A savage?") I'd arrive early and sit at the bus stop waiting for the exact time to walk up to Rechy's apartment. At the precise moment I'd knock on his door (his doorbell never worked—eventually it was covered with a piece of tape). From the window on the door I could peer into his living room and the short hall leading to the other rooms. A few seconds after I knocked I would see Rechy emerge from his office where he'd been working. He'd stop in the bathroom leaving the door open. From where I stood I could look directly into the bathroom where Rechy gave himself a little primp in the mirror. He wasn't primping specifically for me—Rechy, I'm sure, would primp for the mailman or a troop of girl scouts selling cookies.

Usually we would drink white wine and chat for an hour or two with the tape recorder running. Suddenly it would become dusk and we would finish our discussion in shadows. Once, I remember as Rechy eloquently talked about a young hustler he befriended in Pershing Square, an automatic light turned on suddenly by a timer, and I was startled to be brought back into the present time.

Rechy began to trust me and the book grew into a full biography. We are alike in so many ways. We're both the typical artistic, brooding, neurotic, self-centered people that Pisces are stereotyped to be. We both like to draw and dream and write. We were both fascinated with Marilyn. Each of us recognized that desirability could be a weapon. We're both, at heart, loners.

Sometimes I would call him on the phone just to see how he was doing. Something in the conversation would jog his memory and he'd start talking about an incident in his life. Like the time Liberace—who had become fascinated with Rechy's hustler image—invited him to discuss "loneliness" in his Hollywood Hills home. I would scribble notes on a nearby envelope or receipt.

In the three years I worked on the book I saw Rechy often. I went to his book signings and speaking engagements. On a number of occasions we had takeout dinner at his place. One time I saw him lecture at UCLA.

Audiences are there to see the mysterious and hip character of his books and Rechy doesn't disappoint. As you get to know Rechy you soon discover that he's many different personalities happily inhabiting the same buff body. He still can fall into a hustler's stance—the casual lean of the hip and macho coolness that, after years of practicing, comes to him naturally. His body remains remarkably youthful, lean and tight. Usually he wears jeans and a tank top or a tight spandex shirt. Often he wore a white muscle-shirt with black strips down the sides. Once he told me, "I hope you know I have over ten of these shirts and it's not always the same one."

One of Rechy's main themes is that narcissism is healthy. My own confidence was much more fragile. He was always trying to get me to value myself more. I do have a gigantic ego, it's just sometimes it's too shy to come out and show itself. One night we were having dinner at his favorite restaurant on Vermont Boulevard. The waiter complimented my appearance and I was flattered and humbled in front of John Rechy. I quickly glossed over the compliment and began telling Rechy about breaking up with a boyfriend I was still in love with who wanted to remain friends. But now our "friendship" consisted only of my ex telling me about a variety of sexual conquests, which hurt me terribly. Rechy immediately saw what the guy was up to. "He's using you to stroke his ego," Rechy scolded. "You're much too special to let people use you that way." That was very sweet and I felt we were genuinely close.

I told him about how, when my ex and I were dating, he often engaged handsome waiters in long, involved conversations—leaving me sitting there totally humiliated, slowly turning to stone. "Oh I never tolerated that," Rechy said angrily. "I wouldn't if I were out with a man, or even just with friends."

A little while later, when a waiter asked me if I wanted more coffee I replied, "Yes, I'll have a little more." Even wanting more coffee sometimes embarrassed me. Rechy was vexed. "Don't say you'll 'have a little more!' Tell him you want more!"

I said, "See, John? That's just my natural meekness."

"I know," Rechy said, "and there's no need for it, Charles. You have to be more assertive! You see how you ignored him when the waiter complimented your appearance. Instead you changed the subject!"

I always wondered how Rechy had grown so confident. We were alike in so many ways but, even though his childhood was far more painful than mine, he never doubted his sexual appeal or his talent. Never. That's where we were different.

But it's the paradoxes in Rechy, his assertiveness and vulnerability, his street tough image mixed in with his intellect, the respect of a renowned author combined with the isolation of a little boy, that makes him such a compelling writer; a distinction that started with his very first book.

Over forty years after its publication *City of Night* remains a remarkable achievement. It has since gone on to influence every generation of writers that followed. There are no computers in it, no cell phones, no explicit sex scenes, but its sad and funny characters reach out to anyone who has ever donned a mask to cover up scars, anyone who has tried to maintain integrity while searching for himself, anyone who has ever felt utterly and helplessly alone—calling to readers with the astonishing power of an artist who has the remarkable ability to transform all of his life experiences into immortality.

The Tale Of An Angry Heart

For Nelson

First of all let me tell you I was not cruising. I was simply waiting on a subway platform, boozy and tired and hungry and, maybe, a bit melancholy. It had been a long unsuccessful night for the usual reasons—not meeting anyone I liked and missing out on a few of the promising opportunities that the night might have possessed. And, also, I was still slightly agitated because of an argument I had had earlier that night at an upscale midtown bar where the men are well groomed and everyone is on their best behavior. It was a crowded night. Packed in fact. And as I passed by a group of pompous men who were blocking a main passageway by talking, drinks in hand, in the narrow space between the bar and the wall the oldest man of the group snapped,

"You could at least say excuse me."

"I did say excuse me," I said turning to face him.

I had said it.

And he, still in a very nasty tone, said: "Well I didn't hear you. You should learn to speak up."

Now I was angry. I could not understand why he was being so obnoxious. He didn't know me. I had been minding my own business and that was the main reason for my own anger. The bar was jam packed. He was the one who was in the wrong for holding a conversation in the middle of an area that should be kept clear in order for people to pass by. And yet he has the nerve o turn on me.

"You should learn to listen," I answered. "Especially before passing judgment on someone." Now I was the one coming across as bitchy and I hated it. I didn't ask for this.

"You should learn how to talk to people," he said without missing a beat.

"No," I said with force. "*You* should do that. I should do what I want to do and YOU should stop telling people what you think is right and wrong."

It was, of course, a minor incident but I was still smarting over it as I waited for the subway. Even though New York was making me more and more jaded, I still considered myself far too timid. I considered it a major flaw but, hey, I'm flawed. In my way, I'm the type of guy who always tries to play fair. Wait my turn. Be polite. "Thank you." "Please." "Excuse me."

85

These are all words I overuse. A resentment forms when life always treats you the same, no matter what you say or do or how you act—that's why the scene with the older man had affected me so.

I had to wait a very long time before the train pulled into the station and when it did at last, at 2: 15 AM, I was grateful that at least there was a place to sit down. It was one of those subway cars that has a long bench under the windows of either side of the train facing each other. I sat down. The people, like me, had been out all night and were drained of energy, half asleep, eyes closed or half-open, couples quietly leaning into each other.

Suddenly, just as the doors were closing a young man rushed into the train discombobulating the late night, sleepy energy. He had an aura of danger and the whole car filled up with it. Buzzed blonde hair. Snapping gum. Crude tattoos, open shoes, a baggy T that hung to his knees. He was singing some rap song with filthy lyrics at the top of his lungs, his way of marking the space, like a dog peeing. Eyes slowly scanning each passenger—assessing their vulnerabilities. Sitting here then springing up and sitting there. Owning the car. He eventually settled on the seat to my right and stopped singing. He was very near me and I was on guard. In previous years I had been constant contact with this aura—this lack of respect-rules-empathy-compassion-aura. And I was afraid of it, although I didn't run from it anymore. I was tired of running. I braced myself for the long ride from Manhattan to Queens.

It was supposed to be an express train but the conductor, or God, or the mayor, or the NYC Metro, system decided it was going to go local and add 45 minutes to my ride. This news made me very tired again. It was going to be a long trip.

At the next stop a young woman entered and the atmosphere in the subway car was at once charged with energy, for she was the kind of woman you take notice of. Ah, lovely she was—dark and exotic, with gold in her eyes, perhaps Italian, a young Sophia Loren. She sat in the just vacated seat on my left and, although I had no desire for her, beauty is still beauty no matter what sort of life you lead. I stared at her the way one would stare at a particularly lovely painting in an otherwise ordinary museum. Her ass, if you are interested in that sort of thing, was full and round and firm. Her breasts were filled with the milk of youth. She was a sweet peach. A sweet kid. Overflowing with good thoughts and plans and chatter and desire and the children that would come.

When I turned away from her at last I could feel the young man on the other side of me staring at her too. I understood that but he was not, I think, seeing her the way I did. Physical beauty is not an uncommon thing, especially in New York City, but, oh my friends, the emotions it can bring up to the surface. He smelled her sex like nectar wafting over the seats—and I, a vile obstacle between them. The woman meant no harm. She probably wasn't even flirting when in all innocence she asked me, "Does this train stop at Union Turnpike?"

"Yes," I replied. "But it's quite a ways off." It was a popular stop in Queens where I was getting off as well. Just then the man at my side loudly cleared his throat and spit into the center of the aisle. I glanced at him. It's not unusual to see people on the subway spit, or throw their garbage on the floor, or put there feet up on seats so others can't sit down, but still these are not things you ever stop noticing. But let me also note, for this might be important later, that I did not click my tongue or shake my head in disgust or sigh audibly—just a brief glance and a dismissal and then back to my private thoughts.

"Why are you looking at me?" the young man said a few moments later.

I didn't hear it the first time, he was still speaking softly. I leaned in closer as if to say, "Excuse me?"

"Why are you looking at me," he said very loud now, getting the attention of everyone on the subway. Now I understood the situation. I could have tried to explain it in several different ways but I opted for the truth. "I saw you spit," I said. "And I wondered why you were spitting on the train." I smiled, though, to show that there were no hard feelings about it. I mean, come on, I hated the idea of someone spitting in a public place but I'm still a chicken shit.

"Why are you looking at me!" he said again as if I hadn't spoken. After trying out two more sentences of explanation I knew it was useless. His mouth was the turning blade on a lawnmower. My explanations were like grass.

""Did you want me to put my dick up your ass?" he asked me in a mock-awed voice. "Is that it? Did you think I would want to do that to you?"

I was shocked and afraid. I became aware that people were aware of what was going on. "Look," I said quietly, looking at him, "I don't want to fight with you. I wasn't looking at you."

His blue eyes blazed at me with hate. Hate raw and undiluted. Plain and simple. Fierce and forceful. I was paralyzed by his hate.

"Stop looking at me!" he screamed.

My entire body froze. My loyal ol' heart kept beating, though. Have you ever seen a pulsing heart? It keeps on beating and beating while they operate, even when the chest is cut open, the skin pinned back.

I looked away from him. There are certain people with hate in them and make no mistake. There are people without places of human feeling that can be reached or appealed to. I realized this was one of them. I decided to just ignore him. Now I see this was my first mistake. I should have been a man. Defended myself. He wasn't that much bigger than me. I could have probably fought him. But I hadn't had a fist fight in many, many years. I hate confrontations, especially with people. And, of course, there's always the chance of a gun or some other type of weapon. He looked like he might carry one. So I remained silent and since I let him get away with it from the very beginning it made him savagely curious and gave him courage, as well as the fuel to push the situation further. He wanted to see how far he could take it.

"I don't want you looking at me!" he shouted, even though was no longer looking at anything. "Look over there!" he said pointing to my far right.

I wouldn't allow him this indignity over me and instead I continued staring ahead.

"No! Over there," he said pointing across my face to my extreme right with his outstretched arm, his wrist inches from my face. His wrist had a do-it-yourself tattoo of moss green going around it like a bracelet. It made me think of prison cells. I did not follow his pointing finger with my gaze.

"Look over there! Look over there!" he persisted. He would grow tired for a moment or so and fall silent, but he would not, he could not, let it go. Still I stared ahead. He then spewed out a litany of clichés: "Did you not have a father? Did you mother raise you? Turn you into a mamma's boy? Are you a pretty little mamma's boy? Whatsa matter, you had no one to teach you how to be a man? Did you grow up in a house filled with girls? You are a pussy!"

He was emptying the pockets of his mind of everything he'd ever heard about homosexuality. It sounded like he had at least read some outdated books on the subject or talked to people with volumes of misinformation.

In the bar I had defended myself to the older man because I was not afraid of him. When I tried to rationalize why that man had been so harsh for such a minor thing I guessed that I had looked so stuck up and cocksure with my hands in my leather jacket that he thought I needed to be knocked down a few pegs. What he didn't know is that I certainly wasn't on any high horse. He could have gotten to know me. Instead he snapped at me. His friends, who had probably heard me say excuse me in the first place, said nothing and I decided to let it go. Why explain myself? It's all bullshit anyway, I reasoned.

If there's one thing that being in the gay scene has taught me it's that no matter what argument you present, somebody will find fault with it. I knew my night was ruined and so I decided to just leave the bar. Yet as I walked away I heard the man say "Asshole!" in a very loud voice to the room at large. I stopped dead in my tracks and, because the people in the bar didn't know my side of the story, I was really enraged now, with the rage of being unjustly accused. I felt my own hate for this man for making me seem like something I was not. I thought of waiting for him outside and if he didn't get in a cab, following him down a dark street and terrorizing him. Maybe breaking a bottle behind him and threatening him with broken glass. I shocked myself just by entertaining these thoughts.

Incredulous that I did not react to the young man on the subway kept taking it further and further with violent words that hacked open the cicatrix of my scars that I had kept hidden in me for years.

"You fucking pussy! You wanted to suck my dick, didn't you? You wanted to swallow the shit that comes out of it! You thought that I would let you?! You're a woman, you know that? You're a woman! You're lucky that you have something between your legs because you're nothing but a woman! You fucking bitch! That's all you'll ever be! You know that? How does it feel—to know that you'll always be a woman?"

It was a badgering, a badgering, a badgering. He would not stop. He would not stop! I stared straight ahead. Watching the blackness pass outside the windows—he, however, continued badgering, badgering, badgering.

I was no longer drunk. I tried to summon that numbness but found none. Still my face stared ahead and betrayed nothing. But in some vacuous black area of my soul—a place I hate to visit—my arms were flailing, my heart ripping, my voice screaming ... torrents ... were pressing against my sinuses. I wanted to kill him. If I had been carrying a gun I would have. I begged my nose not to start bleeding, as it usually does in emotional situations. The young woman at my other side silently placed her hand over mine. Her act of sympathy set me on fire. I didn't see how I would stop tears now.

"Are we almost at Union Turnpike," she asked gently, pretending that nothing was happening.

"Yes in two more stops," I said. My voice did not crack and I was grateful for her kindness, although I would rather have taken the blows in private than this public humiliation. I wasn't ashamed of being gay. I wanted to explain that to her and to the people who watched my silence. What degraded me was that he was making them all think that I was on a sex prowl and tried to pick him up. For the sake of fairness I wanted them to know that I wasn't looking at him with desire. I wasn't cruising. I wasn't anything but tired.

The young man watched the beautiful woman's warmth towards me, flowing like a gentle balm, and he kept spitting on the floor in front of us with disgust. I hoped he wouldn't get the idea to spit on me. He seemed like he might think that would be a good idea and I don't (didn't) know what I would do if he did it. Spit back? (Probably not). Throw a first punch? (Doubtful). Wipe it off and continue staring ahead? (Probably). I didn't need the further humiliation.

Because my facial expressions throughout barely changed he thought he wasn't getting to me and so he changed tactics.

"You're not white," he said. "You're a spic! You'll never pass. Why are you trying to pass? Filthy spic!"

In a way I was weirdly relieved—not because he had switched subjects but because, by him mistaking me for Puerto Rican, I realized that his incredible hate did not stop at what I was but was a toxic smoke, slogging across the world, trying to whither on contact everything that was not like him. Yes, I said to myself. There are people like this. This is the reality. This is the reason for war and atrocities. This is why children are kidnapped and raped and butchered. This is why women are slit from belly to neck and left in garbage dumps wrapped in plastic. There are hearts like this that, for whatever reasons, do not feel and cannot be reached.

When he wasn't spewing the young man stared at me intently looking for something to pick out—some way he might reach me and get a reaction. And I tried to ignore it. I tried to display dignity. This was not the first time I was forced to be stoic as bombs dropped all around me. These were harsh but I did not flinch. Practice had made me perfect. But the subway lights were merciless and I was a specimen under them.

Stop looking at me; I wanted to say to him as he had said to me. We may be totally different but there's nothing extraordinary about me. I am only a man, just like you. I will perform no miracles.

I hoped that he would forget about me and go back to admiring the beauty of the woman beside me. She is a girl and I am a boy, my mind said.

"Do you want my dick in your ass," he asked mockingly, back on that tired jag. I have never met a fag basher in my entire life (and I've run into more than my fair share) who did not ask me this question. It makes me wonder about them.

"No man will ever respect you," he was saying now. "No real man will ever be you're friend. Maybe women will (this was said glancing at the

90

woman beside me), but no real man. Because you're nothing. You fit in nowhere. You never will." Did people still think this way? In this day and age? With *Queer as Folk* and *Will & Grace*?

My stop, Union Turnpike—which was also the beautiful woman's stop—came up and, as these horrible coincidences sometimes happen, the young man was getting off there too. There was no question of me getting off, of course. I mean, who knew what could have happened with movement? He might strike me on the platform, mock the way I walk, humiliate me in front of a new batch of people. As the train pulled into the station he stood up to leave but did not stop his tirade. My passivity became his target now.

"Any other man on this train," he said with a sweeping gesture as I stared ahead, "would have defended himself. But you are a pussy. You are a fucking woman who eats dicks and swallows the shit that comes out of them. Always remember that!"

And as he stared into my face with those blue, blue eyes that saw nothing but hate—no childhood, no love affairs, no tender nights holding someone, just holding—I was ashamed suddenly because maybe, for one brief moment when he first entered the train, I did check him out. But without, I swear, any passion all. With fear. His was definitely a look that some people go for. I am not one of them. He probably knew that but sat there with the patience of a spider simply waiting for someone to turn on, to release the overpowering anger in his heart. And I felt shame because I should have stood up for myself. I should have defended my dignity... whether there would have been punches, or knives, or death.

The beautiful woman, the catalyst, stepped off the train and turned to look at me. Our eyes met for a moment, hers seemed to be filled with compassion. I did not want her to have sympathy for me but, I thought, it might have been nice to have known her. I knew that I would never see her again, but I also knew somehow that because of her presence on the train, our brief interaction, my life would never be the same.

"Hey everybody! That guy sitting over there is a pussy!" The young man shouted as he held the doors open to get in his last licks. "He sucks dicks! He wanted to suck mine!"

"Yeah?" someone said sarcastically and I was grateful for that too. Apparently everyone saw him as the asshole, not me. As the train pulled away he punched the window as if it were me (or he) with a force that was extraordinary. He would not be ignored. But I noticed, now that he was off the train, that the remaining passengers went out of their way not to look at me. I always thought of people as cruel, but that was misplaced. You never know what lies beneath the surface.

So I looked all around the subway at all of the people who were left and there were blacks and whites and Orientals and Puerto Ricans and Indians and young and old and vagrants and ruffians whom, once, I might have been afraid of or despised in my own way. Yet none of them looked at me. It made me feel somehow exalted. In one of those enlightening moments in life where everything that happens seems to have some higher purpose I saw, or thought I saw, my own misplaced hate and released it as if it were the infectious poisons from a swollen boil. My own eyes at last were cleared. I had been a fool. And with my eyes finally open my heart also opened and a feeling of tremendous LOVE for each and every one of these people on the train, and everyone like them washed over me because they new I was ashamed and they did not want to remind me of my humiliation or even let me know that they had witnessed it and so they did not look at me. And the love that filled up in my heart was so comforting and so great that I let go of the tears I had more or less been holding in check for so long and they escaped down my cheeks with relieved abandon.

"I think I won that one," I said quietly to myself. And it was true.

Now when I looked into my new heart I was glad that I had left the bar without taking the argument with the older man any further. I remembered turning to look at him one last time before I left and I saw at once that he knew he had gone too far and he looked frightened although he tried to stare me down defiantly. He was probably in his mid sixties. He looked so sad and somewhat ridiculous in his loud-colored vest and trendy haircut surrounded by the incredible beauties that this bar attracted and, taking in his full image, I thought that I saw a reason for his anger. It wasn't just unexplained hate for me; it was anger at the sense of the loss of his own valuable youth. And because I saw an explanation for his anger I didn't feel the need to return it with violence anymore. He had unknowingly reached a place in me that confirmed that I was human. The beautiful woman knew that place. The people on the train also knew that place of human empathy. Perhaps by now, with the alcohol wearing off, even the older man in the bar had thought about our unfortunate incident and was sorry. Maybe he really didn't mean any harm.

And what of my young nemesis you might ask? If given the chance I would say to him: Your eyes are lovely but too clouded with hate to see, strangling you, limiting your life to a single emotion. If only you could look at what's troubling you. If only you could say to someone, "I don't know how to fuck another man, will you tell me how?" Or speak of whatever else it is that frightens you; you would find a place that would make it possible for you to live at peace (with all kinds of people.) Open your eyes and there will nothing to be afraid of. Face your own hatred and be free.

92

But as always when these gilded, lovely, enlightening thoughts present themselves, the tarnish of reality also settled in. The subway car was pulling into the next station and the bright advertisements and movie posters rapidly flew past my eyes reminding me of the real world outside. Again I found myself wondering if I had been duped. If the man in the bar really did lash out at me because he was bitter at life rendering him old, unable any longer to pass—or was he simply filled with selfishness and tried to provoke me in the bar because my passing by him had interrupted his conversation? And even if he was angry because he was old, why did he have to start with me? Why couldn't he find solace in the fact that his present physical state is what waited for all of us—if we were lucky.

I wondered, also, if the beautiful woman had really felt compassion for me or was she just being nice to nullify any guilt she might feel, for starting the scene on the train for the sake of a good night's sleep. If the people who diverted there eyes from my humiliation did so in sympathy or in boredom—just another vicious situation on the subway. And maybe even I had just as much anger in me as ever; my hate dormant in a smaller corner of my heart simply waiting for another provocation to spring forward, ferocious and alive. It was up to me to decide. Life is what you make of it. "Beware my foolish heart."

The train was stopping and I decided to leave these incomprehensible thoughts behind. The night had been grueling. I needed to rest. The next stop would leave me at an area that was nothing but empty fields, which led to an ancient cemetery and then to the main road that would take me home. I was relieved at the thought of this place for at this time of night everything would be covered in complete darkness and the walk from there to my house wasn't so terribly far.

The Finer Things In Life

For Rick Brooks

Let's say you're twenty-two. Say you have aquamarine eyes and tousled blonde hair and a surfer's hard body—lean and smooth and tight. And a nice dick. And let's add that you can string two sentences together because—lets face it—if you have all the rest, that's all the conversational skills you need. And imagine some man, some older man, some older man with a lot of money, offered you a life filled with partying and expensive cars and exotic travel and designer clothes. Would it be worth it to trade your best years, the prime years, the years you're at your most energetic and alive and beautiful, the only years you can experience young love at its purest, for the finer objects in life?

"Why not," chirps one young man—who's been there, done that—when I encounter him at an upscale bar in Beverly Hills. I had been recently assigned an article investigating "kept boys," or "trophy boys," the upscale version of the hustler. Brad recently got out of a long term "kept" situation, and was now in search of another. "It doesn't hurt me to go out with someone and make someone laugh and have a good time and travel and look around and see and feel and touch. It's not harming me. So why not do it and get a house and get a car or whatever while I'm at it?"

The thought of having a weekly allowance, a kick-ass apartment and expensive toys, all in exchange for supplying a little piece of ass, has sent hundreds of boys from New York to Los Angeles to bars like the Town House in Manhattan and Numbers in West Hollywood in the hopes of snaring a live one, preferably barely alive. Bars where upper crusty gentleman drink cocktails mixed with the most expensive liquor and scour the surroundings like vultures in search of tender flesh. And where tender flesh, with comb grooved hair and porcelain smiles, set their traps in the hopes of snaring a wealthy score.

In a town like Hollywood, where networking is part of survival, it's not difficult to come across someone who, at one time in his life or another, has been provided for by an older mentor.

At first Brad is not sure he wants to be interviewed, but he agrees to have a drink with me. As many people in Los Angles do, he describes himself as looking like a certain movie star, in this case "a young Robert Downey Jr." and, for once, the person lives up to it. He has tousled dark hair. His abundantly lashed eyes are big and brown and sad. Like a puppy

94

dog—he wants to be loved. That's part of his marketable charm. And I might have given in, warmed to him, but something about him made me keep my guards up. Sometimes, without warning his eyes turn hard and shrewd and impenetrable. I could see him slamming doors on lives without warning.

"Let's go back to your place and talk," he says after awhile. "It will be a good place to break the ice." So we drive over to my place and when we're settled in on my couch, I switch on the tape recorder. Brad didn't object.

Today he is a successful makeup artist in the film industry, but five years ago, when he was twenty-eight, Brad was living in Europe trying to be a writer and living on a shoe string budget. One night in a bar he met an older man from Eastern Germany, a professor of English literature. "I was hurting and he alluded to the fact that he was well off," Brad recalls. "I had some money in savings but I was going through it fast." It started as a one night stand, but Brad soon saw the potential in the situation.

"His house was just amazing—fantastically beautiful," he says. "When he offered me to come and visit him for a week I said, 'of course.'" The week stretched to six months. "It was basically understood that this was a business proposition," he explains.

The professor even told him, "I know you're not that attracted to me but I'm very attracted to you and I'd like you to hang around here for awhile and I'll give you some money, every week, so you'll have an allowance." Brad tells me off handedly that the sex was okay. "But," he adds with a straight face, "I really didn't care for an Eastern German mentality. I don't like their politics."

Politics aside, the terms were agreeable to Brad. Soon the professor was buying him expensive clothes and "taking care of everything." During the whole time that he had been living in Europe Brad couldn't afford to eat out now, suddenly, every night it was a different restaurant.

Okay, everyone knows that life is a hell of a lot easier when you have someone with big bucks footing the bills, but are there any inner conflicts that come with the territory of exchanging the most private and intimate part of yourself, your sexuality, for a more comfortable way of life? "No," asserts Brad. "Actually I felt quite lucky. I knew who I was and no matter what else was going on it was definitely temporary. I knew the boundaries. This was just a self experiment on my part."

The experiment started to go haywire when Brad found that he couldn't live up to his part of the bargain any longer. "I tried for a really long time but I got to the point where I just couldn't have sex with him anymore. Perhaps he could fool himself into thinking that this was anything else but business, but I knew better."

One minute Brad seems vulnerable and almost soft, the next extremely hard, totally in control. Lighting a cigarette, exhaling slowly, studying my reactions, flicking an ash haphazardly. "If you're not in love with someone and you're looking at thirty—which I was—you start thinking beyond temporary and you start thinking about permanent."

In addition to his waning sex drive and encroaching maturity, Brad started missing his friends and hanging out with people his own age. "It had been fun but it was starting to get irritating," he says. "So on an emotional level I just abused him a little and stepped away from it."

He had gotten what he needed from the experiment. Slam went the door to a life but, Brad says, "I could call him up tomorrow and he'd be thrilled to hear from me. But it was just an American in Paris type of situation. It was temporary. It was a fantasy"

I say to Brad that I see that mentality even in Los Angeles. That the older men here feel certain expectations are on them. I'm not that old and I'm in okay shape and I've had offers here from very well off gentlemen to help me out, when I was in between freelance jobs and things weren't going quite as well as I would have hoped. It's almost as if it's expected. Therefore the older men in the scene accept their duties, which is, if they're going to date someone younger, they're going to pay for it.

I tell Brad the story of Michael, a fifty-eight-year-old lawyer who allowed me to interview him at his house in the Hollywood Hills several days before. He lives with a young man, an "actor" barely out of his teens. The actor is the latest in a long line of actors and models and writers who have lived with Michael over the past fifteen years. Michael demurred, however, when I bring up the word "daddy" and muttered some things about being a "mentor."

"I have a low self image and I'm doing a lot to change that," Michael told me. "But when I'm empowering the low self image then it occurs to me that it's going to be difficult for a man in his late fifties to find a lover. That's why I use the trappings that come with wealth to attract people to me."

But, I pointed out, wouldn't it be easier to meet men somewhere of his age range for a relationship that's more genuine? He shook his head. "When I look at people my age they look old and tired," he replied. "When people meet me they say, 'You're fifty-eight? You look about forty-five.' And I feel thirty-five, and I think of myself as in my thirties, so when I date someone who is in their twenties it doesn't feel that different."

This isn't an uncommon phenomenon. You see it online. Did you ever browse the online personals? Men in their forties and fifties will often list the age bracket that they'd be interested in meeting as being between eighteen and thirty-five. They'll say something like, "I'm fifty but don't look it." But, as Gloria Steinham once famously said, "This is what fifty looks like." You can't judge these older men too harshly for their wants, though. After all, we don't choose what we're attracted to. And, let's face the brutal facts: most of us become slaves to what we desire.

For instance I would find it hard to date a guy who showed up for a first date without wearing cologne. I'm well aware this seems stupid, but to me it's very real and valid. When I mentioned this to a friend he said, "How utterly and completely shallow—to miss out on what might be a good opportunity because of the way a person grooms himself." But when I ask the same friend if he would date someone with a potbelly or a hairy back he blurts out unabashedly, "absolutely not!" It *is* utterly and completely shallow. On both our parts. But we want what we want and we love what we love and to overlook that fact is to be untrue to ourselves and to simply settle.

Some men desire younger men. They can't help it. So they do what they have to in order to have them young. Often they're embarrassed by the fact that they're simply not attracted to people their own age. Usually a sixty-year-old will explain his relationship with a twenty-year-old by saying something like, "Joe is a nice kid with a good heart and he just needs a little guidance." At the same time failing to mention that the good heart comes with monthly bills for acting classes and car payments and teeth veneers and rehab clinics.

"Even with fifty-year-old men today taking care of themselves and looking better," I say to Brad, trying to sound like a know-it-all even though I know very little, "with workouts at the gym, Botox, healthy living—even with their life experiences and knowledge and money—they still crave in a lover the one thing they can't buy. Youth."

Brad listens to me talk about Michael and then nods his head knowingly. "I call them youth vampires," he says. "I avoid them in bars because I see them coming. I haven't set myself up for that here. I think they miss their youth and I think there's always—especially with gays—an element of living vicariously through younger people. Young people have sex, they have boyfriends, they're healthy, they have energy, they go out partying all night, they recover very fast and they get up and start all over the next day."

But aren't the "trophy boys" vampires in their own right? Frantically flapping their charms, sucking out the wealth, the fame, the glamour from the men they sleep with, rather then working their way up to that lifestyle themselves. Case in point, the ghoulish and now legendary serial killer Andrew Cunanan. Lacking the real beauty, charm and intelligence needed to break into the circles he longed to be a part of, he tried to cheat his way in by making up an interesting past for himself, putting on facades and trying to absorb the lifestyle from the men he bedded. When he couldn't make it even that way, he murdered his way to stardom.

Ironically, a long time ago, while attending college in San Diego, Brad knew Andrew Cunanan. Years ago, when he was a hot news item, Cunanan himself had been built up in the media as this great beauty, this charmer, this near genius, articulate and gorgeous enough to bewitch several wealthy men into taking care of him. But with the hysteria surrounding him almost forgotten, some who know him paint a very different picture.

"He just was an asshole," Brad informs me. "I don't want to toot my own horn here, but I'm very smart. Amazingly astute, and the guy wouldn't have gotten anything over on me. He was always really loud. Always gesticulating in a way that showed he was trying to get attention. He was always talking in a way that just showed me he was a fake. As far as appearing intelligent—he appeared more intelligent than a lot of the people he was talking to, which let's just say wasn't a very bright crowd to begin with."

But what about the legend of Cunanan's studying up on the finer things in life in order to polish a fatal charm and attract a higher caliber of older gentlemen? "That's a load of shit too," Brad asserts. "There's someone in La Jolla who gave him this car and everything and that's fine. It's not hard to hook up with an older person who's got money and get things from him in exchange for sex if you're a lot younger. And from what I understand that guy was much older, not very attractive, so if he was willing to settle for Cunanan, fine. But charisma didn't have anything to do with it."

"One thing that I did agree with regarding what the media said about Cunanan," Brad adds, "is that he took on different personas but they were all easy to see through as far as I was concerned. I dealt with people that were of a much higher caliber. I was once at a party where he wasn't invited. He came with other people and then just tried to sweep the room, being loud and boisterous. He always seemed to be trying to say, 'look how wonderful I am. Can you see?"

In the world of trophy boys, as in all professions, there are those who master the game, who become so skillful at their job that they rise to what can be considered the top of the field.

"I was a courtesan before courtesan became well known," says Troy, a six foot-six inches bleached platinum blonde with a sky blue stare and a statuesque appearance. He is strikingly handsome and—speaking of look-al-like actors—he resembles Dolph Lundgren in the 1980s. But he looks very, very tired. Like all the kept boys I talked to, Troy thinks of himself as different from the rest. "I wasn't really kept," he says, "in the sense that my Daddy didn't give me a salary."

Troy has come to visit me and tell me the story of his life, which now he informs me, is in development for a major motion picture. Like a hip Norma Desmond, he carries with him the mementos of his spectacular career: photos in *Architectural Digest* of the extravagant homes he has lived, newspaper clippings from gossip columns detailing the troubles with his obscenely wealthy sugar daddy, court papers, and the script telling the entire tale. And oh what a tale he tells. Lust, greed, ambition, vanity, and revenge—the kind of story that would keep Jackie Collins in material for several novels.

Troy, whose mother was an actress and father was a professional athlete, started his career at fifteen when, while walking down the street he encountered a fifty-two year old billionaire. "The naiveté that someone has is priceless," Troy says, attempting to explain the particular allure that can be properly marketed by a fifteen-year-old boy-toy. "So the trick is to maintain that naiveté and yet become educated at the same time. I am a master of that."

"But," I ask Troy, "doesn't that make it a false naiveté?" He considers: "Well it becomes a false naiveté once you know what you're doing. But that's where the blonde hair and the whole bit comes in...(laughs)...makes it easier to pull it off."

And pull it off he did, dating a string of wealthy men one after another. But, he assures me, only one at a time. "With those kinds of people if you're dating more than one of them they're gonna find out," he explains. "And you just don't want to do that because then you're an old, tired piece of meat."

Armed with this knowledge Troy managed to keep his freshness and, in the world of kept boys, his false naiveté, baby blues and blonde hair made him very much in demand from powerful men in the Velvet Mafia to the real Mafia to lawyers because, as he puts it, "you can fuck the muscle boys and the pretty boys but you can't take them out. I was the one who went with them to public places. I was the one who traveled. I could hold dinner parties and they wouldn't have to worry about me knowing what fork to use."

Although, I would think, give some of these men a young, masculine, buffed stud with a three days growth and a washboard stomach and they wouldn't care if he ate his salad with a serving spoon, Troy assures me: "I'm not stupid. I know how to use what you've got to get what you want. I was educated. They could talk to me about more than just going to the gym."

The script, Troy carries with him, aptly titled, *Daddy's Boy*, tells of his nine-year relationship with an Aspen multimillionaire. One afternoon in the late eighties the nineteen-year-old Troy got a phone call that would win him the trophy that all trophy boys strive for in the kept boy Olympics. The caller was a world famous, jet-setting hairdresser—apparently in high society there is such a thing—flying around the country for a color here a comb-out there. Who better to hear of a position opening up?

"There's somebody you've got to meet," the excited hair burner told Troy, "he's straight now but he needs somebody to help him out of the closet. He's gone all over the world looking, looking, looking."

Ten minutes later Troy got a call from this straight "somebody," who turned out to be an Aspen property developer. A few hours later he was on a private jet. The proposition was simple. Troy would be flown in for a cocktail party being given that evening. He could leave that night if he wanted to—have the pilot fly him right back. But with Troy, being a four year veteran of this sort of thing, that wasn't likely to happen.

"He wasn't the most attractive man in the world," Troy (also a master of understatement) says, "but I knew I could learn a lot from him." For a boy who was using his "friendships" with older men as stepping stones, capturing, the attention of the affluent Aspen developer must have seemed like reaching the top of the ladder.

"Jackie Onassis was there, Lee Ioccoca all of the Aspen elite," Troy gushes, "I was being judged by everyone. They had been pre-warned. They knew what was going on. Here we have this man with all this money who wants to come out of the closet and he wants someone to be one on one with. And it could be me."

He passed the test and the developer made him an offer to stay. "After the week he laid it down on paper," Troy says, "and he said 'what I want

100

is what you could give me, which is just constant attention, not embarrassment, and sex.'" Sex, when and where he wanted it.

"And what would you get?" I asked Troy.

He doesn't even pause for a moment: "Everything in the world I ever wanted."

"Which was?"

Now he does pause. "We traveled all over the world. Every place we ever lived was in *Architectural Digest*. We had accounts everywhere. If I needed things to wear there were a couple of designers that I could call directly. I was given a platinum American Express card."

So was this part of the agreement? Did Troy spell it out what he expected in exchange for his sex? "No. I didn't," says the master. "The thing was I never asked for anything. That's the tackiest thing in the world, when a boy says, 'well, I could really use a piece of jewelry.' You know? Hinting around. I was at Numbers the other night and I actually overheard that conversation happen. And I just rolled my eyes. That was one of the things, you know, don't ask for it and you'll get it. And so I never asked for anything. And I was given everything."

Priceless naiveté indeed!

Numbers is the popular West Hollywood male prostitute hang-out which, several years back, moved from a quiet spot on Sunset Boulevard to Santa Monica Boulevard in the heart of Boys Town. With the trophy boy craze the bar/restaurant has become less of a meat market, more of a trendy spot where modern day clones bring stylish lady friends to gawk at the older gentleman patiently shopping for just the right boy. "Vegas-y," is how one friend describes it enthusiastically. But in spite of the new touristy flavor the place now has, there is still an underlying buying and selling atmosphere.

I'm not a stranger to places like this. In New York and in Los Angeles, long before this article, even before I passed twenty, I knew such places. I never considered my self a hustler because I never asked for money. But then I never turned it down when offered either

My last time at Numbers was only a few days before my meeting with Troy. I wasn't going to go out. I had not been going out too much recently, but at the last minute I changed my mind, reasoning to myself that it would be research. But the real reason, I guess, is that we're all lonely and horny anyway.

Plus, I was a reporter being sent into a scene I was familiar with but was constantly surprised by. I hated it because it highlighted the march of time. I hated it because of the lack of respect for rules, the ferocious competition. I hated it because it was only facades that mattered, not a person. And I was drawn to it for all these reasons too.

I've always found the atmosphere fascinating because the night offered so many little adventures. Once I met a gentleman who, to my alarm, asked me to walk around his lavish bedroom using a pair of crutches. Later he cleaned my feet with his tongue. I lost any attraction I had for him but a hard-on wasn't necessary. As I was leaving, he offered me a large some of money. I took it. I guess I felt I earned it because the evening wasn't what I had in mind, any feelings I had for him were destroyed. But I didn't feel bad.

And here I was years later. Still fascinated, watching, watching. A couple in their late fifties silently ate dinner with a sullen twenty-year-old who looked like the type of guy who wakes up beautiful. Witty conversation and clever remarks were obviously not the order of the day at this particular supper party. Not a word was said, but the couple watched the boy as if they wanted to tare into him as fervently as he devoured his sirloin. They didn't seem to mind what fork he used. Sexual desire brings everyone down to the same level.

Here, amongst the gawkers, the real trade is certainly competitive. When the kid excused himself to go to the men's room, another young man, almost identical in looks, immediately sat in his seat. But this one was definitely more experienced. From my vantage point he seemed quite charming—thin and cute like a breath of fresh air—and the atmosphere at the table changed. The couple greeted the additional dish warmly. And the new boy soon had the couple smiling and laughing and he seemed to do it with an unselfconscious ease.

I can't deny it. I truly think there's something innately unlikable about most hustlers. They look so damn good. I want to like them. I try. But they're hard. I try to imagine them as lost, but they're not. They're not lost at all. Am I simply jealous because I'm getting older and my days of competing on a physical level are numbered? But isn't that true of all of us? How very difficult it is to no longer be the most beautiful boy in the room fifteen years after the fact. And how quickly fifteen years goes by.

With thoughts like crowding my head, it was getting congested in the bar, so I moved on, not waiting to see what would happen when the first boy returned to find his grave jumped in. I walked out to the balcony, the

102

latest addition to the new Numbers, which fits in nicely with the "outdoor only" smoking laws in the Los Angeles bars and clubs. My motive was to spot someone that I'd like to talk to.

Before long, I was approached by Jake, a handsome older man in a tasteful suit. His hair was thinning but he plastered what was left severely back as if what hair he did have was a nuisance. He had the kind of carved features that could pull off thinning hair. He looked like the type that the numbers at Numbers would really go for because he exuded money, was in buying mode, but was also masculine, sexy and attractive.

"Are you working?" he asks me.

Actually I was—looking for material for this article, but no need to tell him that. I decide to be evasive. "What makes you think that?" I ask him.

He shrugs equally ambiguous.

I shoot back with, "Are you buying?"

This leads us to a conversation about buying company for an evening. Jake is handsome and smart. I would think he doesn't need to use his money to attract people to him. But, he says, he doesn't have a problem with younger men who are drawn to him for his wealth. "Having money is no different then having a big cock or a six pack or a great face," he informs me.

He also tells me that he lives in Beverly Hills. He says he's a television producer. He invites me to swim in his pool.

It was while I was talking to Jake that I got the journalistic coup of a lifetime. I met Andrew Cunanan. Well, at least as I imagined Andrew Cunanan—brought to stunning life in the reincarnated form of a hustler named Christian. Dark and exotic—just attractive enough to be several steps away from beautiful—Christian compensated for his lack of wit and beauty with a ballsy behavior so intense that it snatched my breath away and left me in awe.

He sniffed out at once the fact that Jake was a prime catch and he couldn't resist the challenge that the catch was already talking with me. Christian saw what he wanted and felt totally justified to intrude on a pick-up in progress, putting himself in the middle of Jake and me, barging right into our conversation. He was turning it into a competition. But I refused to get involved. And the more quiet and reserved I became the bigger the show Christian put on.

The one thing Christian had in his favor was his utterly indestructible confidence. His weapon was his bulldozer personality, which he kept pushing between any chemistry that was connecting Jake and myself. If there was an awkward silence or an uncomfortable glance between Jake and me, Christian plowed right over it.

He was being playful too. He would disappear for a while, and Jake and I would resume our conversation, only to reappear, maneuvering his lithe body between us. Hairless and fatless with Teflon exterior that coated, as far as I could tell, nothing but ego. Perhaps another reason I resented hustlers so much was that they were better at it than I. There wasn't a true feeling involved. Not even a thought. No integrity. Pretty monsters! Their conversation is dialogue. Attraction is beside the point. For them, sex is only an exchange of money and some fluids.

But Jake was intrigued enough to, from time to time, give Christian enough encouragement to come back and join us. He was getting a kick out of it. Jake would say something to both Christian and me and then lean back and wait for our responses. I was wounded and remained silent. Christian would sense my rage and leave. Only to return moments later—energized by the rivalry.

"I was standing at the urinal," he said on one presentation, "and the old guy standing next to me asked if he could jack me off." A lie, I believe, because I had a view of the men's room and no old man went in or came out all the time Christian was in there. This provocative statement was his way of metaphorically flashing open his raincoat in front of us: "see me see me I'm a desirable person!"

If his looks didn't get him the attention he felt he deserved, he would say something or do something to catch it: a slinky move, a suggestive dance, a very wide grin, a double entendre. The real Andrew Cunanan put a bullet through a famous man's brain.

I liked Jake. I didn't want to go home with him (okay, maybe I did). But I also wanted to talk to him. Sure I'm a journalist, but I'm also a human being, and he seemed like an interesting person and a nice guy too. But you either want me or you don't. What you see is what you get. If there's more attractive guys around, for a price, good luck. Don't think you're going to play us against each other in a sort of competition for your own amusement. I won't play that. I won't sell that part of myself.

I lost interest and patience and walked silently away, leaving Jake to deal with Christian/Cunanan on his own. To my surprise Jake followed and stopped me at the top of the steps leading down to the sidewalk. It's always a game. We're all aware we're playing. I got tired of it though, and left the table without officially quitting. I'm not a kid. "You must think I'm an asshole," Jake said

"You keep talking to boys with the depth of a puddle" I sighed wearily, "I'm left to draw my own conclusions."

104

"He told me he's very good in bed," said Jake

How was I supposed to reply to that?

"Well, what do you expect him to say?" I answered at last. "It's like a used car salesman saying, 'she purrs like a kitten.'"

We both laughed and I gave off the wrong signal. Jake leaned in closer for romance but I received the wrong signal.

"Goodnight," I said and slunk away.

Let Jake have the viper, I said to myself. But let him know I was the one who said 'no.' Still, I didn't feel like a winner.

I imagined them in bed that night. Of course that's where they would end up. Throughout the time we had been together Jake was laughing and being a captivating fellow, but all the while side glancing body parts and wondering about my bedroom performance level. What crap! But what was I doing looking for boyfriends in a place like this?

Sex, of course, is the glue that holds these relationships together. A lot of that kind of setup is about pretending. From what I know about any of those situations, it always is an act. "Let's not act like we have a business proposition. Let's act like we have a real relationship." And I definitely think the fantasy is much stronger in the head of the person who's paying the bills.

Although, according to Troy, the kept boy also has to do his share of fantasizing in order to maintain any level of success. "In bed people say close your eyes and think of someone else. You gotta find something about that person. As troll-y or as awful as you may think they are, they're not stupid and if you're not into it they can tell. So you've got to find that one thing about that person that turns your crank. Other than his pocketbook. Because that's not there on his naked body when you're in bed."

"I read an article once that pertained to my life so much," he continues. "It was about a photographer who shot Marilyn Monroe. Marilyn's thinking was: pretend like the camera is your lover, and just do whatever you have to do in your mind. Take away your vision. It's the same way with a guy. Take away what they look like and be passionate—if you can do it without closing your eyes, that's the trick."

Yet even using the tricks of the trade, there were problems. The developer developed a coke habit and Troy tells tales of mental and physical abuse: "He tried to strangle me. He tried to bite my fingers off! I just had surgery because my nose was broken more times than I can count. I'm having my eyes done in a month because they're so swollen for being beat up so many times from trying to stop the drugs." (Actually the bags under his eyes seem to me to be, perhaps, due more to the passing of his own youth but I'm too polite to say. Ahem!). All of which, as horrible as it all sounds, should make for highly dramatic scenes in the story of his life.

"I wanted out at any cost," he says. "But when someone's involved in the Mafia you don't just say good-bye and leave. So I just wanted to do anything I could do to get out."

Troy pauses to fiddle with a glass of water, then he goes on: "When I tried to leave him all I asked of him is five thousand dollars, my car, and my belongings. Not furniture or any of that. I wanted out that badly. Five thousand dollars—he drops that much at lunch. But he wouldn't give it to me."

Dubious, I say to Troy: "In all the time together, even though you were living the high life and had everything you possibly wanted...when the time came for you to leave you really hadn't amassed anything."

"No one ever does," he says, shaking his head at the unfairness of it all. "I mean, apartment buildings with your name on them, and cars with your name on them. I had for example dozens of Bulgari watches, which is what I wear. My net worth in watches was more than most of these current queens make in a year. But what are you gonna do with all of that? Hock it? Oh, that's very chic."

But, being the resourceful type, Troy did what any self-respecting kept boy would do. He sued his Daddy's ass in court. He shows me the settlement: $500,000 down, and $150,000 a year for life, provided that he doesn't live with anyone else.

"Gulp," I say, "not a small consolation for a little solitude."

No wonder he could afford to have his eyes done. In a few years I could imagine Troy being the guy doing the buying—yet knowing the score. Giving out as little as possible and getting as much as he can in return. Still he will be tragic. It's a vicious cycle.

I'm trying to understand why the hustlers I encountered for this story infuriate me. Often, more than the money, the idea of being paid feeds into their already over puffed egos. It makes them feel superior and they have an undeserved superiority, just because they're young and were born with a certain amount of looks (although I've seen many men horny enough to pay toothless crones for a blowjob when desperate enough). It's nothing to be proud of to be a paid as a temporary receptacle for someone's passion—but they crow about it as if they were twenty-million-dollar-a- picture movie stars. But how will they feel when, inevitably, they're on the other end of the transaction?

I find it hard to believe that these wealthy men who are able achieve such great success in their professional life, who take the time to build up a career and master their crafts and with all their smarts and ambition and worldly possessions, are unable to develop the real thing. I can't understand why they wouldn't strive for a loving relationship.

"Because they don't know how," Troy says. "There's one particular individual here in Los Angeles who has the biggest house on the top of the hill, more money than he can count, but he can't keep anybody because he doesn't even know the first thing about affection."

"Is that part of becoming successful," I wonder aloud. "One of the things you drop along the way to the top?"

"Yes," Troy replies. "And if you don't know anything about affection how do you know about love? You don't. You have to pay someone to love you. To show you that. Because you just don't know get it."

As long as we're on the subject of love, did, I ask Troy, he ever love the developer? He did, after all, live with the man for nine years. "I have to say that I did grow to love him," he says. Then musing on the nature of love he adds: "And everybody always asks, 'if he didn't have all that money, would you stay?' And the answer blatantly is 'no' but if I was paralyzed in a skiing accident, he would have gotten rid of me in a second."

I guess love can go down many different pathways. The thought of this kind of love, on so many different levels, in so many different kinds of relationships makes me feel sad, and lost and terribly alone. Yet, I could understand the attraction of entering a situation where both roles are so clearly defined. There is no game playing. There is no guessing. Both parties know their roles and must stick to them or it's over. And when you walk away from it, there isn't the kind of hurt that real love brings. You ask for paradise, you end up with court settlements.

Certainly Troy is shrewd enough to have set himself up for life by the time he was in his 30s. But I can't help but ask him that, even with the fabulous settlement, even with the world traveling, the spectacular homes, the expensive jewelry, was it worth trading off those prime years, his 20s. Years that should be filled with true love and romance and the kind of passion you can only feel with someone you have a real physical and mental connection with.

"There were two realities the whole time," says Troy. "One reality was what's happening. The other reality is what's happening when I'm in a room by myself with the door closed. I would call my old friends just to see what was going on and to get a reality check and they'd talk of one night stands and leaving without saying anything. Writing down my phone number and handing it to somebody. I never had that life. I lived that life through my friends."

Troy breaks off for a moment then continues. "But then they would quiz me about my life. And then when I would hang up the phone it was always putting things on that scale. Is what I'm doing worth it? And it got to the point where I would just brush that thought off and go back to what I was doing, because it was all I knew. All I knew how to do was suck and put my ass in the air in exchange—look nice in public and be able to speak eloquently and have a dinner party hear and there. What else was there?"

Well, there were, of course, a lot of different directions he could have gone with his life. But Troy seems happy with the way his life is going. And certainly he is a connoisseur of the lifestyle he has chosen.

Yet hearing Troy talk about the other boys with ambitions to be kept, who he observes with a shrewd scrutiny, there seems to be an element of blindness about himself: "It just kills me to go all over the world and see these young guys who want to be kept, they don't want to work. As I say they take the short cut. It's just taking a short cut to the great things in life. And it just kills me to see them go to the gym for 25 hours a week, buy all the right clothes, watch the news so they can drop certain names at a dinner conversation, and go out and try to be this pompous little prick. And I just hate seeing that and I see it time and time again because they never get taken."

Brad again. The one who called the Los Angeles sugar daddies "vampires." The one that told me he stays clear of them in bars and clubs. The one who makes a decent living as a make-up artist.

"I dated an attorney for three or four weeks," he tells me closing the subject by telling me a story about a man he met at a place he calls The Troll Bar. "Not great looking by any stretch. I went out with him a couple of times and he was so intent on spending money on me. He didn't have any idea that a cappuccino, a good conversation, a cigarette, that is all I need. I don't need to go to Beverly Hills Hotel and have dinner...I'm not really impressed with all that."

But there are so many good looking men in Los Angeles. And so many places to hang out that wouldn't be considered "troll bars," so why go out with the guy in the first place?

Brad looks sheepish when I bring that up. "He had money," he says finally. And then he laughs as if he just said the funniest thing in the world.

Body of Work

For Stewart Penn

Nick was a very beautiful boy. People were always telling him that. As a result he sometimes believed it and he even managed to get a few modeling jobs along with the satisfaction of seeing his face and body in a couple of international fashion magazines. He had muddy black eyes and dark lashes and in one ad, for a designer leather jacket, they had combed his hair in such a way that it tousled over his forehead covering one eye and people thought that it was sexy. It was this ad that became the first page in his portfolio.

Nick often thought back to the day the photograph was shot. It was the happiest time of his life. There was a commotion of activity and he was the center of it, the total focal point, the only thing worth observing. Loud, energetic music was piped into the all white studio. There were big umbrellas with light bulbs. Light meters were held to his face. Everything was adjusted to benefit Nick. The makeup artist lined his dark eyes and glossed his pouty lips. A hairstylist fussed with his hair. The stylist adjusted his clothes and added the right accessories—a necklace, rings—opening buttons. The photographer shouted out compliments. Everyone wanted Nick to look good. To be his best. To support him. Nick couldn't get enough of that feeling. He wanted it always.

Sometimes when you're on a roll you think that things will always be that way. A few good things come along, a couple of lucky breaks, and you feel like, wow, I'm right around the corner from the big breakthrough. Because of this you're not prepared for the dry spell that follows.

When Nick went on other go-sees he was always surrounded by a herd of arrogant urbane gladiators. How can there be so many beautiful boys in the world, he would ask himself. Luscious hair. White teeth. Lean muscular bodies. Nick was one of many.

Nick wasn't like the others. For him it wasn't only about the thrill of seeing his image in a magazine. He sensed he wasn't strong enough to hold himself up for very long. He was looking for something to sustain him—at least until he was strong enough to discover something else about himself he could value.

This is what happened to Nick: things had been swinging along for a while. He was getting some decent modeling jobs here and there, but he didn't take into consideration that he was without representation. He still didn't have the protection of a big time agency. So, after the jobs stopped rolling in, he found himself floundering and searching for a score to help him make it to the big time or at least to survival.

He was at a club in West Hollywood—the kind of bar where people hoped for scores of various kinds—vacantly wandering around, waiting for something to happen. He knew he was supposed to be having fun. This was a trendy place. This was Los Angeles. The music was up. The lights were down. There were a lot of pretty people and Nick was getting his share of side-glances and double takes—of course these looks were quickly diverted. No one in West Hollywood ever wants to convey yearning. It's all about being the desired, never desiring. Still, on the surface the club was everything he had always wanted but he couldn't let loose and be free on the dance floor like the others.

He watched them. Up to the minute shoes. Creative body piercings. Muscles. Tribal tattoos. Dressed in jeans and tanks—nothing new there. Never anything new. Or so it seemed. Nick wasn't sure he liked them—but the fact that he didn't fit in with the crowd bothered him. He longed to be part of them. Or at least a part of something. Yet if his eyes met someone's for more than one second the guy did a head flick and scurried away. Why such attitude? Nick wondered. Strip them of their trinkets and there's nothing so spectacular or different.

What was the key, the key, the key? To their confidence? Their ease? He watched their silhouetted heads bobbing with animated conversation. It kept on going and going. What could they be talking about that held each other's interest for so long in such an environment with the music blaring its distractions? Usually in such a place, Nick felt like he was running out of steam after two minutes of fertile and amusing banter.

What was it, Nick wondered, that made them so comfortable with themselves? With each other? Drugs? Nick could easily buy some but they usually just made him feel more alienated.

It should be easy. It was to so many. People would meet for the first time and—presto!—they were at ease. Yet when someone talked to Nick he found the loud music intruding and he could only make out every third word the person was saying to him. Disoriented, he became conscious of shouting. He kept his sentences short. How was intimacy possible? How could he convey who he was? Nick sighed and took a sip of his beer. He felt as if he would never be informed enough to exist in the world. But was it too much to ask to achieve just the right balance of mediocrity and quality that the public could relate to?

Somewhere inside of Nick he knew he was as good looking and interesting as the best of them—but there was always a little voice in the back of his head telling him that he wasn't. This little voice was the problem. Nick discovered through years of self-analysis that this voice is what held him back. You're not as attractive as the others are, the voice chanted to him. They are smarter, more talented, much more clever. And then it would taunt: They know things you don't.

Nick believed this belligerent voice all through his childhood, his teens, and most of his early twenties. Now at twenty-four, he began to realize that the voice's campaign was a fraud, planted in his head at birth to keep him from getting ahead, perhaps by some monstrously jealous fairy godmother. Still, the voice had power over him. People did think of Nick as beautiful but he didn't rely on it. Since he didn't project he felt that way about himself, others downplayed his beauty. Instead he encouraged people to recognize him as a lost lamb: the most undesirable thing in the world.

There's a terrible, embarrassing, unhappiness, inside me, Nick noted. There has to be. Or why else would everyone else around me—human beings—be so happy and carefree. But surely it is more complex than that. What people say to you, present to you—the happy content exterior—is very different than what they are feeling. Who knows the secrets that people take to bed with them? Oh! A moment to be away from my merciless self. My mind.

Just then he noticed a female—the perfect prototype of a fag hag—dancing with a gaggle of five svelte, attractive boys. She was at least fifty pounds overweight. Her movements were self conscious and clumsy and Nick could tell that the handsome boys made fun of her when she was not around. They tolerated her, he knew, because she stroked their ego. They thought she was a hoot. She was wearing shoes several years out of style, and a dowdy plaid skirt. Yet she was trying. Her makeup was careful and her hair was dyed a snazzy red. Nick, who had several girls in high school who had the same demeanor as this young woman follow him around and leave notes in his locker, knew that she was in love with one or several of the boys who she was dancing with. He knew that she chain smoked and kept little chocolates in her handbag.

Nick felt so warmly towards her he wanted to go to her and ask her out for coffee and conversation. I never love the svelte beauties, he said to himself. The perfect desirables. They don't need my love. I always love the overweight. The girls who are a bit off. Those are the ones I want to hold and protect...and they are the ones my mind sends silent good wishes to.

But when he caught her eye she looked away quickly with something that conveyed fear. She didn't want his good wishes. He had to accept the fact that he wasn't a likable character tonight. Sometimes his persona worked. Sometimes not. "Although I'm not doing anything different!" he noted.

Amidst the chatter in his head Nick noticed someone studying him. Because the voice in the back of his head had often told Nick that his entire value as a human being rested on how many people wanted to go to bed with him, when someone did display an overt attraction for Nick, the taunting voice in the back of his head was momentarily stunned into silence.

This man who was craving Nick now would certainly be considered "quality," by most standards. He had luxurious hair—blonde highlights of course—which he flung about with jerky head movements—like a teen idol posing for frantic paparazzi on a red carpet. The kind of guy who, from a very early age, was constantly told he was gorgeous; probably by his family but also by the little voice that lived in the back of his own head. It sunk in. Now he found himself irresistible to others. When he looked at Nick it was unflinchingly. When he approached Nick at last it was with a self-assured stride, his cock leading the way.

Having spent a lifetime cultivating a mask of complete indifference, Nick mastered the art of recognizing other peoples more flashy masks at once. Just by looking at him for a second Nick could tell that this man wouldn't have anything of interest to say. But he made up for it with an obnoxious, sexy quality

"Do you know that you're the most beautiful boy in here," was his opening line to Nick. "Adorable," he added. From a lesser entity a line like this would have meant very little to Nick—they are tossed around at attractive and semi-attractive boys in trendy West Hollywood nightclubs as easily and as freely as a Frisbee on Venice Beach. But the fact that this supremely confident man, sensitive to nothing, found him attractive gave Nick a "who me?" attitude which swept over him automatically no matter how hard he tried to keep it down. Even his little voice kept mum. The compliment became a suit of armor for Nick's ego, protecting him from the other attitudes, comments and glares that came flying like knives from all directions.

The guy's name was Bo Trent. He was thirty-one. He was visiting Los Angeles from Manhattan. He was the type of guy who always managed to keep a laid back attitude amongst the disorder of life, along with a year-round tan and a twenty-nine inch waist. He was a booker at a new modeling agency—Rager—which, he assured Nick, was going to be the next big agency back in New York. Bo was in town now, scouting for new talent, both male and female for the agency. Nick could see his own career rising like the sun in the east.

And Bo said all the right things to Nick, his words slithering through the complexities of his mind, dodging through suspicions, weaving through doubts, snaking between his hard earned common sense—gaining his trust. "I'm a regular nice guy," was the attitude Bo interjected between his lines. "You have a special quality," was his message to Nick. "We could make beautiful music together," was the ultimate goal of them both (although both of them had different concepts of the music). After twenty minutes Bo hit him with the inevitable invitation. "I'm staying at a friend's condo," Bo said to Nick. "He's in Europe at the moment. Would you like to come back for a drink?"

The fact that Bo was a winner, at a promising new agency back in Manhattan, and that he was so self-assured about his own brilliance—even though he didn't have any—turned Nick on. He had so few winners in his life. He could really fall for a guy like Bo. He imagined himself being held by Bo each night, protected by his confidence, at the same time being shown the ropes.

But even with Bo's expertise, his compliments, his positive energy—in spite of all that—Nick was picking up other vibes that made him hesitate—and even before he agreed to go home with him, before they were undressed, before they lay side by side facing each other, he got the feeling that he really wasn't Bo's type. That he'd do for now because Bo saw him as the "most beautiful boy in here" but tomorrow there would another variety-pack to choose from, from another club, or another gym, or another street corner, and it would be "good-bye Charlie."

Oh shut up, Nick scolded the voice in his head, which had started babbling again. And he brushed off his doubts like dandruff from a black coat, blaming his qualms on his viscous doubt-spewing voice and other complexities he was trying to shed, and he smiled at Bo and said: "Sure. Let's go."

The fact that Bo had a friend in Europe with such a magnificent condo in Century City did indeed prove to Nick that he was a winner. They sat on the friend's living room couch. Conversation had suddenly evaporated. Bo put his hand behind Nick's neck and at first Nick was thinking, Oh. This is romantic, this is nice. But soon Bo was pushing him down towards his crotch, trying for an impromptu blowjob. But we're both still dressed, Nick thought. He hasn't even kissed me yet!

So, so! His voice had been right. He was to be a quick trick, a one-night diversion, a receptacle for Bo's passion. Nick didn't lower his head to Bo's crotch, he resisted, but Bo applied pressure on Nick's neck trying to lower him to the target. Nick kept his head rigid. How did he get into this? I know better, he said to himself. I always fall for it, though.

114

Eventually Bo gave up, removed his hand and started to undress himself. Nick's mind started playing the soundtrack from *Gypsy*. This seemed like the perfect time for Nick to leave, but Bo was already taking the pillows off the couch and unfolding it into the bed. He's not even taking you into the bedroom! The voice mocked Nick, incredulously.

Nick tried to override his humiliation, with endless tickertape of advice from his heart. Oh, Nick, Nick, Nick...just give it another try, his heart advised him. Maybe he just doesn't know how to get started, romantically. And then Nick's brain spoke up: But why give him the benefit of the doubt? Nick's final conclusion was: Shit, you're here now, just do it. It was very difficult to concentrate on the task at hand with all his various body parts chiming in their advice.

They were undressed, lying side by side facing each other on the couch-bed. Let me entertain you, let me make you smile, a whispery songstress sang in Nick's head.

But soon it was apparent to Nick that this wasn't mutual sex. It was the feeling of being disconnected from the actual action like being at the club earlier—he was a part of the experience while simultaneously, most definitely separate from it.

Of course, he knew everything he was supposed to be feeling—Bo was handsome, Bo was confident, Bo was smart—but Nick didn't feel actual desire. Bo touched him and he touched Bo but they were simply objects. Nick tried to put some tenderness into his touch but Bo's body refused to accept it. From Bo there was no tenderness at all. This was an inspection. Pecs. Ass. Shoulders. Thighs. Touch. Smell. Taste. Was Nick Grade A or Grade B, he wondered?

Let me do a few kicks, some old and then some knew tricks I'm very versatile...

Nick decided that he wouldn't let Bo fuck him, even though Bo had already sneakily slipped on a condom. Nick still had his pride. Or at least some of it. Actually, though, the rubbing of Bo's cock against his crack felt wonderful. It would be so nice—delicious really—to just give in and let him fuck him without emotion. But no. The little voice in his head was on again, drowning out the soundtrack, (or was it the voice itself singing the soundtrack in an imitation Ann-Margaret voice?) Bo views you as only an object he doesn't really like you—because you're not worth liking, the little voice said.

But what do you know? Before he could object, Bo was in him, pumping hard—a Singer sewing machine, needle in motion. Unfeeling. Mechanical. Nick wanted to protest, but it was too late. Wasn't it? Deal with it, stupid! The voice said. Or learn how to speak up sooner.

The piston motions continued but it wasn't going anywhere. No one was feeling anything. No one was cumming. After a while they both stopped trying. Bo withdrew. Nick glanced over at him and peered through the darkness. "The condom!" Nick said, alarmed. "It's ripped!" Bo peeled the torn rubber off his cock. "Don't worry," he said. "I didn't cum."

There was still a danger in this. There was always a danger. Even though people weren't thinking about getting sick so much nowadays, Nick new of enough people on a cocktail of drugs. Bellies bloated from the cocktail. And the fear flashing through Nick's veins, the careless, foolish moment was now a shocking reality. Pre-cum. Drops. Leaks. Into the blood. It only takes a drip. This was the danger he always lived with. Pass the gun. Click. Your turn.

There was no conversation about this; they just understood. The silence was a fucking nightmare. Nick wanted to talk about something. Something to make them both human again. Something. But what? He longed for a moment of shared vulnerability. Yet he only felt his own. He certainly didn't want to talk about people in Los Angeles feeling loneliness, because that would expose his own.

"Why don't you have a lover," Nick finally thought to ask.

"Because I'm not like anybody else."

Good answer, Nick said softly after a weary pause. Or, he then wondered, did Bo say: because I don't like anybody else.

Nick got up and started searching for his underwear. Calvin Klein, as they were supposed to be. There was a globby stain on the front of them. See, I did like him at first, he thought. The pre-cum was evidence of the desire he had felt in the beginning. He dressed quickly. There would, of course, be no sweet morning-after cup of coffee. No cute good-byes. No follow up calls. Bo didn't even ask for Nick's number. He's perfected his act with so many idiots like you, the voice in Nick's head said, returning. And you were the most convenient object around tonight.

Still, Nick hated being a disappointment to anyone and he didn't even take into consideration what a disappointment Bo was to him.

"I have to get up early and go to the gym," Nick said fully dressed, still trying to find a thread that might lead them to a pleasant camaraderie before saying goodbye. The gym always was a good thread in LA. Bo replied, rather curtly, that he wanted to do the same. He walked Nick to the door naked and took a business card from a wallet on a desk along the way—he handed it to Nick. Just a courtesy, the voice in Nick's head said. "But still..." Nick argued.

And we'll have a real good time, yes sir!

116

Bo stepped into the hall and watched Nick wait for the elevator, seemingly unaware that he was nude. Why was it taking so long at this time of night? The bell rang. Their eyes met. Bo looked exhausted too.

"If you're ever in New York, stop by the agency and show me your book," Bo said before disappearing behind his apartment door. The elevator brought him down. So, Nick told his voice, maybe he wasn't a total jerk.

Nick lay on his bed and called his mother in Baltimore. He hadn't worked as a model in months but he told her that his modeling career was looking up. People, big people, in high up places, were taking a real interest in him. He said he would try to get home for Christmas—but even as he spoke he knew he couldn't face his family unless he had some new achievement, some new photo of himself in some prestigious magazine to make his life legitimate.

"I may go to New York for a few weeks," Nick told his mother. "I have some really big opportunities there."

"We're already so proud of you," his mother replied. "I just know were going to see you on television someday."

After Nick hung up he lay curled in the sheets for a long time. He had never felt so far away from his goals. Waving his arms amongst a crowd of beauties, all shrieking, all waving, all pointing at their thrilling selves. Look at me! I'm more amazing than that one! See me! More fabulous than that one! See me! See me! The growing mob screamed. The crowd grew larger every day—a whale—swallowing more and more of Nick, inch by inch, making him more and more obscure. Soon his whole body would disappear. Yet he couldn't think of any new ways to wave his own arms—to make himself stand out amongst the noise. And always, always, always, time ticking away and the new boys arriving each day in Los Angeles and New York, all of them so gorgeous and eighteen.

Sometimes Nick was afraid. What am I doing in an adult world, he'd ask himself. I really don't want to be here. I want to be at my parents' house, twelve-years-old, safe in my bed, reading a Tallulah Bankhead biography.

He picked up his diary from the floor and scribbled rapidly: Everyone looks so good. I am sick to death of beauty. Of tight bodies. Of fashion.

Of going out for breakfast after clubs. Of being asked how old I am. Of everything, everything, everything...

He wondered if he should get tested for HIV. Okay, people weren't dying from AIDS anymore but, if he was positive, where would the money come from to take care of himself? No medical coverage. It was getting better for people who were sick...but still there was the upkeep. Where would Nick get the energy? Nick had no savings in the bank. No way of making a living except for waiting tables. He worked in an upscale restaurant and the tips were good but that could end any time.

Would he die alone, an unknown, before he got a fair amount of time to hack himself into something? Nick knew that if he became successful everything would be all right. Success would elevate him to a higher level of desirability than the others. He would be protected. He would be safe.

Sometimes he thought of his night with Bo. As unpleasant as it was... as much as he hated that night...the promise of Bo, or someone like him, made Nick work harder. Next time I'll be ready, he told himself. What he felt about anything didn't matter to anyone. He worked on his body. His stomach was flat, but maybe if it was flatter. His waist was thirty-one—he got it down to thirty. His muscles were hard—he made them more defined. He ate lunches of green salads or protein bars. Dinners of grilled chicken. The next time a Bo came along he wanted to be prepared.

The body is important, Nick would say as he examined his reflection adjusting his underwear in his bedroom mirror. If he tilted his body this way, with the light coming that way he looked just right. Where is the photographer when you need him? The voice in his head asked sarcastically.

It was weeks before Nick was able to talk himself into actually flying down to New York to check things out and stop by Bo's agency. That was one of the benefits of waiting tables—it may not have security but it was flexible. He finally did go because he kept hearing other models talk about it. RAGER. RAGER. RAGER. It seemed like it really was going to become big. And, hey, Nick did have an "in." He paid his dues on that horrid night. And why not take advantage of it?

Nick checked into the YMCA in the West 20s. He spent an entire day working up the courage to visit the RAGER office in Tribeca. Getting his hair right. His dark, dark hair. Slicking it back with heavy gel. But then, no, manipulating that messy look over his forehead. Putting together just the right guise. Another button open? A T-shirt underneath? Cologne or no? And of course, some scotch, to loosen him up. Not enough to get drunk. Just enough to feel normal. One more check to the mirror. Hmm...not bad, the voice in his head had to admit, but not good enough, of course.

It was late afternoon by the time Nick stepped out off of the subway car, up the platform stairs, into the summer heat. He had miscalculated the agency's address so he had to walk quite a few blocks and it was late summer so he had to deal with New York's famous humidity, his anxiety about seeing Bo again making it seem even hotter. The scotch was making him sweat even more. The sun did not appear behind a cloud of haze, but the air was heavy with sticky moisture, and this did its number on his hair—making it frizz through the gel—and added that oh so unattractive shine to his skin. When he arrived at the building Nick stood out front afraid to go up. Maybe Bo's busy, the voice volunteered. Maybe he won't remember you. He didn't like you anyway...

"But I'm here now," Nick replied out loud. He had come all this way. And so, he had to go through with it.

The office was the entire top floor of the building. "RAGER" was written on a brick wall in a hip hop style. There was a haughty he/she receptionist who stared at Nick coldly. Used to beauty coming in and out of the elevator—and having none of his/her own—he/she didn't even raise his/her eyes. And the other assorted mod types, dressed in black, bustled, shifted papers, snuck glances but ignored Nick too. Or at least they did their best to.

New Yorkers, Nick thought. With their mod hair-dos and their earrings and their pseudo-sophisticated bullshit. 'Wake up!' my mind screams. But am I talking to them or me?

Someone went to look for Bo. Nick thought of a handshake and wiped his palms on his pants leg. Eventually Bo sashayed up front—dick first. His eyes rapidly flicked up and down Nick's body.

"Hi. Remember me," Nick said. "You told me to stop by if I was ever in New York City and...um...here I am with my book for you to take a look at if you've got a minute."

Nick was aware that he was talking too fast. Slow down boy, he told himself. He held out his hand, Bo was looking, or pretending to be looking, at something in the back— beyond Nick—or he was simply preoccupied with something in outer space, and Nick's hand was left stupidly in mid air. He quickly hid it in his pocket.

"Yeah. Great. Thanks for stopping by," Bo said. "The thing is we're not really taking on any new guys at the moment." It was obvious to Nick that Bo wasn't even looking at his face; instead he was looking directly into his skull to the little doubtful voice that lived in the back of his head. See me! See me! Nick wanted to scream. Instead he said:

"I thought you would take a look at my portfolio."

"It's really slow during the summer. We're not looking at portfolios."

"We met in West Hollywood," Nick managed to blurt out. "We went to your friend's condo. You gave me your card."

Now Bo took a look and Nick watched recognition jump into his eyes. And everything in his expression said he didn't want to be bothered with one night tricks from one of his distant boozy nights in faraway cities.

"I'm really busy right now," Bo said, backing away. "Thanks for stopping by."

Nick said: "I was just on a go-see in the neighborhood and I...I remembered you told me to stop by and..."

"Later dude! Much later," Bo said firmly. Nick was shocked at this lack of humanity—even from Bo. And then at the general burst of laughter from the office staff. They had done such a good job at pretending to be disinterested. But "hurt" got their attention. Can't they see I'm more beautiful now?

Sure enough, humiliation seized Nick's body. And held it. Nick was left standing there, portfolio in hand. Bo—who had tricked him, fucked him, put his life in danger—was not even going to give him the courtesy of flipping through his book to save him from embarrassment. Obviously he wasn't worth it. He felt judged and embarrassed and ugly. Modeling sets you up for that. Even his little voice was silent and contrite—not gloating.

What had he done wrong? How should he have dressed? How different could he possibly have looked from the night Bo told him he was, "adorable," the most beautiful boy in the club? But why think about it? Why question it? It was just another rejection. Everybody goes through it. It was part of the business, no big deal. But he had hoped that Bo really saw potential in him, and he had gone to bed with him, and Nick was giving him a chance to redeem himself.

Nick became aware that, for the first time since he arrived, everyone in the office was looking at him all at once—these people who were cool and trendy, but undeniably un-beautiful, they had no heart, no soul. They were unusual things to look at but not to be desired. Peculiar ceramics in a stylish museum. Yet Nick was almost always sexually desired (as if that were a plus) by everyone who saw him. And they knew it. Yet he felt their condescension. He saw their smirks. In their eyes his beauty had just been knocked down a few pegs and that was food for their egos.

"Does that make you feel good?" he said hoarsely to the room at large. He bowed. He turned. They went back to what they pretended to be doing.

Nick waited for the elevator. It took forever. People it seemed, were always trying to get the better of one another, rather than just being themselves and letting life happen naturally. You can do your best to have dignity but you can't stop people from hurting you.

It's not so bad to be humiliated, Nick reasoned. There are people dying and suffering all over the world. And you are healthy. Don't you dare be unhappy, he warned himself. It was no use, though. He couldn't fight it off.

When the elevator came he rushed in and slumped against the wall. "Someday..." he whispered quietly. "Someday..."

Yeah, yeah, he had been used for sex. Big deal. Learn from it, dude, the voice inside his head said. Maybe, maybe, maybe he'd been too giving with his flesh—the only thing he had that people valued, even if only temporarily. Others, with less to offer, had risen faster because they prized themselves more.

Look, Nick said to the voice in his head. I know you're right about some things. But I'm really not all that bad. Maybe we could work together?

This seemed to be what the voice wanted to hear and he responded with some advice. Nick! Oh Nick, the voice said. You've been a fool for listening to me. People aren't any better than you. I'm sorry I made you think that you were so inferior. You're value doesn't depend on how many people think you're sexy. From now on sleep only with people who you really know and like. Let them get to know you inside and out. It's not just about sexual desire for you. You're different. So you have to make them see YOU. Use this advice in all your life and stop being shit on so much. It's not good for either of us.

Nick realized this was true—he was different—but part of him still wanted to be like the rest. He wanted to be tough. He knew he should be stronger if he really wanted to make it in Hollywood and New York.

Someday I will shed my sensitivity like so much dead skin...and they will all want me...and for more than just one night...and I'll fuck them without a condom...and I'll flush their phone numbers down the toilet...

Maybe this would come to pass. Maybe not. Even with all the ugliness he experienced around him Nick was not full of hate.

He stepped out of the building into the stifling afternoon. A father was walking down the street with his small child unwrapping a sandwich for the little boy. Nick need only see some expression of tenderness, even in others, and he was ready to forgive. His face was young. His body a commodity. And there was time to decide what he would be like when his moment arrived.

Nick knew, in spite of his own ceramic covering, that on the inside, he was still a pretty good guy. He had a soul. He treated other people's feelings so gently—his own had been hurt so often. The sun had appeared from behind its protective shroud of clouds and the rays were merciless. "Are you a model?" a homeless woman asked as Nick hurried down the street and he handed her his singles, smiling contentedly.

What he looked like in this lighting, and in this heat, he didn't want to know—certainly not his best. But then he thought of his soul and how it would look at the moment if it were visible—and that was beautiful. If only that were enough.

The Legend of Denham Fouts

For Frank Fischer

"Did you ever hear of Denham Fouts?"

I was walking to a restaurant in West Hollywood the other night with a friend and I brought up the name.

"No," my friend said. "Who is he? It's an interesting name."

An interesting name for an interesting man. A very beautiful man. In the 30s and 40s Denham Fouts, or Denny as he was known on two continents, was famous simply for being desirable or, more to the point, for being the "best kept boy in the world." Starting as a teenager he learned how to use his looks as a lure, and the pleasure of his company as a hook, enabling him to go very quickly from candy bars to kings. Born in a conservative small town in Florida he managed to maneuver himself into some of the most rich and powerful beds of the era. Truman Capote used to say that if Denny had gone to bed with Hitler—as Hitler desired—he could have prevented the Second World War.

"He was a famous beauty of his day," I told my friend. "A boy whore. A prostitute. But..." I added, because I wanted to acknowledge his importance, "...he was friends with the greatest writers of the time. Capote. Christopher Isherwood. Gore Vidal. They all wanted to know him and they all wrote about him"

"But what did he *do?*" my friend pressed.

"He didn't do anything," I said "That's the whole point. That was his plan. It was his ambition to be taken care of. And for as long as his life lasted, which wasn't very long, he succeeded."

"Oh," my friend said dismissively. "He was just a beautiful thing."

"Well, no," I said. "There was more to him than that."

I didn't want to think of Denham Fouts that way. I had been reading about him. In the photograph often used to illustrate anything written about Denny he sits with the innocent look of a schoolboy, his starched white shirt opened provocatively at the neck, but there is no hint of the dark haunted quality that lived under the austere and lovely shell. He looks appealing, sure, but without the contemporary power projected by the dark, slurry, sexual danger in, say, the Calvin Klein models of today.

But it was, perhaps, that ambiguity between gentleness and hidden darkness that Capote, Isherwood and Vidal found fascinating. All of them used Denny, barely disguised, as characters in their fiction—yet he still remains inscrutable—none of them were able to re-create him in anything near his entirety. But, mystery, of course, is also a power.

"A lot of people knew Denham Fouts, but very few knew him well," the writer Gerald Clarke told me when I called to ask about him. "But once a legend gets started it continues rolling along and then people become interested in the person behind the legend."

Yet there's no real way of getting behind the legend of Denham Fouts. He had no children. He wrote no memoir. He gave no interviews. He left behind no immortal quotes. What is left of Denham Fouts, the famous boy whore of the thirties and forties, exists only in the musings of the great writers who knew him, but in these works he will live forever—loved and youthful.

If we believe Capote's account, Denny was sixteen when he was swept up by a cosmetic's tycoon who was passing through Denny's hometown of Jacksonville Florida. Although twice married, the Big Daddy millionaire had a hankering for boys between the ages of fourteen and seventeen. On seeing Denny working behind the counter at his father's bakery—and recognizing something sweet—he offered to take him for a spin in his convertible. Denny took off with him without so much as a change of underwear or a note to his parents.

In his Truman Capote biography, Gerald Clark—who gives the most cohesive narrative of the Fouts Saga—says that Denny turned up in Manhattan in 1932, apparently after the tycoon tired of him. He was eighteen and worked briefly as a stock boy—one of the few legit jobs he would ever attempt. By this time Denny was aware of his impact on people. "He was about the most beautiful boy anybody had ever seen," remembered Jimmy Daniels a singer at one of Denny's favorite Harlem nightclubs.

"His skin always looked as if it had just been scrubbed; it seemed to have no pores at all, it was so smooth." Using his looks as a resume Denny's only ambition was to *not* work. As a means to this end he consulted his roommate's worldly friend, the writer Glenway Wescott. "Now Glenway," Denny said, "you know everything. I want you to tell me: how does one manage to get kept?"

Taken aback by the crudeness in such a blunt question Wescott appraised anew the innocent looking boy in front of him. "He was ridiculously good-looking," Wescott remembered years later. "Unattractively good-looking from my point of view. The only thing I liked about him was that he had the most delicious body odor; I once swiped one of his hand-kerchiefs." But he did recognize that Denny had more than enough poten-tial to achieve his goals. Wescott told him that, if he wanted to be taken care of, subtlety was the ticket. "Never use the word 'kept,'" he advised. "Think of something you want to do that takes money to learn. Then ask someone for help and guidance. You'll get much more money that way than by coming at it straight on."

The delicious smelling boy learned his lessons well. Soon after talk-ing to Wescott he met a German Baron who whisked him away to Europe. Evidently one of the things that Denny wanted to do with other people's money was to discover what life was like abroad. Certainly he became an expert at manipulating people. "He invented himself," said one of his friends, John B. L. Goodwin. "If people didn't know his background he would make it up."

In Europe Denny began a remarkable series of adventures in trade. After a falling out he abandoned the baron in Berlin and, with extraor-dinary confidence, walked out on him with only the clothes on his back; his man-trapping abilities apparently undiminished in the process. While hitchhiking to Venice a big car pulled over to the side of the road. The driver called Denny over, explaining that the owner of the car would like to give him a lift. The owner, as it turned out, was a Greek shipping tycoon who not only drove Denny to Venice but also took him traveling aboard his yacht.

But Denny was repulsed by the Greek tycoon who was "very old and very fat." In Capri he abandoned ship taking a sailor and two thousand dollars out of the Greek's strongbox with him. Denny and the sailor set up house in a suite at the Quisisana Hotel on Capri, living the high life. When the money started to run out, though, so did the sailor.

Undaunted—with the cocksure arrogance which is in the make-up of any successful hustler—Denny continued to show up every evening for din-ner. Because he wasn't paying his bills each night his table became smaller and smaller, yet he was always beautifully groomed in splendid evening clothes. Finally, when it became apparent to management that Denny had no means to pay his bills the police were called in.

But Denny's personal gods once again surrounded him with an aura that gave off a sticky, sweet, seductive pull, as potent as any Venus Flytrap. According to Gore Vidal, he was being led through the lobby of the Qui-sisana when Evan Morgan, the Lord Tredegar, saw him and called out,

"Unhand that handsome youth, he is mine!" And so he was. For a while, anyway.

Paris! Berlin! St. Moritz! Istanbul! Bombay! Athens! Morocco! Heroine! Cocaine! Opium, opium, opium! For a time Denny moved in the glamorous world of European aristocracy, being passed from one titled bed to another. His sexual successes included wealthy connections of both sexes that took him round to the glory spots of the world. One of his conquests was the Shah of Iran. For a while he cruised on the yacht of the American Singer Sewing Machine heiress. Eventually he became lovers with Prince Paul, later the King of Greece. They were closer in age than most of his paramours and they traveled extensively together until the affair ended when they quarreled bitterly over Denny openly sniffing cocaine in the bar of the Hotel Beau Rivage in Lausanne. It was just as well for the time had come for the Prince to marry Frederika.

In Paris, shortly before the war Denny met Peter Watson, heir to a margarine fortune. "One had to have experienced Denny's stranglehold, a pressure that brought the victim teasingly close to an ultimate slumber, to appreciate its allure," Truman Capote recalled in his fictionalized account of their relationship. Denny exercised his power to enthrall on Peter Watson, who was to learn first hand the potency of the Fouts stranglehold. It was said that Watson could not be in the same room with Denny without getting an erection.

Carson McCullers once wrote "that in every relationship, there are two roles, that of the lover and that of the beloved." Denny, was the beloved in almost all his relationships, and because of this he maintained the upper hand. Watson, a charming, wealthy man who was used being the one who was pursued, fell in love with Denny's cruelty. Denny even used his drug addiction as a weapon: Watson was forced to supply the money to support Denny's drug habit, which he despised.

It was during this time Denny supposedly caught the eye of Hitler. Apparently that pairing never occurred—Hitler just expressed an interest—and in 1940, when the German attacks on London intensified, Watson became concerned for Denny's welfare and insisted that he go back to America.

When you're handsome at twenty-one and twenty-two you don't think much about age and accomplishments, you inadvertently know that you still have years left just to be beautiful. In the later twenties, while you still might be beautiful, you begin to realize that it's only a matter of time before you move into the next stage of beauty, a diminished form of it—"attractive" for instance. And there's always the younger, more desirable boys just showing up around every corner. Resourceful beauties, at

126

this age, start thinking about developing inner qualities and building up on their character.

And so it was with Denham Fouts. When he arrived in Los Angeles—tormented by drug addiction by this time—he was in a state of quiet despair. He had become hard and cynical and embittered. "He thought that the world was made up of whores," said a long time friend, Bill Harris. "To be a successful whore was all there was, he said. He didn't brag but he felt he had done pretty well at it."

Years later Christopher Isherwood would describe Denny in his novel *Down Their on a Visit*: "His handsome profile was bitterly sharp, like a knife edge. And goodness, underneath the looks and the charm and the drawl, how sour he was."

Certainly he realized the clock was ticking. During his years in Los Angeles, though, he would begin a rigorous campaign of self-improvement. He formed a close friendship with Isherwood—then working in Hollywood as a film scenarist—who introduced him to the Hindu philosophy Vedanta, which teaches man to recognize his real divine nature

Anxious to start a new life as soon as possible Denny expressed his desire to try the Yogi life of meditation and ritual. He already knew all to well his visible outer self: the calculating playboy. But his quest, through meditation, would be to discover his hidden self. He wanted to give up drink and drugs and compulsive sex. Or so he said.

However a meeting with the Swami Prabhavananda, set up by Isherwood, turned out to be disastrous. Denny, who always came on strong with strangers apparently did so with the swami. In this case the swami was not charmed by his surly behavior and he told Denny what he needed was not meditation but a job and a little hard work.

Afterwards Denny threw himself on his bed, in front of Isherwood, and burst into tears, sobbing that he was rotten, that everybody despised him and that he would be better off killing himself by an opium overdose as soon as possible. Isherwood was moved by this display and believed that he was sincere in his desire to change, in spite of the fact that on his first visit to the Temple, Denny commented on what a wonderful place it would be to have sex.

When in March of 1941, Isherwood moved into a new apartment he invited Denny to share it with him and join him in an experiment of strict Yogi observances as if they were in training to be "monks." Isherwood has said that those first few weeks were some of the happiest of his life ("real happiness is simply the absence of pain"). For a while Denny tried to live entirely without sex, but at the same time he couldn't resist giving his friends lurid accounts of his struggles and temptations.

It seems, by trying to embrace a new spirituality and taking a new interest in education, Denny was trying to shed his old whore persona to get to the purer self, his core persona, who mostly remained masked. He had become chronically suspicious of other people's motives but now he wanted to search for the good in people. He recognized the fact that in spite of his jaded way of life, a part of him remained compassionate and innocent. When he found a seagull on the beach with a broken wing he amputated it to make the bird more comfortable. It was this part of him he set out to unearth and understand. His body, which had been touched by many with desire, now ached to touch with tenderness.

And so it seems Denny's two selves battled for dominance. He would still go to parties, get shit-faced and then talk of nothing but religion. His amused friends jokingly called him "The drunken yogi." He applied for the service as a 4-E conscientious objector, which meant that he was not prepared to serve in the military at all, even in a noncombatant role. As a result he was assigned for service in a forestry camp but he was quickly expelled for being a homosexual when he was overheard talking about his gay life in Paris.

Eventually, though, he buckled down and found an evening job at a bookstore in Hollywood. During the days he worked as a janitor, but he used his off duty hours to study algebra, German, and Shakespeare in the hopes of gaining a high school diploma through a correspondence course at UCLA, something he had never had time to acquire during his world travels. He moved to a small apartment near the beach at Santa Monica. Every Saturday in the summer of 1943 he and Isherwood would go swimming.

Denny's studies were successful and soon he was able to go to college where he studied medicine. A whiff of his decadent past always remained around him though—like the scent of opium—along with the trappings of his affluent conquests. The main room of his tiny flat was dominated by a giant Picasso, a sinister painting of a girl reading which Peter Watson presented to him and had shipped over to California from the Museum of Modern Art. Isherwood wrote of having nightmares about Nazi Germany while sleeping under it on Denny's sofa. Denny later sold the painting in New York.

Many of Denny's friends at this time were black and he claimed to be having an affair with Lena Horne. One afternoon, after a long bicycle ride, he brought Isherwood to her house just above the Sunset Strip calling out "Lena, darling, I brought a friend in to take a shower." Lena, still in bed, took it in stride. "She's a very nice girl," Isherwood reported in his diary. "Not in the least grand or affected."

Denny's grasp at Religion eventually slipped away from him completely and his life once again became bohemian and full of affairs. "I've decided to hold on to things I could see," he told Isherwood. His studies in LA had not brought him any new insight to who he was. Or he had resigned to the fact that his only role in life was that of the "Beloved." His quest had left him exhausted and disillusioned. He gave up his studies and, during the latter half of 1945, returned to liberated Europe.

In Europe, Denny's hard cold mask seems to have once again been placed over the more tender side he'd spent so much time trying to uncover. His drug intake, particularly of opium, increased. "If it's good enough for Cocteau, honey, it's good enough for me," he reportedly said. He stayed in bed most of the days in a drug stupor and then in the evenings, like some nocturnal vampire, he would emerge to walk Trotsky, the large dog he had found in California. He was living in an apartment on the Rue du Bac, a fashionable area in Paris, paid for by Peter Watson who remained fond enough of Denny to keep paying the bills but fed up enough with his drug abuse to keep an emotional distance. Watson more or less abandoned him in the sparsely furnished flat.

In his memoir *Palimpsest* the distinguished writer Gore Vidal, then considered an enfant terrible, recalls encountering Denny there. A lifetime of being beautiful and pampered had rendered Denny demanding and helpless. He still wanted to be taken care of, in spite of the fact that he was now a man in his mid 30s. Even when he was feeling physically well, Fouts behaved like a demanding little boy, always commanding full attention. He received Vidal in his great bed, propped up by pillows, under a magnificent Tchelitchev painting of a nude male. His dark eyes were half shut and watering. As a result of constantly smoking opium the light hurt his eyes.

Vidal, for one (and a beauty in his own right), did not find Denny handsome. "Denham's legendary beauty was not visible to me." Vidal wrote. "He looked like the ghost he would soon be."

He did, however, find him fascinating. Languid and heavy lidded, a male Camille, a glamorous invalid, with a big fluffy white dog sprawled on the far corner of the bed, Denny lay there, his opium pipe at arms length away, and babbled a steady stream of consciousness. He spoke of his desire to meet Truman Capote—whose photograph he had on the night table under his opium pipe. He spoke of friends making spectacles of themselves in elegant restaurants. He spoke of his ex lover, Prince Paul, now the King of Greece.

Eventually, Denny prepared the pipe, a complicated process that involved melting an opium pellet in a metal dish over a flame, and then placing the pellet in the metal end of his ivory pipe—the color of which now matched his skin. He inhaled deeply, holding the smoke deep in his longs, and exhaled slowly.

"Here," Denny offered, handing Vidal the opium pipe, and although he had never even inhaled cigarette smoke, he tried it, only to end up having a coughing fit.

In his short story *Pages from an Abandoned Journal* Vidal describes their meeting: "I can't remember a word he said. I was aware, though, that this was probably the most brilliant conversation I'd ever had. It might have been the setting, which was certainly provocative, or maybe I'd inhaled some of the opium which put me in a receptive mood but, no matter the cause, I sat listening to him, fascinated, not wanting him to stop."

One hot summer night on his way to meet Denny for dinner Vidal saw in the headlines of the Paris papers that King Paul was gravely ill with pneumonia. Vidal hadn't been sure whether or not Denny's stories of his affair with the King had been true. They could very well have been inspired by an opium delusion, but Vidal told him of the King's illness anyway.

"I must wire him at once," Denny said. And together Denny and Vidal went to an all night Western Union on St.-Germaine.

Vidal was to find out that, unlike most hustlers, Denny was truthful. The following day Denny showed Vidal the King's reply: "My dear Denham so thrilled to hear from you I am much better than the papers report I hope you can come see me in Athens. Love Paul." The address on the telegram noted "Royal Palace." Denny didn't have to exaggerate his conquests. They were real.

Hafiz, the thirteenth century poet, once wrote "a boy who is loved can never grow old or die." Some of the great writers of his generation would render Fouts immortal. And it was as if the large doses of love he received from admiring gentleman kept him youthful. In his story Vidal writes of encountering the Denny character on the beach: "I noticed with surprise how smooth and youthful his body was, like a boy. "

Isherwood, who was visiting Paris, noted his spookily un-aged appearance in his diary: "Denny met us for cocktails at the Ritz—like Dorian Gray emerging from the tomb. Death-pale and very slim in his dark, elegant suit, with black hat and umbrella. He looks like the necropolitan ambassador."

Addicted to drugs, wan, sick, Denny Fouts, in spite of his corpselike pallor, managed to keep his youthful looks. Certainly, sexually, he felt most comfortable with young boys, perhaps because, in his heart, he remained one himself. He always kept his door unlocked and as a result he was robbed many times over. For some, this innocence remained his most endearing quality. His dark, lank hair still fell boyishly over a pale forehead.

Even in the swell circles in which he moved his booming South Florida accent remained, like some swaggering, corn fed buck, which of course he was. Denny's occupation was older gentleman in varying degrees of unattractiveness, but his personal taste was for pubescent flesh.

And it was this attraction for adolescent boys that probably led to his obsession with Truman Capote.

Most people today remember Capote in paunchy middle age—balding and gnome-like, employing a slurred, but potent wit on television talk shows. It's difficult to imagine him as the angelic blue-eyed blonde that he was for about three minutes in extreme youth. At twenty-three he was causing a sensation just coming out with his first book, the homosexual, gothic novel *Other Voices, Other Rooms.* Capote, always a master at self-promotion, was many things—subtle was not one of them. For his book jacket he posed sprawled out seductively on a couch, staring into the camera with a languid come hither look, casually touching himself as if the photographer had caught him in the beginning stages of masturbation.

On seeing this photo, Denny became so enamored with Capote, legend says, that he sent him a blank check with one word written on it: "Come." Capote was in the early stages of a long career of seeking out the most fascinating, the most colorful, the most damaged people in the jet set, which in those days was called Cafe Society. A society Capote very much wanted to be a part of. A meeting with the legendary boy whore of fashionable circles was irresistible. He went.

Denny fascinated and terrified Truman. It was like being close to a fabled character from a decadent storybook—a character Truman would years later re-create in *Answered Prayers.* But it was Denny's drug intake that Truman found terrifying. All day long lying in his bed, smoking his opium, his hypersensitive eyes watering and half-closed, like some dark, exhausted angel trapped among mortals. By now even his body—which once exuded a scent so heavenly that a friend stole one of his handkerchiefs—gave off the pungent medicinal scent from his intake of the drugs.

The relationship became lover-like without the sex—the drugs had destroyed Denny's libido to the point where he couldn't even get it up. But Truman lies beside him in the darkened room—talking to him, reading to him or just listening to his stories.

Occasionally in the late afternoons they would venture to the movies were Denny would invariably break out into a sweat and have to retreat to the men's room to replenish his system with the drugs. In the evenings he would smoke opium, or make an opium tea, which consisted of boiling the crusts of opium which had formed around his pipe.

But, after a time, even dark angels lose their fascination. Truman grew restless. As a young, attractive hotly discussed author, he himself was a legend in the making. He wanted to be on the receiving end of lots of attention—not the giving end.

Yet he was very fond of Denny and didn't want to hurt him or leave him high and dry, so to speak. He soon devised a scheme to free himself. He talked Denny into going to Switzerland to a clinic for 'the cure" to get himself off drugs. Truman hinted that they could then meet and start a new life together, perhaps in the West, which Denny loved. "He had a fantasy of buying a gasoline station in Arizona," Truman told Gerald Clarke. "The sort of place that has a sign saying, 'Last Chance for Gas for Fifty Miles.' I was going to write, and he was going to run it and be cured of all the things that were wrong with him. I very foolishly let him go on about it because I knew that none of it was ever going to happen."

So he packed Denny off to the Swiss clinic and ran off to Italy. It was just as well since Denny soon changed his mind about the clinic and called Truman to tell him so. "What can I do now but wash my hands of the whole affair," Truman wrote to a friend.

Eventually Denny was forced out of his Paris apartment and he moved into a tiny flat in Rome, where he was looked after by a devoted Englishman—the last to be held in the Fouts stranglehold. In December of 1949 Denny failed to show up for a date at the Opera. His friend went to his apartment and found Denny dead face down on the bathroom floor.

Denham Fouts, a man who had lived his entire life off of the love of others, died at thirty-five—ironically of a malformed heart. After years of excess, as he sat on the toilet taking a crap, his heart stopped beating, giving up on a life that each day grew bleaker, opting instead for the possibilities in death. A place where there are no wrinkles or hair loss. Imagining it, perhaps, not as an occasion for repose but as something unblemished and thrilling. Like an eternal cocktail party charged forever with the kind of excitement that something new always brings. A non-stop stream of exceptional mouths and kisses that taste of martinis. Or maybe he saw it as a continuous sublime feeling, like the blinding first moments of an exquisite orgasm. Like perpetual love from wealthy admirers. Like Paris when it's new. Beautiful things. Tender flesh. Opium. Paradise!

The Excitement Of Newness

For Bernie, Gregg, and Marc

1. BOYS TOWN

I was in a bad mood. My heart had been broken.

I was in Los Angeles, not a place you want to be with a broken heart, sitting in a Starbucks, not a place you want to be in a bad mood. The pain was getting so awful that I was planning a trip back to New York. I hoped to find something there that would jump-start my life. Give me a boost in the ass of confidence, good cheer, good will—anything that would give me some energy required to deal with the broken-heart pain that would surely continue to infect my body in the coming months.

It was, perhaps, stupid to think that NYC—my hometown—would do it for me. There was nothing new there. My good family and good friends would greet me with open arms and that would give me a boost in the ass of comfort and love—but probably not the energy I needed to survive

Los Angeles wasn't all that bad for my life. My writing career was going well—at least on paper. But it wasn't a city to be in if you were any kind of lonely. I was all different kinds of lonely, mostly lonely for a romantic relationship. And I had just ended one. I didn't ask for much for a thirty-something year old: I simply wanted the kind of relationship where we—just the two of us—understood each other, comforted each other, inspired each other, craved each other, and just generally enriched each other's lives.

Broken heart aside, I was in a melancholy mood for other reasons too. I'm always shocked and saddened by people's cruelty. Example: the night before I had watched a news item in which a Eurasian man, irate that his dog would not get into the car on command, tied the pooch to the back of the car and dragged him. The doggy, a Chow mix, struggled to stay on his feet, while the padding of his paws wore off. Then he flopped down and was dragged until a motorist pulled his car in front of the driver, forcing him to stop...in which the hero motorist picked up the bloodied pooch and carried him off to the safety of a caring vet.

The news showed videotape footage of the sad eyed Chow in the pound, his legs bandaged to the knee, looking at the camera with these big, dark eyes. My family had a red Chow once, who I loved dearly. Oh, I wanted this dog who had been hurt, but the news correspondent said

133

there were hundreds of people who offered to adopt him and my life was far too disorganized, my demeanor too distracted, to throw my hat in the dog adoption arena. Plus, with a recently damaged heart, I didn't have the energy for the phone calls it would entail to go through the screening process. What if I was rejected? I couldn't take another. Besides, there were better homes with more stable owners much more equipped to deal with the responsibilities of owning a traumatized Chow. I figured he'd get a good family with a lot of love. I hoped so. I prayed so.

The day following the dog tale, I sat in the Starbucks in West Hollywood looking through the pane and watching life going on around me. Outside it was January. Still, the weather was warm. Muscled men in tank tops and tans at nearby tables looked up from their newspapers, cruising, in an overt style I didn't care for. Exhibitionists walked into the coffee shop past where I was sitting, with bared torsos, their tank tops hanging from their back jeans pockets—stripping themselves of any mystery or dignity and putting themselves on vulgar display, much to the delight of the throngs.

Unfortunately for me, most of what was considered desirable in West Hollywood wasn't what I wanted. When I swung open the door to Starbucks—in the area of the city called *Boys Town*—down came the dam of a stereotyped ghetto. I walked into a flood of scraggily goatees, a waterfall of earrings—if you'll excuse the poetry—a cascade of buzz cuts. Everyone had these accouterments—whether they were twenty or sixty—they called each other "dude" they described things as "kewl." Many of them were beautiful, but they were not my particular type. At this point in my life I don't consider myself a "dude," and I find very little, if anything, that is "kewl."

These were men who are thin. They count calories. They measure body fat. They are in excellent shape but to my critical eye, fifteen pounds under a normal manly weight and if they approach a proper body weight, well, that's a sign for them to diet.

It's not a bad look, it's just that everyone tries to look the same, whether it's part of their personality and comes from within or whether they see it on everyone else or in a magazine or on a television show that dictates the fashion and then acquire it for themselves.

After awhile it was meeting the same person over and over again. Someone would send me a photo on the Internet and they looked somewhat different from the rest, but with every meeting the same person showed up. I thought that maybe these first dates wanted to see me again only because I didn't go to bed with them. They couldn't believe that someone would choose not having sex with a stranger as opposed to having it.

Here we are, the most talented, creative, intelligent, artistic food group on the planet and yet we all feel we have to look exactly the same in order to be devilishly desirable and sexy. Or am I wrong? Perhaps everyone in the gay scene is cloned from one master cell flown back and forth, at great expense, from West Hollywood California to Chelsea New York? These are the questions that one has to ask oneself but to which ones' self never replies.

This sounds bitter and horrible and makes me sound like a terrible person but, let's just say, I'd reached the point where I could no longer sugar coat my feelings. Perhaps by the time you're reading this, the particular clone-look I'm talking about—which came into vogue in the late twentieth century—will be long gone. Although for the past five years the look hasn't budged.

There were exceptions of course—and the exceptions were very appealing indeed, but difficult to come by. And because the men, who were different from the rest, were in such short supply, there were not enough of them for the demand from guys like me who was always on the lookout for something distinctive. I was something different so was somewhat in demand, but the people that demanded me were usually from the clone group who were not interested in other clones. But I, not being interested in clones, made us incompatible. So you see how it went?

Oh, how I longed for a little bit of a beer belly, a slicked back head of hair, maybe in a pompadour, and some Old Spice aftershave. Nuts, I know. But that's me for you.

No one in the coffee joint had a day job but everyone was so filled with purpose. They were festive and happy—the way they had the right to be. The way they should be. They were on their way. They knew what they were doing. They were confidently typing film scripts into laptops and preparing for movie stardom. What did I care if the well-worked out man at an outside table smoked a cigarette simultaneously eating a chocolate chip cookie and drinking coffee? It was what he wanted to do. I was so separate from them. So much not a part of any of it. Yet by now I was wise enough to realize we all feel separate. That's what encourages togetherness.

Still, I felt as if I couldn't possibly go on much longer. But, on second thought, something had always come along in the past. An appeal. A temporary stay.

"Just ride it through one second at a time. Remain in the moment."

Here love is just some sort of distant relative to pleasure. Sex was here and available. And sex with such desirables! It's Hollywood. I lived in West Hollywood on a street called Hayworth which in its own way is relevant and may come up later. Step foot outside of my apartment and there were outdoor cafes were you could sit and watch an assembly line of cuties walk by and eventually, sooner than later, one would hook you with a stare. And away we go.

Every good, good-looking, confidant boy in the world comes here at one time or another in the hopes of becoming a movie star. The lure of Los Angeles is that it's a rambling city with the promise of making a lot of easy money with adoration of the masses as an added bonus treat. Aside from youth and beauty, it asks nothing in return...not hard work, not talent. Maybe just luck (timing) and connections.

How quickly they become addicted to the available sex. And drugs. And bars. Sex sex sex. On every street corner. Every turn down the aisle in a supermarket. With every switch-on of the computer. It was still a new enough concept. Imagine being able to go on a computer in your bedroom at two AM in your boxers and being able to find sex in the matter of minutes. Guys couldn't get over it. They were giddy with it. And every man's nervous system becomes rewired to detect, hunt, and accomplish new sex with new men. More important than writing a wonderful movie script or doing a compelling acting job in a small but well-made movie—finding something new to have sex with is every day's goal. Still, these boys talk about writing and acting because they should be doing something in between working out and looking for sex. But sex is really all that matters.

I wanted my life to be different. I was very sad when my relationship with Kurt didn't work out. I missed him terribly and, like God, I looked around and saw that it was not good for man to be alone. There was one guy, Todd, who I met on a personal site who had seemed promising.

Todd and I exchanged photos and seemed to be each other's type. He told me he was a screenwriter. That sounded interesting and glamorous, even though I, by this time, realized that most people who called themselves screenwriters were not really screenwriters, or any kind of a writer, and in actuality had never even written anything, but merely had an idea. But since there was no word for a profession for a person with an idea who would like to make a movie someday—and even if there was one there would be no prestige or glamour attached to it—every person you met upped there status to screenwriter and the market was far too overcrowded.

Meeting Todd: I was jumping the gun and I knew it. My heart was still torn up over the breakup with Kurt. I'm not one of these guys who goes from relationship to relationship—moving in with a guy for six months, breaking up, finding my own place, meeting someone a couple of weeks later, and moving in with the newer model by the end of the year. Still, I needed a distraction. Kurt was haunting my dreams, and although I prayed to God to get rid of him, night after night after my sleeping pill did

136

its number, he kept coming back—gloating in a dreamscape McDonald's where he ignored me and flirted with handsome waiters (in a McDonald's?), or rejecting me in other various surreal settings with unlikely casts of characters.

So, desperate for a distraction, something that might end my dreams, I jumped into the online dating pool again and met Todd. We had many telephone conversations in which it seemed to be established that, at the very least, a great friendship was possible between us

Todd lived in the Valley, which could be up to a half-hour drive depending on traffic, but he agreed to drive to the Starbucks in West Hollywood to meet me. Anticipation was high, but from the moment he sat down at my table, whipping off his sunglasses, I could tell he wasn't attracted to me. You just know these things. Sometimes it only takes a moment. It happens. No chemistry. I didn't feel it for him either. He was too tall. Too bony. Buzz cut. Goatee (neither of which he had in the photos he sent). He had a tribal tattoo that wrapped around his bicep, of course, for this is a result of the cloning process. But I gamely got up and ordered for us, bringing two coffees to the table, smiling, looking forward to some pleasant chitchat with an affable fellow with whom I had a lot in common.

Unfortunately his negative thoughts were so loud I could hear them perfectly as he sized up the real me and then quickly looked away with controlled fury. "You looked okay in your photo," Todd thoughts said, "but now that I see you in the flesh I can see that your eyebrows need waxing, the hair on your arm needs trimming and I thought you'd have the sense to get a buzz cut by now."

Luckily his mind didn't say anything about the extra ten pounds I had put on since I broke up with Kurt because the pictures I had sent him were up to the minute and showed me with the excess baggage, and Todd had liked them anyway.

When we had talked on the phone, conversation went on for a long, languishable time. As I told him about my recent breakup, described why I thought men were so difficult to meet in Los Angeles, or described my career as an entertainment journalist, I could feel his delight leap through the earpiece of the phone, wrapping me up in a warm and comfy bear hug. He seemed to never run out of things to ask me—for he was a writer and I was a writer in a kingdom by the sea.

One of the stories Todd had loved was how I had discovered early in my move to California how the collective consciousness of my neighborhood in Los Angeles and the reason why I felt so alone could be summed up at the post office on Fairfax in West Hollywood. It is at this post office you see all kinds of people in most kinds of behavior extremis. And it also illustrates how and why I had reached my present state of bafflement and anger.

On the day in which my story took place, the line was just not moving, as it is often not moving in the Fairfax post office, the line grew obscenely long, extending to the door and then circling along the wall. Everyone was very disgruntled, holding big packages and checking their watches.

I needed to get two money orders. Every once in awhile I'd take a look back to check out the status of the ever-growing line, and I noticed that the guy directly behind me (he drew attention to himself) was filling out the paperwork required for a huge box he was sending—this man was exceptionally angry.

Along with his anger, he looked like many other twenty-something, thirty-something, forty-something, and fifty-something men who live in Boys Town. He was dressed in the standard uniform: baseball cap, skin-tight tank top and jeans. His earrings were of the usual design. Dark sunglasses covered the windows to his soul. Physically he was as expected: at least twenty pounds underweight, he had a tribal tattoo that wrapped around his well exercised bicep, and any trace of body hair had been waxed from existence at first sighting. There was nothing unusual.

But he was angrier than the usual homosexual and his anger emanated from him like white heat. We all were angry, for we were all waiting and we all had lives as important to us as his was to him—only no one ever informed him of this. We kept on waiting. The guy behind me in the baseball cap, with his sunglasses still on, kept sighing and shifting his weight and moving around really impatient.

And he was growling and huffing and puffing. And just about ready to blow the house down. During one of my discreet glances back at him, I noticed that the form he was filling out was for an Express Mail package. Having that sort of transaction myself only a few days before I had discovered that if you have something going Express Mail, you don't have to wait in line. Because they are charging you an arm and a leg to get the package to the addressee overnight, you can, in spite of many dirty looks from others waiting on the line, march right up to the window and say, "I have an Express Mail package, please" and they will put everyone and everything else on hold and take your money immediately.

After learning this, I wished I had known this info before I waited on line for twenty minutes so now—being more knowledgeable of post office rules and regulations—I figured I'd help this impatient man out and let him know the secret. I turned around and said, "You know if you're sending that package Express Mail you don't have to wait in line." He paused, looked me up and down through his sunglasses and bellowed, "I

138

HAVE OTHER TRANSACTIONS TO DO!!!!! IS THAT OKAY WITH YOU??????"

Now I don't think I am exaggerating when I say the force of his words caused my hair to become windblown. Everyone turned to look. My mouth was agape but I couldn't think of anything to say and everyone was staring so I decided that turning around, closing my mouth, and keeping my eyes straight ahead was the best course of action.

The affect his contempt and aggression had on me felt very much like a drop kick to the stomach in the way that, after the initial shock of his comment and tone, I was physically ill. My gut was trembling and I felt nauseous and I was also very dizzy. I wanted to sit down. I knew it was wrong to feel like this. To let something so minor, so stupid, so inconsequential upset me so much, yet I couldn't wait to get done with the post office so I could go home and cry. But there was still a lot of waiting left to be done.

I have spent most of my life alone. Being afraid of people. Not trusting them. Trying to befriend them and understand them and be accepted and feel part of them. I grew up in New York. I know that people are often cruel without explanation. Still, I do want to believe in goodness and kindness and fairness. Since I'd moved to Los Angeles, I had been making a real effort to join the human race and be normal. And yet I found that the gay population in Los Angeles was the cruelest of all people I'd ever come in contact with.

Maybe I should just mind my own business, always, but I wanted to prove that this instinct was wrong. But every time I turned to sneak a look at the guy behind me on line there he stood—exactly the same. Angry. Defiant. Scowling through his sunglasses

Most of the time I am a well-meaning person. This day, I swear, I meant well. I kept thinking that he had to realize that my comment was innocent. After all, there was nothing for me to gain by telling him that he didn't have to wait in line. In essence I was telling him to go ahead of me. This guy realized this. And yet, although his reply was only a few words, his tone clearly said, you are beneath me. You are annoying me. How dare you speak to me? I am beautiful and witty and clever and yet I have to wait in line with the rest of you, people like you—so incredibly beneath me.

I thought that, perhaps, he was having a bad day. Surely, while we waited on line together for many more minutes, he would realize that I am a nice guy and he would tap me on the shoulder and say, "Listen, guy, I'm having a bad day. I didn't mean to take it out on you." And I would smile good-naturedly and say, "no prob, bud," as is dictated in the vernacular. I waited and waited as we waited, but he never said a word—he just kept on huffing and puffing—and I was just one more annoyance in his long day, a day in which all sorts of unimportant people kept getting in the way of his urgent business of thinking of ideas for screenplays before he would be able to settle down to his well deserved life of fun and drugs and sex and rest and relaxation

As luck would have it we were both called up to windows, side by side, at the same time. As we did our transactions I kept looking over at him, trying to catch his eyes. I was so sure he was going to apologize. It was important. He never did. Yet, I kept looking over at him trying to penetrate the secrets of cruelty and hardness. Nothing outstanding. The usual mixture of impatience, superiority, cartilage and aggression. I wanted a little of that in me.

I could not stop thinking about this incident. It took up my entire day's limited amount of energy. Should I have answered him back snottily, that I was "only trying to help?" Should I have said, "Fuck you," in my toughest Brooklyn accent? Or was I right to remain silent in a situation that defies explanation?

I had several conversations with myself about this incident before telling various friends the story and they listened to the tale with a bemused smile that conveyed: Oh, Vince is having another one of his operatic moments!

Was I being hypersensitive?

"The legacy of that awful guy," I told Todd in one of our late night conversations, "is that now, I'm less likely to offer assistance to someone who might need help. The world is an uglier place because of him. And I am an uglier person. More like him. And that's sad for everyone, myself included."

Todd had loved that story and I thought, maybe, it was because that it illustrated that I was somewhat sensitive and looking for something different, and because he related to it, maybe he was somewhat sensitive and looking for something different too.

Now, however, as we sat face to face at Starbucks he let every comment I made hover over the table like an overweight, exhausted bird—till it fell dead, with a thud, on the table between us.

Actually, my unattractiveness to him caused him to reel back, as if at the entranceway to some hideous thing with hair of snakes. He seemed unable to look at me for more than several seconds at a time (fear of really turning into stone?) opting instead for the passer-bys and making sure he exaggerated his goggle-eyed stares when a muscle boy to his liking passed. I tried. Oh lord how I tried! I asked questions. When those only brought

140

forth one-word answers, I blathered out a sequence of pop culture consciousness, hoping I'd hit on a subject he could pick up the thread of.

When I asked him about what he was working on he testily replied that he had a great idea for a new screenplay.

And then there was awkward silence after awkward silence as Todd stared off into the distance at the windmills in his mind. Now I was feeling bad. I was hideous. Yes! But more than that, I was selfish. I forced him to come out and meet me all this distance under false pretense. I was a fake. I wasn't his dream boy after all. I was only me. Pathetically flawed and undreamlike.

I could have, should have, would have gotten up and said, "nice meeting you, thanks for coming, ciao bab-eee" hitting him with a dose of his own rudeness. But, I decided to see how long he would drag me behind the car.

Finally, I couldn't stands no mo' so I swallowed down the rest of my ice coffee in two huge gulps and put on my sunglasses to show that I was ready to leave.

Now, freed from the clutches of the horrible hairy toad, Todd was big about it all. He stood up. He smiled. For the first time he could look me in the eye: for he was free to get the hell out of there. "It was so nice meeting you," he beamed, convincing himself that, unlike the guy in the post office, he was a decent fellow, even managing to be polite towards an undesirable. "Good luck with everything," he said. And then he escaped into the sunshine and the muscle men and dream boys and an endlessly interesting freedom.

I decided not to leave. Instead, I sat there, very still, for a long time. Recovering. And I kept thinking about myself, about the guy in the post office and all the work. All the work I've been putting into toughening myself up, and preparing myself for anything. All the talking that I've done to myself in the past years—reasoning in the dangers of being sensitive—has led to nothing. I was exactly the same. Still quite bonkers—so much so that I could allow a stranger, wielding no weapon except his own persona, to have so much power over me. The power to hurt me so incredibly much.

I got up to leave. A robust, young man with gelled hair and better shoes than I walked towards me with his hand outstretched. "Spare change?" he asked in a fake whiny voice. "No thanks," I replied, "I've already got plenty."

To keep myself from being completely taken over by sadness, I reminded myself that some men find me attractive. They enjoy my company, miss me when I'm gone, call me, and would very much like to spend a lifetime with me. Unfortunately these are not the men I usually fall for. I go for the ones who are a little off. Not up to date—but timelessly masculine. The guy who wears Brute as opposed to Krizia Uomo. The wrong shoes. A shirt that doesn't quite match. Someone who doesn't quote Madonna and own the first seasons of *Queer as Folk* or allow *Queer Eye for the Straight Guy* dictate to him how to wear his hair. The type who usually doesn't totally go for me.

Enter Kurt.

In LA, for a brief time (for in my lifetime love has almost always been brief) I thought I found love with the right man. It was Kurt. We met in October, we broke up exactly two years later... last October. Now it was already January. January. January. The time for starting over, resolutions, new beginnings. January was a clean white piece of paper. Kurt had called me earlier that day, after the dog-dragging incident on the news but before my meeting with Todd. January.

The conversation started with him saying, "I uh...uh...uh..."

"Just say it very quickly," I said. I thought he was going to tell me he had a fatal illness or some other atrocious news.

"I met someone else and I'm moving in with him," he blurted.

Ouch! Ouch! I would have rather taken a brick in the face. I was stunned and silent amongst the mess of my apartment. I hadn't made the bed. Dishes were piled in the sink. Kurt, a neatness fanatic, would have hated that. I twisted my finger around a rubber band. I noted I needed to dust the television set. My phone table was a tower of notes and papers and napkins with phone numbers that needed to be sorted. I was letting myself slip. Buy a new filing cabinet, I reminded myself. If I concentrated on mundane things, maybe the impact would lessen.

"Who could be better than you?" he had said to me a few months before. Okay. We broke up in October. As recent as September we had been making plans to buy a condo. To open a joint bank account. To start businesses together. To be married. To spend our lives entwined. Forever and ever. I had not yet removed from my dining room table the photo of us together—in a sterling silver frame—taken several months before in Mexico. Some of my clothes still hung in Kurt's closet. There must have been traces of me, other than just DNA, in his bedroom and bathroom and other places of his apartment. Moving in with someone? Someone else? But it was only January.

"I'm telling you this because we're so close and I don't want you to hear it from someone else," Kurt had added on the phone. In fact we had not been close recently. In fact I had recently asked him to please not call me anymore. And what did he mean he didn't want me to "hear it from somebody else?" Were our lives so fascinating to the residents of Boys

Town? What did he think? That he was Richard Burton? That I was Elizabeth Taylor? That this was 1963?

I could catch up to Kurt! My personals were online on various websites in case anyone was looking for me. I was here—ready to connect with the right one. When we hung up I immediately called Todd.

"How about finally meeting face to face," I said. And in Starbucks a mere hour later, Todd gone, I squeezed my eyes closed very tightly to stop tears. Don't look like such a sour puss, I scolded myself. But how could I not react to the loss of Kurt. The dragged dog. The failed hope of Todd. The daunting, exhausting, overwhelming prospect of having to start over again–the only possible way to have a second chance, a new beginning.

2. WHEN WE FELL IN LOVE

Recently while browsing an Internet dating site I came across a profile where the guy began his introduction to his profile by saying "Since none of us are really who we think we are..." and, startled, I stopped reading. I glanced at the man's photograph. Perhaps he was on to something. He did look like someone who might have lived on top of a mountain for many years, eating grass and wild roots, studying the meaning of life with someone named "Oh Wise One." I found this concept—that none of us really know ourselves—very discombobulating. Could it be true? What if I spent all these years scrutinizing every detail of myself trying to get to know me, only to discover now that I am an impostor?

By the time I met Kurt I thought I knew myself pretty well. I figured I knew what I wanted and that I'd recognize it when he came along. With Kurt, at least I thought there was a potential for love everlasting. Eternity. But eternity, and whoever runs it, God I suppose, does have to keep Himself amused. I can't blame Him for that, but I wish my sitcom would get canceled for a few years. I had taken more than my share of unprepared left hooks from love's "let me knock you flat on the mat" main event, and I was always on my guard.

Kurt was from Chicago. That's one of the things I liked about him. Not Manhattan. Not Miami. Not Los Angeles. The other thing I liked about Kurt is that he was so "non-scene," and this is probably one of the reasons he was not hip. Not trendy. At least not as hip and trendy as he would have been by now had he originated from New York or Los Angeles or Miami. He was a corporate type. He had been married for six years and recently divorced. He had experimented a little with men and now he wanted a life outside of bars and the Internet. Or at least that's the way he seemed on the surface. When we met, he had been in Los Angeles for about one year.

At the time that time, although Kurt explained what he did for a living at least a dozen times, my mind could not process or retain the information. It had something to do with finance and it afforded him a luxurious Beverly Hills lifestyle. What he looked like was what really reeled me in. Thick brown hair, the kind that was streaked naturally from living in a constantly sunny climate. He had cheerful brown eyes and his eyelashes, both upper and lower, were so thick that people would often mistakenly think he was wearing makeup. A mischievous grin. Perfect white teeth. And he was successful, to boot.

There was another quality—not a physical characteristic—but one of those unexplainable electric chemistry things that you feel with certain people of all physical types. It might be an abrupt charge you feel with someone you're simply passing on the street or a diner you lock eyes with momentarily when exiting a restaurant. I hadn't yet been able to pinpoint this attribute in Kurt or the other men I felt it with. The root of this chemistry was still, to me, of unknown origin.

But what was most important to me was that he wasn't like the other West Hollywood guys, and that was my main attraction. He had some muscles but he was a bit husky and was not one hundred percent fat free. He had a strong masculine face, but he didn't come with arty facial hair experiments. He dressed in smart, classic clothes, but they were not too tight or, more importantly, Lycra. There wasn't a piercing on his body. Nor a tribal tattoo around any of his biceps or anywhere else.

Kurt was short, about five feet, seven inches but he made up for his lack of height with his charisma and his incredibly strong and appealing voice. He had a deep, gravely, masculine voice—a voice-over voice—with just the right amount of velvet—filled with arrogance and swagger and good will towards men. I could imagine him reading the evenings sports news on television. Actually, with his fastidiously groomed and styled appearance, he looked like a sports anchorman. And Kurt cleverly used his voice as part of his considerable charm—it added about five inches to him. Kurt's voice worked like an aphrodisiac and everyone—sales clerks, waiters, operators—fell giddy in love with him a little on a first hearing of that voice.

We met on an Internet dating site—both of our ads said we were "tired of the scene" and were looking for something lasting—then we took the proper steps. Exchanged more photos. More emails. All was A-Okay. Then phone numbers. When I called him and received his voicemail I was

144

stunned and delighted by the sexy voice that greeted me—as I am sure it has stunned and delighted many before and many after myself.

We met at a bar not far from where I lived. Still, I arrived slightly late. Breathless. I can see him now, sparkling at the end of the bar. Handsome and smiling. He felt a delight with me as I entered. I felt that. I hadn't disappointed. I was delighted too! He looked better in person than in his photos—usually it was the other way around. His hair was neatly combed, parted on the side. Glittering eyes. He had a suave and debonair air, very reminiscent of George Clooney in *Ocean's 11*—which is definitely my type. Skip ahead a few months: I wrote on his fortieth birthday card in all honesty: "there hasn't been a moment since I first laid eyes on you that I haven't been totally and completely in love with you."

It had been like that.

Ah, the recognition of something rare! There was that exceptional moment of joy. We both lived up to the fantasy we had built around each other. I knew it. He knew it. As I took a seat on the stool next to him I noticed we were both wearing the same thing: black T-shirt, black leather blazer, black jeans. I ordered scotch on the rocks. He was already drinking that—the same brand.

My charm comes in very limited supplies, but I used it all up on him, telling him the stories that are real and a part of me and that never fail to seduce. I do usually have a certain power in the beginning.

It was supposed to be a meeting for a drink. That's what all online "old hands" do: set up a meeting for one drink or coffee. This is one of the major rules. It's an escape hatch. If there is no spark, you can smile charmingly, tell an anecdote, listen to one, and then shake hands and call it a night. Nothing is lost and no feelings are hurt. But our one drink turned to two. Then another. He told me the anecdotes that made up his life. Neither one of us was a clone, yet we were still compatible!

The gods, or God, was smiling. I wasn't getting any younger and my time left on earth wasn't getting any longer. I hadn't felt this was for a long time. A few years actually. Maybe this was the one.

We got pleasantly drunk, Kurt and I. When we left the bar we knew where we were heading. Laughing, we walked the long walk down the street to his car our arms wrapped around each other. I pushed him into another neighborhood bar I frequented. Kurt had never been in there. In this tiny, old, quietly decaying bar, in front of the sad Friday night crowd, I kissed him. He seemed surprised. He seemed thrilled. We kissed again and then walked out amongst stares and envy—there were cartoon hearts bursting from our heads.

Next door to this bar was a wretched little Italian restaurant. The Non-English-Speaking waiters were sweeping and putting the chairs up on the table. They allowed us to order anyway, the only customers in the place. The chicken parmigiana was a colorless slab of poultry, tasteless sauce, with a plastic coating of "mozzarella." We thought it was delicious.

Later, on my leather sofa, he stripped my foot naked. For some reason, I don't know why, I picked up the new digital camera on my coffee table. I snapped photos of Kurt, my bare foot in his hand, then, continued snapping away when he took it into his mouth. It was strange for me to allow my foot to be photographed in such a compromising position. What would happen if some time in the future these pictures ended up in the wrong hands? What damage might it do to my foot's—and the other parts attached to it—career? Various celebrities, I recalled, had posed in the nude early in their climb, and when the photos were discovered it had turned into an advantage, so maybe it wouldn't be so bad for my foot, after all.

"When We Fell in Love" I'd name this picture file on my computer months later when I came across this series of photographs. I thought it was the most romantic night I ever had.

We entered my bedroom. Kurt pushed me down on the bed with one hand and I landed flat on my back. I felt completely out of my own control. I wanted him so badly I could feel my body begin to tremble. With my help unbuttoning, he pulled at my clothes. With one swift yank he got off my pants. In no time at all the rest of me was as naked as my foot. He undressed hurriedly.

Through the years, after failed relationships, knives in the back placed by trusted cohorts, betrayals, and disappointments of various kinds, I'd come to consider myself a sealed off residence. The doors were firmly shut. The windows nailed down. My body, and what it contained, was safe, secluded and very well protected.

Now, though, when he joined me on the bed he entered my home. The investigation began. No warrant was necessary. I invited him in. We lay with our arms around each other's neck, our faces close together, panting, taking in each other breath. Our hands explored each other's body. Kurt was strong. Solid. Everything about him was perfection. He kissed me, exploring the interior of my mouth. His kisses sucked out my past. He was rubbing himself all over me and doing this he found a way inside of me. He swung open the doors to my closets pulling out my clothes—my Communion suit, my Calvin Klein jeans, a rumpled red silk shirt. He rummaged through my drawers and examined each item one by one—each failure, every success. "Ah," he said. "Ah!" He placed his hands on my inner thighs, spreading me apart. His fingers entered me too. I accepted it as fate. There

146

were secrets there for no one else. He was knocking down walls. Breaking through windows. Tearing off wallpaper—it had little baseball bats, hardballs and mitts on it—the coverings of my childhood. The kids in high school stopped laughing at me. He lowered his head and took me into his mouth. Another door was opened. My photo albums were piled there. My family at weddings, Christenings, birthday parties, anniversaries. Parents, grandparents, uncles, aunts, cousins—and they were not ashamed. They waved from snapshots in a friendly manner. I kissed a trail down his neck, his chest, his stomach—taking him in my mouth. He tasted somewhat salty. "Oh," he said. "Yeah." I could have stayed there forever. He lifted himself so we were face to face. He rummaged through my file cabinets and found things that were meant for no one to ever see. He discovered my diaries and ripped them up page by page. A shudder ran through my body. My fingers clawed at his back. History didn't matter. He ripped up the carpeting and saw what lies beneath. There was so very little left of my old self. "Yes! Yes! Yes!" I said. We came together, first in little spurts and then one enormous outpouring. My past was destroyed. It was time to begin.

In the present I lay side by side with Kurt, both of us panting. "I feel strange," he said. Something in both of us had changed. I had found a different kind of shelter. I was ready for him.

The next day he told me he was supposed to have another date, a coffee date, with some guy he had been corresponding with from the same personal site we had met on. But after meeting me, he said, well, there was just no way had he wanted to be with anyone else. He insisted on calling the guy and canceling their meeting from my place, right in front of me. A great show of it. A great show indeed. I have to say I felt good. My ego was stroked. It was romantic. It was sweet. He stayed the rest of the day with me. Drinking coffee in our underwear and listening to music. Sinatra. We both loved Sinatra.

From that night on, for the next two years, there was not a day we didn't speak on the phone at least three times; there was rarely a day (except when I was out of town) we didn't spend together.

I told him my dreams and my fears. I had moved to Los Angeles in the hopes of bringing my writing career to the next level. He had been reading my stuff.

"What if I never really become successful?" I said. "What if I remain obscure and talented?"

"You're already an excellent writer," he said.

"Thanks. But the real money is in television and movies."

"What do you want out of life?" he asked.

"Everything. But I'm willing to negotiate a percentage."

Kurt understood wanting to make more money. It had always been important to him. "Then you'll get into those industries. Just envision it for yourself."

"Oh it's that easy, huh?"

"Yes it is," he replied. "Let me give you an example. When I'm driving down your street and can't find a parking space I just imagine a space in my mind, and when I circle around the block for the second time the space becomes available. Always. That's how it will be for you. You just have to learn how to believe in yourself—now you have someone who believes in you too, so it will be easier."

"I want to have an apartment in New York and a house in Los Angeles," I said. "I'm envisioning that."

"Can I live with you?" he asked, smiling.

"Yes," I said.

In the beginning, I knew he was infatuated with me. All day while he was at work, I knew he couldn't wait to be with me and that felt nice. A little scary—only because it had been such a long while since someone felt that way—but nice.

Kurt loved to have sex with me. He couldn't suck my cock enough. He would come home from work in the afternoon to have sex during his lunch hour. At night we'd watch television, have sex, go back and watch television and he'd say, "Let's go do it again." He'd wake me up in the middle of the night. He liked to suck my cock and have me suck his. He'd kiss me a lot. I didn't know how much I would miss his longing once he no longer felt it.

At night, from his office, he would come back to my apartment and bring little treats for us. Tiny loaves of bread you had to put into the oven to warm and a funny little pate he liked made of olives. Tapanade. A couple of months after we broke up I found a package of those tiny loaves in the back of my freezer. I gasped with recognition. There was only two left in the package. Why would I save this? I held the package in my hand, staring at it, and that first October came back to me, quickly. Sweetly. Of course, of course! It wasn't the bread I was freezing. It was the moment. The way we felt for each other. The delight. Everything was good. If only we could have been frozen in that time and never left the moment. How happy eternity would be.

We kept separate apartments. It just seemed easier that way. I worked from home and needed a lot of office space. We lived only a few miles apart so it seemed almost as if we had one extended apartment. After awhile, though, I noticed he preferred to spend evenings, together, at his place.

That was fine with me. I liked having someone next to me in the night. Someone who didn't disgust me after the sex.

Oh, I thought to myself, this is why heterosexual couples feel they can marry and spend an entire lifetime together. We could have wonderful sex sessions, but didn't feel as if we couldn't wait to get away from each other after it was over. We could have long discussions in the morning or do nothing but sit quietly and listen to music. We could make plans for further down the line than one week.

I loved his apartment. It was like living inside of him. His love of luxury extended throughout his apartment. The immaculate tiled bathroom. The high, lush bed. I still shopped for bargains but for him everything had to be top of the line—dishes, wine, cigars, desk chairs, cutlery.

I was sloppy. He was the neat type. He taught me how to make a bed "properly," so that there wasn't a single wrinkle in the sheets, the pillows plump and lineless, the blanket smooth. The toothpaste had to be squeezed from the bottom. I looked at these lessons as self-improvement. I was happy to find myself wiping spots off of the mirrors in my own apartment, as well as making sure there was no residue hair in the shower at his place.

We had been together for a few months when we started going to Christmas parties together. Up until the holiday season we were in our own little world. Just the two of us. But, even though he had been closeted at work, he brought me to his corporate office celebration. When the people there asked me what I did for a living I told them I was a writer. Kurt noticed their skeptical looks.

"You must read Vince's piece in the current *Vanity Fair*," he informed them proudly. "It's absolutely stunning."

They stared at me and nodded blankly.

"And I have a great idea for a screenplay," I quickly added, and suddenly the conversation became lively with discussions of ideas for movie scripts.

Now he met the staff of the various magazines I wrote for. Kurt was a great success at the *Los Angeles Times* editorial holiday party—he was supposed to go to a big clients holiday party, but gave it up to go to this bash with me. We seemed to be a couple people wanted to meet.

"You two look adorable together," an editor I respected told me. When we separated to wander around the place by ourselves—I didn't worry about who he was meeting or talking to. I didn't want anyone else in the room or in the world. I know he felt the same. Of this I was certain.

Someone once told me the way you spend New Years Eve—the kind of time you have on that evening will set the tone for the rest of the year. Kurt and I spent it alone. I made baked brie on Italian bread and he made a special kind of pudding with noodles—a recipe from his mother. The apartment was lit by dozens of candles. We wore t-shirts and sweat pants and bow ties. We put on music and slow danced. We sang along with the CDs. Don't go changing to try and please me...

That night, when we were in his bedroom—in the middle of making love—I had a vision. Maybe it was the champagne. I closed my eyes very tight and I saw blue dots that slowly shifted, became sharper, changed colors and formed into the shape of a teased-haired, blonde woman in a mini-dress and white go-go boots singing a duet with a heavy set, handsome, older man in a tuxedo. I fought my way through an imaginary audience getting closer and closer to the stage.

Oh my God! It was Nancy Sinatra with her legendary father, Frank, in a Las Vegas auditorium singing their popular 1960s duet *Something Stupid*. Something about the stars getting red.

I'm sure the apparition was sent to me for some divine reason, but this was not, by any means, the proper time to for me to interpret visions. Kurt was going down on me, roughly, passionately. He gave up important plans to be with me tonight. I thought of him at the party, in the car driving me home, his hand on my thigh. And then I said it—exactly at the same moment Frank and Nancy were singing the second chorus.... then I go and spoil it all by saying something stupid like...

"I love you," I whispered.

Kurt stopped looked up. Bewildered. Surprised. Ecstatic. A pause. And then he said it back. "I love you too, Vince." And, although neither one of us had an inkling at the time, that moment was the beginning of the end for us.

Love addresses many situations in different ways. Actually, I'm not sure how long we would have stayed together if things didn't change so drastically and so suddenly. Unlike me, Kurt didn't open himself up to me so fully after our first meeting. I discovered dark corners in his psyche that weren't immediately apparent—areas that he did not allow many people to see. We all have these places but I allowed him to explore many of mine right away.

During that first year together, within a matter of days Kurt lost a lot of money. I suppose his manic depression temporarily blocked him from envisioning good things for himself and his life nose-dived.

Stocks he had for years plummeted. Investments went bust. Because of alimony and credit card payments he had very little available cash. I made a decent living so I wasn't all that worried. We couldn't afford to live the way he was used to, but we wouldn't have to worry about rent or food or an occasional dinner out. His money problems affected me, only because I

150

saw how unhappy it made him. He stopped going to the office. He'd spend long mornings in his underwear checking stocks on the Internet but not doing much of anything else.

When he lost his job and the health insurance that went with it, he stopped taking his antidepressant medication.

I'm not a take charge type but one of us had to take charge. I called his ex-wife and explained the situation. She seemed to feel no ill will towards him. "He certainly thinks the world of you," she told me. Literally and figuratively he needed his hand held. I was happy to do it. It sealed our love. It showed that love, when the right person is involved, conquers all. Together we could withstand anything.

After many phone calls, hours on hold, we discovered a free clinic, and he agreed to go for a consultation: a great humiliation for him, but he was able to get his (substantial) depression medications without cost. In need of a new career, I encouraged him to take a real estate course when he mentioned it was something he had always been interested in.

"I wouldn't be able to get by without Vince," I heard him tell his mother on the phone while I was half sleeping one morning. "He's everything to me."

Man, he really went broke. Many times he couldn't afford to fill up his gas tank. I wasn't hurting, but supporting two rents and two cars did put strain on me financially. I took a job ghostwriting the memoirs of a world-renowned porn star. Kurt would do the same for me. There was no worry on my part. In my heart I knew that he would eventually make back his money. I used to tease him and tell him the list of plastic surgery procedures I wanted and would have him pay for when he made back his fortune.

"You can buy whatever you want with my money, Vince," he would say, just as confident as I was that he'd have it all again someday, "But the one thing you don't need is in this life is plastic surgery."

Meanwhile, I taught him how to hunt for bargains. He was hesitant at first, but then he actually delighted in finding something new. His first trip to a 99-Cent Store was like a religious experience. "This is the same toothpaste I always paid $4.99" he exclaimed in wonderment.

Perverse as it sounds, some of our happiest times as a couple were spent during his recovery—emotionally, financially and physically. Struggling along with the day to day effort, but together. Facing armies.

Sex had petered off. "It's the medication," I told myself. But he was on anti-depressants when we first met. We both were. Antidepressants. Tranquilizers. Sleeping pills. Basically all my life I had been afraid of situations and people. Sure, I could have gone through years of psychoanalysis to work my way through it. But pills were so much faster.

Yet, at first, that didn't stop him from having the strongest libido I had ever encountered. Now that his drive had died down, I had to come up with other excuses to placate myself: How could he be interested in sex with all the stress he has on his plate?

Plus, the phenomenal sex we once had was replaced by an emotional warmth. A bond. Comfortableness. A tender feeling we had for each other as a team. An entity. There was no one else on the planet that mattered, really, more than the two of us.

During the day, he'd study for his real estate license at his apartment. I'd go home to my apartment and write. In the evenings we would go grocery shopping. He loved to cook. He'd make homemade pizza, pasta dishes, elaborate salads with a variety of cheeses or fruits. "I love cooking for us," he'd say. When he had first moved to Los Angeles, as a newly single guy, he had never bothered to buy a dining room table. We'd sit on the couch and watch news analysis shows with food trays in our laps.

Even though we talked on the phone several times during the afternoon, when I arrived at his apartment in the early evening he'd say. "All day long I look forward to the evenings when you come over." He'd say, "Just come over here and let me hold you." He'd say, "Don't turn on the television yet. Just talk to me."

I'd say, "I love you." And he'd say it back. But he'd never say it first. There are some people this wouldn't bother. But it began to worry me. Only slightly, of course. Anything even the slightest bit negative I'd push to the back of my head because, how dare I be negative when I was finally in a loving relationship?

At night we'd take our sleeping pills at the exact same time. Or our tranquilizing medication prescribed to each of us for anxiety. Once when he took his before I took mine I called out, "Now we won't be in synch!" And we both laughed.

But after awhile his lack of initiative in the "I love you" declarations bothered me enough to bring it up. "Why do I always have to say I love you first?" He made a joke out of it. Somehow the movie *Ghost* came up in which the main character can never tell his partner I love you. Demi Moore always says I love you. Patrick Swayze's reply is always "Ditto." Now it was a private joke. Often when I said, "I love you," he'd come back with "Ditto." I would smile but I didn't think it was funny.

But he would send me email cards that said, "I love you." One I was particularly moved by was an image of a dark ocean. A lighthouse suddenly brightened on the monitor, beaming out a searchlight on to the dark terrain. Then the words slowly appeared on the monitor: "You are the light in my life."

On the weekends our social life was a walk to the neighborhood video store. It was so much fun. We'd choose a movie. Our deal was that each alternating time one of us would get to pick what we wanted to see. Kurt would cook a restaurant-quality dinner and we'd sit in front of the television with our trays and a scotch. Or, sometimes as a very special treat, we'd go to the movies and bring our flasks, sipping throughout the movie, laughing at ourselves for being juvenile and naughty.

When I went for a visit to New York, he came with me. For the first time I introduced a man to my parents with the explicit understanding that we were a couple. This must have made them feel uneasy, but their love for me would not allow them to show it at all. We shared a bottle of wine at dinner and we all got along and had a wonderful time.

My parents viewed me as a rather ridiculous person and I don't blame them. If I were they, I'd think I was a ridiculous person too. I had been a mystery to them as a child—although I clung to their love.

Now I worked as a freelance writer, rather than have the safety and security that my brothers had being partners at my father's successful automotive body shop chain. I didn't own a house or even a condo. I went from periods of being very comfortable to very broke, from relative happiness to theatrical despair. I could be warm and kind or sharp tongued and short-tempered.

I had a longing to know them better—as adults—and have them know me but too many revelations would unearth pain. And didn't we have enough of that?

Still my parents tolerated me, and even loved me. They would never understand how I could choose the temporary joy of seeing a byline in *The New York Times* over the lasting happiness of seeing a newborn in a hospital window, yet, together they were the one thing in this world I could always count on. They felt an unchanging rock solid love, different from romantic love, but potent and necessary all the same. I felt it for them too.

Kurt and I slept in my childhood bed. "They make wonderful in-laws," he said that night.

One of my good New York friends Gabrielle threw a cocktail party for me to introduce all my East Coast friends to my West Coast boyfriend. Gabrielle and I had met many years before when we were both aspiring models. She made it. I did not. She went to Europe, walked on celebrated runways, posed for international magazines and returned to the USA to marry a successful investment banker aptly named Rich.

She's one of the people in my life, Gabrielle, who loves me without any restrictions or conditions put on our love. She has for many years. Even though I'm often morose and self absorbed and don't give her very much to love about me—she always does anyway.

Blonde and blue eyed, full-lipped and long legged, Gabrielle is rare because she is one of these people whose soul is so stunning, so good, that, as you get to know her, her personality becomes more overwhelming than her physical self. Everyone sees that Gabrielle is beautiful. But nobody knows it like I do. When I used to describe her to friends who didn't know her I'd use the word "Christ-like," and they mistook me for being a religious fanatic and Gabrielle as a martyr, not realizing that I meant that she was so kind and gentle and loving to all people—whether she was talking to a world famous celebrity or an impoverished Mexican immigrant who washed dishes at the restaurant her husband had recently invested in.

Gabrielle loved Kurt because I loved Kurt and Gabrielle loved me.

"Swear to me," Gabrielle demanded to Kurt in the kitchen where the three of us had drunkenly gone to spend a minute away from the party. "Swear to me that you love Vince."

I swear," he said.

"Tell him that in front of me! Look into his eyes. I want to watch the two of you together."

"Vince, I swear to God I love you," he declared.

And Gabrielle hugged us both and she had tears in her eyes because I had spent so many nights long distance crying on the phone to her about this or that. She wanted so much for me to be happy. And I was.

Although the party was for me, most of the talk was about Felicia, a big, funny, boisterous, pretty girl who had been a part of my New York circle. Felicia had died the month before the party after lethally mixing, alcohol, cocaine, unhappiness, and many pain killers. The doorman called the police the following day when they could hear the dog barking but no one answered her buzzer. The cops found her dead, in her pajamas in bed.

There are always mysteries in death. When someone young dies suddenly, unexpectedly, they are instantly held up to icon status. Everything about them becomes a mystery. Where had Felicia gotten the fatal dose of cocaine? Why was she unhappy? Was there someone in the apartment with her earlier that evening? These are some of the mysteries she took with her.

Everyone was still stunned at the news of her death. Even though Felicia and I weren't all that close, by some strange twist of fate, I was the last person she had talked to the night she died (she called me very late in Los Angeles, New York time, stoned and in a depressed mood). The police and

154

friends alike had studied her phone, and my number was the last one dialed. As a result everyone wanted to know what she said to me.

Felicia had been in a vicious mood the night she died and since most of our discussion was fairly negative gossip about everyone at this party, I revealed very little of our conversation. I didn't want to hurt anyone's feelings nor betray Felicia. I know for a fact Felicia loved them all. The thing is we all talk about each other. That's what we do in life. We all give our own versions of the story. Our opinion. Then we fight about it, discuss it, work it out, and life goes on and things are resolved. But when someone dies in the middle of a life, in the middle of the daily intrigues, heartbreaks and disappointments everyone experiences, all the last things she said becomes gospel, frozen in time. Even though, had she lived, Felicia's opinions would have been altered the following week.

I thought the entire party would turn into a sort of memorial for Felicia, but later, I overheard two of my other friends, longtime lovers—Justin and Christopher talking about me in the kitchen.

"Well, what do you think?" Justin asked Christopher. They didn't know I was standing right outside the entranceway.

"The minute that Kurt guy gets back on his feet," Christopher replied, "Vince will be history."

3. ONE VERY CONFUSED BOY

I have a tendency to think too much. This is something that, after much thought, I've concluded is wrong. Because if it's true that change is the only constant, then by the time you think you've got something you've thought about too much all figured out, everything is different anyway. At least, I think so.

When we returned to Los Angeles after our New York visit, Kurt seemed happier and more assured than he had been in weeks and what he was feeling on the inside projected on what was happening with the outside, and his luck did a full circle. As I suspected he was a natural at real estate. On his very first interview, he signed with a renowned agency. The charming extrovert. The people person. The ambitious dynamo. The velvet voice. All of these things made him the inherent salesman.

Now, instead of checking stocks and bonds, he'd spend long hours on the internet looking up prime properties in the area—learning the value of hot commodities, comparing prices, memorizing proper procedures. He loved his new profession.

At night, now, instead of taking our nighttime meds, or "dolls" as I called them together, he would often stay up at the computer. "I'm coming to bed in a minute," he'd say. But most of the time he didn't come. I'd fall asleep and wake up in the middle of the night to find him sleeping with his back to me. Then when I woke up in the morning, I'd see that he was already at the computer. "There's coffee made," he'd call out when he heard me moving around.

We continued spending every night together but now his days were spent out in the field, showing properties to perspective clients. His calls would come in but they were "in between chats," while he was waiting to show some bigwig a house in the Hollywood Hills. He wasn't yet making lots of money but the potential was there. He was getting exclusive listings on very expensive properties.

At this phase, there was a shift in our home life together. I wasn't the focus of his world anymore. That was normal and expected but still...

When we rented movies, if I chose something he didn't want to see, he would let me know. "This is shit," he'd say. He'd jump off the couch huffily after five minutes and go on the computer. "I'm listening to it," he'd call from the next room. I sat in the couch in silence watching the movie, which I could no longer follow. Rats! I chose wrong. He'd been working all day—this was supposed to be our "alone" time. I was upset, but to bring any negative feelings up would be to show the universe I was ungrateful. I remained silent.

And he'd do things that would negate my intruding qualms. Calling me to the computer. "Look at this condo," he said showing me a recently listed property. "White marble tile—the kind you like! Check out the fireplace! And it's two bedrooms so you can have a big office. This is the kind of place we should put a down payment on."

But—even if we ensconced ourselves in a beautiful condo—there wasn't just the two of us anymore. There were young men in his office. Very bright. Very successful. He'd tell me about them at night over our salads and pasta. "Kyle isn't even thirty yet and he takes home three million a year. Attractive too."

He didn't see me anymore. He felt my love—and it's lovely to feel love—but it was love in the abstract. It was a comfortable cloak he could wrap around himself when needed without ever acknowledging it or returning it. How I looked, what I had to say, what I was doing wasn't all that interesting to him anymore. Love was nice. But there were so many other things presenting themselves with clarity each day.

Actually, now that he was out on a daily basis, meeting dozens of new people per day, his universe was filled with new men. Hey, we're men. We notice other men. But Kurt became a bit extreme and it began to set off little warning bells. He acquired the uncanny ability—unique to the men

156

I've loved—to make me feel as if every man in the world was attractive, with the soul exception of me.

The technique was easy. He simply described every male he came in contact with in excruciating detail, never failing to leave off how cute/hot/handsome the guy was. It was mind-blowing, the handsomeness of other agents, landlords, building maintenance men, a man on the street who had stopped to asked directions—all were worthy of note. Every man who crossed paths with him during his busy day to day schedule were so uncommonly gorgeous they could not escape being commented on to me, whether I was with him at the time, or later in the day by a telephone call. He would call me to say that the guy in line in front of him at the deli who turned to him and recommended the turkey was "so cute!" What did that have to do with the sandwich? Was the turkey good? These kinds of details were often left out.

Of course, Kurt, being a man, was also irresistibly handsome, so they all ogled and eyed and flirted with him—a crucial part of the story that had to be told to me. If he thought these stories and descriptions made him more desirable to me it was a miscalculation on his part. It made me feel bad. But then many things make me feel bad, often as a result of me thinking too much, so I tried to ignore it.

When I brought up the subject of Kurt's need to tell me about his daily flirtations to his ex-wife, who I continued to talk to long distance from time to time, she told me that this was due to his own insecurity. It certainly fed into mine. If he was commenting on others, obviously he wanted them. Why was he with me?

My own insecurity began to turn into indignation, then anger. There's always going to be men who are better looking than I am, who exercise more, who are younger...more educated. But I was willing to compete with any man on an individual, total package level. But...but...but...how could I? How could I...compete with every man in the world? An entire scene, the male population of a city, a state, a world? No matter what kind of package I presented, no matter how loyal or attractive, there was no possible way to compare myself to the excitement of newness.

There was always a man in line in front of you like an ornately wrapped package waiting to be opened. If there was junk inside—so what? Down the street at the coffee shop there's another, and then another. There's always someone to take your place—superior or inferior—but with a cock and a promise of sex nevertheless.

While other men once again came into focus for Kurt, I faded. The posh veneer of newness started to rub off. The silvery surface began to tarnish. I tried to polish myself, but I noticed he stopped noticing. If I got

157

my haircut that afternoon, I'd arrive that evening beaming. He wouldn't comment. It didn't matter if I wore cologne or not. If I wore a new shirt. It was all the same to him. When even the occasional cuddling stopped, I said, "We should join a gym."

"That's a good idea," he said. But somehow we never got around to it.

We were putting on weight too. I liked being a handsome couple. "We should start eating more healthy," I suggested. "Maybe we should cut out bread and so much pasta for awhile."

"I'll make you a salad if you'd like," he said. "But I'm going to keep eating the same way. I can't focus on changing my diet at the moment. There are too many things going on." He loved pizza and made it so well. There was no way I could resist. And who cared? We had each other.

Sometimes, though, I would think about what I overheard my friends say at the party in New York. "Once Kurt is back on his feet, Vince will be history." He was up and running now, but I was determined to stick it out and remain in the present.

"What's the matter," Kurt asked while we where out driving one Sunday afternoon.

"Do you belong to me," I asked. It was, I realized, a stupid question. By this point in life I had done enough thinking to know that nothing belongs to anything.

But what I wanted to know was, if we were at a party and there were plenty of hot guys around on the prowl, would he be pleased to let them know that we were a couple? Or, while we mingled separately, would he allow a man to flirt and come on to him while the guy cast one gloating eye in my direction. And of course, being in sales, he always had an excuse to give out his business card. Would Kurt put a stop to the touching and walk over to me and let the room at large know that he was proud we were together?

The answer, sadly for me, was no. At an outdoor party given by one of his clients later that week he let some guy go further and further—touching and feeling and rubbing each other's shoulders—until I came over to join the conversation. The man smiled in my direction. "What did you say your name was," he asked. He had a victory over me. Feeling ignored by a lover at a party is cliché but this was a bit much, you must admit.

But in the car Kurt had said, "Yes. I belong to you. Why do you ask?"

"I just worry about what would happen if you met someone you liked better than me," I said and swallowed. It's not easy to say things like that.

"Who could be better than you?" he said.

I had to go to New York for an assignment in August. I was going to be gone for awhile but, much of the time, I still felt so close to him, so in tune, so right, I wasn't really all that worried. Well, maybe just a little. Kurt drove me to the airport, one early morning before going to his new office

"A month?" he kept saying. "What am I going to do without you for a month?" We took the luggage out of his trunk together, like an old couple, but there was something new about him. He had his confidence back, that potent aphrodisiac. His unflagging, unflappable, unyielding assurance that made him such a good salesman, such a hot commodity.

"Did you get your haircut," he asked.

"Three days ago," I said gathering up my bags.

"I love you," I said.

"Ditto," he mouthed back. There was bustle all around us. It had the sweeping, melancholy feel of *Casablanca* but for some reason I bordered the plane less confident then I had been a few months earlier.

After a few days in New York I could sense more changes in our long distance communication. You just know. When there are nights you don't hear from him until a call the next morning and then there are no explanations. I'd lay awake in bed, sensing that he was with someone else. But I tried to put the blame on that perception on my mind. My mind had instigated trouble in my relationships since I started having them. And yet, his calls did not come exactly at the same time every morning—sometimes they even came in the later afternoon. I tried to call him in the morning a couple of times and I landed directly into voicemail. How did I get here? Also, I couldn't help but notice his emails were not as ardent. Sometimes the ended signed simply "K." No "love." No "miss you." Just the initial.

I suspect that it was during that month, my time away, he met someone else. How could he not with hungry eyes everywhere, waiting to be shown hot properties by a masculine man with a rising career and a terrific voice?

When I finally did get back to Los Angeles, he picked me up from the airport. When he spotted me, he ran his hand over his new buzz cut as a way of greeting. Actually his head was almost completely shaved.

"I know you don't like it," he said. "I know how you love my hair. But it's so much easier this way." I smiled, blinking very rapidly and didn't say a thing.

Back at my place we hugged each other for a long time. We went to my bed and fell asleep just holding each other. Just holding. The love was very real. But the times, they were a-changing.

We no longer spent every night together. He was busy. He was exhausted from a long day of work. "Do you mind if we don't see each other tonight," he'd ask late in the afternoon. "I'm whipped."

"I don't mind at all—you've been working hard." But the telephone calls didn't come that evening, not even to say goodnight. He's with someone else, he's with someone else, he's with someone else. I knew it was true but I told myself I didn't know everything and maybe he was just tired. But I knew. I knew.

"Did you sleep with anyone while you were in New York," he asked me one night out of the blue as we sat on his couch eating dinner.

"Of course not," I replied. The question shocked me. What did he think of me, that he would even consider asking such a thing? I'm not a prude by any stretch. I'm very upfront about the fact that I've been through my promiscuous periods. All along, though, I had been hoping, even thinking, that I was with someone who had reached the same point that I was now at. I felt that I had already dated everyone there was to date, been to every bar there is to visit, seen all the strippers, tried the drugs, been in all the beds.

I had been looking for one person to be with so we could get into each other. I thought I had found him. After thinking about his question for several seconds I realized he brought up the subject for a reason. He wanted to tell me something I couldn't bear to hear. Instead I asked, "Would you be jealous if I did sleep with someone else?"

"I don't believe in jealousy," he said.

Another blow. I would have preferred for him to feel jealous. There was nothing left to say, except for me to ask him if he slept with anyone while I was away. I knew the answer. I didn't ask the question.

Soon I was to discover—to my great dismay and embarrassment—Kurt didn't desire me at all anymore. The sex had started to peter off when his depression started. But now, it seemed, he felt nothing for me at all physically. Oh we still slept in the same bed four or five nights a week—but it was rare that he even put a hand on me. Once in awhile he'd hold me with great affection. Never was it with desire anymore.

I was always reaching for him. Kissing him. His shoulders, his cheek. I kissed him on the lips but now always with my mouth pressed tightly closed. I could tell he didn't want to kiss me. If I lingered too long with my lips, even closed that way, he turned his face to the pillow. Sting, sting, sting! Ouch.

It seemed so strange, outrageous, shocking, that two gay men, not too old, relatively horny, can climb into the same bed, sometimes drunk, in our briefs, sometimes naked, legs touching...and nothing happened. I mean, there would be nights in the past that, even with someone I found disgusting, SOMETHING would have happened under similar circumstances. With Kurt, nothing nothing nothing. He no longer viewed me that way. And that's the truth. I typed it. I mean it. It hurts admitting it. But there it is.

We tried a few times but it was awkward and obvious that we were both pretending. I was too preoccupied with pleasing him to enjoy it myself. He was eager to appear to be enjoying it. In fairness to him, what could he do? He had lost that loving feeling for me. It happens to couples every day. Songs are written about it.

Shame is also an emotion.

We never went to bed at the same time anymore. He'd say that he had to get some emails out before hitting the hay. I'd take a shower and brush my teeth. I hesitated getting in to bed. I sort of dreaded the rejection I knew was coming. Kurt, I knew, viewed me as a very nice guy, very interesting, who a lot of people found attractive—but, alas, he was not one of them anymore. The one who mattered the most, the one I wanted to please more than anyone, was sitting at the computer totally uninterested. I was truly horrified to be on the undesirable end of the spectrum

I'd crawl into bed. From previous nights I knew that, when he did come to bed, he wouldn't make a move—but there was always a chance, right? But I became so overcome with humiliation and shame for my body. I debated whether or not I should take my t-shirt off. If I took it off he might think I was trying to entice him. There's nothing more pathetic than someone who is not attractive to a person, trying to seduce that person into physical contact. Then I thought, if I don't take off my shirt, maybe he'd think I didn't want him to touch me. Often, I'd take off my t-shirt, but keep on my underwear, and lay in my corner of the bed. Then my medication would take over before he came to bed and I'd fall asleep. I'd wake up hours later, whisper his name, but I'd look over and see that he was not there. Not even his back. He was still at the computer.

I was so preoccupied with his dissatisfactions that I ignored my own. Other times, in the middle of the night, when I'd wake to find him snoring with his back to me, I'd get out of bed and lay on the cold bathroom floor staring at the ceiling—tears streaming down the side of my face, feeling like a fool for wanting him so much.

After a very long while, I'd get up off the floor and stare at the big mirror behind the sink. What was wrong with me? What should I change? I had to deal with the reality that I may disgust him now—and he was just waiting it out for a convenient getaway, a time to cross to a new place in his life. I was working out some, but not as much as I should. My body wasn't as nice as so many of the other men in the neighborhood. Still, eyes still went up and down my body when we were out together. When I was having coffee alone at Starbucks, handsome men continued to sit down at my table to strike up a conversation. So I concentrated instead on the idea that other men found me attractive and maybe someone would rediscover me. But while other men commented on my gorgeousness, my waning gorgeousness, he stared the computer screen and scrutinized real estate.

And what about my cock, my cock, my cock? My dick is okay by normal standards in regards to the number of men I've compared it to—which is substantial—but it's still not MASSIVE by any stretch. I studied my cock in the mirror. Poor shriveled little guy. It had the ability to scrunch up to one inch in the cold or to grow to what some men pronounced "huge." It was never really huge, but nicely average and there was no amount of work I could do on myself, or money I could spend, that would change that. I'd like to add on an inch if such things were possible. One always wants another inch. If there was some scientific breakthrough concoction to swallow or inject to make it bigger I would. I would if I could but, you know, I can't.

A couple of times he brought up the fact that we weren't having sex. The first time he made it out like it was my fault. "Are you not feeling sexual," he asked. I was absolutely dumbfounded. For weeks I had discretely rubbed him, rubbed myself against him, tried to kiss him...and it was like... well...I wasn't there.

I said, "Um. I get the feeling that you don't feel that way about me anymore..."

"THAT'S NOT TRUE!" he yelled.

"...and I've been thinking that maybe it's a phase and it will pass?"

"I think you're very sexy and desirable," he said.

It baffled me and I knew it wasn't true...but I didn't know what to do. I couldn't bear being alone at this point and I loved him enough to be content, for the time being at least, just being near him.

Another time, the one other time, we were talking about sex during a conversation and I said, "...and I know you don't like to kiss."

"That's not true!" he said again. "I love to kiss." I was really, well, sort of blown away. If he did love to kiss it most certainly was not me any longer. By now we kissed each other only hello and goodbye—but in the same way you'd kiss a very dear, close friend.

Yes, it hurt me—but he knew how to make me feel good too. In ways other than sexually. But the signals were mixed and life had left me too exhausted to have to try and figure everything out.

I remember he got angry with me because he woke up and saw me huddled in my corner of the bed hugging a pillow as if it were a human being. "Why can't you hug me instead of the pillow?" He asked, chagrined. "What am I here for?" But he hadn't been there when I fell asleep.

After he received his third big commission check he booked a vacation for us to Mexico. We stayed at a luxury hotel. We swam in the aquamarine ocean or the sprawling pool that circled around a full-service bar. We drank sweet drinks out of coconuts. We photographed each other with our latest digital camera. The (mostly gay) staff ogled us and grinned with admiration and, when we were alone, flirted with us individually. Once when we arrived for dinner very late at our hotel restaurant, the waiter smirked and said with his accented voice, "Hmm. You two were busy with *other* things tonight?"

"Is that any of your business," Kurt joked with a twinkle. The truth why we were late was I hadn't been able to find my expensive watch and we spent a substantial amount of time looking for it until it was discovered in one of my suitcase compartments.

When we came back to Los Angeles I viewed all the vacation photographs very closely. We look like we're on a honeymoon, I thought. Yet another part of me, either more pessimistic or more realistic—I couldn't decide—thought of the whole trip as a parting gift.

Sometimes, in his bed, while I was sleeping, I would feel him put an arm around me. Holding me close to him. He was comfortable with me but he was no longer in love with me. I was comfortable with him too, but I was also in love. Is that it? Is that what life gives you? A year? An hour? A moment?

He was dieting now. "Have you noticed I've been working out," he asked one night as we were finishing our dinner. We hadn't seen much of each other after our trip because he was working on four new deals.

"Yes," I said. "You look great." He did indeed, and I couldn't help but notice that I wasn't included in this new plan for self-improvement.

"It's hard to get back into shape at this age," he added.

I smiled, nodding. There was someone else, of course. Someone whose significance warranted looking good for. Someone with a body to be reckoned with. Someone worth keeping up with. I put my tray down on the coffee table and stared at the television screen.

After a very long time passed with neither of us saying anything he looked at me. "What?" he asked.

There was no answer to that.

We had been to all the cool restaurants in the neighborhood. We'd met each other's friends. He knew where I stood politically. We had watched all our favorite films together. We'd listened to all our favorite music. He'd looked in all of my closets. I had said, "I love you." The wine bottle was empty. The cheese and crackers had become a tray of crumbs.

What in him continued to hold me? I knew it was illogical to stay in the relationship at its current status, but logic had never played an important factor in my decision-making and I had long ago grown used to my actions making little or no sense. What if this bad spell passes? I reasoned. What if he starts wanting me again? What would I be throwing away?

I loved him so. It had nothing to do with the kind of love that asks for something in return. He didn't have to make me happy. I loved him regardless. I loved him for who he was. I loved everything about him. And there were faults and I loved those too, even the ones that made me unhappy, because they were part of who we was and I thought perhaps together we could help correct each other's flaws.

It will pass, I told myself again and again. The bad patch will pass. The new guy will pass. There was evidence of this. Sometimes he would still call me several times a day. At times he would send me unexpected emails saying, "I love you" in various different ways. One time it was a cartoon Elvis who sang to me from the computer screen: I will love you longer than forever.

On the nights we were together he continued to cook for me, dishes he thought I would like. Now that he had some money again, he would pick up little things for me, little presents. Expensive gadgets to show he valued me. That he appreciated me. Elvis sang: Promise me that you will leave me never.

What was really painful, though, was that—even while being kind to me—more than ever he conveyed that he desired every other man in the world.

One night, pushing our cart in the supermarket some average looking thing caught his eye. The guy was ten years younger than we, with a great head of hair, sure, but he was 30 pounds overweight, was dressed in a very tacky, tight sweat-suit, and looked somewhat like a plump aardvark with

164

nice hair. The guy glanced at Kurt. Kurt stopped dead in his track, did a full turn and gave a come-hither look worthy of Theda Bara in *A Fool There Was*. If I wasn't there surely he'd pick him up, bring him home, and have a mind-blowing fuckfest. The thing was, well, I had been blaming it all on my body—and here was someone who made me look like a *Fitness* cover model in comparison. So that wasn't it. Was I so undesirable? Was this guy's saliva so much cleaner than mine?

I love to look at guys too. I appreciate handsomeness of the face, sexiness of cologne, brilliance of a smile. But when I'm with someone I really like, or love, the other men take on the quality of a very fine masterpiece I'm looking at on a museum excursion. I admire it, I enjoy looking, but I don't want to take it home with me and hang it behind my couch. If someone caught my eye I took it in, felt good about it, and put my hand on Kurt's arm to let the other person know where I belonged. I never would want the person I'm with to think that I'd want to be with anyone else but him. Kurt made me feel that way in the beginning, but things were very different now.

Now that he was making money again we'd go out to bars on occasion and he'd flirt and make suggestive comments to anything male. If he wasn't getting the attention he craved he'd do something to get it. Walking home from a trendy bar one busy Friday night, he stopped in the middle of the crowded street, flexed his arm—we were in Boys Town—boys all around us, and shouted out, "Feel my muscle!" And there were some takers and he let whoever wanted to touch him, touch him...in front of me, his lover. This gesture hurt me more than anything he could have said. He was trying to push me away. And I knew that if I wasn't there he'd invite one of them back to his place. It didn't matter if they were smart or appealing or young. They were new. They were not me. They were exciting.

And I started to walk away, as he stood standing there with some guy accessing the muscle in his arm. "Vince! Vince!" he called out after me. But he didn't follow me. I didn't have my car and had a two-mile walk back to my place, but he didn't get in his car and drive my two-mile route home to find me. There were messages from him when I arrived, but I deleted them without listening, switched off the ringer, and went to bed.

I have to be careful here. I want to be fair. I want to stress that Kurt was a good guy. You might like him. You should like him. It's just that his personality is being refracted through my pain. Maybe I'm emphasizing the bad things because they affected me in such a way. Maybe. Who knows? Aww—he *is* a nice guy. I like him. He hurt me though.

When he called me the morning following the muscle-flexing incident, I knew it was time to stop prolonging the inevitable. I felt as if I had been dragged behind the car long enough.

"What happened last night," he asked, as if stopping in the middle of the street and having other men touch you in front of your partner was the most natural thing in the world.

"I think we need to talk," I said. "Let's meet tonight."

"Can't you tell me now?" I could hear panic on his end of the line.

"I think we should talk in person."

"We can talk tonight too. But at least give me an idea of what it's about."

"I don't think we're really in the kind of relationship we started in…" I began.

Did he love me? Sure he did. I'm not that stupid. He just didn't want me in "that way" anymore. But he didn't want to let me go—completely—either.

"What are you saying?" he asked.

"I think we are very close and have a remarkable friendship." Friendship? What *was* I saying? "So no matter what happens with us I'd like to remain friends."

There was a long pause. "I don't know where this relationship is going either," he said at last. "But as long as we remain—I don't even want to call it 'friends' because what we have is so much stronger than friendship—but as long as you are in my life, always in my life, in a special way, I can deal with anything."

Of course he could "deal." I supposed he was thinking about whomever it was that he had on the side—and who he'd be free to be without the hindrance of my expectations. Now he'd have the best of both worlds. I'm sure he viewed me as a very nice warm interesting person. And certainly he recognized that I loved him more than anyone in the world. He was terrified of losing that. But at the same time he was relieved that he was free again.

"So we're not in a relationship any more…okay?" I said very softly.

"Okay," he said.

And we hung up.

So it was over. Two years. So simply. So finally.

The pain was very bad but it was not annihilating. It was not terminal. I guess I had been preparing for the break up for quite awhile—lying drugged in Kurt's bed at nights waiting for him to join me. Sprawled on the bathroom floor, cold and ridiculous at two in the morning while he slept in the bedroom a few feet away.

166

With, all that in the past, free now, I went about my activities. I continued to hand in my articles without missing a deadline. I watched *Judge Judy* in the afternoons and, through her sardonic, biting, sarcastic wisdom, I often found keys to life and behavior I had been looking for all my life. I made my bed, the way Kurt had taught me to in the mornings, and there was rarely a dirty dish in my sink.

No, the failure of this relationship was more of a steady constant hurt that I carried around with me like a wound hidden under my shirt. Some days it burned and throbbed more than others. But it was always there, alive.

I talked to my family and friends in New York telling them Kurt and I were no longer together. That was hard. I managed to cover up enough so that no one was overly concerned. "We're still close," I was sure to add.

But soon out of the relationship and into the friendship with Kurt I began to realize my mistake. He took to our "new" relationship wonderfully. After all, he already was involved with someone—it had started while I was in New York. And he couldn't wait to tell his new friend—me—about his new love.

In our first time out as "friends" we decided to go to brunch. It was a noisy place in Beverly Hills. People chatted animatedly, they dropped silverware, they called out to the waiters/actors/models for more coffee. The mannequin-like waiters were tersely polite.

Kurt told me all about the guy he had been seeing (without of course saying that the relationship had been progressing for weeks while we were still officially together). They had met on the Internet. The guy was a bit older. He was an executive in the television industry. He wanted Kurt to leave his new line of work and join him in television, where they would work together and divide their time between New York City and Los Angeles.

So Kurt went from me to the ready-made life I had once dreamed of for myself.

He couldn't intentionally be telling me this to hurt me. Could he? No, no, this was chatter amongst buddies. But what a mistake I had made in suggesting we remain close friends! Unlike me, he didn't seem to need a period of adjustment. He felt totally comfortable about the fact that we spent two years together making plans—sharing dreams and a bed—and were now simply "buds."

How was I going to deal with this kind of talk? I hadn't had time to modify my feelings. I needed time. I couldn't, I discovered, consider a man a life partner one day, and discuss his love life over omelets the next.

Changing the subject, I told him about a movie I thought he might like to see, a documentary about religious Jews who were having trouble dealing with their homosexuality. I brought a review, which I pulled out of my bag. He seemed interested. "Do you mind if I read this now?" he asked—our food had just been served.

"Not at all," I said, pleased that I knew he would be interested. I was proud of myself for knowing him so well. My Kurt.

He scanned the review and then looked up. "We should see this together," he said.

Still, I couldn't sleep that night. I relived the brunch in my head rather than imagining the wall to my crypt closing me in—a surefire way for me to fall asleep. In the morning I called him. "Look," I said, "if we're going to be friends...I'm not ready to hear about your dates. About your relationship. About the new men in your life. About the men you meet on the internet."

"Fair enough," he said. "As long as you don't tell me about yours."

I had no intention of doing that.

"Oh, by the way," I said, cheerfully, lightening the mood. "That movie we talked about is playing up the corner from me at the Lumley Theaters." There was a pause. "You know," I added, "the one about the religious Jews? The one you said you wanted to see."

Awkward silence. And then. "Oh Vince, I saw that already." He had to have seen it the night before. How quickly they forget.

I was hoping that my own depression would have the effect of me losing weight, as I had when I was feeling particularly gloomy in the past. To my horror I was actually gaining weight. I was in a tough place. I needed to find comfort wherever I could. If I wanted to eat a box of Coco Pebbles for dinner, so be it. But that wasn't enough. One of the symptoms of my sadness was a newly developed eating disorder. I'd go on late night binges, shoveling food in my mouth with something that didn't even resemble hunger, but had more to do with anger and disappointment. There was no rhyme or reason for what I consumed. A package of raw turkey hotdogs would be followed by three bowls of pasta with butter, a hunk of cheddar cheese, chased down by a jar of peanut butter.

I began to gain weight and feel awful because, as that world famous philosopher, my girlfriend Gabrielle, always said, "You can be happy and overweight but if you're depressed you simply must be thin, because to be depressed and have on extra poundage at the same time is just too awful." She was very wise. Plus she had been a model so she knew about such things.

As a man in my mid thirties—thirty-five to be exact—I hated the idea of going back to the gay bar and club scene. I had been a part of it back in New York when I was a model and twenty. I continued to be a barfly at twenty-five, even twenty-nine. But now? Well. Okay. I needed to meet someone to help me over the hump so I had to rejoin the living.

Frankly I didn't have the energy to put too much of an effort into my first night. I chose a nearby place. Actually it was the place where I first kissed Kurt—that night we met. It was no more or less difficult than anywhere else, since almost every place in the neighborhood had a memory for us by now.

Walking in, I immediately felt ill at ease. There were faces there that I recognized but had not seen since the last time I had been there, two years before. Now everyone was two years older. As I was two years older. The martini glasses were very small. Always a bad sign. Lots of the faces looked younger than mine, something I had never noticed before.

But the night started off good anyway. You know how sometimes you have a good night and everyone thinks you're really hot and the hottest guys in the world are buying you drinks and strangers are walking up to you and handing you their number scribbled on a napkin.

And then there's bad nights when you're horny as hell and willing to kiss the toadiest of toads, and even the toadiest won't come near you and you go home in tears...after spending way too much time trying to attract some toad...who goes home with the Hunchback of Notre Dame...you stay just long enough to watch them go as they throw a sneering side-glance look of triumph back at you and waltz out the door.

Well this was a good night. I was feeling good. I had been off the market for a while, but as I stood there with my teeny martini watching the fellows play pool, men who I considered quality were approaching me. I could have had any one of several—my absolute fear making me come across as exotic or mysterious. Like something they wanted to conquer. They didn't now I was already conquered. I wasn't looking for a pickup. I was looking for a nice conversation, an ego boost, a pleasant diversion.

Because I was out, and I wanted to do all there was to do, I found myself on the dance floor and a sudden clap of loud music made me feel like I had been swallowed suddenly and landed in someone's noisy digestive track. I didn't know whose. Maybe my own. Dancing was no fun tonight. Big mistake to go out with a broken heart. Someone will pick up on the vibes and sniff you out. Before long, someone did.

Here's what happened: This guy approaches me with the idea he's smarter than me. This wasn't likely considering the place I had arrived in my life in general and the bar that I was in at the moment specifically.

He's an older guy, meaning a couple of decades older than most of the guys in the bar. But well preserved in the way that—even though he has a shriveled face, and a wispy gray buzz cut, and scraggily goatee—his body is very worked out and muscular. He's about twenty-five pounds underweight but considering where we are that's considered about right—the standard

Here's where he thinks he's smarter than me: This guy wants to insult me, see? He doesn't know me but he doesn't like my look. He's got the idea that maybe I'm stuck up and I need to be knocked down a few pegs. Not true, of course. But, then, he doesn't know me as well as I do.

He wants to knock me down by hurting my feelings but to walk up to me and just insult me would make himself look bitter and mean. He is both these things but he doesn't want to admit it to himself or to other people. So, he comes up with a subtle plan to bring me down.

He walks up to me and says, "You're a very good looking guy. Really beautiful...." Blah, blah.

And I'm, you know, hooding my cow-eyes and saying things like "aw shucks" and "aren't you nice." And it's all happening really fast and the music is playing loudly, as it always does, and I'm a little high and he is very drunk and suddenly the conversation is turning...'cause when I tune in again he is saying: "...but, man, you gotta lean out." Those were his exact words: "lean out"

And now I'm really paying attention because his compliments have turned into this: "because you're a gay man, man, and this is West Hollywood, and men are really fixated on lean, hard bodies. And, oh man, you got a beautiful face...(see how clever he thinks he is... throwing in these little compliments so I don't just walk, which I would be smart and right to do) "...and, you know..." he is saying, "if you aren't making out, and you're alone, it's because guys' are turned off by your body. Now maybe you make out fine, I don't know, and if you do...you can tell me it's none of my business..." Here I try to interject "it's none of your business" but his mouth is going faster than the hoof taps of a runaway horse or something else very fast.

"If you would like," he went on, "I could work out with you everyday. I'm a personal trainer. I wouldn't charge you of course. I can whip you into shape in no time."

170

He had been holding some sort of coffee related drink with a huge cream topping. Now he licked at the topping obscenely, staring at me with a come-hither look. I didn't want to be whipped into shape by this man. He saw himself as an object of sexuality. I thought he was tragic and ugly. Would that be me someday? I didn't think so. I didn't act that way when I was twenty so why would I at sixty. Still I worried.

And basically what he wanted to do is walk up to me and say, "You're a fat pig and no one in the world wants you." Whether he believed this to be true or not isn't the point. The point was he wanted to say it.

You know what? It was one of those situations that, five minutes later, you think of everything you could have said. But in the moment you're just so...flabbergasted!

Well, see here, the thing is that after all these years I like to think that I've become pretty impenetrable when it comes to insults. Starting out at the age of zero being gay primes you for that. In high school I was the male equivalent to Stephen King's "Carrie," without the telepathic powers. "Gay boy, sissie, faggot"...and all sorts of sticks and stones like that.

But every once in awhile someone manages to be sneaky and think of a way to break through my armor and hurt hurt hurt. Now please don't think that my iddy biddy feelings got hurt because he called me fat and undesirable. I mean, I didn't have the greatest body in the world, but...just for the record...I was okay.

What knocked the damn wind out of me was the fact that he was using all of his limited intelligence thinking up schemes trying to think of a way to make me—a total stranger, mind you—feel horrible.

In my more sensitive, vulnerable, wussy moments I feel hurt that he'd want to hurt me. In my more lucid tough guy moments I think: How the fuck do you dare? Where do you get the balls to walk up to a stranger in a bar and say something like that?

Maybe I just am way too thin-skinned, maybe I just have the kind of looks that rub people the wrong way and make them want to attack...or maybe I'm the only normal fucking guy left on the planet and everyone else is wrong. I'm opting for the latter.

I left the place soon after thinking, wow, that's not going to work anymore. But I wasn't sure what to do. I came home alone to the sound of nothing—a deafening silence. Like a scream.

As if I had never asked him not to talk about his romantic life, Kurt plunged full steam ahead and continued to call me with daily updates about his new and improved life. Oh, it wasn't always improved. He was truly devastated for a week when the fling with the television producer didn't work out, meaning he would not get a free pass into the television industry, nor an apartment in New York. For a week he couldn't get out of bed and I feared a repeat depression like the last one that was so debilitating. Then what would become of him?

His depressions would come and go. I somehow felt responsible for him. Often behind his bravado was a scared little boy who clung to my love—just as I clung to his. Even after he began meeting new men.

He implied that he felt so bad that the thing with the producer didn't work out that now he felt the need to be promiscuous—to prove himself to himself. These weren't his exact words, but it's what was coming across, to me at least. I heard about each new guy he met on personal websites, or on the job, or simply driving down the street, in agonizing detail.

Many of his conversations were like baskets of figs with a serpent on the bottom. He'd start off with sweet figs, telling me about his family in Chicago, asking my opinion on the latest political development, telling me he had burned me a new CD filled with rare songs I'd love. These were the kinds of conversations I had in mind when I agreed to be friends. Eventually, I hoped, I could view him as a very special and close friend and we'd begin to talk about our love and lives. "You're the kindest person I ever met," he said. "The only person in this town who really cares for me. I never had this kind of connection with anyone else." But then would come the serpent.

"Oh I met this really hot guy who wanted me to show him a property in Beverly Hills the other day. There was an instant attraction between us—no use trying to fight it off. We started having sex right there and then in this beautiful, empty house!"

I began praying that he wouldn't go on.

"He blew me right there, I knew it was crazy—someone could have walked in at any minute—but how do you control yourself in that kind of situation? I invited him to come back to my place later that night."

I thought of his apartment, which I, not so long ago, considered my apartment. The pictures of him and me together must have been put out of sight long ago. But still there was the cream leather couch and always-vacuumed area rugs. I remembered the blue pottery barn dishes piled up in the clean, tiny kitchen, waiting for me to wash them while we finished watching some show on television, the immaculate tiled bathroom with our toothbrushes hanging side by side, and the toothpaste tube correctly squeezed from the bottom. We had been happy there. The beginning of a relationship, before all the complications set in and all the baggage is revealed, can be so very lovely.

"He wanted to lick cocaine out of my ass..." Kurt was saying.

I was wounded, but he kept right on telling me and I kept right on listening. On the one hand it made me feel like a good person—like a good friend to someone in need, a friend somewhat out of control. But when I really stripped through that enamel coating of our friendship, I realized that what I was doing was allowing myself to be a fluffer for him—the guy who keeps the porno stars dick aroused before actually filming the scene with a different model.

He knew that I didn't want to hear about him having sex with other people. But as long as he knew that it was still reaching me—even if it was through pain—he had the satisfaction of knowing that I still loved him. That made him feel secure. It stroked his ego, allowing him to go to his various lovers with a self-confidence that swelled on par with his cock. He knew that I still had feelings for him. He'd be a fool not to. Yet, when he weighed what was more important, not hurting me, or getting the rush of the ego boost, he chose the rush.

I suspected that he might use me as a weapon against his new lovers in a similar way. "This is my ex-Vincent," he would say, working in a way to whip out a photograph of me at my best. "He's a writer," he would add showing my latest article in a current magazine—letting the other know that he attracts quality and he was loved by someone of value.

Would his comments about an ex-boyfriend hurt his new boyfriend, I wondered? Or is it that I am just overly sensitive? Everyone in the world thinks they are sensitive—even more sensitive than everyone else in the world. Maybe I'm not. Maybe everyone is as hurt as things as I am. As troubled. This is something I did often—compare my own sensitivity status with those around me to check and see if I was abnormal. I was never quite sure if I was sensitive or insane. Certainly, since childhood, at various stages of my life, I had been called "neurotic."

Once, on a dinner-date with a wealthy orthopedic surgeon, I brooded because I couldn't tell if I had unintentionally insulted the waitress when I had meant to give her a compliment. The compliment was, "you have wild hair." She looked stricken. Because I had been chewing on a piece of bread at the time, ignoring the old rule not to talk with ones mouth full, I thought that maybe it came out sounding like "you have weird hair." I became so concerned with the idea that I might have hurt her feelings that the surgeon paused in his calves-liver eating to observe, "That sounds more neurotic than sensitive." This was when I was an adult, not a child. I'm not sure what an orthopedic surgeon's qualifications are for diagnosing mental disorders, but surely in his years in medical school he had been required to take a few psychology courses.

I could have cut the friendship with Kurt dead in its tracks but it was too late for that. I had already made my devil's pact when I agreed to be friends—and now I felt our lives were too intertwined to just cut my losses and move on.

The reality was, even with all his hurtful sex talk, Kurt was a good guy and I loved him as a friend. The problem: I was also *in* love with him and I couldn't separate the emotions.

He'd call me to see how I was feeling. He'd say, "Do you need a ride anywhere?" He knew well how I hated to drive. "I know how anxious you get before you interview someone—just let me know if you ever need a ride. Or if you ever need to be picked up." That was very sweet.

He'd stop by with groceries. "You never shop enough," he'd say. He'd stay for a drink and I'd put on some music and we'd relax and chat and I was reminded of how I once wanted to spend the rest of my life. "I never feel as comfortable with anyone as I do with you," he'd say.

Still, as time went by, our friendship disintegrated into Kurt mostly telling me about a series of sexcapades for which he wanted me to bear witness. I hated listening to these stories but it came with the package when I agreed to stay friends with him.

Each story was a reminder that we didn't work out. He told me these tales like a magician in a black cape and satin top hat throwing sharpened knives at me. I listened perfectly still, trying not to recoil, but they hit my heart every time, which, of course, was the target in the first place. Maybe he truly told me these things because he thought we were so close.

When defending Kurt in my mind, as was my wont at times, I thought: he thinks of me as a brother. Or a very special friend. The things he confessed to me were the kinds of subjects you'd gossip about with a brother or a pal. A brother was someone you'd flake out on seeing a movie with, if a better offer came along. A pal was someone you'd want to tell about the hot sex you had in an abandoned house. The thing was, you see, I already had brothers—mechanics living in Brooklyn—and I didn't want to hear about their sexual activities in empty houses either, if they were having any. I had close friends as well, but I wasn't in love with any of them, so that situation wasn't really comparable either.

Once I had a place in his life and I served a purpose. Now I couldn't find a place, and my purpose had become destructive to me.

"Tell him to fuck off," was the advice my friends would give me when I told them what was going on (from my point of view, of course). This was solid advice, and advice I would have given to any friend in the same situation. But being in the situation myself, I couldn't follow my line of reasoning.

What I wanted most was Kurt out of my life—at least till I could recover. This whole friendship business was affecting me to the point of causing suffocation and panic attacks. But I was so in love, so concerned with trying not to hurt his feelings that I totally forgot about hurting my own. I continually allowed him to, and yet I had no one else to blame because I set myself up for it and there were no orthopedic surgeons around to label me neurotic.

I stopped returning Kurt's calls. I thought he'd get the message and leave me alone. But no, no, he continued to call me several times a day. "You never call me anymore," he'd say. I loved the idea that he still wanted me to call, but I hated the idea of what he'd want to talk about. The dilemma was that although his calls did indeed hurt me—very much—when I didn't hear from him I missed him—or at least the Kurt I once knew. Which was worse? This temporary, pathetic faux friendship or not having him at all? I couldn't tell. It would take strength, a tremendous amount of strength, to tell him "Fuck off." I didn't have that kind of strength yet.

But the hits just kept on coming. Once he called with a particularly vicious snake at the bottom of his gift basket of figs:

"Remember the day after the first night we spent together?" he asked.

"Yes," (a whisper).

"Remember there was some guy who I had a date with who I had exchanged emails with on the computer and I cancelled from your place after spending the night with you? Well he answered my personal ad again, not remembering my face but maybe I shouldn't be telling you this, Vince?"

I could not speak. He might as well have been strangling me with his necktie.

I would get off the phone and wonder what to do with my loneliness. I could take it to a bar, but it would only get drunk with me and we'd end up doing something seedy that we'd regret completely in the morning.

I dreaded his calls yet spent my days waiting for the phone to ring, so I switched off the ringer—beating it at its own game. Sometimes when I thought I'd have something to say, I switched the phone back on. It would start ringing immediately. The person on the other end—usually Gabrielle—would say how difficult I was to get a hold of. Now that I was able to talk, I'd yammer on and on...and Gabrielle, would think what I was saying was amusing. Although most of my conversation was about how unamused I was.

Afterwards I'd go to my bed to recuperate. I asked God to join me there. I'm sure He came and He helped me a lot, but the relationship wasn't physical and He didn't wear cologne.

I kept on seeing Kurt. Each time, I guess, in the back of my head was the hope that he'd realize that he still loved me. How could I still feel so strongly while his feelings had changed so much? Eventually he'd see that we were meant for each other and things would go back to the way they were.

Occasionally when we were out I'd be astonished when we ran into one of the boyfriends he had been taunting me with. They weren't the strapping, masculine, assured studs I had imagined. Each time I was confronted with frail, prissy, little numbers—slightly passed their prime. The type of guy who had been taunted in the schoolyard, but instead of retaliating by growing up to be kind and brilliant, they remained shallow bitchy and whiny. Although they never fulfilled their dreams of becoming Madonna, they did make some money by sticking with the same job for many years. They were able to get by in Boy's Town year after year by relying on their diminishing boyishness. In a few years, though, they would have to depend on their money in order to remain in that scene.

Since they weren't men who had any qualities I neither wanted nor desired, I tried to name what I was feeling. A distant cousin to jealousy—disappointment and anger. I was certainly humiliated.

Once at a popular outdoor bar we met one of Kurt's "last week" boyfriends. Kurt introduced him as Tripp. They talked stiffly for several minutes, as Tripp looked me up and down. He prattled on about an article that recently appeared in a gay magazine about his new business (a facial spa), and the amount of phone calls he received asking him out for dates because of the published photograph accompanying the piece. We listened politely.

"I know you from somewhere," Tripp said to me when he finished talking about the article. Kurt glanced at me with renewed curiosity, and then returned his attention to the bartender who was provocatively shaking a martini, not wearing a shirt, smiling, and appearing oblivious, all at the same time.

"I don't think so," I replied.

We all turned our attention to the bartender. "I thought that he was interested in me when I ordered my martini," Tripp said, "He was really coming on to me. But then you never know with people." You never know with people! I thought that was wise beyond his intelligence.

While Kurt wasn't looking, Tripp handed me his business card, which I later tore up—I was already trapped enough in this quagmire.

Another night, at dinner with Kurt in a Chinese restaurant he said out of the blue, "Did I tell you about Tommy?"

And I braced myself for the snake. There were no figs anymore—our conversations had become baskets of snakes with an occasional fig thrown

176

in. "Tommy is in college and he is under a lot of stress," he said "and I help him."

I knew what was expected of me in the friendship, so I played the role—after all I had allowed myself to be cast in the role so I had to go through with it.

"Help him how?" I asked, putting my acting skills to use and sounding genuinely bewildered.

"Well, like I said, he's under a lot of stress and I, you know, help him...release it"

"I see."

"Don't you think it's unusual for a forty-two-year-old man to be fucking a twenty-four year old?"

"No, I don't."

It was hard to believe this was the same person I had loved. This was a completely different dimension to the man who had brought me loaves of bread and olives when we first met. Sometimes he seemed like a stranger I didn't even like. If this had been the character he had presented when we were first getting to know each other, we would have never had become friends, let alone shared a bed. And I mourned the loss of my lover and my friend.

After many drinks at the Chinese restaurant, Kurt was going to drive me home, but on the way he decided he wanted to stop for one more drink. Ironically, or maybe not, he chose the bar where we first kissed, the bar where I had recently been insulted by a treacherous goat. I hated the place now, but as painful as my relationship with Kurt had become, I was rather fascinated by all the twists and turns and curious to see how it would play out.

He brought us our drinks and we stood there, in the back of the bar, looking at each other. Once I thought I'd never run out of things to say to him. Now I couldn't think of a single word.

Suddenly he kissed me.

I stepped back startled—as surprised as he had been when I kissed him that first night we had stumbled in here after our initial meeting.

"Do you still love me?" he asked. My mind was racing for the correct thing to say, but all the while I remained speechless.

Finally I said: "In a different way now."

He looked at me with something that I interpreted as anger.

"Come on he said," swallowing his drink in a few quick gulps. "I'll take you home."

When we pulled up in front of my apartment I was one very confused boy. Actually I usually don't like it when men over twenty-five call themselves "boy"—but sometimes it's appropriate, although usually it's when under a muscular, hulking, cigar-chomping brute.

"Do you want to come in and talk?" I asked.

He did. But when we couldn't find a parking space, even after he envisioned one in his head, we both began to feel tired. Eventually we tried to squeeze into a spot between two cars and couldn't. We switched places, I got on the drivers side, and I nicked the back of his car trying to park it in the too-small spot. We both decided it was too late and we were too drunk and it was better if he went home.

Needless to say I entered my apartment in an extremely agitated state. I looked at myself in the mirror and saw myself for what I was: The type of guy who had been taunted in the schoolyard. But, I thought, instead of retaliating by growing up to be kind and brilliant I remained shallow, bitchy and whiney. What to do? I could have gone online and found sex in a minute but I wasn't horny in that way

During various crisis phases in my life, sometimes one old movie or another comes to weigh heavily on my mind when I associated my predicament with a particular film. If I could not think of any films the situation paralleled, I usually could find a similarity in an *I Love Lucy* episode. This time, however it was not Lucy I related to but a movie entitled *Gilda*—a 1948 *film noir* set in Argentina.

In the movie, the fetching Rita Hayworth plays Gilda. Glen Ford is Johnny, a man utterly obsessed with Gilda, but for reasons too complicated to explain here, they pretend not to love each other, instead opting to hate each other with a sizzling passion.

They flirt. They insult. They say one thing to each other, while meaning something else. They are always one-upping each other when it comes to trying to see who has the ability to hurt more.

Gilda has married another man who Johnny had also been flirting with (extremely daring for a movie made in the 1940s). When her new husband mysteriously disappears, Gilda and Johnny get together at last—then he suddenly deserts her. Finally she has had enough of all of this pretending and she tries to get away from Johnny. She flees Argentina, but Johnny, who has become a powerful man, keeps finding her and bringing her back until she collapses to a heap on the floor in front of him, clinging to his legs begging him to "Please let me go. I can't stand it any more! I don't want anything from you. Just please...let me go."

And it's those lines—going through my head each night over and over again—that made me feel like Gilda, even though she was a woman and I was a man and this was Los Angeles rather than Argentina. Still, like the character in the movie, I didn't know what Kurt and I were feeling for each

178

other anymore. We weren't lovers and it wasn't really a friendship, and I was tired of pretending and tired of trying to figure out what it was—I just wanted to be let go.

"Please let me go." I whispered in my bed that night. There wasn't anyone there to hear me. I just thought I'd put it out there into the universe to see where it got me. It got me nowhere fast and after a few days I realized I had to do something.

Unlike Gilda, however, I did not throw myself at Kurt's feet and beg him to let me go. Instead, I decided to try my own version of Gilda's plaintive plea with Kurt and one morning, without warning (even to myself), I called him. I knew I wouldn't be able to stand to look at any pain on his face. He was in the car.

"I need a break. I think we shouldn't see each other for awhile," I said very quickly.

I could hear his speeded-up breathing on the other end.

"And not talk to each other," I continued. "And maybe we shouldn't even email."

"Why do you feel that way?" His voice was hoarse and low.

"I'm not saying we can't *ever* be friends. That we can't be in each other's lives some day. But right now I'm having a hard time adjusting to the friendship thing. You have a new life and I can't really find my place in it. Maybe when things settle down for me...when I feel comfortable in my own skin...we could find our way."

I could hear that he was crying quietly. "How long are we talking about?"

"In six months," I added quickly, "we can meet for dinner. Everything will be different then. And I can see us through new eyes."

"I understand how you feel," he said sadly. "And I'll respect whatever you want to do."

In the movie *Gilda*, after Gilda falls to the floor in a wasted heap of crumpled, glamorous flesh—begging Johnny to let her go—he scorns her claiming that he will never let her escape him, yet he will never want her and he won't allow her to be with other men either. Johnny makes Gilda believe she is forever trapped in his apathetic limbo and the scene ends with her defeated—lying and crying and quivering at his feet. But Gilda is much too gorgeous, sexy, and fiery to let that stop her. To reach Johnny where he lives, in the very next scene, she triumphantly appears at the club he owns and operates. She has pasted herself back together, makeup fastidious, her beautiful hair hanging densely to her magnificent shoulders. She is wearing a strapless black satin evening gown with elbow length gloves. Prancing confidently onto the nightclub's stage she sings *Put the Blame on Mame*

Boys, doing a mock strip tease, peeling off her gloves, tossing around her unbelievable mane of red hair (in glorious black and white) and completely bewitching the audience, while Johnny simmers in her afterglow. Because everyone else in the world wants her so badly, so furious and turned on is he, that Johnny has her dragged off the stage, into a corner where he slaps her. But she's made her point. Marvelously.

It seemed that Kurt was going to let me go without the dramatics of this classic film. I was simultaneously relieved and heartbroken. Kurt would go on with his life and I would move on to find what glamour and excitement I could. With one uncomfortable, semi-poignant phone call it seemed I was able to make my escape.

But several weeks later, on that fateful day in January, he called me with the slap in the face. "I met someone else and I'm moving in with him," he said. It was my turn to crumple to the floor again.

It must take a tremendous feeling of love and solidarity to make the decision to move in with someone after a couple of months. Kurt and I had been together for two years and never got around to actually go out condo hunting—although we had talked about it on and off throughout. Of course I was injured. It's no fun thinking of yourself as a two year pit stop. Was I so replaceable?

He went on talking about the new place. The great neighborhood. The big rooms. "And I finally bought a dining room table," he said. "At last I can eat like an adult." I'm positive he wasn't saying it to hurt me, but the nights we sat in front of the television set with trays in our laps flashed before me with useless clarity. It had been one of the happiest times of my life.

I wished him well, and I meant it too. Kurt really didn't do anything wrong, except fall out of love with me and in love with someone else. And that's not a crime. In my heart I truly wished him happiness. I loved him. And I also felt a bit of resolution. I had no responsibility towards him—or anyone else for that matter. Maybe now I really could be free. But I was also terribly alone.

Although Kurt had once again one-upped me, I did not feel the need to go out and sing a seductive song in a sultry way in front of him at a neighborhood nightclub. I had already degraded myself enough and, besides, my body wasn't in as good condition as Rita Hayworth's was at the time of the making of *Gilda*.

This was another thing that worried me. The insult from that stranger at the bar was never far from my mind. As my friend Gabrielle had always counseled—it is imperative to remain thin during a crisis. If you are starting a new life it's better to do it with a better body. But there I went think-

180

ing about things too much again. At the moment I had to book a flight for a visit to New York—to heal. To stir up the energy to start over. There was a new life to plan, a self to recast, preferably in something light and frothy, in glorious Technicolor—I had done enough drifting through black and white *film noirs* for the time being. Those dark, dangerous things.

4. NEWNESS

I want to tell you about my terribly exciting weekend.

A simple letter from an old boyfriend is what led up to it. I had already booked a visit to New York and was sort of counting the days. There were three days left before my flight, when I received the letter from Jared. It was a shock to my already mixed up system. I hadn't heard from Jared in a couple of years. Jared was my first love—our relationship had begun many years before when I was just a kid really. He was approximately twenty years older. I never knew for sure. Although it wouldn't have made a difference, he would never tell me his age.

Because I spent much of my childhood feeling so dim-witted and worthless—so much so that I could hardly string two coherent sentences together at the time that we met—an overly confident, Harvard educated billionaire was just the medicine I thought I needed to boost my confidence and help me work my way towards mental health. And I truly fell for him, unable to understand that there was absolutely no future for us.

Once, in a flash moment of complete sobriety while being very drunk, I realized that ever since Jared—every man who has held my attention had has this incurable desire for all that is new. Currently these guys are called "players." This was an unfortunate type for me to choose because, even back then, I was very much a romantic. Yet, because Jared was the specific type I wanted to have a romance with, I could never be successful. I was unable to win my competition with newness for Jared's affections. He always opted for the unopened goodies.

The clue to the pattern of our relationship should have been in the place we met, which was a hustler bar in Manhattan. The place had a tawdry elegance that, at the time, I mistook for sophistication. The kind of place that uses shiny surfaces—chrome and mirrors—the way old time bordellos used crushed red velvet and crystal chandeliers.

This was a bar where delicious boy delicacies could be bought like items on a first class menu. After you tire of a particular dish, you could go back another night and order entirely different entree with a flavor tantalizingly not the same. Jared would have happily kept me a leftover in some corner of his refrigerator, probably for years or forever, if I would have turned my face blindly to the new items that he'd continue to order up and sample with annoying regularity. Whatever budding ego I had, however, wouldn't allow that. Even back then I wanted some sort of integrity involved in my relationships.

He refused to commit, broke my heart, and we both moved on. After we were over, we kept in touch sporadically. For the first few years after meeting him I didn't want anyone else. Well, at least not for very long. We'd run into each other at a bar and start talking and before you knew it we'd have plans to grab a bite to eat and see a movie. I loved him in that "first love—blind-to-all-else" way.

Occasionally he would call me out of the blue and I'd be excited. He wanted me back. He'd impress me by taking me to a fancy restaurant and the symphony, but soon the same relationship that we started out with would repeat itself. We'd end it on a bad note. His game with me always remained the same. He viewed me as an intriguing and appealing side dish that would be nice to keep around, but whenever it seemed like I was getting too close and our relationship was becoming too "real," he'd do something so appalling and I was forced to flee. I think he was relieved when I did. He had escaped the clutches of love again. Love is something he found both seductive and grotesque. For him love was something better to hunger for rather than actually have.

Once—during one of our "on again" times—I was meeting him for dinner. I arrived at his majestic apartment building, naturally expecting to be sent right up. I remember the doorman telling me, "Mr. Grey is in the shower. He asked that you take a seat and wait for him here." Me? Vince? Wait in the lobby? Had this doorman confused me with one of Mr. Grey's takeout callboys? I, who had been in that apartment hundreds of times through the years, slept in the bed, taken showers, eaten breakfasts, was being asked to wait downstairs for Mr. Grey to appear? I was no longer a self-conscious kid (about twenty-five by this time), yet, for about a half a second, I actually considered waiting on one of the sumptuous, velvet covered love seats in the lobby. Confused and embarrassed, I looked around.

This was the kind of building that had many doormen—opening doors, accepting packages, greeting dog-walking tenants. Various celebrities—from both the movie and sports worlds—lived on various floors. Each floor was an entire apartment. You were given a credit card like key and put it in the elevator and the elevator would automatically stop on the correct floor, which would open to a sprawling apartment with magnificent views of Central Park West.

The doormen and the celebrities had all come to recognize me over the course of time. Now I realized that, in their eyes, I wasn't something special in Jared's life. I was just one of many. I suppose that was the truth. If I could only see myself through a doorman's eyes!

"Oh the humiliation," I remember thinking on the subway ride home. (Ultimately I simply turned around and walked away without comment, the doorman calling after me, "What shall I tell Mr. Grey?").

I came home to a number of messages from Jared: "What happened? I told the doorman to send you right up! He said you left without a word!" See? Part of the game that Jared played so well was to make it seem like I was a nut case. That each failure was my fault. Actually I *was* nutty—for allowing it to happen to me over and over—with Jared, and all the men I met who were cut from his cloth

I had never been able to breakthrough and make Jared love me completely. And now, at this susceptible period in my life, he had contacted me again.

"I would like to see you the next time you're in New York," the letter said. It was hand-written on his fancy, pale blue, engraved stationary. Everything about Jared exuded his station in life—which was a high-end, successful, tycoon. He made his fortune in Manhattan real estate. Now Kurt, who shared many qualities with Jared, was making a fortune in real estate. It seemed like karma that he would be in touch with me at this juncture.

As I carried the letter with me from room to room, reading and re-reading the few lines, I began thinking about Jared and it all seemed to fall into place.

The bad qualities of Jared spilled out onto the coming years of my life, staining everything. Even if I didn't notice it at first, I now realized that all the men who held my interest—Kurt included—had some of the main characteristics that made up Jared. He had been the prototype. I spent many years trying to recreate him in others—shackled to an image. Trying to beat newness at its own game. To make the Jared-prototype forget about all the others, at least resist them, because I wanted each one to feel that what we had was worth preserving with dignity. I think I felt if I could conquer those "player" characteristics now, in another man, I could win. I could be at peace with myself. My love life could work.

Such was my obsession with winning that, if I was involved with some good man and love came too easily, I stupidly rejected it. I wanted it to be a competition and I wanted to win. Whenever a man has loved my fully, treated me well, and was, in essence, perfect partner material, I'd quickly grow bored and restless. I figured there must have been something wrong with him if he loved me. How dumb I had been! How clear it all was now!

This is not a phenomenon unique to me. I've heard various people discuss their heartaches with various distressing anecdotes. It's Cupid's sick little sense of humor that makes him shoot his golden arrows into the heart of the sensitive ones, making sure they fall for the ones with the capacity to hurt them the most. Maybe Cupid sees this as a learning experience and growth potential. I say enough is enough.

Yet the letter from Jared affected me. What if he had been the one all along? What if I had been trying to recreate the man who had been the real soul-mate but our timing had been off? We were in a new time. I was in a new space. Perhaps Jared was too.

I dialed Jared's number with the intention of telling him I could meet with him the following week, which was the equivalent to putting on a strapless black satin evening gown and elbow length gloves and singing *Put the Blame on Mame.*

"Jared? It's funny I got you're letter today," I said. "I'll be in New York next week."

"Vince! How wonderful. We must get together for dinner! Hold on a sec, let me check my appointment book." (Pause. Rustling pages) "How's Wednesday?"

I had nothing planned for my trip back to New York other than flopping into my childhood bed in my parents' house for an indefinite period of time. I used their place like a hospital, only better: the food was great and the staff loved me.

"Wednesday would be terrific."

Yeah, I could have, should have, pretended to check my own schedule but, hey, weren't we adults by now? There was no need for foolish games. I was available.

"Come over at my place at eight and we'll have a drink first," he said.

I was lightheaded with the thought of seeing Jared. What would have happened had our affair worked out and we stayed together, was something I couldn't stop thinking about. Would I hate him as much as I do? Would I love him as much as I do?

The one you love first always makes an imprint. All the others that come after will have to, in some ways, match up to the first one. So when the original comes back into your life, it's too much of a temptation to try and win this time, because it's sort of like trumping all the others.

I spent the first couple of days at my parents house recuperating. Lying in my bed re-reading the books that had taught me so much when I was a teenager. My parents knew something was up. That I was down. They were used to my moods. They had picked up on my depressive state from the anguished tone in my voice and my general lethargy when they called and checked on me in LA. "Don't do anything to break our hearts," my father had said during one conversation when he picked up heavy doses of grief in my chatter. That comment broke my heart.

The last time my mother had asked about Kurt I said, "We're not in each other's lives anymore," and left it at that. While I was staying with them, she knew enough not to probe further.

I was concentrating on diet and exercise. When I first met Jared I was an actor and I was modeling a little and was in pretty good shape and considered quite a dish although I was too stupid and to low on self esteem to appreciate it at the time. I was 170 pounds. I had gained some weight, since my heyday of twenty. Oh, I was still considered a dish by some but I *never* felt it now. Mostly because I currently lived in West Hollywood, which made me even stupider and made my self esteem even lower than when I was a kid.

After I broke up with Kurt I had to put my energy into survival. I didn't have the will to exercise. I didn't have the want to eat healthy. Instead I chose to eat cookie dough ice cream for dinner, and make grilled cheese sandwiches at 3 A.M. I was tipping the scales at 185. In the gay scene it is absolutely unacceptable to have an extra fifteen pounds, a little beer gut, or to be slightly out of shape in any way shape or form. I always found this sad, since I personally don't mind if my lover's body isn't "International Male" catalog perfect. Sometimes it's the very imperfection that I find appealing and sexy; the flaw endears him to me, because it's something that is his alone.

After thirty, you might be able to get away with a slight beer belly or a hint of love handles if you are very rich or famous or both. But the chances are if you are rich or famous you won't have either because you have the money to hire an expensive trainer at a trendy gym, have excellent exercise equipment at home, and to have the plastic surgery required.

Now I had a major reason to whip myself into shape. I had started on the road back to health by pure starvation in the days before I left Los Angeles. In New York, I asked my mother to make me small portions of steamed vegetables and brown rice for dinner. That was all I ate—all day. I jogged for several miles every night. I exercised with the free weights leftover from my youth. I didn't expect a miracle. But luckily I could shape up fairly quickly. Still, what used to take a few weeks now took months. By Wednesday night, the night for my meeting with Jared, I weighed in at 178. Not perfect, but better. Everything seemed a little better.

I know, I know, I wanted to tell you about my weekend. I'm getting there. This must be the longest set up you've ever read for a story—but sometimes the anticipation is even more satisfying than the real event.

When getting anywhere in New York you have to take a lot of things into consideration about how you will look by the time you get to where you're going. If you look a hundred percent perfection when you leave the front door you have to factor in elementary factors: if it's raining, the humidity level, if it's over sixty-five degrees, and if you'll be taking the subway to get to your destination.

Conditions were favorable that night weather-wise. We were having an unusually mild February and it was a cool fifty-five degrees, low humidity, no rain. But—and this is no small "but,"—I would be taking the subway to Manhattan from my parents place in Brooklyn.

The gods of New York were smiling on me for a change. With the favorable weather conditions, and a ride from my Dad, I arrived at the subway platform pretty much intact. While waiting for the train, I noticed a young girl, about twenty, watching me as I walked down the platform in her direction. She was very pretty with her perm and blush.

"Do you have fifty cents," she asked.

"Yes, thanks for asking," I replied, breezing passed her. I always gave my spare change to the elderly or infirmed. Did God look askance at me because I wasn't an equal opportunity giver? Perhaps this sweet young thing was actually God in disguise trying to trip me up. I thought of that old song *What if God Was One of Us?* I didn't want to spend too much energy worrying about it, but I did want to score brownie points with God. I could take no chances. I called out to the girl. She turned and approached me with a look as blank as a sheet of Xerox paper. "Here," I said, handing her a dollar. "For your Victoria's Secret fund."

The good deed paid off. The subway was quick in coming, not crowded. I took a seat, un-harried, somewhat calm. I was still at about ninety-eight percent of as good as I could look

I took a seat. On the New York subways the people spread their legs wide and look at you like they want you dead. Just as the doors were beginning to close a gang of rowdy kids ran into the car in a rattle of distraction. Drinking orange pop. Holding the doors open for more friends as they ran down the subway steps. The signal bells were going nuts—off on, off on. I felt queasy. The doors were trying to close. They were delaying the rest of us. Giggling.

I was nervous—excited about seeing Jared but I still couldn't get Kurt out of my mind. The conductor mumbled something about letting go. The high-spirited kids herded into the car and found seats. The doors closed. We were on our way. "Close your eyes," I commanded myself. "No looking at the doors opening and closing, opening and closing."

The doors closed. I opened the newspaper to see what New York was up to. The same old scandals. Politicians in extra-marital affairs. Movie-Star-Couple breakups. Some songstress exposing her nipples on a cable award show. I turned the page. The usual assortment of rapes, murders, and new reality television shows. My horoscope, on the other hand, was interesting: "A friend may need you more than you thought. Saying 'no' once in a while doesn't make you a bad person. When people act strangely, don't take it personally. Distance yourself—it could be a healthy reaction."

I didn't really believe the horoscopes in the New York daily newspapers. After many years of research I now knew that only the *TV Guide* horoscope and the inside of fortune cookies told the truth. All other forms of astrology were pretty much hit or miss. You had to wait and see.

When I got off the subway I still had time to get a mid-town drink. Actually I had planned it that way. I knew the exact concoction of Scotch and Xanax that would put me in the perfect personality mode for Jared. For my pre-dinner location, I chose a nicely decorated, spacious, somewhat fancy midtown piano bar. The *très chic* decor, however, was misleading. The clientele was varied. Sure there was plenty of what I called "after business mints": handsome professionals in expensive suits. But there were many other characters as well: rough trade, flaming queens, artistic Madison Avenue types, blue collar guys, hustlers, and preppy collage boys. Everyone mixed splendidly together and it usually made for an interesting cocktail hour.

As soon as I walked through the door, even before I had time to take the Xanax out of my wallet, an older gentleman who looked and sounded like a 1970s version of Lauren Bacall with red hair approached me. I had about an hour to kill before I had to head up to Jared's Upper West Side apartment. I was up for anything.

"Do you have plans for later, young man?" he asked.

"I'm having dinner with a friend," I replied.

"Well I would hope so!" he said, tossing his flame, pageboy. "You don't want to have dinner with enemies—they'll think you're trying to sell them something."

I smiled and continued towards the bar drinking it all in again. So many familiar faces. There was Daryl talking his trashy philosophies and picking up older men. I took out my Xanax and popped it like a breath mint. After I ordered my drink I also noticed that Beth was still hanging around the bar. Beth was a lonely, Jewish, sixty-five-year-old widow who, in her mature years, decided to turn herself into a fag hag. For years she liked to hang out in gay bars and coffee shops and engage sympathetic homosexual men in LONG conversations, spending the evening telling them her sad sack stories. One unhappy night, years before, I fit the bill and listened to the vignettes that made up her life, including a recent trip to Atlantic City: "I hate to travel alone but what could I do? I have no one. My children? Ha! I'm lucky if I get a card on Mother's Day. You take a chance..." It made me miserable and impatient. Now I noticed she had trapped someone who had obviously been her captive before. Her mouth was spewing out a steady stream of unhappiness, while his eyes frantically roamed the room, looking for an escape hatch.

I slinked by, rattling my ice.

"That one," a man said to his companion as I passed.

"Which one," the other asked.

Then, through the corner of my eye, I saw him see me. "Oh! Him! Yeah!" he exclaimed. "I noticed when he walked in!"

This was like the old days. Before I moved to Los Angeles. It was a good idea to come here before seeing Jared. I wasn't *that* beautiful, but the New York crowd made me feel as if I were. Some trick God played in my favor made them view me as one of the most interesting and desirable guys in the room, which I was grateful for. Usually I felt God's tricks were not in my favor.

"Life is a cabaret old chum," the piano player sang with a chorus of chorus boys. And I had to admit, I do love a cabaret. Every time I took a few steps I was drawn in to another conversation. Being back in familiar surroundings, I remembered how much I enjoyed witty repartee.

The place was crowded and jolly and men grabbed me by he waist as they squeezed passed and copped an extra feel or patted me on the ass—behavior that could sometimes be annoying but was medicine I needed on this particular night.

Everyone wanted to touch my body—even though it wasn't that great. A power that I used fraudulently. Everyone wanted to meet me and know me. They smiled at me and I relished the return of the muscle of confidence that Kurt had stripped of me recently. A youngish Latino guy pointed me out to his older Caucasian boyfriend—a man who looked like Dracula. A few minutes later they approached me and invited me into a threesome, which I smilingly declined.

Even though I felt I wasn't in my prime—unsettling stories on the evening news, miserable Internet dates, heartbreak, and time had all taken their toll—I still had "it" and that was important to me. At this age I wasn't going to be getting any better looking. It was probably down hill all the way from here.

"Luck be a lady tonight..." the piano player began.

Feeling cocky and sure—which is something that does not mesh well with my true personality at all—I approached the only one who seemed not to be paying any attention to me at all. In fairness to myself, he wasn't paying attention to anyone. Facing the door, he watched anyone who entered with an intense stare, then looked down at his drink again. He had eyes similar to Kurt's—brown and thickly lashed. I had to meet him.

He was wearing a white dress shirt open at the neck. I rarely have the guts to approach anyone but the Xanax and alcohol urged me on and I figured fashion is always a safe topic.

"I like the way that white shirt with the black sports jacket looks on you," I blathered. "I saw it the other night on a news anchorman on the sports channel and I thought, 'it looks so good I'll wear it the next time I go out, if I have a tan.'"

He looked at me with a brilliant, tile-white smile that clearly conveyed, "Please leave me alone" and amazingly still managed to be a smile anyway.

"Let's keep the party polite..." the piano player sang in his Sinatraesque voice.

I smiled back sincerely, said, "You're welcome," and turned, leaving him to whatever he was waiting for. I had meant my comment and didn't regret saying it. I know that at times I come off as snotty and aloof, and sometimes people give me a compliment anyway. And that always means a lot.

I wanted another drink but the bar was mobbed and the waiters had gone on vacation.

Beth, the gloomy widow/fag-hag, had trapped another victim in her web of despair. Obviously he too had been snagged before. They were standing a few feet away.

"I don't want to hear anything bad," he exclaimed. "Tell me about the last show you saw."

"I couldn't remember," she said grimly.

"The last movie!"

"I haven't seen any."

"About how happy your life has been!"

"Well it hasn't been happy. But it's a life...."

"Why do you come out, Beth?" he asked her, finally. She could tell by his tone he was getting annoyed.

"I'm just looking for a date," she said.

"You think you're going to get a date here?" he asked incredulously.

"Oh you never know. It's better than the senior citizen dances at the Y." Now, in the hopes of holding him in conversation, she had a big, dentured smile and was trying to make her chatter bright, but her loneliness was so substantial that my body received it physically rather than emotionally.

I glanced down at my watch. Oh my! How time does fly when you're having interesting experiences. I had to leave right now in order to continue the festivities with Jared.

It was seven forty-five and I was meeting Jared at eight. What I didn't take into consideration was the not-able-to-get-a-cab factor. Standing on a corner trying to flag down a cab—and they're all occupied—fifteen minutes before your destination arrival time, is bound to knock down a few points in your level of attractiveness. Buses passed spewing me with heavy gray exhaust fumes. Cars were everywhere. Vultures! They swarmed and looked for parking places. What happened to the city? Usually, in all the years I lived in New York, I could get a cab easily at seven forty-five PM. I don't know. I don't know. It was cool but I was beginning to sweat, as various percentage points were being shaved off of my looking-good chart.

At last a limousine pulled up. The accented guy (Israeli?) said he would take me across the park for twenty-five bucks. More than double it would cost to take a cab. But it was after eight and I had no choice. I was already down to eighty-five percent of looking my best.

The limo driver was unusually chatty. He was either hitting on me or he thought I was rich enough to afford riding around in limousines and was a possible steady client. He gave me his business card. He wanted to know where I lived. What I did for a living. My name. He was attractive and had a comfortable way to get around the city but I was going to meet Jared for god sakes. Other men didn't matter at the moment.

We pulled up in front of Jared's imposing building. The limo driver was impressed. Hell, I was impressed again. I was forced to revisit my initial attraction. Surely the comfortable safe haven Jared represented had always been part of his substantial appeal. But the night I met him, at that hustler bar, I didn't know anything about him. I was attracted simply because of the way he looked. The way he spoke. Certainly he must have been giving off success vibes, and that drew me in. But I had no idea of his wealth and power. I think that if he had turned out to be a mildly successful insurance salesman I would have felt the same.

I slammed the limo door and, once again, headed towards Jared. I looked about 83 percent. Perhaps I could primp a bit in the elevator.

The doormen greeted me with the same haughty air I remembered, but the one at the desk didn't ask me to wait. He told me to go right up. Cocooned in the elevator I quickly ran a brush through my hair and blotted my face with a tissue (I would have used some blot powder but I knew the doormen were watching me on the monitors). Then the bell rang.

The door opened and there stood the culprit. He looked terrific. Jared had to be at least in his mid fifties by now, but he looked almost exactly the same as the first time I met him over fifteen years earlier. The last time I saw him, several years before, although I was still mad with that "first-love" madness, I could see that he had started to deteriorate with the hanging flesh and paunch that awaits everyone. Now I accessed his plastic surgery. A facelift. Liposuction under the chin. Hair transplant or weave. And, I'm certain, whatever other modern, fountain-of-youth procedures that lots of money could buy

Jared always had a certain masculine, corporate businessman appeal. If Kurt looked like a sports correspondent on ESPN, Jared had the quality of a senior news anchorman on CNN. Or he could have been your best friend's successful father getting ready to run for political office. The debonair guy sitting at the next table at an expensive restaurant, ordering his dinner in arrogant detail. The sophisticated and sexy uncle you burned for as a child.

We hugged a bit awkwardly, but he held the embrace and it grew welcoming.

"You look wonderful," I said.

"No, no—you look wonderful! It's so good to see you."

He poured us drinks, and we sat on the fawn-color, suede sofa. Jared redecorates every other year or so. Last time I had been here it was in various shades of white and eggshell. Now everything was done tastefully in beiges and tans and light earth tones. There was an elaborate mirrored bar I didn't recognize and some striking, new modern art paintings. Another difference I noticed was that there were photos of his mother all over the place.

"She died," he explained. And I saw a look of real love, longing, and sadness cloud his eyes. Funny, he had never talked about his mother much before. "She had been suffering from Alzheimer's for years. But she was wonderful to the end."

Now she was gone, out of reach, and she had achieved that special place in the heart that only the unattainable can inhabit.

We sat there like two mature adults with complicated histories. There was a formal feeling, yet a genuine pleasure shimmered between us, the delight to be in each other's company again. He asked me about my work. He commented on some of my recent articles, which he had read. He made flattering comments about my appearance. "You're still so sexy," he said.

Eventually, he asked if I had been seeing anyone. I explained my two year relationship with Kurt thusly: "I was seeing a guy from Chicago for awhile—we were very close but...it didn't work out. He was a nice guy. You would have liked him. Very sharp. A lot like you, actually. He's in the real estate business too."

Jared didn't ask for any more details and I didn't offer any. Instead he launched into a story about an "affair," he had been involved in for a number of years. "He's an Asian doctor, which was interesting to me because I'd never been attracted to Asians before, but I saw him at a gallery art showing and there was an immediate attraction. We began talking and soon his lover joined us. During the course of the conversation I discovered that they had been together for many years."

"How old is he," I asked.

"Oh, Jim is in his late thirties. His lover is somewhat older. The physical attraction between us continued to develop and grow throughout the evening. To avoid suspicion I gave them both my business card, but it was obvious where my real interest was. I had dinner with the two of them soon after, but shortly after that, Jim and I began seeing each other."

Immediately I wished I could meet Jim. I wanted to observe the attributes he possessed to capture the heart of a man I had given my very best to, on and off, throughout my adulthood. But when I thought about it, sipping my scotch, I understood perfectly why this particular relationship had worked for so long. Jim, the partnered doctor, would rarely be available. He had to be on call for patients, and accessible to his long time partner. He and Jared probably snuck around clandestinely for years—a dinner here, a night together there. Perhaps a weekend when they could both arrange it. His unavailability—the gaps in the time they saw each other—allowed him to continuously renew himself. He was always exciting because he was never permanent. I took note of this. An important tip for future reference.

"Finally, I gave him an ultimatum," Jared continued. "His lover or me. And although he loved me very much by this time, he explained that he and Lloyd had been together for too many years to walk away from each other. So we agreed not to see each other any more."

This was Jared's version of the facts. I wondered what Jim's were. I felt somewhat jealous, but fairly certain, that if Jim had left his lover and chose Jared, in time Jared would have grown tired of him and the two of us would now be sitting exactly where we were. But who the hell was I to think that? I didn't know everything. I didn't even know anything. It was my ego chiming in, trying to placate me and make me feel that, if Jared couldn't love me, he couldn't possibly love anyone else.

There was something about me—something in me—that made Jared not want me completely. I never could clearly identify this something. My best deduction was that it was because, from the very beginning, I truly wanted him. I was won over too easily. Everything seemed to be in place for a long-term relationship, but I never made him have to work at winning me. So, no matter how much he liked me, somewhere in his mind I wasn't worth having.

Or perhaps I was thinking too much again and it was something easier. Maybe he didn't like the shape of my ears. It could very well have been my temperament—he was happy and carefree most of the time, I was filled with brooding demons. Or it could have been something else entirely. He believed he was a gentleman, maybe he preferred blondes.

But, yes, I always sensed that there was something lacking in me as far as he was concerned. Something not quite right. The way he'd draw me in, only to do or say something that was guaranteed to push me away again.

It made me think of Brett, another Jared-clone I was involved with several years before I met Kurt. Brett and I had a wonderful surface relationship. We had similar family histories. We loved going to movies and talking about them for hours afterwards. We cuddled on the couch. We had fantastic sex. We shopped together, worked out together, breakfasted together. Yet... yet... there was something, I felt that he felt, I was lacking. I could feel this deficiency in me as much as I could feel a bruise on my forearm or a nagging toothache. To boil it down to a main component, Brett simply didn't look at me the way men who have truly loved me did.

After awhile we broke up, obviously. We didn't really stay in touch. But here's the kicker: several years later I noticed Brett's screen name on AOL and I wanted to say "hello." First, though, to make sure he wasn't busy, I did a check to locate him online. And he was in the *Black Men for White Men* chat room. The proverbial light bulb! My mind suddenly became excited. I had the answer! Now I could recall all the times he would fall silent, his mouth slightly open, when a handsome Afro-American man walked into the steam room at our gym. The extra attention he gave our waiter if he happened to be a young black man. From then on, whenever I saw Brett online, I noticed that he was in that chat room and I felt vindicated.

So you see? It could be something like that. Brett realized that I was a pretty good catch. A nice guy. A cool person. Sharp too. And it's rare for two people to have such a great connection. To enjoy such special times together. For those reasons he was hesitant to let me go. The bottom line, however is, we had everything except for the fact that I was white and he was craving black.

How could I know what it was in me that Jared found lacking? Or what repelled Kurt for that matter? I'm sure there was a thing or two about me that disgusted him but that was for him to know and me, likely, never to find out. The curiosity, I'm sure, is part of what held me.

While I was lost in these thoughts Jared moved in closer and cupped my face in his hands. "You know," he said suddenly. "I've always been in love with you. Every man I've met through the years I've silently compared to you. And it was you I wanted, Vince. Always." He looked at me for several seconds, released my face, took a sip of his drink. "I still jerk off thinking about you, you know," he added.

How could this possibly be? The man who had so infected my life and my relationships with his ever blasé attitude towards me, his continuous slights and humiliations, his forever searching eyes, was telling me that I, somehow, had an affect on his? I felt like Bette Davis at the end of *Whatever Happened to Baby Jane*. I wanted to say, "You mean all these years we could have been friends?" I was open to it. He was the one I wanted from the beginning. He was the one I had recreated and hoped to win over in relationship after wretched relationship. I, however, felt it was one of those moments that anything I said would be wrong, so I instead said nothing and let him read into my thoughts what he may.

Soon after we left for dinner. Jared chose an expensive, low-key, French restaurant, walking distance from his apartment. The attractive waiter's politeness was so rehearsed and artificial that it almost seemed like an insult. I don't know much about French food. The prices were outrageously high. The portions were very small. During the course of the meal we each ordered two drinks. As always, when the check was brought I reached for it and Jared snatched it insisting it was on him. "You get it next time," he said, looking over the bill.

Afterwards Jared invited me up for a nightcap.

When we plopped down on the couch again we were both slightly drunk, and it amused me to discover that Jared was still the type of guy who, with all the money he could possibly spend in many lifetimes, would complain about the price of ten-dollar drinks. "That's the last time I go there," he grumbled. "Those drinks were mostly ice, weren't they?" I had to smile on the inside because I knew for a fact that he thought nothing of dropping three grand for an amusing lamp to place in the second bedroom in his Hamptons house.

"Why don't you move back to New York," he asked unexpectedly. "It would be good for us to be together again." Funny, this was the sentiment I wanted to hear from him since I was in my early twenties. Years before I would have accepted, without question, that we had a chance to make it. If

194

I had been living in another city at the time, I would have been mentally going through my closets deciding what to keep and what to discard. I would be thinking about what would be the best month for me to move. I would be willing to give up everything to give us a try. Now, I'm sad to report, I wasn't as much of a romantic. I was leery. I was weary. I still wanted and hoped for good things. But I knew they usually didn't come easily or, like this, out of the blue.

He sensed my confusion in my hesitation to answer.

"I'm much different now," he said. "You'd be surprised."

"Surprise me," I sighed. I wanted to be surprised.

He leaned in for the kiss. I leaned into him. I kissed Jared with a mixture of emotions that expressed the tenderness and dreams and need left over from my relationship with Kurt, and combined with memories of feelings I had leftover for Jared. I could feel Jared respond and he kissed me back with an expression left over from whatever had been going on in his recent life, merged with whatever remaining feelings he felt for me.

"Let's go to the bedroom," he said.

On his big, soft, opulent bed, his kisses were very open and receptive, mine were too, and together they formed the perfect kiss. The embraces were so warm, so comforting. It had been a long time since I had sex (made love?) with so much tenderness and expression. As always, Jared's body was far from perfect, but it retained tone and he felt very familiar and very nice. He still didn't clip his body hair—there was more gray mixed in now of course—and it grew over his torso like a rough terrain that I had often explored in the past. I was too woozy in the moment to call up the bad things about my times with Jared that I was also very familiar with.

Our hands languidly ran over the other's body and the time we took, the sounds we made...well...there was no doubt we were both enjoying it. It brought me back to my youth and the excitement I always felt when I was with Jared.

It felt so right. Did it ever feel like this before with him? I was trying to remember. It was so long ago. I had done so much growing and changing since then. I've been involved with so many other people. It was always good in bed between Jared and me. Sex was never the problem. Is that why I had hung on so long, even though I was constantly being let down? Is that why I never forgot him? Or was making love with him now really more affectionate? Had he really changed?

The pleasurable tenderness soon grew into intense desire. My dick, my nipples were precious to him and he sucked greedily. Then it was my turn and I returned the favor. Soon we were 69ing, that favorite of positions. I had every intention of swallowing—something I saved only for the most special of my loves.

In the extreme insatiable moments before orgasm, he began giving me little slaps on the ass. That was something he had always done, but I had forgotten about.

"I want to fuck you," he said.

Wasn't gonna happen. Never had happened. But for a moment I entertained the thought of letting Jared fuck me some time in the near future—if there was a near future. He wasn't so huge that he would hurt me. At least not with that thing. I had already stupidly surrendered myself to him in every way. Why not make it literal and experience the submission in total?

Not tonight though. We came simultaneously swallowing each other. And then, with something of each other inside of the other, we lay languorously in a half slumber state for quite awhile.

"Did you know you'd be staying here tonight?" he asked.

"No, I didn't," I said. I really didn't. I had brought a bag that consisted of only reading material for the train and a hairbrush and a pen. There was no toothbrush. No change of underwear.

"I knew you would be here with me tonight," he said. Then he asked: "What made you have any doubts."

"You invited me to dinner, Jared, which was nice. But we could have been meeting as old friends. You could have been involved with someone else. Maybe we wouldn't have had a good time. The chemistry might have changed."

"The chemistry between us will never change," he said. "It's always been there and it always will be."

"Then why haven't we been together?"

He paused considering whether to tell me what he'd probably been considering. "To be honest, I've always been afraid of you."

Jolted out of my dreamy haze, I had to laugh out loud. "You? Afraid of me?" Something was up with the universe and I wasn't in on it. I was the one who was always frightened.

"You were a baby when I met you," he said. "And you were so intense. So smart. I was afraid of what would happen if I let myself go completely with someone like you."

"And now I'm a man. But I'm still basically the same person."

"I've been through therapy for many years," he said carefully. "I've done a lot of growing. I don't obsess over work as much as I used to. I understand there's other things in life."

So, was Jared telling me that he was, at last, ready to love?

196

The idea of me moving back to New York to live happily ever after felt, by this phase in my life, farfetched and unlikely. Yet many things in my life had seemed much more farfetched and had become likely and later even came to fruition. I didn't really think that a life with Jared was going to happen. But, I thought, as I felt myself drifting under, maybe now that he's asked for me I'll be free of him and his kind. Now I can truly seek out love without the Jared-blinders on. We fell asleep holding each other.

The next morning we both rose early. He had to be at the office and I had to get back to my parents' house, I hadn't told them I'd be out all night and even though I was a grown man, in their eyes I was eternally fourteen.

"Can I call you at you at your parents' place while you're in New York," he asked.

"Of course. You can call me anytime."

We took a cab and he dropped me off at the subway. In order for it to be real, I always have view my life as Hollywood movie. I was no longer in *Gilda*. I couldn't think of anything, really, that fit the situation. But as the subway carried me home I said to myself, "well, this ends the story of Vince and Jared with a much happier slant." If only I had left it there. If only I didn't feel the need to take everything to the absolute limit.

The following day, Jared did indeed call me at my parent's inviting me to his house in the Hamptons for the weekend. It wasn't the season, he explained, but some good friends who lived up there were having a dinner party and there would be people attending that he wanted me to meet.

Wanted me to meet? But I never socialized with Jared. Whenever we had gone out, it had always been just the two of us. Another way, I always thought, from keeping me from becoming enmeshed with his life. He had owned this Hamptons house throughout the years we were together—as well as a house in Florida. I had never been invited to either house, although I was positive that other, less central boys were part of his seasonal location changes.

I should have resisted but I couldn't resist. It was a major step for Jared to say he loved me. It must have been hard to tell me that he had once been afraid of me. Now he was going further by inviting me away for the weekend.

"I'd love to come," I said.

Because I already had dinner plans with friends, we couldn't leave for his house on Friday night as he had hoped. I arrived at his building early on Saturday morning in a state of excitement. I even shampooed my asshole. I was carrying a little overnight case with a new outfit for the dinner party—I hoped to leave tons of excess baggage left over from sixteen years of relationships like the one that had started out with Jared in the first place.

"Please have a seat," the doorman said. "Mr. Grey will be down in a moment." I looked up at the ceiling and smiled. I was determined not to let pessimistic thoughts destroy our chances. I had to put part of the blame on negativity for my past failures. Jared was simply running late and if I came up it would only cause more delays. I sat on a corner chair and waited. Ten minutes later the elevator door opened revealing a smiling, cool, calm and collected Jared.

The drive up was pleasant enough, although the passion and intensity we expressed—both physically and emotionally—earlier in the week left us somewhat subdued and shy. We listened to music and chatted about our families, his corporation, and a book I was working on set to be published the following year. The book—a mystery based on a true story involving the murder of a bewitching young actress and the effect her death has on her family and friends—had grown out of an long magazine article that had published months before. I felt proud that I was no longer a struggling actor sitting next to the successful tycoon. My accomplishments were not as rewarding financially, but they were creatively fulfilling and worthy of note.

Jared's Long Island house was a large, beautiful, rambling thing. It had two floors, three fireplaces, and four bedrooms. There was a library, dining room, sprawling kitchen, and much more. Hallways led to anterooms that opened to larger rooms. Every time I turned a corner I found myself in a room I hadn't been in before. I did a lot of the exploring myself since Jared explained that he had a morning appointment with the guy who had installed the stereo system. The man, who showed up fifteen minutes after we arrived, would be installing flat-screened televisions in all of the bedrooms in time for summer. They began discussing—in great detail—what would be the best size, style, and quality for each room.

198

I walked the grounds. There was a large, stone barbecue and a built-in curved pool, with a Greek statue in the middle—winterized of course, but I imagined the "theme" parties that Jared held each summer. I had never been to one. When that time of the summer rolled around, Jared and I, ironically enough, were never together.

After my survey, I returned to the house to see that Jared and his electronics man were still deep in conversation. I sat on the couch and listened for a while—talk of gadgetry always bores me—and drifted off into a fitful sleep.

When I awoke the handy man was gone. Jared was on the phone. He made a sign that he would only be a moment. It sounded like a business call. I snapped a few photos while I waited. "I just have to make one more call he," he informed me when that call ended.

Perhaps childishly, I thought, since we arrived he hasn't paid any attention to me at all. It was after noon and, after all, we were leaving the following morning. Being alone in a strange house gives a person a lot of time to think, something that has always gotten me into trouble. But the wide screen TVs hadn't been installed yet and I didn't feel like reading. Jared had invited me here. He even seemed to be looking forward to it. "What is going on?" is one of the questions that I asked myself. Now, while I waited for him to finish conducting his business, the time had come to analyze, or re-analyze, Jared and his motives.

He had spent his life in luxury—able to have whatever he wanted, except for one thing. The Beatles seemed to have said it best, at least in modern times: money can't buy love. Jared was getting older. Maybe, through his years of analysis, he had explored the reasons why he had never been in a committed relationship. Perhaps he thought the time to experience it was now. Since it wasn't something he could put on his MasterCard, he went back to the one person—me!—who he knew at one time truly loved him. But this was simply an experiment. He had probably fantasized for weeks about what it would be like, the two of us, being a couple. By this stage in his life he should have been prepared for the difference that awaited him when comparing the fantasy to reality. Probably he was still scared to death. Not only of me—but also of the idea of a relationship of any kind. In fear, he turned to the two things he had always used to distract himself from me. Business and pleasure.

An agitated feeling was starting to force its way up, memories of the bad things about Jared, but I quickly forced it down. I didn't want any negative molecules to escape from me into the air—Jared would breathe them in and, as it had in the past, the day would become an endless game of tit for tat.

"So what would you like to do?" he said, snapping the phone closed, with the second call complete. The winter day was still clear and sunny, although there was rain in the forecast for the following day. We could have gone for a long walk or even a bike ride—I noticed he had two bicycles. But then he decided to take me for a drive to see the town.

We drove around admiring the views.

"Those sun glasses look great on you," I said.

"You think so?"

"Yep. Really handsome. You look like a heartthrob."

We had lunch in a charming little bistro. It was cozy and dark—fireplace, stone walls—it could have been romantic but it really wasn't working. It was as if we were actors playing the parts of two men in love. But I was so eager to make it work I threw myself into the character and tried to keep up the fourth wall.

After lunch he explained was having trouble with his television cable bill and wanted to take care of it in person. We set off for the cable company's main headquarters. The young man at the front desk was short, blonde and handsome—he had on a blue shirt opened to the navel, revealing a smooth sculpted chest. I could feel Jared's excitement swell up and fill the room. The eternal cockeyed pessimist, I made a bet with myself that the apprentice cable company worker would not escape comment somewhere down the line. When he heard Jared's problem (he was being charged for a network he hadn't ordered), apparently it was out of his range, and the worker disappeared into a secret back room and a matronly woman appeared to take over and settle the dilemma. After much discussion and explaining, the problem was resolved.

"I wouldn't mind it taking so long," Jared said as we headed back to the car, "If that cute guy had taken care of the problem. Anyway it's nice to know he's there if I have any more trouble." Bingo! I won the bet with myself. But by making the bet did I bring it on myself? I wasn't about to start on that jag again.

I wondered if he meant it as a joke. He probably did. But not a very good one and at the expense of me again. I nodded sadly. News flash, Vince, I said to myself, this is how men are. You aren't the only man in the world. Get over it! To keep the anger from surfacing, I reminded myself not every man in the world acted this way, this wasn't the usual, and it kept happening to me as a result of my own poor decision-making.

Remarking on the desirability of other men in my presence had always been Jared's way of verbally giving me little slaps on the ass to show that he was in control. To keep me in check. That I had no real power here.

"Yep. He was very dreamy," I agreed.

Oh what was wrong with me? The same bullshit scenario that had been going since my first years with Jared, through my bad times with Kurt, was replaying itself. Even after all I had learned. All I had been through! How had I allowed myself to be trapped into this again? I may have put myself in new environments but it was still, more or less, the same body and soul that I dragged around from situation to situation.

After that, the day disintegrated into a series of contests. In order for me to win I had to remain cool calm and collected and nice and not to let anything he said or did wound me. For Jared to win he had to reach me in a way that hurt. If I showed a reaction, if he struck some inner cord, he won. If I remained pleasant and unaffected, I was the winner.

Having not reacted to Jared's comment about the possibility of a future tryst with the cable guy put me ahead. He wasn't about to let that happen. Driving back to the house, we passed a place that sold decorative stone and tiles. "Last summer my friend told me that the hottest man in the world worked in that place," Jared informed me. "All summer long he kept urging me to go in there, to go in there, and I resisted. Finally I went in to check the guy out."

"And?" I urged.

"And when I went in there sure enough, he was this incredible man. Absolutely perfect."

Competition number two. I looked back at the place we just passed and turned to Jared. "Well," I said grinning, "aren't you going to take me in there to see him."

Pause. "Well, I don't know if he works there now. It was last summer."

"Too bad," I said. "I would have liked to have seen the hottest man in the world." I won that one too.

When we arrived at the house, Jared wanted to take a nap. That was fine with me. It gave me a chance to reassess the situation. So far, so bad. But it wasn't too late to turn the situation around. I browsed the library. Many classics, which didn't look thumbed through. Mixed in with a stack of magazines, there was a book on current plastic surgery techniques—confirming my suspicions. Eventually I sat down with the weekend edition of the *New York Times* in front of me. Perhaps the key to winning was to win over Jared's friends. If he saw how much people who were in his life, people he loved—liked me—then maybe he'd stop treating me with such contempt. This defied common sense. The real question being: why did I still want to win?

I dressed very carefully that evening. I had a new cream silk shirt. I had brought a tiny iron to be sure I would be wrinkle-free. "I have an iron here," Jared said when he saw me unpack the appliance. I smiled.

"Why don't I go to an upstairs bedroom so you can get ready in privacy?" I suggested.

I always like to get dressed alone. We all have our little grooming secrets. I was sure Jared had some of his own. It was cold upstairs but I took a long hot shower. I shaved carefully. Trimmed my eyebrows. Made sure there was nothing growing out of my nose. I put some gel in my hair and mussed it a bit. I put some bronzer on my face. I was happy to see that the new thirty-three inch waist black pants I had bought fit me comfortably. My goal was thirty-one ... but this was a size smaller than the previous month. I looked as good as I possibly could at the given moment. The weather conditions were perfect—cool and brisk. And there were no subways to take.

The dinner party—at a house even bigger and more lavish than Jared's—consisted of fifteen of his best friends. They ranged in age from thirty to sixty. There was an art dealer, but most of the others were in the real estate business. Two of them were still a couple but I suspected that many of them dated each other at one time or another. Somebody's sister was there, a sweet young woman named Julie. She had short blonde hair, a strong nose and resembled Princess Diana, which made me like her the way you just do some people on first meeting. She sensed I liked her and she liked me back.

I had been to elegant dinner parties like this a hundred times in the past ten years—some leaving an impact and some disappearing from memory without the faintest of impressions. The only reason this one was different was because it involved Jared and his click. I wanted in. Wrong or right.

Apple martinis were served along with a lot of complicated and delicious *hors d'oeuvres*. I was nervous. But everyone treated me kindly. They were all jovial and joking with each other. I got the sense that they were politely including me, but at the same time I was not accepted as a member yet. Jared and I separated for a while. I looked at the magnificent modern abstract art that hung at every turn.

I was going into the kitchen to see if I could find Jared and I saw him standing there with one of his friends, Fred, a realtor in the same age category who, while he talked, was smoking a cigarette as if he was afraid of it.

"...you like Latin men, I like Latin men," Fred was saying. "This cruise is supposedly filled with them. What's to stop us from...?"

They saw me standing there.

"Hi Vince," Jared said.

"Hi," I replied. And the subject was changed until we were called to dinner.

What do I remember about what was being served? Zucchini soup. Filet mignon. Baked potato. Sour cream. Caviar. German chocolate cake. But I was very high by now. Desperate to be affable and charming I was drinking a little too much too soon. Someone brought up the subject of the drug Ecstasy. In my eagerness to dazzle and seduce the crowd, I admitted I had taken it once, years before, and that the sex I had, with a stranger, that night had been incredible. This anecdote lasted less than one minute. Then other people at the table told their Ecstasy stories and it was then, while listening, that I realized how disrespectful I had been telling my story in front of Jared. I had been an idiot. I was so ashamed of myself. I was always judging others for hurting me. I was no better. Now I was determined to make it up to Jared in some way.

I wanted to go over to him right away but after dinner his art dealer friend told me a long complicated story involving an affair he was having with a married man, which I managed to follow even though I was comfortably numbing. I could always bring myself out of a stupor if the need should suddenly occur.

"Why do you stay with him?" I asked

"Some Italian men are very attractive."

I went into the open living area to find Jared. I sat next to him on the couch. I wanted to indicate to everyone that I was proud to be here with him. I put my arm around him. We seemed to be a real couple. He rubbed my back. I thought we were having a good time. Somewhere there's photographic evidence of this. Someone was snapping pictures.

The host asked me what I did for a living and I knew I was being given my moment. I talked about my writing career and the book I had coming out based on a murdered actress and her stricken family. Everyone listened with silent concentration.

"You're very quiet and shy." Julie said when I had finished, "but when the subject turns to something that you're passionate about, you are so compelling and interesting—I can't take my eyes off of you."

"Oh, Vince and I have had a connection for many years," Jared remarked.

But then, soon after, Jared unexpectedly and without and perceptible reason, started a discussion of someone named Miguel, apparently his most recent boyfriend. It seemed he wanted me to know a lot about Miguel:

"young," "nice little body," "tight" are but a few of the words that were used to describe him.

"I can't remember him," Julie said.

"Of course you remember him, Julie," Jared said. "He was at my New Year's Eve party."

"The little guy," Julie replied (God love her). "He was nice? I don't remember him."

"I don't remember him either," someone else chimed in.

I think they were all a little shocked that Jared was talking about this, like this, in front of me—his date for the party. I remained silent at his side. I'm sure he had been to a lot of parties with a lot of dates, but he probably didn't demonstrate his cruelty so openly with them—not having any real feelings for him—they wouldn't have allowed it. But I figured it was my due for telling the Ecstasy story at dinner. Maybe after this we could call a truce.

Two neighbors, aware that there was a party going on, came over for a visit and they were very hot indeed. They were what we used to call "fresh meat." The party was suddenly recharged. The older of the two (and in my opinion the more handsome) was wearing sky blue shirt and black jeans. His younger, lover was a dark-eyed, full-lipped Latino—in white T-Shirt and banana-colored leather pants. And believe me, his banana was very apparent through the leather. Everyone noticed. I took a step back. I saw all the others take two steps forward, Jared too, asking questions and being delightful.

We left soon after. We didn't speak much in the car. It had begun to rain, as had been forecasted. I had disappointed Jared in some way but I couldn't think about that now. He had disappointed me too, in hundreds of ways. The same old ways. But I was too preoccupied with being a disappointment to consider that.

Jared led the way down a hallway, to the bedroom. Along the hallway there were some shelves with a lot of framed photographs of family and friends. He paused quickly, almost imperceptibly, to adjust the position of one if the pictures. I glanced at the photo and there he was on the beach with a young, dark, nice-looking boy with a tight body. Miguel I assumed. And in the moment I looked, I saw that he resembled me. Ten years before.

I was hoping that the night, which had ended drunkenly for all concerned, would be viewed as a success with morning sobriety. Nothing really so terrible had happened. A good sex session in the meantime might put us back on track and we could still end the relationship, for all time this time, on a positive note. But, if there's one thing I've learned after all these years

204

of having sex—and doing everything else—is never expect anything. And since I was going to bed with the original version of Kurt, I stripped, kept on my black briefs, and hopped into bed. I was ready to go right to sleep or have sex. After months of not knowing with Kurt, it really didn't matter. Whatever happened, happened.

"Why are those still on?" he asked, indicating my underwear.

"They can come off pretty quickly," I replied.

"Take them off," he said.

"Okay," I said, but it was so softly I wasn't sure if I was talking to myself.

I checked my hard-on status. It was limp. But I am a man of many moods and the status can change quickly. He stroked my cock while it was still soft. He kissed me and, sure enough, I immediately got hard. He stroked me again.

"That was quick," he said.

So it was going to be sex after all. I was ready and moved into it. But, even though he was naked, he had something up his sleeve. He moaned. Not in pleasure. It was the kind of moan that would come out of a sick child. I ignored it. He kissed me again. He groaned again—this time like a cow caught in a tar pit.

"What's the matter," I asked.

"Ohhhhh, I ate too much!" he said.

So we weren't going to have sex? Like I said, that would have been fine. We both ate and drank too much. Still, I was embarrassed.

"Me too," I said. "Why don't we get some sleep?" I turned. I gave him my back. This was turning into some sort of trend. The more I was in bed with someone, the more I was ending up alone.

I really was very exhausted and I felt myself falling fast. Just before I blacked out I could feel him snuggle up against my back. Spooning. Talk about mixed signals. I was sick of mixed signals! I didn't respond as I normally would, mostly because I was just too sick and tired to stick around in the conscious world to discover what his next plan of action would be. What I wanted more than anything at that moment was delicious oblivion. I fell asleep that way, with him holding me. I was holding a pillow.

But when I woke up again, a few hours later, I could hear the rain beating against the windows and—just like in the old days with Kurt—we were back to back.

His phone rang. Jared, although sleeping, jumped up quickly and answered. Suddenly he was wide-awake, speaking with exaggerated glee: "Hello? Oh yes. Hi! Oh no! Don't let the weather change anything—I'm still planning on being home tonight. Yes, I'm leaving right after breakfast and I'll be home by mid afternoon. No, no ... come over! We can order in and rent a movie. Okay? Promise? Okay. See you then."

And then he added the sucker punch: "I love you."

I wasn't going to think about who was on the other end. Okay, okay, okay, okay. You win. Uncle. I give. It's over. The entire conversation had obviously been for my benefit (as much as the adjusting of the framed photograph the night before was) but I was out of the game. If it was some new boyfriend, or even Miguel, on the phone, I didn't think of it as Jared cheating on me, since we weren't really together. But, with me in the bed, wasn't he cheating on someone else? I had no intention of showing any kind of emotion. He lay there waiting for me to ask, "Who was that?" Instead I jumped out of the bed and ran for cover to the shower.

If all these stupid hurts, all these days and nights of game playing and ridiculousness didn't add something to me, build character or something, than so much of my life has been such an incredible waste.

When I returned, he was sitting on the bed putting on his shoes. I walked passed him, wrapped in a towel, and he grabbed me, pulling me to him and, to my extreme discomfort, he started pinching and poking at my stomach, and then kneading it very quickly as if I were dough being hastily prepared for the oven. It was rough and graceless and crude—there was nothing sexual about it. Unprepared for such sudden intimate contact, I felt self-conscious and uneasy. My poor stomach wasn't at its best—I had I still had about eight pounds to lose—but even a tight stomach would feel ungainly and compromised under such savage scrutiny.

Then Jared commented on my middle section by saying this: "Hey, what is this? I'm supposed to be the older one here."

Several weeks before, while I was making a salad in my kitchen, I opened an upper cabinet and a can of olives dropped to the floor. I bent down to pick it up and when I rapidly stood again—BAM—I conked myself incredibly hard on the forehead on the corner of the open cabinet door. There was a forceful unexpected blow to the head, excruciating pain, and then a momentary disorientation of not knowing where I was or what had just happened. Jared's words gave me these kinds of unexpected, severe sensations which I hadn't experienced since that time.

For a few seconds after the sudden blinding, shock of pain there was nothingness. I had to coax myself back. Slowly ... slowly, I saw a dresser and a lamp, a long row of mirrored closets, a painting on the wall of a sunny beach and a colorful umbrella in the sand. Oh! I was in the Hamptons, in a house that had been built by Jared.

Here were my fingers. I gingerly felt for each one and they were all still there. I wiggled my toes—they seemed to be intact. When I came completely to, though, I was so shell-shocked and insulted that I could think of no appropriate response and, even if I could, I couldn't speak anyway.

I pulled away from him and tried to think of what to do next. The deal I had made with myself earlier about not becoming angry—introverted and sulky—seemed nearly impossible. But I could hardly bear to live in this moment with Jared, or with anyone including myself, as witness. I would have rather been anywhere else. Yet there was breakfast to get through and a three-hour drive. Impossible!

"Just ride it through one second at a time."

I wish I could have brushed it off and said, "That big dinner last night didn't help, but when I get back to Los Angeles I'll be working on it," and smiled and walked away. I couldn't though. It's not in my nature. And although I didn't become rancidly silent, every move I made, every word I said, from that point on, had the facade of a crumbling house garishly covered with a coat of bright, cheap paint and plastic shudders. I tired hard to come across as devil-may-care, but Jared felt my fake gaiety, and I was now the kind of house he didn't want to visit, let alone live in.

He had enough money to get away with doing things like that—to most of the men he dated it wouldn't matter if he insulted them in such a way because they wouldn't have cared for him and his opinion would mean nothing. They only wanted the life that happened around them while they were in his life. Besides, they wouldn't have seven extra pounds and a little potbelly. Their exteriors were merely facades, too, but constant and more expertly built. Not me, but strangers who looked like a better version of me. How easy it would be for Jared to comfortably spend some time in one and then start looking for another house, a newer model, of a different architectural design when the atmosphere became boring—as mine had become. I deserved what I got. What else could he feel but condescension and contempt, for me, the only one ever stupid enough to have ever felt real love for him?

He finished dressing and told me he had to go to the store. There was nothing in the house. He asked me if I wanted anything with my eggs. "Cheese?" he asked. I almost laughed, but it wasn't funny.

"Plain will be fine," I managed.

"Plain?" he asked.

"Just plain.

When he was gone, I went directly to the liquor cabinet and poured myself a drink. It wasn't yet nine AM. If I took two of my tranquilizers and swallowed them down with scotch, I might be able to bear this and not call a taxi before he returned. These fucking relationships were going to put me in the Betty Ford Clinic. But that was a concern for another time. By the time he came back I'd be able to disappear into a mythical world in my mind—and Jared would be little more than an extra player there.

He cooked the breakfast in silence. The atmosphere was that of a house with terrible secrets. Yeah, we both felt it. The horror was in not being able to escape the moment. He switched on the stereo to a Sunday morning jazz station. Even drinking all that Scotch while he was out getting the eggs didn't help in making me feel any more at ease. My casual comments about the music were tainted with unnatural enthusiasm.

Breakfast was a series of starts by me and finishes by both of us.

"It's not much of a breakfast," he said.

"It's not the breakfast that counts," I replied lamely. "It's who you're eating it with."

I thought about his final blow. "Wow!" I said to myself. I had to feel it fully now and get it over with. I let it run through me. I rolled it around on my tongue to taste it. Then I swallowed.

For what reason? I had done nothing but propped him up all weekend. Complimented him. I was as charming and nice as I could be. Certainly his friends seemed to like me. The sting didn't go away, not so much for the insult itself, but for the thought behind it. Was he crazy saying something like that to me? If nothing else, his friend. His guest. Did he find himself liking me more than he wanted to, so he thought he should be put in my place, end everything, before feelings started to emerge? That almost seems too flattering an idea to entertain. Was he really suddenly repulsed by me and my lack of a six pack that he felt the need to voice his opinion—if he was, though, couldn't he have kept his opinion to himself? We almost made it. I was leaving for Los Angeles in a few days. It would be extremely easy for him to never touch me again. Couldn't he let me go and let me go unharmed?

The pills and liquor finally kicked in and I slept in the car most of the way home. Well not home. He dropped me off near the subway station in Manhattan. "Thanks for an exciting weekend," I said, with not a little irony.

It was still pouring rain. I was heading towards the subway when I realized that I was very near a bathhouse, a sex club that I used to go to many years before. Was it still open, I wondered?

What the hell. I walked the one block east to the location and sure enough, there in the directory in the lobby of the building was the name, Midtown Sauna. I decided to go in. Here I could become anonymous. I would have no history. I paid the entrance fee. I gave my wallet to be locked up at the front desk. I left my clothes and overnight bag in a locker. I began wandering around.

It was a bleak Sunday afternoon but the place was full of activity. There were many men in towels of varying ages and sizes posing dreamily in corners or walking down the long corridors looking into the cubicles where men lounged on cots waiting for the right man to enter. Some were sitting in the steam room patiently hoping to lure their prey in the camouflage of hot mist. Other's were languidly eating snacks from the vending machines and watching porn on the monitors.

If seen from an aerial view from many feet away, the place would resemble an ant farm with every entity moving around with a purpose and intent. I joined in the activity. Just one among many.

I looked around. Corny love songs were being piped through the sound system. Elvis: Welcome to my world.

I found the bathroom. Sometimes when I'm peeing at a urinal I hear Kurt's voice asking, "Do you think we should still be together?"

"No," I answer. "You're with who you're supposed to be with and I'm with who I'm supposed to be with. But we did have fun sometimes, didn't we?"

Bittersweet fragments of me with Kurt inevitably attacked my memory: someone commenting that we looked good together, him looking into my eyes at a party in front of my best friend and saying, "I love you."

I didn't want to become one of those guys who always talked about his "ex." Yet I wondered if something of him would touch me every day for the rest of my life. Maybe not a full memory, exactly—but a shared moment, a song, or movie, or food, or smell, or joke. We shared a lot, comparatively speaking.

I couldn't have done a thing differently. I loved him dearly. I tried my best to make him love me. It was an honorable failure. I simply was not the one for him. Somewhere in the world, as I stood there, or as you read this, Kurt may be with a new lover—committed and happy. A man who makes him feel like a billion dollars. A man he flatters and lifts up and adores. And he is happy. They both are. I hope so

There were oceans and cities and mountains and misconceptions and many bodies between us. Although I felt very sad, I had some of my happiest moments with him. For a brief time—while we were together—I was less lonely. I don't know if the love was real or fake on his part, but for me it was real and that's what I remember. For the time being, chaos was my lover, but that too was always changing and if I only had the guts to wait it out for a while my situation would be altered. I had guts. Or I was developing them.

As I investigated the various hallways of the bathhouse, I noticed many men stop at one cubicle room in particular, stare into it for a long time, take a hesitant step forward, then dejectedly walk away. I knew the room would contain something spectacular. I had to see for myself.

I walked quickly passed the room and gave the occupant a cursory side-glance, but even in that instant I knew the man was indeed extraordinary. It was like turning the pages of a magazine and coming across an especially striking model who makes you stop suddenly. He was sitting on the edge of the cot stroking a semi-erect cock. I saw full dark hair. Thick eyebrows. Large eyes. A sculpted face. Muscles. I took in all of this in a fraction of a second. God only knew what I'd see if I lingered there. I figured, in my current state of mind, it would be better not to try for him. Another rejection would be really bad. But, as I wandered around, up and down the stairs, passed the rows and rows of rooms, the wandering men, I kept getting drawn back to the page. The next time I stopped at his room I paused at the door.

Now he was lounging comfortably, leaning back with his hands behind his head, his semi-erect cock resting on his thigh. I stood tentatively at the doorway. After many moments of staring at each other, he made a motion for me to enter but I still wasn't sure he wanted me. I didn't move. "Come in" he said quietly. I sheepishly stepped into the cubicle.

"I'm Fernando," he said, and smiled. "Fernando from Brazil." Frequently in these kinds of situations no words are spoken. But here I was, with the door still open, and he had already introduced himself. Sweet. I closed the door.

Closer, in the half-light coming from the little lamp, the glowing moon next to the cot, I concentrated on his face. I saw his huge brown doe-eyes, long lashed, dreamy, interested. The flawless nose. The masculine jaw. Full dark lips.

Sheltered in the warmth of the tiny room, in the dim light, I dropped my towel, and leaned over him. He raised himself up and he kissed me on the side of my lips and then opened his mouth and sucked, very lightly at that place, the corner of my mouth. He made room for me on the cot, and I pressed next to him, bodies touching. His fingers traced my eyebrows, touched my eyes, my nose, moving down my jaw line. He put a huge hand on the back of my neck and massaged the muscles there.

He smelled like soap and perspiration. It was nice. My anxiety turned to anticipation. I moved my face closer to him and he kissed me dead center on the lips. We kept our eyes open, staring deeply into each other, until we broke up laughing.

He was lovely. Fernando was. Fernando from Brazil. Anything anyone could ever want. We continued to kiss and he touched me tenderly. I felt his muscles—but gently, I didn't want to encourage him to probe me too roughly.

"What is your name?" he asked.

"Vince," I whispered, and saying my name sounded strange too. As if I were saying it for the first time.

We lay down on the sad little cot and kissed some more, playfully biting and licking at each other's mouths. We held each other very close, nuzzling skin in various places, and I knew I'd never see him again. This was a gift, a remarkable moment in time. Soft tan flesh, a kiss, a touch, a smell, an unintelligible whisper. This was Fernando. And it was exciting. Terribly exciting.

Books Available from Gival Press

A Change of Heart by David Garrett Izzo
  1st edition, ISBN 1-928589-18-9, (ISBN 13: 978-1-928589-18-1), $20.00

A historical novel about Aldous Huxley and his circle "astonishingly alive and accurate."
— Roger Lathbury, George Mason University

An Interdisciplinary Introduction to Women's Studies Edited by Brianne Friel & Robert L. Giron
  1ˢᵗ edition, ISBN 1-928589-29-4, (ISBN 13: 978-1-928589-29-7), $25.00

Winner of the **2005** DIY Book Festival Award for Compilations/ Anthologies.
A succinct collection of articles written for the college student of women's studies, covering a variety of disciplines from politics to philosophy.

Bones Washed With Wine: Flint Shards from Sussex and Bliss by Jeff Mann
  1st edition, ISBN 1-928589-14-6, (ISBN 13: 978-1-928589-14-3), $15.00

A special collection of lyric intensity, including the **1999** Gival Press Poetry Award winning collection. Jeff Mann is "a poet to treasure both for the wealth of his language and the generosity of his spirit."— Edward Falco, author of *Acid*

Boys, Lost & Found: Stories by Charles Casillo
  1ˢᵗ edition, ISBN 1-928589-33-2, (ISBN 13: 978-1-928589-33-4), $20.00

Casillo's boys are hustlers, writers, models, cruisers, lovers— complicated, smart, cool, witty, lusty, and romantic. "...fascinating, often funny... a safari through the perils and joys of gay life." —Edward Field

Canciones para sola cuerda / Songs for a Single String by Jesús Gardea; English translation by Robert L. Giron
  1st edition, ISBN 1-928589-09-X, (ISBN 13: 978-1-928589-09-9), $15.00

Finalist for the **2003** Violet Crown Book Award for Literary Prose & Poetry.

A moving collection of love poems, with echoes of Neruda *à la Mexicana* as Gardea writes about the primeval quest for the perfect woman. "The free verse...evokes the quality and forms of *cante hondo*, emphasizing the emotional interplay of human voice and guitar."— Elizabeth Huergo, Montgomery College

Dead Time / Tiempo muerto by Carlos Rubio
1st edition, ISBN 1-928589-17-0, (ISBN 13: 978-1-928589-17-4), $21.00
Winner of the 2003 Silver Award for Translation—ForeWord Magazine's Book of the Year.
This bilingual (English/Spanish) novel is "an unusual tale of love, hate, passion and revenge." — Karen Sealy, author of *The Eighth House*

Dervish by Gerard Wozek
1st edition, ISBN 1-928589-11-1, (ISBN 13: 978-1-928589-11-2), $15.00
Winner of the 2000 Gival Press Poetry Award.
This rich whirl of the dervish traverses a grand expanse from bars to crazy dreams to fruition of desire. "By Jove, these poems shimmer."— Gerry Gomez Pearlberg, author of *Mr. Bluebird*

Dreams and Other Ailments / Sueños y otros achaques by Teresa Bevin
1st edition, ISBN 1-928589-13-8, (ISBN 13: 978-1-928589-13-6), $21.00
Winner of the 2001 Bronze Award for Translation—ForeWord Magazine's Book of the Year.
A wonderful array of short stories about the fantasy of life and tragedy but filled with humor and hope. "*Dreams and Other Ailments* will lift your spirits."— Lynne Greeley, The University of Vermont

The Gay Herman Melville Reader Edited by Ken Schellenberg
1st edition, ISBN 1-928589-19-7, (ISBN 13: 978-1-928589-19-8), $16.00
A superb selection of Melville's work. "Here in one anthology are the selections from which a serious argument can be made by both readers and scholars that a subtext exists that can be seen as homoerotic."— David Garrett Izzo, author of *Christopher Isherwood: His Era, His Gang, and the Legacy of the Truly Strong Man*

The Great Canopy by Paula Goldman

1ˢᵗ edition, ISBN 1-928589-31-6, (ISBN 13: 978-1-928589-31-0), $15.00

Winner of the 2004 Gival Press Poetry Award & Semi-Finalist for the 2006 Independent Publisher Book Award for Poetry.

"Under this canopy we experience the physicality of the body through Goldman's wonderfully muscular verse as well the analytics of a mind that tackles the meaning of Orpheus or the notion of desire."—Richard Jackson, author of *Half Lives, Heartwall,* and *Unauthorized Autobiography: New & Selected Poems*

The Last Day of Paradise by Kiki Denis

1ˢᵗ edition, ISBN 1-928589-32-4 (ISBN 13: 978-1-928589-32-7), $20.00

Winner of the 2005 Gival Press Novel Award.

"...Denis's debut is a slippery in-your-face accelerated rush of sex, hokum, and Greek family life. A little bit Eurydice, a little bit Chick-lit, with non-stop riffing on reality...."—Richard Peabody, editor of *Mondo Barbie*

Let Orpheus Take Your Hand by George Klawitter

1st edition, ISBN 1-928589-16-2, (ISBN 13: 978-1-928589-16-7), $15.00

Winner of the 2001 Gival Press Poetry Award.

A thought provoking work that mixes the spiritual with stealthy desire, with Orpheus leading us out of the pit. "These poems present deliciously sly metaphors of the erotic life that keep one reading on, and chuckling with pleasure."— Edward Field, author of *Stand Up, Friend, With Me*

Literatures of the African Diaspora by Yemi D. Ogunyemi

1st edition, ISBN 1-928589-22-7, (ISBN 13: 978-1-928589-22-8), $20.00

An important study of the influences in literatures of the world. "It, indeed, proves that African literatures are, without mincing words, a fountainhead of literary divergence."—Joshua 'Kunle Awosan, University of Massachusetts Dartmouth

Maximus in Catland by David Garrett Izzo
1st edition, ISBN 1-928589-34-0, (ISBN 13: 978-1-928589-34-1), $20.00

"... [an] examination of the idea of the Truly Strong Man—or, in this case, Cat—which is one who would give his own life for the sake of transpersonal good...This book is a treat—with a truly mystical message.—Toby Johnson, author of *Secret Matter*, winner of the Lambda Literary Award for Sci-Fi

Metamorphosis of the Serpent God by Robert L. Giron
1st edition, ISBN 1-928589-07-3, (ISBN 13: 978-1-928589-07-5), $12.00

"Robert Giron's biographical poetry embraces the past and the present, ethnic and sexual identity, themes both mythical and personal."— *The Midwest Book Review*

Middlebrow Annoyances: American Drama in the 21st Century by Myles Weber
1st edition, ISBN 1-928589-20-0, (ISBN 13: 978-1-928589-20-4), $20.00

"Weber's intelligence and integrity are unsurpassed by anyone writing about the American theatre today..."— John W. Crowley, The University of Alabama at Tuscaloosa

The Nature Sonnets by Jill Williams
1st edition, ISBN 1-928589-10-3, (ISBN 13: 978-1-928589-10-5), $8.95

An innovative collection of sonnets that speaks to the cycle of nature and life, crafted with wit and clarity. "Refreshing and pleasing."— Miles David Moore, author of *The Bears of Paris*

Poetic Voices Without Borders Edited by Robert L. Giron
1st edition, ISBN 1-928589-30-8, (ISBN 13: 978-1-928589-30-3), $20.00

Winner of the 2006 Writers Notes Book Award—Notable for Art & Semi-Finalist for the 2006 Independent Publisher Book Award for Anthologies.
"...This book is edgy with a literary inclusiveness...Each voice is unique, yet together they create oneness even as they individually represent societal diversity."—Lucinda Farrokh, LareDOS: A Journal of the Borderlands

On the Altar of Greece by Donna J. Gelagotis Lee

1ˢᵗ edition, ISBN 1-928589-36-7, (ISBN 13: 978-1-928589-35-5), $15.00

Winner of the 2005 Gival Press Poetry Award.
"...the journey of our time at this altar offers us a striking, immense set of views of a world we thought we knew, and still, wonderfully, do know in much richer ways by the end."—Don Berger, author of *Quality Hill* and *The Cream-Filled Muse*

On the Tongue by Jeff Mann

1ˢᵗ edition, ISBN 1-928589-35-9, (ISBN 13: 978-1-928589-35-8), $15.00

"...brilliantly pagan eroticism, at once tender, yet forceful and hard, like the hard-shelled seeds that spring from the fragilest of flowers. These poems are both, and in that breadth, nothing short of extraordinary..."—Trebor Healey, author of *Through It Came Bright Colors*

Prosody in England and Elsewhere: A Comparative Approach by Leonardo Malcovati

1st edition, ISBN 1-928589-26-X, (ISBN 13: 978-1-928589-26-6), $20.00

"To write about the structure of poetry for a non-specialist audience takes a brave author. To do so in a way that is readable, in fact enjoyable, without sacrificing scholarly standards takes an accomplished author."—Frank Anshen, State University of New York

Secret Memories / Recuerdos secretos by Carlos Rubio

1ˢᵗ edition, ISBN 1-928589-27-8, (ISBN 13: 978-1-928589-27-3), $21.00

Finalist for the 2005 ForeWord Magazine's Book of Year Award for Translation.
"From the beginning, the reader feels pulled into the narrator's world and observes, along with him, a delicate, beautiful, and vulnerable universe as personal and intimate as a conversation between lovers."
—Hope Maxell Snyder, author of *Orange Wine*

The Smoke Week: Sept. 11-21, 2001 by Ellis Avery

1st edition, ISBN 1-928589-24-3, (ISBN 13: 978-1-928589-24-2), $15.00

Winner of the 2004 Writer's Notes Magazine Book Award— Notable for Culture & Winner of the Ohioana Library Walter Rumsey Marvin Award.
"Here is Witness. Here is Testimony."— Maxine Hong Kingston, author of *The Fifth Book of Peace*

Songs for the Spirit by Robert L. Giron

1st edition, ISBN 1-928589-08-1, (ISBN 13: 978-1-928589-08-2), $16.95

This humanist collection invokes a new vision, one that speaks to readers regardless of their spiritual inclination. "This is an extraordinary book."— John Shelby Spong, author of *Why Christianity Must Change or Die: A Bishop Speaks to Believers in Exile*

Sweet to Burn by Beverly Burch

1st edition, ISBN 1-928589-23-5, (ISBN 13: 978-1-928589-23-5), $15.00

Winner of the 2004 Lambda Literary Award for Lesbian Poetry & Winner of the 2003 Gival Press Poetry Award.
"Novelistic in scope, but packing the emotional intensity of lyric poetry..."— Eloise Klein Healy, author of *Passing*

Tickets to a Closing Play by Janet I. Buck

1st edition, ISBN 1-928589-25-1, (ISBN 13: 978-1-928589-25-9), $15.00

Winner of the 2002 Gival Press Poetry Award.
"...this rich and vibrant collection of poetry [is] not only serious and insightful, but a sheer delight to read."— Jane Butkin Roth, editor, *We Used to Be Wives: Divorce Unveiled Through Poetry*

Wrestling with Wood by Robert L. Giron

3rd edition, ISBN 1-928589-05-7, (ISBN 13: 978-1-928589-05-1), $5.95

A chapbook of impressionist moods and feelings of a long-term relationship which ended in a tragic death. "Nuggets of truth and beauty sprout within our souls."— Teresa Bevin, author of *Havana Split*

Books for Children

Barnyard Buddies I by Pamela Brown; illustrations by Annie H. Hutchins
1st edition, ISBN 1-928589-15-4, (ISBN 13: 978-1-928589-15-0), $16.00

Thirteen stories filled with a cast of creative creatures both engaging and educational. "These stories in this series are delightful. They are wise little fables, and I found them fabulous."
—Robert Morgan, author of *This Rock* and *Gap Creek*

Barnyard Buddies II by Pamela Brown; illustrations by Annie H. Hutchins
1st edition, ISBN 1-928589-21-9, (ISBN 13: 978-1-928589-21-1), $16.00

"Children's literature which emphasizes good character development is a welcome addition to educators' as well as parents' resources."
—Susan McCravy, elementary school teacher

Tina Springs into Summer / Tina se lanza al verano by Teresa Bevin; illustrations by Perfecto Rodriguez
1ˢᵗ edition, ISBN 1-928589-28-6, (ISBN 13: 978-1-928589-28-0), $21.00

Winner of the **2006** Writer's Notes Magazine Book Award—Notable for Young Adult Literature.
"This appealing book with its illustrations can serve as a wonderful learning tool for children in grades 3-6. Bevin clearly understands the thoughts, feelings, and typical behaviors of pre-teen youngsters from multi-cultural urban backgrounds...."
—Dr. Nancy Boyd Webb, Professor of Social Work, author and editor, *Play Therapy for Children in Crisis* and *Mass Trauma and Violence*

Inquiries: 703.351.0079
Books available
via Ingram, the Internet, and other outlets.
Or Write:
Gival Press, LLC
PO Box 3812
Arlington, VA 22203
Visit: *www.givalpress.com*